PLEA OF INSANITY

PLEA OF INSANITY

JILLIANE HOFFMAN

THORNDIKE
WINDSOR
PARAGON

This Large Print edition is published by Thorndike Press, Waterville, Maine, USA and by BBC Audiobooks Ltd, Bath, England.
Thorndike Press, a part of Gale, Cengage Learning.

LIBRARY OF CONGRESS CATALOGING-IN-PUBLICATION DATA

Hoffman, Jilliane, 1967–
   Plea of insanity / by Jilliane Hoffman.
     p. cm. — (Thorndike Press large print basic)
   ISBN-13: 978-1-4104-1770-1 (alk. paper)
   ISBN-10: 1-4104-1770-0 (alk. paper)
   1. Women lawyers—Fiction. 2. Large type books. I. Title.
PS3608.O478P56 2009b
813'.6—dc22   2009012562

BRITISH LIBRARY CATALOGUING-IN-PUBLICATION DATA AVAILABLE

Published in 2009 in the U.S. by arrangement with Janklow & Nesbit Associates.
Published in 2010 in the U.K. by arrangement with Penguin Books Ltd.

U.K. Hardcover: 978 1 408 43123 8 (Windsor Large Print)
U.K. Softcover: 978 1 408 43124 5 (Paragon Large Print)

LP HOFF- MAN
Hoffman, Jilliane, 1967-
 Plea of insanity

Printed in the United States of America
1 2 3 4 5 6 7 13 12 11 10 09

*For Rich, Amanda, and Katarina,
my beautiful, daily inspirations*

*And for those who face the world
when reality goes missing,
may you find peace, tolerance,
understanding, and a cure.*

CHAPTER 1

The old, two-story Spanish-style house sat back away from the street, nestled behind lush tropical foliage and towering palms. Halloween decorations dotted a manicured lawn, where a six-foot, hooded Grim Reaper waited menacingly to scare trick-or-treaters from a flowerbed filled with impatiens. Homemade ghosts with Magic-Markered black eyes dangled from the branches of an oak, twisting in the gusty breeze that had come in overnight, courtesy of an early-season cold front. In the moonlight they glowed an odd, bright white. Somewhere up the block a dog barked as night yawned toward morning.

The short whoop of a police siren broke the sleepy quiet as the car turned onto Sorolla Avenue from Grenada. Rookie Coral Gables PO Pete Colonna ignored the long cobblestone driveway and pulled the cruiser over at the curb. Stepping out of the car, he surveyed the house for a moment and then made his way up the winding brick walkway to the front door. When he spotted the abandoned tricycle with silver racing stripes, he moved a little faster. He rang the bell and pounded on an impressive mahogany front door. *Obviously a big-money house,* he thought as he knocked. He could hear the loud chimes inside, but no one answered.

"8362, Gables," Pete said into his shoulder mike.

"Go ahead, 8362."

"10-97 at 9-8-5 Sorolla. There's no response."

"Stand by, 8362." After a moment the dispatcher with the Coral Gables PD came back on. "BellSouth's checked the line. It's open, but there's no convo. They're not getting an answer."

"I don't hear any ringing inside," Pete said, putting his head close to the door. "I'm not hearing nothing in there."

The voice of his sergeant crackled to life on the radio pack. "8362, this is 998. Go to channel 2."

Channel 2 was the talk-around channel, where you could speak without going through dispatch. Pete switched over. "G'ahead, Sarge."

"What've ya got?" asked his sergeant,

Ralph Demos.

"I'm checking the residence," Pete said as he moved off the porch and about the front yard, parting the elephant ears and traveling palms that hid too many French windows from sight. "There's no evidence of a break-in that I can see, nothing broken, but . . ." He hesitated.

"Yeah?"

"Something don't feel right, Sarge."

"What was the call?"

"Burglary in progress."

There was a pause. "All right. Trust your gut. I'll come now, then."

"I'm gonna take the door."

"The hell you are. Stand down. Wait for me," his sergeant said sternly.

Pete looked through shrubbery that hid a black iron fence and back gate. Forgotten toys drifted lazily across a still pool. A wooden swing set the size of a small house sat on a patch of perfect grass. "Kids live here," he said. Pete's wife was pregnant with twins. In just a few weeks he'd have two little ones of his own.

"Wait for me. Don't go in there alone, Colonna. You may find a confused home-owner with a shotgun in hand who didn't hear the doorbell. 10-23 for backup. I'm there in five."

Pete clicked back over to dispatch. His sergeant's voice radioed in. "998 is 10-51 to 8362's location from UM." UM was the University of Miami. The campus was only a few miles away.

Pete checked the rest of the ground-floor windows and the backyard sliding glass doors before walking back around to the front of the house. Next to the tricycle he spotted a spilled tub of sidewalk chalk. The black night sky had begun to warm to periwinkle, and the birds hidden in the oak tree started to wake up and chirp in the soft darkness. He tried the front door again. Still no answer. A cold, anxious feeling spread through his bones as he waited on the porch.

It seemed like a lifetime, and definitely more than five minutes, before he saw the squad car pull down the street and park at the curb. Sergeant Demos was a large man, and with just weeks to go before his retirement party, things moved at a slower pace for him, both physically and mentally. It was another minute before the car door finally opened.

"Still nothing, Colonna?" Ralph asked with a huff as he lumbered up the walk.

"Nah, Sarge. No sign of life."

"It was a hang-up, right?"

Pete nodded. "Dispatch said it sounded

10

maybe like a kid."

"Yeah, yeah. Could be a prank," Ralph said, scratching his head as he looked up at the dark windows on the second floor. "Great. Everyone's in bed except for Junior. Kid's sweating it out right now, watching us from behind Bugs Bunny curtains."

"Line's alive, but no ringing. No one's answering the door. I got a feeling, Sarge."

"You and your feelings. I got a feeling you're looking for some OT, pay down the college fund for those new babies you got coming." The sergeant used his baton to bang on the door. "Police! Anybody home?" After a moment he looked at Pete again. "Any history on the house?"

"Homesteaded to a Dr. and Mrs. David Marquette. Dispatch didn't say nothing about a history, and I know I ain't been here before," Pete said, looking around at the stately homes that lined the block. "Nice 'hood."

"Don't let the address fool you, Junior. OJ lived in Beverly Hills."

"Actually, I think it was Brentwood."

"Same damn difference. The point I was trying to make was domestics happen everywhere. You'd do good to remember that." Ralph sighed. "A little kid? All right. Minimal damage. Take the pane. The city's paying for it, so don't go Rambo."

Using his flashlight, Pete broke out one pane of the frosted etched glass that framed the front door, reached in, and unlocked the lock. If it was a kid messing around, he was probably shitting his drawers right about now.

"Police! Everyone okay in here?" Pete yelled into the dark house. He pulled his Glock and stepped inside, his sergeant breathing like a porn star behind him. Shards of glass from the windowpane crunched under his feet. He shone his flashlight into the room.

Twenty-foot ceilings loomed over an elegant living room. A staircase zigzagged alongside a wall, and an ornate iron railing stretched across an overhead balcony. Past the balcony and down the upstairs hallway Pete could see a light. "Police!" he yelled.

They moved quickly through the first-floor rooms. Laundry sat piled on a washing machine, and toys cluttered the family room. In the kitchen, cleaned baby bottles were lined up neatly next to the sink on paper towels.

Pete stared at the bottles. The house was too quiet. Someone should be up by now. Either they had the wrong house and no one was home, or . . .

Pete ran for the stairs, taking them two at a time. Behind him he could hear the labored breathing of his sergeant as he tried to keep up, the jingle of the cumbersome equipment belt under the sarge's belly, the heavy click of his heels on the stone steps.

Dull yellow light spilled softly onto the landing from a back room whose door was partly closed. A nightlight? Family pictures smiled at him from every angle. All the other hall doors were shut tight.

"Anything?" called Ralph, still on the stairs.

Pete moved slowly toward the open door, snaking his way along the wall. Pieces of the room slowly came into view. Butterflies dancing across a purple wall. A Hello Kitty mirror. The edge of a Disney princess comforter. "Kid's room," he called out.

"What the fuck did you step in?" Ralph asked suddenly.

Pete turned around. He shone his flashlight where he'd just walked. Dark smears that looked like footprints followed him down the carpeted hall. He slowly spun and looked at the floor in front of him. Small red puddles with the sheen of fresh paint stained the mint-green hall carpet. But Pete knew it wasn't paint he was staring at. He moved his flashlight about. Tiny red droplets

13

had splattered up onto the white baseboard and crayon-yellow walls.

"Jesus Christ!" Ralph exclaimed. The sergeant stumbled back, his large body hitting the wall with a thump.

Pete wanted to stop. He didn't want to see any more. A sick feeling churned his stomach and sweat dribbled from his upper lip, for instinctively he knew that what he was about to witness was something he would probably spend the rest of his life trying to forget. He took a deep breath and pressed his head against the wall, his firearm out before him at the ready. His hands shook, and he thought of his wife, Victoria, and the two perfect, innocent babies he had not yet met. From the sonogram he knew they were both girls. "Police!" he shouted again, struggling to hide the tremble in his voice.

Then he entered the room and completely fell apart.

"But I don't want to go among mad people," Alice remarked.

"Oh, you can't help that," said the Cat. "We're all mad here. I'm mad. You're mad."

"How do you know I'm mad?" said Alice.

"You must be," said the Cat, "or you wouldn't have come here."
— LEWIS CARROLL,
THE ADVENTURES OF
ALICE IN WONDERLAND

CHAPTER 2

"*State v. Guarino.* Is the State ready for trial?" Miami Criminal Circuit Court Judge Leonard Farley asked in a disinterested monotone as he stirred cream into his coffee. He surveyed his jam-packed kingdom with a smirk from atop a majestic wooden throne.

The courtroom buzzed with the hushed whispers of prosecutors, defense attorneys, witnesses, victims, cops, corrections officers, and defendants, all of whom were ignoring the many posted signs that prohibited talking, cell phones, and kids. Sudden bursts of frenetic hall noise would break in as the doors opened and closed and attorneys flitted from courtroom to courtroom to handle their Monday-morning cases. Most had several defendants before several judges in several courtrooms, which meant they were going to be late for nine A.M. calendar somewhere, but no one dared be late for Judge Farley, so everyone came first to 4-10 — otherwise known around the Richard E. Gerstein Criminal Justice Building as Siberia.

Assistant State Attorney Julia Vacanti stood at the State's podium, an eighty-six-page calendar before her, four boxes of "B" felony cases stacked by her Steve Madden sling-backs, and a long line of irritated, toe-tapping prosecutors behind her, waiting to call up their cases out of turn. An even longer line snaked its way behind the defense podium. It was the B trial week, so most of the cases on calendar were hers, and almost all were set for trial. Sixty-three, to be exact. She tucked a piece of long, dark hair that had strayed from its clip back behind her ear and stared in disbelief at the *State v. Guarino* Victim/Witness Availability sheet in her hand. Scribbled across the front in her secretary, Melba's, barely legible psycho scratch was: *Victim Johnson MIA — WON'T COME IN NOW!!* Words that Julia knew had not been there Friday night when she'd prepped the calendar. Right below them Melba had scrawled a big smiley face.

Shit. Shit. Shit. Julia hesitated for a moment, thumbing through the rest of the red case file even though she knew there was nothing in there that was going to save the

18

day. The victim on her domestic aggravated battery had just gone AWOL, and the judge was about to pitch a fit — the fiery focus of which was sure to be directed at her, as it always was. Damn, she hated Mondays. "No, Your Honor," she responded slowly, mentally bracing herself for what was coming while trying hard not to actually wince. "I don't think I'm going to be ready for trial after all."

Each of the county's twenty felony division judges had three Assistant State Attorneys and three public defenders assigned permanently to their courtrooms. "A" prosecutors and PDs worked the more serious first-degree felonies; "B"s, second-degrees; and "C"s, third-degrees, like simple burglaries and grand thefts. A Division Chief for each side supervised the letters and worked "no-name" homicides — murders that didn't grab headlines or get snatched up by specialized units like Narcotics or Career Criminal. It was the pit prosecutors, as attorneys in division were known, who handled most of Miami's forty thousand–plus felony arrests each year. In an office of 240 lawyers, it was just the luck of the draw whose pit you were assigned to as you moved your way up the ranks from misdemeanors and traffic in County Court to Juvie to Felony Division and then, hopefully, one day to a cushy spot in a specialized unit. After almost three years climbing the SAO ladder of success, Julia's luck had finally run out. For the past four months, she'd been assigned to Siberia as the B with no transfer in sight.

The judge sighed loudly into the microphone. A squawk of feedback silenced the courtroom chatter. His wiry, coal-black Einstein eyebrows collapsed into a V, and he leaned his whole body on the bench so that he was practically towering over the podiums below. "But you announced ready on this last week, Ms. Vacanti."

"And I was ready, Your Honor. Last week."

"And now?"

Julia cleared her throat. "My victim is apparently no longer available."

"Aah," said the judge, flopping back into his chair and tapping a finger to his leathered temple, as if he'd just invented the lightbulb, "you mean she doesn't want to come in." He looked over at the jury box, where the defendant, Alonzo Guarino, stood in his orange jail jumpsuit, shackled and cuffed next to the other inmates. Sporting at least 250 pounds on his six-foot-two-inch frame, the man was hard to miss even without the citrus-hued prison garb. Colorful tattoo sleeves covered muscular fore-arms; a cobra ran up his neck and onto his cheek. "Misses her man, does she?" teased the judge. "Needs a little help with the rent, maybe?"

The courtroom tittered. The defendant smiled, revealing a mouthful of shiny gold teeth.

Julia could feel her blood begin to boil. Judge Leonard Farley was a jerk, but unfortunately he was a jerk with a lot of power. After spending his first five years on the bench terrorizing the dead in Probate, he'd spent the next ten smartly schmoozing the big-money attorneys in Civil — the boys who, for the right rulings, kept him in the black robes he was accustomed to. He'd stayed relatively harmless messing with people's money until last year, when the voters of the county had screamed enough and elected his opponent, a young Cuban female half his age. A fitting end to the tyranny of a sexist pig, Julia thought. But like a sick twist in a Stephen King novel, the morning after Election Day the chief judge — who was also conveniently married to Farley's sister — had appointed him back to the bench permanently as a retired sitting circuit court judge and dispatched him to the criminal courthouse. Now the man couldn't even be voted off the bench. Since he was completely ignorant about criminal law but arrogant enough to think he wasn't, every day became a battle. "I'm afraid I'm going to have to have her personally subpoenaed, Your Honor," Julia finished.

"That should've been done already," the judge said, grabbing his stamp and waving it ceremoniously above his head. "I'm dismissing."

"What?" Julia shouted. "Your Honor, you set Guarino as number twelve for trial today! I'm ready to go on any of the other eleven. If we can just reset —"

"You announced ready. You're either ready or you're not, State."

"I've never even asked for a continuance before! She's a domestic violence victim, Judge!"

"She's an absentee victim is what she is, sweetheart. And I don't have time to coddle her. As you correctly pointed out, we've got a number of other cases to get to."

The PD smiled at the defense podium.

All the crowd needed was popcorn. The room turned its attention back to her. She stood there, her face probably glowing, staring at the case file and trying hard to think through the pregnant silence. She could do what every other attorney in the division, including her own Division Chief, always did, which was nothing. Lodge a quiet objection for the record, let the judge dismiss, and dump the whole thing on Legal. Let them appeal the old geezer, which, without a victim, probably wouldn't happen anyway. Or just send it back to Domestics. The sad truth was, the judge was probably right. With Alonzo in the can for two months, Pamela Johnson was most likely out of money and needed him to hurry back home with some bacon so she could feed either her kids or her habit. But the problem was, Julia wasn't everybody else. And as her Uncle Jimmy had once told her, the right path wasn't always the easy one. Her jaw clenched. "Then the State's ready for trial," she announced.

"Did I just hear you right?" asked the judge, sitting up straight. "No victim, and you're telling me you're going forward?"

"Judge, Mr. Guarino's a career criminal. He's got priors for resisting, aggravated battery, and aggravated assault with a firearm, not to mention three arrests in the past for domestic battery. He attacked his girlfriend with a razor blade because she looked at the produce man in Winn-Dixie. His pregnant girlfriend, I might add. It took sixty-two stitches to sew her face back together."

"And now she doesn't think it's important enough to come in."

"If Your Honor refuses to grant the State a continuance, rather than see this case dismissed, I have no choice but to go forward without her."

"And just how're you going to do that, State?" The judge was more than mad. He was furious. Domestic violence was a prickly topic. It was not good press for him to look this insensitive. Or stupid.

She swallowed. "I don't need the victim, Your Honor."

"That's a first for me, Ms. Vacanti. Didn't they teach you corpus delicti back in law school last year? The body of your crime doesn't want to come in."

She ignored the cheap age zing. The first two months in division she'd spent fighting off his thinly veiled advances; she'd take the barbs anytime. "Witnesses can testify about her injuries."

"Who's gonna tell me how she got them? Did anyone see her getting attacked?"

"Her statements to the police —"

"Are hearsay," added the PD.

"Are admissible as an excited utterance," she finished.

In the law, people were thought to be much more honest than usual when acting under the stress of certain situations. Excited utterance, as it was known, was a recognized exception to the hearsay rule, which generally prohibited the in-court use of any statement made out of court. Being sliced to ribbons by a tattooed maniac with a razor blade qualified as a stressful event, Julia thought. Maybe it was a stretch to try a case with no victim and just a hearsay exception, but the hell she was gonna let the SOB high-five it out of here while the judge yelled good-bye to him in her face.

"Don't play coy with me, Ms. Vacanti. I won't indulge moot-court trial antics in this courtroom," Farley bellowed. "You damn well better be ready to pick a jury."

"I am, Your Honor."

The judge glared at her. "You want a trial? Nine tomorrow. I'll see you back here." The PD opened his mouth, but the judge waved him off. "Don't bother, Mr. Venema. Ms. Vacanti says we're ready even without a victim, so we're ready. Ivonne," he turned to the court clerk, "set over the rest of Ms. Vacanti's trials to print on Wednesday's calendar. Guarino won't take us long at all." He spun his chair back in Julia's direction. 'If you waste my time with this, Ms. Vacanti, you'll have more to worry about than double jeopardy. I strongly suggest you get on your knees, and when you're done praying, start scouring every damn inch of every damn women's shelter or crack house or whorehouse in this town, for all I care, and find out where it is your victim is hiding out and get her the hell in here so she can tell me what happened. Or Mr. Guarino's going home. And I'm pretty sure that when he does, *he'll* be able to find her."

Julia stepped back from the podium and gathered her boxes as the ASA behind her called up his case. Her blood was racing so hard that she could hear it pound in her ears. She felt the eyes of her colleagues upon her as she packed up her cart. All she wanted was to get out of the courtroom and scream.

"Don't let him push your buttons," her Division Chief cautioned in a low voice as she moved to help Julia load her files.

Julia took a deep breath to prevent herself from saying something she knew she'd later regret. Her DC never pushed anyone's buttons. Farley probably thought Karyn Simms — pretty, busty, blond, and completely non-confrontational — the ideal woman but for the fact that she occasionally opened her mouth and said something.

"He's not going to change, Julia. And you're not going to change him. But from the shade of red you made his tan turn, he just might leave the bench on a stretcher one of these days," Karyn said with a sardonic smile and a shake of her head when Julia didn't respond. "You really gonna try this case without a victim? What's the point in that?"

"I have no choice."

"She does. She's not here."

"If I have to try it without her, I will."

"I repeat, and the point of that is?"

Julia looked over at the jury box. It sucked being an avenger when nobody else saw a problem. "Maybe next time he'll go for the throat."

"I think you're a great lawyer, honey. I do. But even you know the judge is right. Investigations won't find her because she doesn't want to be found. All you're going to accomplish is to piss off the judge. And double jeopardy's gonna prevent you from retrying if your victim ever does see the light and wants to prosecute. Why not just let the judge dismiss? Then hand this off to Domestics, where it should've been all along."

Of course dismissal was the path of least resistance, which was why Karyn was suggesting it. As she saw it, every case had a problem, every victim an agenda, every defendant an excuse. So for her, everything was negotiable, including battery, rape, and even murder. Sometimes at bargain-basement pleas that fell way below statutory guidelines.

"Domestics will be in the same situation as me, only worse," Julia whispered, turning her attention back to the file cart. "Just look at that guy, Karyn. If he walks, he's heading straight back home."

Karyn rolled her eyes. "Don't say you weren't warned. You know, you've got a set of balls, girlfriend."

"Thank you," Julia replied, snapping the bicycle strap across her file boxes.

"And I'm not the only one who's noticed." Karyn's voice dropped even lower. "Listen, while you were duking it out with the judge, Charley Rifkin was in here."

Rifkin was the Division Chief of Major Crimes. Julia felt her palms start to sweat and her heart beat fast. Uh-oh. "And?"

"He wants to see you in his office. Now. Oh, and honey," Karyn called out with a flip of her perfect blond bob as Julia started toward the gallery swing-door, "he didn't look happy."

CHAPTER 3

Maybe it was time to start looking into private practice, Julia thought as she dragged the rickety cart stacked with boxes down the courthouse wheelchair ramp and hurried across the street to the State Attorney's Office. At twenty-eight years old, barely surviving paycheck to government paycheck with a shitload of law school loans to pay back and no time for a social life was a hefty price to have to pay for experience — but now she was about to have her ass handed to her because she didn't want to lie down and look the other way. A gusty breeze threatened to Marilyn-Monroe her black crepe skirt, of course right in front of the steel-barred windows of the Dade County Jail and the leering Sabrett sausage vendors on the corner, and she cursed herself for picking the one suit in her closet that didn't have a tailored hemline.

She knew her Division Chief thought she

was being overzealous and combative. And her judge was mad at her — again. She had a day to prepare for a trial she really wasn't prepared to have, with a judge, a DC, a defense attorney, and even a victim who didn't want her to have it. Now, just when she thought the day couldn't get any shittier, the Chief of Major Crimes was demanding to see her in his office.

In the food chain of the State Attorney's Office, Major Crimes was right up there with administration. An elite, specialized division that handled explosive media cases, complex homicides, and all death-penalty cases, the unit comprised ten of the most experienced and accomplished trial attorneys in the office. Heading it up was Charley Rifkin, a seasoned litigator and the State Attorney's right-hand man for the past five elections. Being summoned to Rifkin's office was not a normal happening for any pit prosecutor — unless, of course, Rifkin had witnessed something he didn't like in court. Or, Julia thought nervously as she watched her boxes go through the office X-ray conveyor belt, had had a judge or DC call him about a problem.

She hit the elevator button and waded back into the crowd of uniforms, attorneys, and assorted interesting persons who packed the lobby. Even though it probably wouldn't have deterred her from pressing forward on Guarino if she'd known the Major Crimes Division Chief himself had been standing right behind her, she still wanted to kick herself for not knowing. Not that she would have recognized him anyway — aside from the occasional elevator sighting, she'd never actually met the man. Major Crimes attorneys tended to hang with their own kind; they even had their own Christmas party that the rest of the office was not invited to.

She got off on 2 with a guy whom she figured for either a drug dealer or a plainclothes narc in need of a shower. She waited in the elevator bay till he disappeared down the hall that led to Career Criminal. Then she wiped her moist palms on her skirt and walked over to the door marked "Major Crimes." The Hallowed Hall. She'd never actually been down it, and she wondered for a second if her ID badge would allow her access. She was slightly surprised when the door clicked open and she stepped into a low-lit empty hallway painted — like the rest of the office — a depressing shade of shipyard gray.

Immediately the air changed. That was the first thing she noticed. The second was the collective blank stares of the secretaries whose lair she landed in when the hallway abruptly ended. A fluorescent-lit maze of Formica and Plexiglas cubbies, and there she was, standing dumb-faced right in the middle of it. Conversation didn't just softly die down — it dropped dead in midsentence.

"Hello," Julia began with a smile. Since no one looked away, she addressed them all. "I'm looking for Mr. Rifkin's office?"

"Is he expecting you?" asked an older woman with a sour expression, doughy cheeks, and a lot of pink eye shadow. Somebody cracked gum.

Julia glanced down. On the desk in front of pink-eyes was a plaque with a plastic manicured index finger that bobbled back and forth. It read, *Don't Mess with Grandma.* "I think so," she answered slowly. "My DC told me Mr. Rifkin wanted to see me."

"Oh," said Grandma. Her mouth slid down until it looked like it would melt into her neck, like a Dr. Seuss character. "You're the one from Judge Farley's division."

That couldn't be good. "That's me," Julia replied. She put away the smile.

Grandma picked up the phone, hit a number, and turned away. "She's here," was all she said. Then she looked back at Julia

suspiciously and motioned down the hall
with a nod. Her throat jiggled like a turkey's.
"207. Take the hallway to the second corridor and make a right. Last office on the
left."

CHAPTER 4

The zombie stares followed her as she walked past, like moving pairs of eyes in haunted-mansion paintings. Forever and a day later, she finally turned the corner and entered another seemingly endless gray hallway, this one lined with closed doors. Apparently no one in Major Crimes was particularly social. Not that it was a constant party up on 3, but among pit prosecutors, doors were always open and attorneys wandered in and out of each other's claustrophobic offices all day long to ask for advice, bitch about a PD, chat up the weekend, or gulp down a quick shot of *café Cubano* — hot, liquid adrenaline made fresh every afternoon by her friend Ileana Sanchez, the B in Judge Stalder's division. Upstairs there was a sense of camaraderie in the gray halls. Here in the Hallowed Hall she just felt shut out from the rest of the world.

"Charles August Rifkin, Division Chief," read the nameplate next to 207. Inside, she could hear Rifkin talking, his words muffled. She hoped he was on the phone because an audience was the last thing she needed. Her Fruit Loops and coffee threatened mutiny, and she prayed her stomach wouldn't start making any weird noises. Wiping her hands one last time on her skirt, she tapped on the door. There was a brief silence before someone said, "Come in."

"Hi," Julia answered cheerfully as she pushed open the door. The file cart she was trying to negotiate behind her nailed the doorframe with a thud.

"Leave that outside," commanded another voice from somewhere on the other side. A voice she immediately thought she recognized.

She nodded with a wince, backed out of the room, and pushed the cart up against the hallway wall. She blew out a slow, steady breath before stepping back inside. The door closed behind her, but it wasn't Charley Rifkin who'd shut it because he was sitting right in front of her behind an oversized desk, wearing what looked a lot like a scowl. The door-shutter moved to one of two small side chairs and motioned for her to take a seat in the other.

Yes, the day could get worse.

"Good morning, Ms. Vacanti," said the Assistant Division Chief of Major Crimes, Rick Bellido, looking cool and reserved in a conservative black suit, white dress shirt, and gray silk tie. The gray in the tie accentuated the silver strands sprinkled throughout his otherwise jet-black hair, but in a flattering way. She stared at him for what felt like an incredibly long moment, but he didn't smile. He didn't nod. He didn't wink. God, he didn't even blink. Even Dionne Warwick and her entire network of psychic friends would have been hard-pressed to guess at that moment that the two of them were sleeping together. Julia herself was now doubting the memory.

"I saw you in court today," Rifkin began. "You like to test old Farley, do you?" Before she could reply, he turned to Rick and said flatly, "She's going to trial on a domestic with no victim. Lenny had a fit."

"Nothing unusual there," Rick replied with a shrug as he sat down.

"How long've you been in his division?" asked Rifkin, tapping his hand against his coffee mug. His wedding ring made a soft, distracting *tink, tink, tink* against the ceramic.

"About four months," Julia answered. Four months, one week, and two days, to be exact. Four months too long, she wanted to say. She sat up straight in her chair and got ready to defend herself, ticking off invisible bullet points in her head. "He was going to dismiss —"

Rifkin cut her off. "That's not why you're here."

She wasn't sure if the weight actually moved off or onto her chest. Rifkin motioned to Rick with an exaggerated wave. She felt her face go hot; her cheeks could probably lead the way on a midnight sleigh ride — a curse of being half Irish and fair-skinned. She recrossed her legs, casually tugging at her skirt so that it at least touched the knee. *Oh, God. Please, please, please don't let this be about the state's policy on dating in the office . . .*

"There was a family murdered in Coral Gables over the weekend," Rick began. "I'm assuming you've heard."

She let out the breath she'd been holding, so hard and so fast it sounded like a sigh. "Yeah, yeah. Of course," she replied. The horrible story had been all over the TV news on Sunday and had made the front page today in both the *Miami Herald* and the *Sun-Sentinel.* An entire family, the victims of some psycho intruder. Other than the names of the victims and the fact that it

37

was a homicide, the news didn't have much to report, as everyone close to the investigation was remaining tight-lipped. But the press was still having a field day, whipping up fears of a serial killer, cautioning everyone to lock their doors and windows and call police if they noticed any strange behavior. In Miami that was sure to have the 911 lines ringing off the hook.

"Jennifer Marquette and her three children, Emma, Danny, and Sophie, were all murdered Saturday night sometime before dawn. Three little kids, all under the age of seven. One a baby," Rick said as he tapped his Montblanc thoughtfully on the top of a yellow legal pad that had appeared on his lap. "It's pretty bad."

"Only Dad's alive. He's over at Ryder," Rifkin added.

"The poor man . . . I can't even imagine," Julia said softly. "He's a doctor, right? Is he going to make it?"

Grandma opened the door at that moment. Apparently no one messed with her because she didn't even knock. "Ruth Solly's headed over to court, Charley. She needs those files."

"Okay, okay. Let me get with her before she goes," Rifkin said, rising, coffee cup in hand. "Excuse me, I'll be back in a minute."

He headed out of the office with Grandma teetering close behind, interestingly enough, in a strappy pair of Jessica Simpson stilettos.

Okay. *Now* Julia was confused. Apparently this little tête-à-tête wasn't about Farley or her combative attitude or her taking Guarino to trial. She didn't know the name Marquette, and she couldn't think of any connection she might have with the weekend massacre in the Gables other than the possibility of one of her defendants being investigated as a suspect. And thank God, as far as she could tell, it wasn't about the SAO policy on sexual harassment and sleeping with one's superiors. But five minutes into a conversation was still a long time to go without knowing if she should be floating a few resumes on Monster.com.

"How was the rest of your weekend?" Rick asked quietly when Grandma and her boss had cleared listening distance.

"Uneventful," she replied with a shrug. She suddenly remembered Friday night — the last time they'd been together, which also happened to be the first time they'd been together. His mouth on hers in the shower, his hands on places she never should've let them go. She felt her cheeks start to burn, and she looked away, finding a gray spot on the gray carpet to concentrate on.

"I was the on-call this weekend," he offered, maybe as a reason why he hadn't called her since then.

"Where in the Gables did it happen?" she managed. "The murders?"

"Off Sorolla, near UM. Oh, I forgot," he added with a touch of amusement, "you're not from around these here parts."

It was no use. She lit up like Bozo at a birthday party. Her shower was in Hollywood, a twenty-mile trip north of Miami.

"Sorolla and Granada, to be exact," he continued. "It's in the older section of the Gables. A lot of expensive historical homes and mansions. 'Course nowadays I don't think you can touch a trailer in Leisure City for less than six figures, so 'expensive' is a relative term."

"Is it going to be your case?" she asked.

"Hell, yeah! I was at the scene all day yesterday. John Latarrino's working it with Miami-Dade Homicide. Steve Brill's with the Gables. You know them?"

Julia shook her head. "No, I don't think so," she answered. Of course she didn't know them; she didn't prosecute homicides. Suddenly she felt very young and very out of her league, and not just because of her

40

age. Senior trial attorneys and Major Crimes prosecutors knew all the homicide cops in each department by name because they worked with them all the time. It was a pretty small, macabre clique that oftentimes spawned lifelong personal friendships among its members. Julia didn't have any of those kinds of friendships yet; most of the time she didn't even recognize the signatures on the bottoms of arrest forms. They changed daily.

"I've worked with Lat before," Rick offered. "He's good. Brill's a character. You know, the Gables doesn't get many murders."

"They don't let them in," Julia mused. "Let me ask you, why would Coral Gables need to call in the county?"

"Like I said, they don't get many murders. Their department doesn't even have a homicide squad, just a Persons. The county has the experience and the manpower. They also have the lab."

Strike one to fitting in with the conversation, not knowing that Coral Gables lacked an actual homicide detective. "Do you have any suspects yet?" she asked.

The door opened again and Rifkin returned with a steaming cup of coffee but no Grandma. "I see you tried a DUI manslaughter last month," he said to Julia as he slid back behind his desk. "Have you worked on any other homicides?"

"No," she replied. "My A passed that down to me because I did DUI when I was in County."

"Misdemeanors?" Rifkin asked incredulously.

Julia shifted in her seat. "That's what we handled in County Court."

"Misdemeanors," he repeated. "What'd your jury come back with?"

"Guilty as charged."

"What'd Farley give him?"

"Five, followed by ten years probation."

Rifkin shot Rick a look and began impatiently tapping away on his coffee mug again.

"It was the defendant's first offense," she added because she thought she had to.

The *tink, tink, tinking* ticked off seconds like a sledgehammer. No one said anything. Then, just as she'd begun to think maybe she should have another lawyer in the room with her, Rick leaned in closer, his elbows resting on his knees and his hands clasped in front of him like a coach about to call a play. "To answer your question from before, Julia," he began, "we do have a suspect in the Gables killings."

"I just took a call from Marsh over at Metro. Our suspect's out of surgery," Rifkin added with a snort. "Looks like he's gonna make it after all."

Rick shook his head, but his dark-chocolate eyes remained locked on Julia's. "That's why you've been asked here this morning, Julia," he said quietly. "I want you to help me nail the bastard who murdered his wife and kids on Saturday night."

CHAPTER 5

Julia said nothing. She couldn't. If she was hearing this right, she was being asked to second-seat a murder prosecution. *A Major Crimes murder prosecution.*

Rick sat back in his seat. "I'm gonna level with you, Julia. I've got a really brutal crime scene. A dead mom and three dead kids with a rising-star doctor playing the role of father, husband, and, right now, prime suspect. I'm gonna need help from the very beginning to work it up right, before Crime Scene mops up the last of the bloodstains and the cleaning crew wipes the print dust off the furniture. Charley and I have been tossing around names, and I thought about you. I thought about that closing I saw you give a few weeks back, your style in front of a jury. Your stats are impressive, there's no denying that. Thirty-six felony juries, thirty-four convictions. You work hard, and you stay late. I like how you push difficult cases to trial, and once you get before a jury, you've actually got the skill to back you up — a talent most attorneys in this office, frankly, just don't have. It's a gift. A sign of a solid, long career as a litigator."

She tried her best to hold it back, but the cheesy smile slipped out anyway. "Wow," she said softly. "Thank you." Maybe Mondays weren't so bad after all. . . .

Charley Rifkin carefully placed the coffee mug back down on his desk and leaned forward. "Rick apparently has a lot of faith in you, young lady," he remarked after a long, purposeful silence, but the scowl remained. He toyed with a paper clip that had escaped its caddy. "I'm going to be honest here, Ms. Vacanti. I asked to see you because, as you well know, I supervise this division. The cases up here, they're assigned by me. Though the personal decision on who one of my attorneys wants to try that case with may be his or hers to make, in the end that case is still *my* responsibility. And while I'm more than confident that my Assistant Chief, with over twenty years in this office and seventeen death-penalty convictions under his belt, is more than qualified to work a quadruple homicide with the media breathing down his neck and a slew of high-paid defense lawyers up his ass, I'm not so sure that this is the murder case I want you cutting your baby teeth on."

Ouch. There was nothing Julia could say without sounding either desperate or defensive, so she bit the inside of her lip and concentrated on the wall of impressive diplomas behind the man's head. The absolute worst thing she could do would be to cry.

"That's just bullshit!" Rick exclaimed angrily. "Other pit prosecutors have second-sat cases in this division, and no one has given a damn before, including you, Charley."

"The stakes are a lot higher on this one, Ricky. This is a death case," Rifkin countered. "We're talking three little kids butchered in their sleep by their daddy. Assuming everything at the end of the day points to premeditation, you're looking at four counts of murder one. If Dr. David Marquette becomes the next Scott Peterson du jour — which he has the face for, and the crime to match — the press will be camping out in both your backyards until Corrections finally sticks the needle in." He looked back over at Julia, obviously disappointed. "She's never even tried a homicide outside of a DUI manslaughter, and you're gonna have her possibly death-qualify a twelve-person jury with you?"

Rick stood up and slapped both hands on the desk. "I think it's shrewd for us to put a woman at the table, Charley. If this does go the distance, a jury's gonna want to see someone young and pretty representing a young, pretty dead mommy and her kids."

"You want a woman?" Rifkin asked. "Why not bring in Karyn Simms? A DC with some freaking experience? Lisa Valentine? Priscilla Stroze? I can keep going. . . ."

Rick shook his head. "I've seen Julia in court. Maybe it wasn't a murder, but you've got to start somewhere, and the girl is good. Damn good. She can give the victims a voice; she can keep a jury in that room!"

"This is not the case to play social experiment." Rifkin looked over at Julia like he'd hidden a camera in her apartment Friday night.

Rick leaned across the desk. "Like you said, it's my case, my decision, Charley. I appreciate your input, I do, but . . ." He paused. "I think you just might be surprised to find that behind that smile of hers, Julia's got some pretty sharp teeth. Just like me. And she's not afraid to use them when it counts. Just like me."

The two men stared at each other. Then Rifkin held his hands up, breaking the deafening silence. "It is your case, pal. But don't you dare screw it up. I like to think that after almost thirty years, I can smell the bad ones. This one, I gotta tell you, it stinks, Ricky. Like the perfect storm, it's got all the ingredients brewing for high profile. Off-the-charts high profile. A fuckup on that can follow you around for the rest of your career." His eyes narrowed, and it was clear that the two men were now talking about something other than the Marquette murders. "It would be in your best interest to remember that."

Rick nodded and straightened his suit as he sat back down. "I can appreciate that." Turning to Julia, he said, "Of course we may be getting way ahead of ourselves. After all this, I don't even know if Julia's gonna want to come aboard."

She had yet to take her eyes off the diplomas, not wanting to interject herself any further into the scary little King Kong–Godzilla go-round that had gone down right in front of her. Even if it was true that opportunities such as this knocked only once, Julia wasn't so sure anymore that she wanted to open the door for fear that it might just slam shut in her face and catch a few fingers in the process. Maybe she wasn't competent enough to try a murder yet.

Maybe she still did have her baby teeth, and everyone would see her struggling to learn the ropes on the eleven o'clock news, like Charley Rifkin was predicting.

She listened to the sound of the wall clock tick off the seconds, like on a bad game show. She'd never really wanted to be a lawyer, to be sitting here with this meaty career decision tossed at her feet. Like a funny joke, it had just happened one day on her way to register for cooking school. Two months after graduation from Rutgers — stupid enough to believe a liberal arts degree would get her a job — she was scanning want ads in Starbucks with a friend and making a list of things she liked to do in the Cinderella hope of finding a way to spend the rest of her nine-to-five life doing something she actually loved while getting paid handsomely for it. She'd narrowed it down to cooking and reading. Librarians were paid shit and required a master's; chefs traveled the world. Cooking school it was. As she was on the phone with the registrar at Johnson & Wales, her unemployed friend started spouting some of the salaries that lawyers in New York City were being offered. A fan of *L.A. Law* reruns and *Law & Order,* Julia put "lawyer" down on the list, hung up the phone, and signed up for the

LSAT. Four years of night school and a shit-load of student loans later, she was an attorney.

It wasn't a New York salary, that was for sure, but Miami was much prettier to look at in February, and it came with lots of crime — great job security for a prosecutor. More importantly, three years later, she still loved Sam Waterston. The pay was definitely crummy, and the hours were long. There were few weekends that she wasn't in front of her computer and few nights that she left the office before seven. But no matter the complaints — from ornery judges to apathetic witnesses — at the end of most days she knew she'd made a difference. And sometimes, when she put a really bad guy behind bars, she knew that the difference she'd made might actually have been one of life or death, even if she never got credit for it.

Now she was being given the chance to take her career to another level. It was an opportunity most prosecutors in the office would never be offered, an opportunity that only an hour ago she wouldn't have hesitated to take. But now she was unsure of herself. Trying her first murder was one thing. Trying her first murder in front of a bunch of cameras, skeptical colleagues, and an administration that she knew was waiting to watch her fall was another. Then she thought of something else just as troubling. Though she didn't believe their recently escalated friendship was the reason Rick Bellido was asking her to second-seat, maybe that thinking was just plain naive. And while she was pretty confident that no one inside or outside the office knew about their relationship, if it continued, chances were someone would eventually figure it out. Gossip ran recklessly and purposefully through the State Attorney's Office, like a match on the trail of gasoline. What then? What would people speculate was the real reason she was second-seating a Major Crimes case? Or worse, *what if it ended?* And even worse than that, *what if it ended badly?* A million questions screamed for answers. All the while, she felt both men watching her, waiting for a decision, as the *Jeopardy!* music played in her head. . . .

Your fear of failure should never be greater than your fear of regret. Another maxim espoused by her wise Uncle Jimmy, the garbageman from Great Kills, New York, who could've been a philosopher. Or a regular on *The Sopranos.* What would he tell her to do now? God, she didn't want to fail, and she certainly didn't want to fail so publicly, but she sure as hell didn't want to look back and see the very obvious fork in the winding road of her career. The prong she should've taken . . . She drew a deep mental breath. Screw Rifkin and his opinion. Screw Mondays.

"I understand your concerns, Mr. Rifkin," she said, moving her stare off the diploma to look the Major Crimes Division Chief right in the eye. "But I have to say that I'd welcome the opportunity to try this case."

"Great," Rick said with a smile. He walked over to the door and opened it. "Drop off your files and meet me down in the lobby in ten minutes. I wanna take you over to the scene."

Rifkin said nothing.

She nodded expectantly. No time like the present to get your feet not just wet, but completely soaked. No time to change her mind. She followed Rick to the door, thanked both men, and walked out into the hall to get her cart. When she heard the door shut behind her with a click, she finally exhaled the real breath she'd been holding and clicked the heels of her Steve Maddens together, even though she knew that the conversation in the room she'd just left was probably far from over.

CHAPTER 6

She pushed the cart up against the wall of her cramped office next to an overgrown stack of dispos — pesky final case dispositions she had yet to get to — grabbed her purse from her desk, stepped over another stack, and hurried out the door. "I'll be back!" she hollered to Melba, who was busy watching *The Jerry Springer Show* on a portable TV stuck up under her desk and who didn't really give a shit where Julia was going or when she'd be back. Then she headed down the hall, hastily trying to retouch her lip gloss and check her cell for messages as she did. It wasn't even eleven yet, and a lot of attorneys were still stuck in court — their doors open and offices empty — but as she rounded the corner past the secretary for Judge Stalder's division, she spotted Ileana at her desk on the phone.

"Oh, good, you're here," Julia said in a hushed voice as she rushed in. She grabbed the *Herald* off the top of Ileana's perfectly stacked inbox. The room smelled of Pledge, Windex, and Cuban coffee. There were no dispos on Ileana's floor. No files waiting to be put away on her file cabinet. Just a clock radio, a Tupperwared bag of Pilon coffee, and an oversized bottle of hand sanitizer. Even on the small table where she brewed *café Cubano* for twenty every afternoon, there was nary an espresso bean or a sugar grain in sight. If the two of them hadn't been such good friends for such a long time, Julia might've allowed Ileana's obsessive-compulsive disorder to make her feel inadequate, but aside from her insane jealousy that Ileana was in a normal division, there was no competition between them. "Can I borrow this?" she whispered, heading for the door without waiting for an answer.

"Hold on a moment, sir." Ileana let the phone slip down into her neck. "I haven't read the funnies yet. Don't crinkle it."

"Not a problem," Julia replied, backing out with a quick wave.

"Are we doing lunch?" Ileana called out.

"Can't. Not today."

"Are you in trial?"

"Tomorrow. Wanna try a domestic on an excited utterance with me?"

"Hmmm . . . no. Where're you off to?"

"I'll tell you later!" Julia called back as she made her way down the hall to the security doors. "But you won't believe it when I do!"

NO SUSPECTS IN GABLES MASSA-CRE blared the front-page headline in her hands. She hadn't had the time to actually read the article this morning before heading out to work, but now every detail mattered — every name, every title, was important to know and remember and catalog in her brain.

Her eyes flew across the page: Jennifer Leigh Marquette, 32. Emma Marquette, 6. Daniel Marquette, 3. Sophie Marquette, 6 weeks. A small, grainy black-and-white picture of a smiling Jennifer ran under the headline. Even though the picture was bad, Julia could see she'd been pretty, with a sweet, infectious grin that took over her entire face. It was funny how the press always seemed to find the happiest-looking photos of murder victims to post alongside stories of their violent deaths.

. . . *found early Sunday morning by police . . . brutally slain at their four-bedroom home in a quiet, upscale section of Coral Gables . . . veteran police chief Elias Vasquez refused to release further details . . . described the scene as "one of the most disturbing"* . . .

watched as Miami-Dade Crime Scene techs removed items from the home all day . . . no suspects have been identified . . . pending the notification of New Jersey relatives . . services have not yet been scheduled . . .

An icy chill ran through her as her eyes caught on the next headline: PHYSICIAN DAD STILL IN CRITICAL; COMMU- NITY, HOSPITAL PRAY FOR RECOV- ERY.

Dr. David Alain Marquette, 38. Another grainy picture smiled softly back at her, obviously a professional headshot — maybe a med school grad photo. Disquietingly normal by all appearances, it was not the crazed Charlie Manson mug she might have expected, given what she knew the man was soon to be charged with. In fact, like his wife, David was good-looking, with an all- American type of boyish charm that jumped out even from a photograph. *Their children must have been beautiful,* she thought with- out really thinking. More goose bumps.

. . . discovered near death inside the home . . . to undergo emergency surgery this morning . . . no further details on his condi- tion . . . the gynecological fertility specialist from Chicago with a growing practice on Miami Beach . . . loving father and hus- band . . . many friends and colleagues still in

56

shock . . . relatives brace for another possible funeral . . .

She stuffed the paper into her purse as the doors opened onto the crowded lobby.

Rick was already there, chatting with the Division Chief of Narcotics and Pete Walsh, the office employment lawyer. "Ready?" he asked, jingling his keys in his hand as she walked up. "We'll take my car."

"Sounds good," she said, feeling the eyes of the other two men follow them as they headed out the door together. She'd have to get used to the funny looks and raised eyebrows. The match had been lit — the rumors would be next.

"Do you have to be back for court?" he asked as they stepped outside.

"No. I have nothing on this afternoon."

"Good. I'm not sure how long we'll be. We may even take a run over to the ME's later," he said, crossing the lot to where a shiny black BMW 525i sat. He clicked the alarm and held open the door for her. "So, you ready for your first homicide?"

A disturbing image suddenly popped into Julia's head. *We're talking three little kids butchered in their sleep by their daddy.* "Are the bodies still there?" she asked hesitantly as she stepped inside the car. "At the scene?"

An amused look crossed his face. "I hope not. They'd be pretty ripe by now. They were found yesterday," he replied, shutting the door.

"Oh, yeah," she said to no one but herself in the empty car. Strike two. Officially on the case less than twenty minutes, and she already sounded like a moron.

He climbed in on the driver's side and looked at her with concern before turning on the engine. "Why? Would it bother you?"

Hell, yeah, she wanted to say. *Four dead bodies and a blood-splattered house might freak me out when the biggest scene I've been to so far is a DUI roadblock on the Fourth of July.* But of course she didn't. "No," she answered with a shake of her head. "I just wanted to prepare myself if they were."

Rick Bellido fascinated her, impressed her, intrigued her, scared her. Long before she'd actually met the man, she'd heard of his reputation. Everyone who practiced criminal law in Miami had. He was arguably the office's best litigator, earning his coveted spot in Major Crimes after less than seven years in the office, and was rumored to be in line one day for even greater things than Charley Rifkin's job. Rumor had it he was being groomed for the spot of State Attorney

He'd tried some of the most notorious, heinous murders in Miami history and had been courted throughout the years by several different U.S. attorneys to come work for the feds. As the stories went, he'd stayed put with the State because he preferred trying murders to prosecuting plumped-up racketeering violations. But it wasn't just his intimidating trial skills that had the feds still asking him out and the governor searching for his name on judicial nominating appointment lists. His age and experience, ethnic good looks, and last name were an asset to any law enforcement office with a South Florida constituency.

Whether it was his reputation or his well-tailored presence that commandeered a courtroom, Julia wasn't quite sure, but she'd seen it happen often enough. Like a TV evangelist, Rick Bellido just had a mesmerizing, authoritative, rock-star way about him. What he said to a judge was taken as gospel; what he asked of a jury was usually done. His days in the pits long past, his colleagues were senior trial attorneys, local politicians, police chiefs, and big-name defense lawyers. So Julia had been more than just surprised when he'd sat down next to her in court a few weeks ago and struck up a conversation as he waited for a defendant to be brought over from the jail. She'd also been flattered. And definitely attracted. Even though he was a lot older than she — seventeen years, to be exact — it didn't seem to matter. Casual cups of coffee had turned into a couple of off-campus lunches and then, finally, and more or less unexpectedly, Friday night. She hadn't heard from him since — not even a text — which made this, their first moment alone, all the more awkward. Even though there were so many things to discuss, she had no idea what to say, so she opted for nothing and looked out the passenger window.

"Don't let Charley get to you," he said after they'd pulled out of the parking lot and onto 14th. "He just likes you to know who's in charge. He does it to everyone."

Somehow she doubted that, but it was still nice to hear. "Okay."

More silence.

"I didn't pick you because of us," he said finally as the car pulled up to a light. "Let's get that elephant out of the way." He turned to look at her, leaning an elbow on the console and taking off his Ray-Bans. "I meant what I said in there. I like what I see in the courtroom, Julia. You've definitely got raw talent, and that intrigues me. You've got this kind of rebellious, take-no-shit, chip-on-your-shoulder attitude that reminds me a little of CJ Townsend, a prosecutor who used to be with our office."

"Thanks for the compliment," she replied with a laugh. "I think."

"You're welcome." He smiled. The crinkle of crow's feet softened his intense brown eyes. "I think you can make things interesting. And I like interesting. Of course what happened the other night was fun, too." He lowered his voice to a whisper and traced a finger over her hand. "And I definitely think we should do that again." Then he leaned over and kissed her, his fingers finding their way through the tangle of her thick, dark waves to the back of her neck, pulling her closer. She remembered how the water from the shower had spilled off his back like a waterfall; those warm, experienced hands in complete control of her body, shampooing her hair, running over her shoulders, rubbing lather all over her skin. The moment felt a little forbidden, a little embarrassing, totally exciting, just as it had then, and she kissed him back, her tongue finding his, her fingers running underneath his jacket, tracing the crisp starch lines in his shirt. The beep of a horn pulled them back to the present.

"I'll do my best," she said softly, touching

a finger to her lips. "That I can promise you."

He slipped his sunglasses back on. "Good," he replied as the car pulled away from the light.

It was all he needed to say.

CHAPTER 7

"Four forty-seven A.M. Sunday, Coral Gables PD received a call on their nine-eleven line. It didn't last long — less than a minute. The caller, who was barely audible, asked for help, said someone was, quote, 'coming back,' then just hung up. It was sent out as a burglary in progress. Dispatch reported the caller might've been a kid," Rick said as he pulled the Beamer up in front of a mustard-yellow Spanish-style mansion. A few brown MDPD uniforms stood smoking on the front porch underneath a witch who'd crashed head-on into the stucco. Crime-scene tape crisscrossed two wooden front doors; blue roofing tarp covered a hole in one of the side window-panes.

"The responding officer found no evidence of a break-in, but since there was no response at the door and no response on the telephone line, he and his sergeant made forcible entry, as you can see, through the front door, breaking one of the window-panes. Inside, they found . . ." He stopped himself and turned off the engine. "Well, we'll get to that inside. Crime Scene's already videoed, so you'll get to see what it looked like yesterday before the techs trampled over everything important."

Handmade pillowcase ghosts with blacked-out eyes danced in an oak tree. Police barricades blocked access to the front walk and driveway, where cop cars with both the Gables and the county boxed in an MDPD Crime Scene van. Julia could see a tricycle on the lawn next to a colorful hopscotch game drawn in chalk on the brick walkway, and through the iron fence that ran along the backyard she could make out the top of an elaborate swing set. A heavy, guilty feeling settled in her chest, as if she'd swallowed an entire jar of peanut butter and it had gotten stuck on the way down. With all the excitement of being asked to try her first murder case, she'd almost forgotten that four people were dead. *Butchered* was the word Charley Rifkin had actually used. Now here she was, in front of this perfect Norman Rockwell house, surrounded by cops and sealed off with crime-scene tape, where only steps away the unthinkable had happened. And she was only moments away from walking right into it. . . .

A sudden hard knock on the driver's-side window pulled her out of her thoughts and made her jump in her seat.

"Hey, there! Eddie Brennan, Channel 7 News," shouted a guy in a slightly rumpled blue suit, wearing a dress shirt the color of chewed bubble gum. Behind him stood Willie Nelson with a camera, faded yellow-white braid and all.

"Shit. I should've figured he'd be out chumming," Rick grumbled in a low voice. "Watch yourself around this guy, Julia. I'll handle all the press on this," he said, opening the door. It wasn't a date, so she opened hers and stepped out.

"Can you identify any suspects for us yet, Mr. Bellido? You looking at making an arrest anytime soon?" the reporter asked, following Rick out of the car and up to the barricades. "How about warning the anxious public with a description, some details? Are we talking an intruder? A psycho here?"

"Behind the horse, guy. I already told you! That's what it's there for," shouted one of the porch uniforms in a pissed-off voice as he trotted across the lawn.

Brennan's face fell like someone had stolen his puppy. Then he turned suddenly with a grin and ran back to where Julia was by the car. "Are you with the State Attorney's?"

She nodded.

"How'd they die in there, huh? Huh? Is it true the kids were mutilated? What about the father? Have you guys questioned him?" He fired questions like bullets. "Is he gonna die, too? Is he a suspect? Why won't your office make a damn statement?"

"Julia!" Rick called from the walk.

Oh, shit. She kept her head down and hurried past the police horse, following Rick up to the house. Just the nod had probably given away too much. She definitely had a crappy poker face. Always had. Heaven forbid it was a look from her that silently confirmed David Marquette was not only a suspect, but *the* suspect.

"This isn't a press conference, Mr. Brennan," Rick called out when she reached the front door. "When I want to hold one, I'll call you."

He closed the door behind them with a thud, and the two of them stepped down into an enormous marble-floored living room. Loud voices could be heard coming from one of the back rooms. "Latarrino?" Rick called out, disappearing down a hallway.

Julia stood where she was in awe. A stunning stone staircase, wrapped in wrought iron, hugged a two-story Venetian-plastered wall. Expensive knickknacks lined the shelves of an antique curio cabinet. Luxurious silk drapes dressed the windows. She'd watched enough *CSI* episodes to brace herself for what a murder scene would look like, and it was nothing like this. But for the thin coating of black fingerprint dust that covered the glass coffee table and windowsills, everything looked set for an *Architectural Digest* photo shoot. Even the throw pillows were arranged on the sofa. She swallowed, trying to force the foreboding feeling back down. It was like watching a horror movie. Any moment now she was going to find out why people were leaving the theater screaming.

"You coming?" Rick called out.

She tentatively followed him down a hallway that led into an all-white designer kitchen, the square footage of which was probably the same as that of her entire apartment. A once-upon-a-time chef herself, she recognized the Viking and Dacor brand names on the professional stainless-steel appliances. Cleaned baby bottles were laid out on paper towels next to the main sink. Gathered around a separate island, their backs to her, were two guys in MDPD Crime Scene polos and a plainclothes detective, the sleeves of his dress shirt rolled up to the elbows, a Glock holstered to his hip. A set of legs stuck out from underneath the island's sink, which rivaled the size of her tub.

"He's having trouble with the trap," said the plainclothes with a chuckle as Rick walked up. "Like you need a degree in fucking rocket science to be a plumber. Yo, Satty, you want me to call Roto-Rooter to help you do your job?"

"Fuck you, Brill," said a voice from under the sink.

"Hey, guys . . ." Rick nodded in Julia's direction. "You wanna watch yourselves?"

"Whoa, excuse me," said the plainclothes in a thick, scratchy New York accent, turning around. Short and stocky, he had an extra-full handlebar mustache and an Elvis pompadour that must have taken a lot of mousse to hold its height. The only things missing were the half-open satin dress shirt, gold chains, and patch of woolly chest hair. "Didn't realize you brought company with you, Ricky."

"Steve Brill, this is Julia Vacanti. She'll be working this with me. Julia, Steve's a detective with the Gables."

"Secretary?" asked Brill.

"She's a prosecutor, you ass," Rick shot back.

"Whoa, I'm sorry," Brill replied, holding up his hands defensively. "I'm just gonna shut up now."

"Finally," said the voice under the sink.

"You got it?" asked Brill.

"No, I don't got it. But you're finally gonna shut up." The room snickered.

"That's it. I'm calling in a plumber, you incompetent —" Brill looked over at Julia again, hesitated, then finished his thought, "jerk."

She turned away, pretending to look out the sliding glass doors that led to a tropical backyard and the pool. No one said anything. Talk about awkward. It was bad enough to be the only woman so far on scene, but she was also the youngest person in the room by at least a decade. And she was a lawyer, another fact she knew didn't win her any brownie points with the boys in blue — no matter whose team she was playing on.

"What're you guys doing?" Rick asked.

"Cleaning out the asshole's sewer line. What the hell do ya think we're doing? We're taking the traps." Brill looked back over at Julia. "Oh, shit," he said, smacking

69

his head. "Sorry for the language. Again. My bad."

She shook her head. "Don't worry about me. I speak French."

"Where's Latarrino?" asked Rick.

"Upstairs. Master bedroom, I think," Brill replied. "Hey, Ricky, thanks for exchanging pleasantries."

"Sorry, Steve. How you doing, my boy? Got enough lift to take off today?"

Brill laughed and proudly patted his pompadour. "That's better."

"Okay, Julia, let's head up," Rick said, heading back down the hall. "That's where the bodies were found."

"Hey, Ricky, can we arrest this asshole yet?" called out Brill.

"Soon," Rick yelled back from the living room. "Let's see what he has to say when the anesthesia wears off."

"Oh, shit," Julia heard the detective say with a chuckle to the guys in the kitchen. "I did it again."

"My kid makes you pay him a dollar in the potty-mouth bucket if you say a curse word," someone said.

"He must make a fortune off your fucking mouth, Lou," joked another.

"College fund's paid off."

Everyone laughed.

" 'Secretary'? You're a fucking idiot, Brill."

"What? What? I think I have suits older than her. Nice ass, though. Woo-hoo. I'm sure liking the looks of that." Then he yelled out, "Hey, Julie, sorry about the language!"

"No problem," Julia called back with a sigh she made sure no one could hear as she followed Rick up the stairs.

CHAPTER 8

Now it was beginning to look like a crime scene.

Julia stepped onto a landing that had once been carpeted. A huge swath of the wall-to-wall mint shag that stretched the length of the long hallway was missing; only the gray padding remained, speckled in some spots with dark blotches. Miniature white easels with numbers on them dotted the floor, marking for the photographers where evidence had been found and seized. The air smelled and tasted like the halls of a nursing home — like disinfectant and chemicals and death. Three doors led off the hall, all of them shut tight.

"The uniforms checked the first floor where we were, found nothing, came up here. We've got two sets of bloody footprints off the landing, one of which we believe is the first responding uniform's, who unwittingly stepped in blood, then walked it down to the last room on the left. That was the first room he checked, the little girl's room. That's where he found the six-year-old, Emma. The other set of prints we think belongs to Dad, but the scene got pretty chaotic once the bodies were found. There was a lot of blood and a lot of people running in and out of the house. Don't know what we'll get from Forensics, especially since the suspect prints were smeared and distorted, and it doesn't help that it's a shag — the long piles don't hold prints as well as a tightly looped Berber would. But we'll DNA to see whose blood it is being trailed, and I made sure the warrant lets us clean out Marquette's closet, so we'll test even his slippers and flipflops and see what we come up with as far as a tread match goes."

"I wouldn't think you'd need a warrant to search the victims' own home," Julia said quietly as her eyes passed over family photos that covered the hallway's pale-yellow walls. A beaming Jennifer and a pink-bonneted baby. A little girl with no front teeth in front of a Christmas tree and a fake fireplace. Another baby, this one swaddled in blue. David Marquette at his med school graduation.

Rick shot her a look. "A dead body might give you exigent circumstances to get into the house, secure it, and wait for the ME, but it doesn't give you the right to do a full search, even if the victim — or in this case victims — lived there, too. Best to remember that. I've watched hotshot veteran cops somehow forget they need a warrant when they respond to a homicide. They see 'dead body,' and that's all they need. What a freaking mess that is to clean up. Especially in a situation like this, where one of our victims turns out to be our defendant."

She nodded sheepishly. Strike three.

"We'll save Emma's room for last. Instead let's start in what we believe to be the order of the murders," Rick said as he turned and walked down another hallway that T-boned the balcony. A set of closed double doors waited at the end. More missing carpet. More evidence easels. More random dark blotches that had soaked into the gray rubber padding. "This is the master." He slipped on a pair of latex gloves he'd pulled from his pocket and handed her a pair. "Even though Crime Scene's been through the upstairs already for prints, use gloves if you touch anything. I hope you're not squeamish," he cautioned as he opened the door. "This is where the mother was found."

Julia swallowed hard and tried to brace herself for something she was suddenly no longer sure she wanted to see. It was one thing to watch *CSI* or *Bones,* to see fake bodies and fake autopsies in all their colorful glory on TV and think you could handle the real thing. Or to sit around and talk about a crime scene with colleagues — discuss the position of the bodies, the entry and exit wounds, the clinical cause of death. It was another to walk among ghosts down bloodstained halls. She had an urge to turn around — to just walk quickly down the stairs, out of this creepy, perfect house and back to the car, back to the office, back home. Take her scolding from Rifkin, kiss her budding relationship with Rick goodbye, and chalk up this overwhelmingly bad feeling that was slowly sucking the air out of the room to inexperience. *Just don't look anymore. Don't see it. Don't open the door, Julia.*

Don't make it real.

But it was too late for that. Dark-red splashes of blood ran up arctic-white walls, exploding into countless tiny droplets on the ceiling. Evidence tape marked where blood and other fluids had presumably dripped or pooled onto the wood floor. Above the antique sleigh bed was an eleven-by-fourteen-inch wedding portrait of a smiling David and Jennifer. Beneath it was the stripped-bare mattress, stained a rich, dark red. Blood had seeped through the thin pillow-top, leaving a jagged line on the side of the bed that looked a couple of inches deep in places. Julia's eyes returned to the happy portrait taken what must've been only a few short years ago. Blood had sprayed up onto the glass, coagulating and then freezing in time as it had dripped back down, like drops of paint stuck forever onto a dry wall.

The ghosts were crying tears of blood, the silenced shrieks of the dead playing over and over again in her head like the violent crescendo of music in a horror film.

That was when Julia realized she'd just walked into the part where everyone starts screaming.

CHAPTER 9

"The body was found faceup, as you can figure out, on the bed. We've got spatter on the headboard and the walls, traveling at a high enough velocity to actually hit an eight-foot ceiling. I don't know how much you know about bloodstain-pattern interpretation, but a helluva lot of force is needed on impact to generate that type of distal trajectory. The spray pattern starts here and travels up," Rick said, motioning to the wall next to the nightstand, "indicating that Jennifer was lying flat when she was first struck. The drops on the ceiling are satellite spatters, most likely the result of an arterial spurt when he hit the aorta or jugular. She was probably sleeping when it happened."

Probably sleeping. The words struck Julia as odd — disconnected — in a room painted red with the woman's blood. Maybe when he landed the first blow, but definitely not the last . . . The bloodstain impression on the mattress was only on one side, in the general shape of a person. Julia didn't need crime-scene photos or video to envision Jennifer Marquette's twisted blue face, her eyes, open and vacant, staring dully up at the ceiling.

"Cause of death, blunt trauma to the head and multiple stab wounds," Rick finished.

"Thirty-two in all," said a deep voice behind Julia, making her jump in her skin for the second time in twenty minutes. She turned to face a young-looking guy, midthirties, in a white dress shirt and Tommy Bahama swordfish tie paired with old Levis and new Nikes. With light-blue eyes, dark-blond hair that definitely went past his collar, and well-tanned, unshaven skin, he looked a little like a surfer who'd reluctantly had to get a real job. A gold detective's badge hung around his neck.

"Just the man we're looking for," Rick said. "Julia, Detective John Latarrino, Miami-Dade Homicide. Lat, this is Julia Vacanti. She's a prosecutor in our office. She'll be working this with me."

Latarrino nodded. "Nice to meet you."

"She's already met Brill downstairs."

"I'm sorry," Latarrino replied.

"I was just showing her the scene. Anything new?"

"Just got the preliminary autopsy report back this morning. Speaking of which, what happened to you last night, Bellido?"

Rick looked around the room. "I had another engagement," he replied dismissively. "I called over this morning, but Nielson wasn't in yet. He was supposed to do the autopsies today, and I was gonna be there. Torie gave me the rundown, though." Rick looked at Julia and explained the players. "Joe Nielson's the Chief ME. Torie's his assistant."

"You know most of it, then," Lat said with a shrug. "Blunt trauma to the head probably knocked her unconscious. At least that's what we hope. Impact slammed her brain against the other side of her skull, resulting in a large hematoma and massive bleeding. Thirty-two stab wounds to the chest and neck — at least three through to the mattress. One hit the aorta, another the jugular, and that was it. She was wearing just a nightshirt, which was ripped open, and a pair of panties. But no other evidence of sexual assault. Nielson did do a rape kit. It's not back yet.

"We think he surprised her here," Lat continued, looking around the room as if the bloody walls could answer him. "There was nothing under the nails, no sign of a struggle. No evidence the body'd been moved. As you said, Bellido, she was probably sleeping, he came in, hit her upside the head, made it look like a rape attempt, and then went at her with a kitchen knife."

"Have you found the weapons?" asked Julia, taking a few steps forward, physically distancing herself from the scene behind her. She didn't want to turn around again or look into the mirror that was directly behind Detective Latarrino, mounted above a neat marble-top dresser dotted with more family pictures, a jewelry box, and some cosmetics. All around her she could see the blood spatters raining down on her. The room was suddenly boiling hot, and she struggled not to gasp for more air. It was getting hard to stay focused.

"We did find a baseball bat in the boy's closet. No blood on it that we can see, but he could've cleaned it up. The lab can check for blood, hair, or fiber."

"What about the knife?" she asked, clearing her throat.

"We think that'll be the one the docs removed from David Marquette's stomach. We also seized every knife we could find downstairs. Nielson says it looks like a straight blade that attacked Jennifer and the kids because he saw no tears consistent with a jagged edge, but that's the best he can do. We'll do pattern testing, but perfect matches only occur on shows like *CSI,* you know. You're not a fan, are you?" he asked, frowning.

"I don't watch TV," she lied with a shake of her head. "The knife that was recovered?"

"A Henckels boning knife. Straight blade, seven inches. Brill's downstairs taking the traps to see if there's blood in the drains, although we found bleach under the upstairs and downstairs sinks, so there's a chance we might not find shit if the guy knew what he was doing with a bottle of Clorox. Rigor had not yet begun, so time of death, based on temperature, lividity, and stomach contents, was sometime between one and five A.M., when uniforms responded."

"That's the best Nielson can do?" asked Rick, exasperated.

"That's it. You must've pissed him off before with that charming personality of yours, Bellido, because he says to tell you that he's not a miracle worker, so don't ask him for the second hand on time of death."

"Fuck him," Rick grumbled.

The detective turned to Julia. "Exact time of death is another fallacy spread to the mindless masses on Thursday nights by Jerry Bruckheimer and his team of writers.

But while we can't tell you the instant Jennifer Marquette stopped living, Bellido, I can share some news I think you'll find probably even more interesting. We have verbal confirmation that Dr. David Marquette was booked at the Marriott World Center in Orlando from Friday night through today to speak at an AMA conference. The front desk manager got a bit nervous when I said the words 'homicide investigation,' so Terri's readying subpoenas for the records."

"Jesus Christ!" Rick barked. "Why the hell didn't you call me?"

"You had another engagement."

"Don't let them touch that room, Lat!"

John Latarrino was the same height as Rick Bellido but somehow looked a lot bigger. He held up his hand. "I've already done the warrant. You can look it over before Orlando PD takes it to the judge for a signature. See, unlike all those other hotshot veteran cops you've had to show the ropes, Bellido, I know when I need to go to the bathroom and when I need a warrant." He smiled and cracked his gum.

An uncomfortable moment passed. "That wasn't directed at you," Rick replied.

"Of course not."

The tension broke with the ring of a

phone. "I gotta take this," Rick said, opening his cell and moving into the master bathroom.

"All right," Latarrino said, looking at his watch. Julia could tell there was a strained history between the two men, but it was too early to say just whose fault that was. After waiting about thirty long seconds, the detective turned and headed back out into the hall. "Bellido's already had his tour. Follow me, Ms. Prosecutor, and let's get this over with," he called back. "It only gets worse from here. . . ."

CHAPTER 10

"We're assuming the caller on the nine-
eleven tape was Emma, although she neve
identified herself," Latarrino explained as
they walked back down the center hall to
the landing. "On digital enhancement of the
final seconds of muffled audio before the
line drops, we can hear a man's voice calling out the name 'Emma,' followed by a crying voice saying, 'No, Daddy!' Based on the
timing of that call, we think Emma was the
last one left alive in the house; that David
Marquette had already killed his wife, left
the master bedroom, and then walked down
this hall here, probably making some of the
prints that we took up in his wife's blood
which he must've been covered in. Then we
figure he entered either the infant's room or
Danny's room. At some point Emma woke
up, probably saw what happened to her
mom or what was happening to her brother
or sister, took the cordless from the hall

charger, and hid back in her own room, where she placed the call to nine-eleven, asking for help. That's when the dad came in and found her, calling out her name because she wasn't in bed like she was supposed to be. When he finds her, she begs him, 'No, Daddy!' and he hangs up the line. We found the phone next to her body."

Latarrino stopped at the first closed door and rubbed his eyes. "Like Jennifer, Danny was found in his bed. God willing, the little guy never knew what hit him. Just went to sleep with a kiss from Mommy and never woke up."

Julia held her breath again as the door opened. Race cars zoomed across blue-and-red striped wallpaper; tiny Matchbox cars lined neat white shelves. Set up in a corner of the room was a loop-de-loop Hot Wheels racetrack with a long line of cars and trucks backed up and waiting to be played with on its yellow tracks. A toddler's bed in the shape of a race car was pushed up against a wall. The bedding was gone.

"This looks clean," she said right away, looking at the tiny bed. "Cleaner than the master."

"We had spatter, but definitely nowhere near the scene we had in there. Cause of death was blunt trauma to the head. Several stab wounds to the torso, but not much bleeding into surrounding tissue, so Nielson says they were made postmortem, which is another reason it wasn't as bloody. No spurting or gushing because the heart wasn't pumping anymore. My take? This guy wasn't as angry with Junior as he was with his wife. He showed restraint, if that makes any sense."

She nodded.

"It also makes him out to be more of a monster in my mind. Bastard tucked the kid in again before he tiptoed out to find his daughter," Latarrino said as he walked back toward the doorway. "This is the one the boys hoped they'd still find sleeping when they pulled back the covers."

"Why isn't the mattress stained, like the mother's?" she asked, following him back out into the hall.

"You're pretty observant. For a lawyer," he said with a smile that was hard to read as he closed the door quietly behind them. "Rubber sheets. The little guy was still in training."

God, she needed to get the hell out of here. Even for just a few minutes, she needed to step outside and suck in some fresh air instead of this stale, heavy, hot substance that now filled every room. She could taste the air now, coppery and bitter on her tongue, like she'd bitten her lip and swallowed a mouthful of old blood. But she knew that even a request for a bathroom break would be interpreted as a sign of weakness, especially by this detective and definitely by the crew downstairs, so she said nothing as she followed Latarrino to the door at the far end of the hall — the one with all the crayon scribbles made by someone who couldn't have been more than three feet tall.

"This is Emma's room," Latarrino said, pushing open the door. "We found her in the corner, behind a box of Barbie dolls and Hello Kitty chair."

Even though the Barbies had been seized and the chair impounded, Julia immediately knew what corner little Emma had run and hidden from her daddy in. Her blood matted the pink carpet and splattered the lilac walls. The ending of the story she'd so desperately begun to tell to a stranger on the phone now left to be translated into words by a specialist in bloodstain-pattern analysis.

It was no use. Julia could no longer maintain the collected, detached persona of prosecutor. She sucked in a breath as her imagination took over, placing the tiny, frightened figure in the scene, racing from room to room, looking for a place to hide from her daddy. Maybe his eerie whispers as he came looking for her; his demands that she come out, come out, wherever she was. The dead were screaming in her head and she could feel the jolt of adrenaline in her own body, the terror that had seized Emma's heart when he'd finally found her hiding spot. And then the sinking, shocking feeling of betrayal when she'd seen the knife, knowing what he was going to do with it before it came down on her, but still not believing it as it did. Still loving him even then. Julia covered her ears and turned away from the gruesome sight.

Latarrino looked embarrassed. "God, this job sucks," he said quietly, turning to look out the picture window that opened onto the backyard. "No matter how many scenes you've been to, nothing ever preps you for this. Nothing." Outside, uniforms chatted and laughed in the sunshine by the pool. The soft sound of their voices drifted up and into the room, filling the void of strained, reflective silence. He turned away from the window to look back at her, immediately frowning. "Enough. Let's get you out of here. You don't look so good."

The truth was, she didn't feel so good

She fought back a wave of nausea. "There's still the baby's room," she said weakly, wiping the sweat that'd gathered on her lip with the back of her hand. The latex from the glove pulled on her skin, and she could taste its chalky bitterness on her lips. She felt incredibly light-headed and could only hope that if she did go down, she'd whack her head on something hard and at least stay unconscious long enough for the ambulance to pull out of the driveway.

"Ain't nothing you need to see in there, Counselor. Just a pretty nursery," Latarrino said softly, taking her gently by the elbow and leading her back to the hallway. "He only suffocated that one."

CHAPTER 11

She sat on the closed toilet lid, her forehead pressed up against the cool marble window sill, a warm breeze from the open window blowing on the wet wad of toilet paper she had packed on the back of her neck.

"Is it passing?" Latarrino asked, looking awkwardly around the bathroom.

"Yes," she said into the wall. "I'm fine now, thank you. I think maybe I'm coming down with something."

"Oh. That's rough."

She hoped her legs wouldn't twitch when she stood. Or at least that he wouldn't see them twitch. "Okay," she said looking up at him, "I can see the rest of the house now."

"You're still a little pale," he answered frowning. "I think you should stay down another minute or two. You know, this happens all the time. It's a tough scene, even with the bodies gone."

She decided not to say anything. And she

didn't get up.

"If you don't mind me asking, how'd you get this case?" he asked, leaning up against the sink, hands in his jeans pockets. "I mean, I haven't seen you before at the State, and I know that Bellido's definitely keeping this one for himself. Plus, he's not the type to share glory. So are you a new hire, or have they been hiding you with the brains up in Legal?"

Julia sat up stiffly. "I'm in Judge Farley's division. Rick and Charley Rifkin asked me this morning to second-seat this case." Not entirely true, but Rifkin had been there when the decision had been made.

He nodded thoughtfully. "I've had a few cases in front of Farley. Is he still an ass-hole?"

She caught herself smiling. "Yes. And like a bottle of cheap wine, rest assured he's only gotten worse with age."

"I thought wine got better with age."

"The cheap ones turn to vinegar."

Latarrino shrugged. "I'm a beer drinker myself. I thought Karyn Simms was the DC in Farley's."

"She is."

"Oh. Then who're you? The A?"

Her back arched. "I'm the B."

"The B? Wow," he said with a low whistle.

"You must be something special then." He looked at her, but differently for a second, as if he'd just figured something out. Call her cynical, but that something was probably that she was a woman and ergo must have used her feminine wiles to climb the company ladder. What really pissed her off, though, was that that guess would be half right since she was sleeping with the lead counsel.

She rose, took the soggy, bunched-up paper wad off her neck, flushed it down the toilet, and closed the window. "Why does everyone think it's him?" she asked, smoothing her skirt. "The dad, Dr. Marquette. Why's everyone so sure it's him?"

"Well, for one, units arrived within about six minutes of the call and gained entry within another twenty. No one else was found in the house, and there's no evidence of any break-in."

"Why did it take them so long to enter?"

"Good question. One I'm sure the boys will be asking themselves for a long time to come. They thought it was a prank. There were no previous domestics, no sign of trouble outside. Hindsight's always twenty-twenty, Counselor."

"Oh," she said, pausing. She didn't want to sound like an idiot again and say the wrong thing, yet she couldn't help but think of JonBenet Ramsey, the seven-year-old in Boulder, Colorado, who'd been taken from her bed and murdered in her home on Christmas night with her parents and brother sleeping just down the hall. The police and DA had instantly focused on the parents, but the murder had never been solved. The Ramsey detectives were criticized for having tunnel vision — focusing solely on Mom and Dad while critical evidence was destroyed, other leads were ignored, and the real murderer long gone and still on the loose. "Could a killer have gotten in some other way?" she asked. "An open window? The garage?"

"Now you're playing defense attorney."

"Someone's going to."

"There were no other signs of forced entry. Nothing missing from the home that we could see, which would eliminate robbery as a motive. The father was supposed to be speaking at some medical conference three hundred miles away, and he shows up here. He's the sole survivor in a scene out of a freaking horror movie. He's got a knife stuck in his gut, but even though that sounds really bad, he surprisingly has relatively minor injuries when the rest of his family went through a bloodbath. And of course we have his crying six-year-old or tape naming him as her murderer."

"That is pretty damning," she conceded.

"And we're pretty sure that when we dig we'll find some other interesting info Always do."

"Like a girlfriend?"

"Or girlfriends. Domestic strife. Money problems."

"Insurance policies . . ."

"Now you're thinking on the right side o the law, Counselor."

"Please call me Julia. So it was a suicid attempt then?"

"Maybe. Maybe murder and attempted suicide. Wouldn't be the first. I'm thinking it was supposed to be just murder. The suicide attempt came after he realized hi daughter had called the cops on him and he was running out of time with an alibi that was still some three hundred miles away."

"Where was he found?"

"Master bath. He was unconscious and naked on the floor, nothing but a towe beside him, knife sticking straight out of hi belly. Shower was still wet."

"What were his actual injuries? I know he had to have emergency surgery today."

"A collapsed lung and a carefully placed abdominal stab wound. Could've been fatal

I suppose — which is what I'm sure his attorney's gonna argue — but wasn't. A pulmonary embolism he threw this morning necessitated additional surgery."

"Sounds serious."

"He'll be fine."

"You obviously think the wounds are self-inflicted?"

"They're too neat for what went on in this house."

She paused again. "What I don't understand is why. If suicide was just an afterthought, why would he do this to his family? To his wife? His kids? Jesus Christ, to a baby? I mean, the man's a doctor. . . ."

"Don't let the MD blind you, Counselor. There've been plenty of murderers throughout history who were smart enough to go to college. Matter of fact, the smarter they are, the more likely it is they'll get away with it."

"Fine. I'll try not to let his profession impress me. But you said it, Detective Latarrino — that's not just a crime scene in here, that's a bloodbath."

"Let us finish the investigation. Maybe we'll find you your why. But I have some bad news for you, Julia," he said, making sure he emphasized her name. "Welcome to the big time, where there's not always an answer that's gonna make sense; that's why the law doesn't make us prove why. Look, people are messed up, and sometimes they snap. Especially in domestics. I'm sure I'm not the first to point out for you the fine line that exists between love and hate. When someone crosses it, nothing's gonna prep you for what he or she is capable of. Nothing."

The room began to spin again — round and round, faster and faster, like a merry-go-round gone out of control. Julia took a deep breath. She tried to focus on counting to ten, like Dr. Weiner had taught her, once upon a lifetime ago. Deep breath, get to five. Deep breath, get to six. The spit dried in her mouth, her heart began to race, the walls closed in. It'd been years since she'd had a panic attack — please, God, not a full-on one now. What she had to do was stay focused. Recognize what was happening and get out of the situation. Get out of here. She grabbed the edge of the sink.

Sometimes they snap. . . .

There was no way to jump off, nothing she could do to steady herself as the awful, strange, fragmented memory suddenly rushed her. . . .

The warm smells of fried bacon, freshly cooked waffles, and brewing coffee filled the air. All around her in the packed IHOP were tables of happy people cheerfully chowing down their Sunday-morning after-church breakfasts, chattering away as if nothing had just gone horribly wrong in the world. The ordinariness of it all made her want to scream.

Uncle Jimmy stared at her with the saddest eyes Julia had ever seen. "Some people just ain't made right, hon," he said quietly while Aunt Nora cried softly next to him. "Only God knows why they do what they do. It's best for all of us not to try and understand, ya know? 'Cause we won't. We can't. It's too horrible to think somebody could . . ." He stopped himself, choking on his words. "Sometimes people," he finished, crying, "well, they just snap. . . ."

". . . and I've seen some bad shit," the detective was saying.

"Well, a jury's gonna want to know why, Detective Latarrino," she started slowly, her breath catching. "Even if we're not required to prove it."

Mercifully, the detective seemed oblivious to what was happening to her, staring instead at something in the shower. "Assuming Marquette wants to talk, we're gonna try. Just as soon as the docs give us the green light. By the way, Julia, call me Lat, please. Or John. Save Detective Latarrino for the stand."

She nodded. The merry-go-round slowed just a little. She continued to count off numbers in her head, adding one more to each count as she clenched and unclenched her fists. "Ready?" she asked, sucking in a final deep breath. Only a few steps to the door, and then she was almost out of here. . . .

"When you are." The Nextel at the detective's side chirped to life. "Lat? You there? Come in." Steve Brill's distinctive voice filled the bathroom.

"G'ahead," Lat replied.

"You still upstairs?"

"Yup. Try walking up a flight next time, pal. It might do wonders on that beer belly."

"Fuck you, you steroid-loving piece of crap. Oh, shit. You still with Bellido and that prosecutor chick?"

"Yup. Wanna say a quick hello?" Lat chuckled. "Or should I just send a tech down to extract that foot from your mouth?"

"Nah, 'cause I'm sure everyone's gonna like what I have to say, color and all. I just got a call from the duty nurse at Ryder."

"We're listening," Lat replied, looking at Julia, his hand on the doorknob.

"The motherfucker just woke up."

CHAPTER 12

Julia sat back in her chair at her desk and stared at the phone in her hand. It was still yelling at her.

"Don't tell me I gots to come down there! I don't gots to do nuthin'! And let me tell you, lady, nobody's done shit for me since Alonzo cut me up. Now you wanna talk all nice and be my friend?"

"What is it that you'd like me to do for you, Pamela?" Julia asked through gritted teeth, still trying her best to sound patient. "I kept him behind bars for you for the past two months. Now to keep him there, you've got to come to court tomorrow."

Pamela Johnson finally stopped yelling. There was a long pause before she spoke again in a much more hesitant voice. "What if I don't want him to stay in jail no mo'?"

Julia closed her eyes. Classic domestic victim. "Pamela, he took a razor blade to your face."

"I got chil'ren. One jus' born."

"We can help you find shelter."

"Bullshit!" The yelling was back. "That's what I mean, y'all don't do shit for me. I need food, lady. My kids need t'eat. They need their daddy is what they need."

"Pamela, I'm sorry," Julia said, her own voice rising, her patience thinning. "I really am. But what damn good is their daddy gonna do them if he's in jail for killing their mommy? Then who's gonna feed your damn kids?"

"Fuck this shit!" Pamela screamed.

Maybe that was a little harsh. "I can arrange transporta—" Julia began, but it was too late. All that remained of Pamela Johnson was the dead hum of a dial tone.

Julia hung up and rubbed her tired eyes. Then she spun her chair around and looked out her rain-streaked window. The streets in front of the State Attorney's Office were deserted, miniature lakes the only thing left behind in the parking lot after the heavens had opened up a couple of hours earlier. Except for a few other diehards and social recluses, she'd be one of the last to leave the building.

She'd forgotten about the Guarino trial until she and Rick had gotten back to the office. By that time it was after four, and

Melba already had her sneakers on, purse on lap. Finding anyone in Investigations willing to serve a subpoena this close to five was just not going to happen. So after prepping the next morning's forty-eight-page calendar, Julia had worked the phone lines herself for the rest of the rainy evening and into the night, calling witnesses and beeping officers, hoping that after she picked a jury tomorrow she'd actually have someone show up to put on the stand. At nine o'clock she'd finally gotten hold of Pamela Johnson. Five minutes later she was talking to herself. She reached for her folder on excited utterances. Farley was gonna crucify her.

Past the twin five-ton air handlers outside her window, directly across from the courthouse, stood the steel-and-concrete mass that was the Dade County Jail. Even now, strange undesirables squatted under its overhang, smoking cigarettes and drinking from paper bags, waiting for a friend or relative to make bond. Behind the razor wire and barred windows were some of the most violent men in the state of Florida. Murderers, robbers, pedophiles, rapists. All caged together, waiting for a trial, or their next hearing, or to finally find out what state prison Corrections would be shipping them off to for the next couple of decades. Alonzo

Guarino was among them. Soon enough, so would be David Marquette.

She rubbed her eyes and thought back to the morning. In her three years as a prosecutor, never had her job affected her the way it had today. Never before had a case or a criminal or a victim rushed back to consciousness the horrible memories her brain had long since purposely displaced. Memories that nightmares were made of. Memories that triggered debilitating panic attacks in the middle of bright, sunny days.

Life was funny, and not always in a good way. Happy childhood recollections were always random and spotty, like miscellaneous snapshots shoved into a scrapbook. The smiling faces were fuzzy, the details slightly out of focus. Why you remembered some and not others was anyone's guess. But the bad memories . . . those were always painfully vivid. They played like a movie in your head — each second recollected in real time, every face still crystal clear even decades later. And the seemingly innocuous exchanges that preceded or succeeded something awful — moments that would otherwise never have formed a memory on their own — they, too, became part of the film noir. Like breakfast with your aunt and uncle on a sunny Sunday morning . . .

Julia scrounged the bottom of her desk drawer for the Tylenol bottle she knew was in there somewhere. That and a full glass of wine when she got home might help relieve the pressure building inside her head. Perhaps the one and only good thing that could be said of Alonzo Guarino was that he'd kept her mind busy for the past couple of hours — far away from places it shouldn't go and people it shouldn't remember. It was hard to believe that only hours ago she'd been so excited to be working her first murder. And now . . . She finally found the bottle under some old dispos and pulled it out. She looked at her hands. They were shaking.

She dry-mouthed four gel caps and pulled the crumpled *Herald* from her purse, staring at the headline that was soon to be yesterday's news. Wrapped inside the paper was the small manila envelope with the 911 tape that Lat had given her before she'd left the house. She hadn't listened to it yet, for a number of reasons. She tapped her fingers on the package, wondering what'd happened this afternoon down at the hospital. She hadn't heard from Rick since they'd returned from the ME's office. Maybe Marquette had confessed. Maybe he was already in custody. Maybe this case would go the way of a quick plea, like 90 percent of all arrests. Maybe that would be a good thing. . . . She looked over at the phone and toyed with the idea of calling him, but decided against it. If he'd wanted to call her, he would have.

Just as she was thinking it, the phone rang. She jumped in her seat. "State Attorney's," she answered hesitantly.

"Julia? You still there?" Rick asked. He sounded surprised she'd picked up.

"Hey yourself. I was just thinking about you. Yeah, I'm still here," she sighed. "Prepping for my trial tomorrow."

"The one with no witnesses?"

"No victim. I'm hoping for a change of heart, but it's not looking good. She just hung up on me." Julia stood up and walked to the window, craning her neck to try to get a look at the parking lot to see if she could spot his car. "Where are you?" she asked.

"Heading home from dinner. I just got off the phone with Latarrino."

She stopped craning. "Oh. How'd it go?"

"It didn't. The boys didn't make it through the front door of Ryder. Mel Levenson greeted them in the parking lot."

Even she knew who that was. Mel Levenson, the self-proclaimed Jewish Johnnie Cochran of Miami. A big-name defense attorney who usually handled big-name celebrities for a big-name price. "So I guess Dr. Marquette's doing okay," she replied. "Well enough to pick up the phone and call a high-priced lawyer."

This was big. Even though legally you weren't allowed to infer someone's guilt because he or she decided to hire a lawyer and not cooperate with the police, everyone in law enforcement did just that. After all, why wouldn't a dad want to help the police find the murderer of his wife and kids?

"It sucks that Latarrino didn't get a statement." There was a brief, static-filled pause. "Let's see what the boys turn up in Orlando tomorrow. Our doc's not going anywhere for at least a few days, and I want to make sure we dot our i's on this one. His arrest is gonna generate a lot of press. I don't want to look like an ass by jumping the gun."

She heard something slam in the background and then the beep of a car alarm. "I just pulled into my building," he explained. "So you're gonna head home now, too?"

"I was just packing up," she lied.

"Okay, well, look, I'm getting another call. Let's talk in the morning. We'll get coffee."

"Okay. Good-night." She clicked off the phone before he could say good-bye. She hated new relationships. She hated the way she felt right now — insecure and unsure, like the schoolgirl who'd fallen for the high school star quarterback. Or in this case, his coach. Rick certainly didn't owe her a phone call or even a good-night before he left the office — although that would've been nice — but she hated thinking about someone who wasn't thinking about her.

She sat back in her chair with a sigh, fingering the manila envelope, then ripped it open. She popped the 911 tape into the boom box on top of the file cabinet and hit play. The crackle of dead air filled the room until the tape began. A long beep signaled the start of the call.

"Police and fire. What's your emergency?"

Silence.

"This is the nine-one-one operator. Is there an emergency?" the dispatcher repeated.

More silence.

"You've reached the emergency line, can I —"

"Help us, please," said the small voice.

The dead were alive once more. Julia closed her eyes. It was being in that house, smelling those smells, seeing the blood on the walls, on the carpets, splattered everywhere. She knew there were places that a cleaning crew would never get to in a death house, where the blood would seep and settle and become part of the walls and the very foundation. When the sun went down and the lights went out, you could hear the screams of the dead, trapped forever in those walls. No matter how much you scrubbed, no matter how much you cleaned, it would always be a house of slaughter.

"I can help you," the operator tried in a soothing, almost mothering tone. "What's your name?"

Silence.

The operator tried again. "Can you speak up? I can barely hear you."

"Help us . . . please."

"I'm going to help you, honey. I need you to stay on the line and tell me exactly what's happened."

"I think he's coming . . ."

Goose bumps rose on Julia's skin.

"Who's coming? Are you hurt? What's your name?"

"I think he's coming back."

"Who's coming back? Has someone been hurt? Do you need an ambulance?"

"Uh-oh. No, no . . . sshh, sshh . . ." the little voice whispered, obviously panicked.

The operator remained silent for two seconds, then started back in. "Hello? Is there someone on the line? Is there anyone there? This is the emergency operator. . . ."

"No, no . . . Oh, no, no!"

The muffled sound of silence, as if someone had covered the phone, then the volume and static got louder, followed by a man's voice.

"Emma?"

"No, Daddy!"

The hum of a dead line, and the tape clicked off.

"Recorded four forty-seven A.M., Sunday, October eighth, two thousand six," reported the digital voice.

Julia opened her eyes with a start and stared once again through the drizzle at the Dade County Jail, glowing ghostly gray in the powerful beams of the searchlights.

It was time to go home.

CHAPTER 13

"What time will you be home in the morning?" Julia's mom asked from the dinette, looking up from her Ladies' Home Journal, which had just come in the afternoon mail. Her glasses slipped to the tip of her nose. Her mom always wore her thick, long hair up in a high ponytail, but tonight it was down, her dark waves spilling glamorously across her shoulders. She'd just taken a shower, and although it was only seven thirty at night, she was already wearing her pajamas. Julia had bought her the nightgown for her birthday. It was pink with delicate yellow satin roses on the sleeves. Pajamas at seven thirty? How totally lame, Julia thought.

She put her fuzzy purple overnight bag on the kitchen counter and sighed loudly because that's what you do when you're thirteen and majorly inconvenienced by your mother. "What time do you want me to come home?"

"Do you have homework due on Monday?"

"Just the report in social studies. But that's easy."

"Then ten o'clock," her mom said, rolling up the magazine.

"But tomorrow's Sunday, Mom!" Julia protested.

"And you have an assignment due. Tell Carly no Saturday Night Live. You need to get some sleep. I'm sure Mrs. Hogan doesn't want you two up after she's gone to bed, anyway."

It was so unfair. "Mom, jeez . . . ten o'clock?" Julia looked around for an ally, but there was no one else in the room.

"You heard me, Monster." She tapped the magazine against her palm. Julia noticed she'd painted her nails a boring shell pink. Her mom never painted her nails. Never wore makeup. Never dressed up or wore high heels or did her hair in anything other than a pony. There wasn't any reason — she never left the house anymore. Tonight must be big. Maybe her dad was gonna break out the Trivial Pursuit. "Besides," her mom said, getting up from her chair and coming around the table to where Julia stood with her arms defiantly folded across her chest, "I'm gonna miss your face tonight. So give me a kiss before you walk out that door."

Julia held out her cheek and gave her mom

a perfunctory peck back. Then she grabbed her fuzzy bag off the counter and hurried out the front door and into the cold night air, crisp with the smell of pine and burning leaves. Carly's house was a few blocks' walk away. She was officially free till tomorrow morning! And she was definitely watching Saturday Night Live. . . .

She walked down the front walk, humming Christmas songs to herself, the crunch of old snow under her sneakers, not once imagining she would never see her mother alive again.

"Know what I think?" said Perry. "I think there must be something wrong with us. To do what we did."

Dick was annoyed. Annoyed as hell. Why the hell couldn't Perry shut up? Christ Jesus, what damn good did it do, always dragging the goddamn thing up?

"There's got to be something wrong with somebody who'd do a thing like that," Perry said.

"Deal me out, baby," Dick said. "I'm a normal."

— TRUMAN CAPOTE,
IN COLD BLOOD

CHAPTER 14

". . . I changed his dressing and emptied
he pan; just keep an eye on his line. Dr.
_orton upped his Valium to two hundred
nilligrams. He'd been pulling at his tubes."

"How long ago was he dosed?"

"Maybe thirty minutes. He's out for the
light, that's for sure."

The voices dropped to hushed, excited
vhispers. "So how'd he take it? God, how
loes anyone take that news. . . ."

"You wanna know? I heard he didn't do
anything. Alice Leighton was in here. Said
ie just stared at the wall. Everyone else was
:rying, even Alice. It's just so sad."

"Maybe he was in shock. He must be."

"I know *I'd* do more than stare at a wall if
omeone told me my family was dead."

"Well, can he talk?"

"He's off the vent. Sure he can talk."

"Tell me! Does he know who did it? Does
ie remember anything at all?"

"Like I told you, he didn't say —"

Beep. Beep. Beep. Beep. Beep. The shriek of an alarm serrated the conversation.

"Oh, shit, he's tachy. I'd better get the doc. This guy shouldn't even be dreaming."

"Is he bad?"

The nurse hit the end-sound button. The alarm stopped. "Nah. Heart rate's one-fifty. He'll live."

The door opened with a whoosh, and brightness rushed in. It just as quickly snapped out as the harried whispers drifted off down the hall.

He tried to touch his face but couldn't move his hands. No, he could move his hands, but they wouldn't go where he wanted them to go. He pulled and pulled, but nothing. He realized then that he was attached to the bed. Strapped down like an animal.

He listened to the blip of his own heart, sure and steady, as it etched across the monitor. In his first year of med school, he'd wondered what it was like when the first flatline happened, when the heart seized and the end was coming. He'd heard stories from those he'd helped bring back. Stories of bright lights and smiling angels coming to escort you to eternity, but no one who made it back to the living ever spoke o anything evil. No black-hooded grim reapers waiting in the darkness to collect the devil's due. Maybe those people, he thought, never came back from the edge. Maybe they went straight to hell for what they'd done.

He closed his eyes and listened to his heartbeat in the pure darkness.

Maybe he was one of the lucky ones.

CHAPTER 15

John Latarrino rubbed his eyes and struggled to focus on the road in front of him. The patter of driving rain and the rhythmic *swish-swash* of the wipers was hypnotic, and right now he was an easy subject. He slugged down a gulp of coffee, turned up the static on the country-music station, and blew the AC on max. In the seat next to him, Detective Steve Bril hadn't even moved — his snoring face was still smashed up against the window, where it'd been since they'd pulled onto I-95 and out of Miami.

It probably wasn't the best idea to drive to Orlando tonight, considering he'd been up for almost two days straight. But i fourteen years as a cop had taught La anything, it was to never trust anyone else to do your job. Not if you wanted it done right. In the event of a screw-up, shit defied gravity at his department and rolled uphill

Rather than let Orlando PD execute his search warrant, Lat knew enough to get his butt in the car and head three hundred miles north to the land of everything Mickey. And after Marquette's high-priced mouthpiece had greeted him and Brill at the hospital door this afternoon and told them that the good doctor would regretably be unable to cooperate with their investigation, Lat had decided there was no time like the present.

Although he didn't necessarily want company on the three-hour ride, he'd invited Brill along for a couple of reasons. First, the long drive could be a hazard on zero sleep, and another body meant another set of hands on the wheel. Second, this was still a Coral Gables case. Officially, Lat's department had been brought in only to assist. Since it was unseemly for anyone to be killed in posh Coral Gables, thoughts were that the county would be better equipped to handle a quadruple homicide, seeing as it actually had a homicide squad, a crime lab, and a lot of experience with dead bodies. Enter MDPD and Detective John Larrino. The reality of the situation, though, was that his department would actually be taking over the investigation, and the responsibility of finding answers would shift to him as the lead detective. Lat knew it Brill accepted it, but out of respect, no one actually said it. Instead everyone just slipped quietly into their new roles.

The silent change of command would definitely not help forge the strongest of bonds between either the two department or the two cops. It couldn't. Even if a department was completely inept, no one really wanted somebody else peeing on their territory and taking charge of their mess. And that no one included Elias Vasquez, the chief of Coral Gables, who himself had been the one to call in the county Sunday morning. That created a delicate and potentially explosive problem for Lat. Because for the duration of the investigation — whether they liked it or not — Brill and he would have to function like partners. Manpower at MDPD wasn't unlimited. Besides an analyst, Crime Scene, and use of the lab, Lat wasn't gonna get any other bodies to help conduct interviews or run leads. That meant he needed Brill, and he needed the Gables, and he needed the two departments to work together. The one thing he didn't need was to take a power trip to Orlando all by himself. Sharing the ride, he'd figured would be the best way to befriend his new partner.

Of course he had no idea if the guy felt befriended, seeing as he'd slept the entire way up. While he hadn't worked with Brill before, he'd heard all about the guy's reputation from those who had. "Hot-headed," "difficult," and "obnoxious" were some of the adjectives. "A cheating, moth-erfucking asshole" offered the most com-plete description, but that came from a female detective who'd actually dated him. Lat didn't count that; God knew what his own ex-wife would say about him behind closed doors. But snoring and abrasive adjectives aside, no one was denying the man was competent. He'd been with the Gables fifteen years, the last three of which had been spent as a detective in Persons, and he had a personnel file filled with com-mendations. Before that he'd put in ten years as a sergeant with FHP, the Florida Highway Patrol. Accomplishments not readily achieved by the lazy, Lat thought skeptically, looking over at the stocky, ag-ing, rock-star wannabe sawing wood on the passenger seat next to him.

Two marked Orlando units and a Crime Scene van sat under the overhang of the Marriott World Center — a sprawling hotel and conference center bustling with tourists and Disney shuttle buses even at eleven thirty at night. "Let's go, Sleeping Beauty," Lat said, pulling in behind a cruiser. Then he got out of the car and slammed the door, stifling another yawn as he caught up with the uniforms waiting for him in the lobby.

The night manager twitched when Lat handed him the warrant, as if it were electric, and quickly ushered Lat, the three Orlando officers, the Crime Scene tech, and a disheveled Brill through the lobby to the elevators and up to the twelfth floor.

Room 1223 was right off the elevator bay. A "Pardon Our Appearance . . . Closed for Renovation!" card dangled from the handle. Lat's stomach knotted, as it always did when he served a warrant. This was the room where David Marquette had stayed only hours before he'd decided to kill his whole family. The missing piece of the puzzle — the why — just might be on the other side of that door, written in bright red lipstick across the mirror, or encrypted somewhere on his laptop, or lying right there in his bed, perhaps, still waiting anxiously for his return.

"You call this secure?" Lat asked incredulously as the manager reached to open the door with an electronic key card.

"Crime-scene tape and police officers make guests very uncomfortable," the man ager twittered in a high-pitched, nervous voice. His name tag read, "Albert Plante, Night Manager on Duty." "Only management has access to this room. The code was changed as soon as the police contacted us today. Housekeeping hadn't cleaned since Saturday morning, as there was a 'Do Not Disturb' sign on the door. It's all documented!"

"Oh. The code was changed. I feel better," Brill piped up as the door clicked open. "You do know this is a quadruple homicide investigation, right, chief? Homicide, as in murder, and quadruple, as in four?"

"Oh dear . . ." Albert Plante muttered anxiously as cops pushed past him and rushed into the room, probably fearing a shout-out any second now that they'd found a body swinging from clean sheets in the shower.

But disappointment quickly replaced anxiety. There was no damning confession taped to the mirror, no sexy girlfriend lying in a negligee awaiting her lover's return. There'd been no maid service, but the bed hadn't been slept in anyway. Two suits and a couple of pairs of slacks hanging in the closet, a shaving kit and assorted toiletries set out next to the bathroom sink. Literature from the medical conference spread out on the desk next to a laptop and a pot of in-room coffee. An emptied suitcase in the corner. That was it. No drugs. No pile of empty beer or alcohol bottles. No suicide note. No leftovers from a violent rage. No evidence of a girlfriend or a boyfriend or a hooker. Lat didn't quite know what he'd expected to find, but since Marquette had lawyered up, he'd hoped for more than this.

The next couple of hours were wasted interviewing a lot of people who'd unfortunately seen a lot of nothing. None of the employees recognized Marquette from his photo, hence no one could tell them shit about who he might've been with, the mood he'd been in when he'd left, or, for that matter, if he'd ever even been at the hotel. The conference he was supposed to speak at Sunday had ended Monday afternoon, and most of the five hundred attendees had already gone home. Hunting them down for interviews to try to find the one person Marquette might've sat next to in his reproductive endocrinology refresher course was going to be a nightmare. The most promising piece of evidence was the bag full of videotapes from the hotel's multiple surveillance cameras. Maybe they could pick Marquette up on one, merrily whistling — large knife in one hand, blunt instrument in the other — as he headed to his car late Saturday night.

"Well, that was a bust," Brill said as they headed out of the now crowded lobby, the evidence bag of security tapes in hand. Lat carried Marquette's sealed laptop and a cardboard box full of nothing seized from the hotel room. Tourists stared as if they were an attraction.

Lat sighed. "Piecing together his last hours is certainly gonna be a bitch."

"Maybe he was just heading home in the middle of the night 'cause he missed his wife. Then something went bad," Brill tried.

"So he could turn around and drive another three hundred miles the next morning and still make his nine A.M. speech? No rookie's that good. Although it does set up a nice alibi."

Brill shrugged. "Maybe he thought his wife wasn't missing him too much."

"Maybe he came down to catch her in the act. That would complicate things." Lat made a mental note to press Nielson for the results of the rape kit.

"That would also at least give you motive, something we both know you're running a little short on, boss-man."

Lat nodded. Usually the hard part of a murder investigation was figuring out who

125

the killer was. You arrived on scene, looked at a dead body, looked at the clues left behind, and started from there. Normally finding out why the victim might've been killed led you to a suspect. Was he robbed? Was she raped? Were there marital troubles? But here things were backward. Here they had their suspect — on scene and with the damn murder weapon in the guy's own gut — but no why. Considering the government wasn't legally required to prove motive, it would seem the easier case. But as Julia had pointed out, just because it wasn't legally required didn't mean that a jury wasn't gonna want to see why all the dots connected back to the smiling dad in the family photos before they agreed to put a needle in his arm.

Outside, the rain had stopped. The birds were up, and the shuttle-bus waiting areas were packed with colorful people ready for fun in the parks. "Hey, don't call me boss man," Lat said quietly as they made their way around a bus.

"Well, it's the truth, ain't it?" Brill replied.

Lat stopped walking. "I ain't your boss."

"And this really ain't my case no more now, is it?" Brill asked.

"That's not my decision."

"But that *is* the decision. And that makes

you the boss." He chewed on the toothpick he'd picked up in the restaurant, and neither one spoke. "So, did you check up on me?" Brill asked finally, turning and walking backward.

"Yup."

"And . . . ?"

Lat stopped again. "You want a quote?"

"Lay it on me, brother."

" 'Hotheaded, difficult, obnoxious,' and, I quote, 'a cheap, motherfucking asshole.' End quote."

"That last one was Patti Corderi. You can't count her. She's a whack job."

"I didn't," Lat said. Surprisingly, the conversation felt less tense than he'd thought it would. Brill had all the personality disabilities everyone had warned him about, yet he still kind of liked the guy. Unlike Sonny and Tubbs or Starsky and Hutch, he didn't have a regular "partner" in Homicide. No one did. Sometimes you worked with somebody on a case, but more often you didn't. And while you could always run things by guys in the squad, it actually felt good to have someone involved on the same case from the get-go. Someone who wasn't trying to climb the same ladder with the same people you were. "No sleeping this time, Rip," Lat warned with a yawn, heading for the passenger door. He dug the keys to the Impala out of his pocket. "It's your turn to drive."

"This new?" Brill asked, running his hand over the hood.

"Just got it. Took me three years to get on the top of the new-car list; I had a piece-of-shit Taurus before this." He tossed the keys over the car. "Don't fuck it up. I don't think other drivers are covered."

"Wow," Brill said, catching them. "Since the accident, I can't take home no more. So I always get the forfeited drug-dealer cars. You know, the fucking Fred Flintstone pieces of shit with the floorboard holes. They never look like the dealer cars in *Miami Vice,* man. I've yet to get a Lamborghini."

"What accident?"

"You didn't know?"

Lat sighed and walked back around to the driver's side, his hand out. "You're a fuck. Give me my keys and get in the car."

"I would've driven, Lat. I'm a team player." Brill laughed, tossing the keys back and heading around the car.

"You fall asleep and I will personally beat your ass," Lat growled, climbing in the car. "I'll play John Denver the whole way home if I have to."

"Now I know you're fucking with me

Ain't nobody got John Denver tapes in their car — not even the guy's own momma," Brill said, yawning, taking off his jacket, and rolling it into a ball. "I guess I can live with *hotheaded* and *difficult*. And coming from that nut, *asshole*'s quite a compliment." He pressed the jacket against the window and tucked in.

"I'm glad you feel that way," Lat said, reaching for the radio dial.

Brill closed his eyes and smiled. "It's still better than what I heard about you. . . ."

CHAPTER 16

Julia watched Judge Farley climb down off the bench and hurry out of the courtroom, his swollen robe trailing behind him like an enormous dark cloud. The door to the judge's back hallway slammed shut behind him, leaving the courtroom in stunned silence. She stared at the empty bench in disbelief.

Alonzo Guarino whooped when his lawyer explained to him that he was free to go. Since nobody had shown up in court on his behalf, he hugged and high-fived the PD and his intern instead.

"Whoo, no, this can't be good now," Julia heard one of the corrections officers say with the excitement of a kid about to watch a schoolyard fight. She looked up to see Alonzo standing in front of her.

"Tough break, bitch," Alonzo said, his shiny gold smile not at all friendly. She was acutely aware that he was no longer wearing handcuffs or leg shackles. The State's table was all that separated them.

"I'm sure I'll get another shot," Julia replied coldly, her eyes meeting his.

"Alonzo, don't talk to her. You don't need any more trouble," Kirk Venema cautioned, firmly tugging on the suede elbow patch of his client's ill-fitting sports jacket. They walked back to the defense table, and a few minutes later Corrections escorted a whistling Alonzo out the courtroom doors.

"I'll be seeing ya, Miss State," Julia heard him call with a laugh. "Tell Shorty I'll be seeing her soon, too, ya know. Real soon." Shorty, of course, meant Pamela Johnson.

Julia just could not believe it. It'd taken her a full day to pick a jury, another to do openings and present her witnesses. And it'd taken Farley just five short minutes to JOA her.

JOA stood for judgment of acquittal. Normally only a jury could acquit a defendant, but in the event that a reasonable jury with common sense couldn't be found, the Florida legislature had built a safety valve into the law. That was the almost-never-used JOA. If, after the State had presented its case, the trial judge felt in his learned opinion that no reasonable jury could find the defendant guilty, he could save *his* jury the time and trouble and acquit the defendant himself. Julia knew it wasn't Farley's learned opinion but his vindictive personality that had set Alonzo Guarino free. And the worst part about a JOA was that there was no right to appeal and hence nothing she could do but hold open the courtroom door as Alonzo headed back home. Of course Farley knew that, too. He'd planned to JOA her from the second she'd defied him in court on Monday. She probably should've seen it coming, but she'd put too much faith in the system. And that was a hard pill to swallow.

She continued to sit there staring dumbly at the bench. Kirk came up on his way out of the courtroom and offered his hand along with the standard postverdict condolences. When he added, "You made your case; I wouldn't have JOA'd you," she bit her lip. It didn't make her feel any better.

After the rest of the court staff emptied out, she quietly packed up her boxes and headed back to the office. That was when she noticed John Latarrino standing by himself next to the courtroom doors.

"You don't look happy," he said as she made her way down the aisle, dragging her pull cart behind her.

"Hey. What're you doing here?" she asked.

ooking around the courtroom to see whom else he might be waiting for.

"I just came from the lab," Lat replied. "I stopped up at Bellido's office. His secretary tells me he's out of town." He reached for her cart. "Can I help you with that?"

"Sure, if you want," she said, handing over the reins. "I think he's teaching at a chief's conference in Jacksonville." They walked out into the deserted hallway. It was almost five, and no one was around.

"I need to run some things by you," he said quickly.

Her hands grew clammy. Obviously this drop-in was intentional. And it was obviously about the Marquette case. Distancing herself from Monday's brutal scene and diving into a difficult trial with an asshole judge had, ironically enough, helped clear her head of ghosts, but she found her nerves once again on edge. She hadn't expected to see Lat here, now.

"Okay," she answered hesitantly.

"We've got some decisions to make, and with Bellido unavailable, it looks like you're the 'it' girl."

Uh-oh. Decisions were something Julia wasn't so sure she wanted her name on making. She didn't think Rick would want her making them, either. "Have you talked to him today?" she asked as they stepped into the elevator. She hadn't, but that didn' mean anything.

"Nope. Left a couple of messages on hi cell, but he doesn't seem to want to call m back. You're still second seat, right?"

She nodded.

"Then you're the one I need to be talking to. Listen, I got some of the lab work bac from the house. The footprints in the up stairs hall — one set was made by a size eleven loafer that belonged to the uniforn who responded. Tread base matches to a T The other set — they're too distorted for comp. Not just smeared, but distorted. N tread at all. The foot was wrapped in some thing, maybe a bootie. Best guess, base upon size and what appears to be weigh distribution, is a size ten, which woulc match Marquette — and half of Miami but I don't think you can use that with jury."

She frowned. "Sounds like a wash."

"Wait. I have good news. A nurse anesthetist at Mount Sinai who works witl Marquette's practice ID'd his voice on th nine-eleven tape. It's not a forensic compari son, but it'll do for PC. Sure as she's breath ing, she says it's him."

PC stood for probable cause, the lega

threshold of facts necessary to arrest a defendant. Was it more probable than not that a crime had been committed and that the defendant was the one who'd committed it?

"We got the phone records," he continued. "Marquette made a call to the house from his cell Saturday night at ten. It lasted six minutes and used a cell tower in Winter Park. That was the last call into or out of the Sorolla house until Emma's call to 911 at five the next morning. So he was definitely still in Orlando when he called."

"Maybe he was trying to establish an alibi."

"My thoughts exactly. Now, prints. We've got sixteen sets around the house that've yet to be identified. Three of those are by and around windowsills. Could be the Terminex guy or a shitty cleaning lady, for all we know, and in the long run it probably won't matter a damn, but a defense attorney's gonna pick up on that and play the fingerprint game, so I just wanted to give you a heads-up. I don't want you saying later that I was holding back."

She nodded as she stepped out of the elevator and started toward the doors that led out the back of the courthouse. "Okay. I think Rick wanted to work up a warrant by the weekend, before Marquette gets released from the hospital."

Latarrino stopped walking. "We don't have that long, Counselor."

"What?" she asked, turning to face him.

"That's why I'm here. Marquette's being released today," Lat replied. "He's being transported to Chicago's Northwestern Memorial on a private plane tonight."

CHAPTER 17

"You're kidding me," Julia said flatly, staring at Latarrino. The clock in the courthouse hall hung right above the detective's head. The numbers seemed to pop out at her, like a cartoon drawing: *BOING! 4:58!*

"A nurse over at Ryder called my LT and gave him the heads-up. Once Marquette's out of our jurisdiction, Julia, it's potentially gonna be very hard to get him back here. And, assuming he doesn't skip town and we can ever find him again, we'll have lengthy extradition issues to contend with, 'cause I'm betting the good doctor's gonna fight us tooth and nail on coming back here, seeing as how Bellido's probably gonna try and fry him."

"What makes you think he's a flight risk?" Julia tried. "Lots of accused murderers hang around for their trials."

"Marquette's daddy's the one who arranged the private plane. Dr. Alain Marquette. In addition to being the chief of Neurology over at Northwestern, and on a couple of big boards, we know Dad's pretty heavy-handed with a checkbook."

"So he's got pull."

"And money. In my book, that makes sonny boy a damn high flight risk."

"I'll need more than that, Lat. Just being rich doesn't make you a flight risk."

"Okay. I'll give you more. Marquette was born in Paris, emigrating here at six so his dad could work at Northwestern. That makes him a French citizen. We found copies of a French passport on his med school application, but we can't find the passport."

"Damn . . ."

"France will not extradite a capital murder defendant, Julia. Like the rest of Europe, they're against the death penalty."

"So if he does go there to get better . . ." she started.

". . . he's not ever coming back," Lat finished.

There was a long silence.

"We need to pick him up."

She looked around the empty courthouse lobby. The cafeteria was shuttered, the courtrooms closed till tomorrow. This was government; at four thirty the support staff here and at the SAO cleared out. By five most attorneys and judges had followed suit. No, no, no. This could not be happening. Not on her shift . . .

Arresting someone was a much bigger deal than it looked on television. Some really important legal clocks started ticking the second the words "You're under arrest" were uttered. First and foremost was the right to a speedy trial, which, absent a defense continuance or a waiver by the defendant, ran out permanently 180 days after those magic words were spoken. That meant, ready or not, you had to bring the defendant to trial within six months. A very short amount of time to investigate, indict, prep, depose, and try a quadruple homicide. Sometimes it took years to see a simple drug-deal-gone-bad murder to trial. And there were no second bites at the apple — say if you screwed up and made the wrong call but subsequently found that murder weapon or missing witness on the 181st day. Double jeopardy — the constitutional prohibition against trying someone multiple times for the same crime — prevented that. As Julia's Crim Law professor at Fordham had stressed, in criminal law the stakes were high for a prosecutor to make the right call at the right time all the time. While Julia had made the decision to arrest someone before, she'd never done it in a homicide.

"Hold on, hold on. I can't give you the go-ahead until I at least try to reach Rick," she said. "Let's head back to the office while I try his cell. If I can't get him, we'll go from there." She speed-dialed while quickly walking across the street, praying like a nun for him to pick up.

"You've reached the cellular voice mail of Ricardo Bellido. Please leave a message after the tone." *Beeeeep* . . .

Shit. Shit. Shit. "Rick, it's me. I have Detective Latarrino with me, and there's a problem. A big problem. I need you to call either me or Lat ASAP. Marquette's getting discharged and flying to Illinois tonight."

They walked the rest of the way in silence. "We don't have time for a warrant," Lat said quietly when they'd reached the glass doors of the State Attorney's Office.

She looked down at the cell in her sweaty fist. "When's his plane?"

"It's already at MIA. Flight plan says eight fifteen takeoff. We have an hour before he leaves the hospital for the airport. Maybe less."

She hit redial. "You've reached the cellular voice mail of Ricardo Bellido. . . ."

She looked around the practically empty SAO lot. If Marquette disappeared, it would be worse than going up against a clock.

"All right," she said nodding. "Go pick him up."

Welcome to the Big Leagues.

CHAPTER 18

Lat waited until the wheelchair was actually pushed out the front doors of Jackson Memorial Medical Center's Ryder Trauma Center before he walked up to the man seated in it. "David Alain Marquette?" he asked, already knowing the answer.

"Jesus Christ! Not here!" shouted an older man, maybe in his late sixties, dressed in slacks and a sports jacket, who walked carefully alongside the chair. He had the slight cadence of a French accent that had been worn away over the years. Lat figured it was Alain Marquette, David's father, who'd been successfully ducking the police since his arrival in Miami. A handsome woman, also in her late sixties — probably David's mom — flanked the chair on the right, dressed impeccably in an ugly but probably expensive suit, her silver hair pulled into a tight chignon. She looked elegant and reserved, but scared. Alain moved protectively in front of the chair.

A private ambulance sat waiting under the awning. The two EMTs who'd moved to assist Marquette hesitated, looking around dumbly for someone to tell them what to do.

Brill held up his badge. "Mr. Marquette and his family won't be needing your services anymore, boys," he said. At that precise moment, three MDPD cruisers pulled up, lights flashing. "We've made other arrangements."

"Are you Alain Marquette?" Lat asked the older man.

"Go to hell!" the man spat back.

"Ooh. Feisty. Step away from the wheelchair, Pops," Brill cautioned.

"I'm Detective John Latarrino, Miami-Dade Police," Lat offered.

"He's sick!" the man yelled, his tone both desperate and indignant.

"Step back, sir," Brill repeated. Family members were always the ones to watch during an arrest. Emotions ran high, and you never knew what someone was capable of.

The figure in the wheelchair was pale. His light-gray eyes darted everywhere. An oxygen tube ran from his nose to a tank on the side. A portable IV connected more tubes to his veins.

Lat was unmoved. Images of the slaughter he'd seen at the house flashed in his head. The crumpled, broken body of a six-year-old hiding behind her Hello Kitty chair in her princess room. For as long as he lived, he'd never forget that scared face, those innocent brown eyes, empty and lifeless, staring up at him. Lat nodded to a uniform. The nurse backed away as the officer took her spot. On the other side of Jackson and only a building away from Ryder was Ward D — the part of the hospital reserved for in-custody defendants who required hospitalization. Marquette would be booked in there, just a few short pushes away. Although a hospital, Ward D was handled like a jail, with bolted doors and high security. But no matter how bad it might be, it still wasn't a cell. For Lat, that just wasn't bad enough.

"Get Mr. Levenson on the phone. Now!" shouted Alain Marquette.

"Alain, calm down!" said the woman.

"Just do it!"

"His lawyer ain't gonna help him tonight, folks," piped in Brill.

A blue Channel 7 news van pulled up fast behind one of the cruisers. A breathless Eddie Brennan jumped out, microphone in

144

hand, Willie right behind him. "Dr. Marquette!" he shouted. "Did you kill your whole family? Why'd you do it? How do you feel right now? Or are you the victim here?"

"Jesus Christ!" Lat waved in the direction of the uniformed officers. "Get them the hell out of here!"

Only a few ears knew about Marquette's arrest. Lat hadn't authorized anyone to contact the news, even going so far as to keep it off the police radio so no one would pick it up from a scanner. It didn't take a quantum leap to figure out the boat had a leak. Another news van pulled up and another reporter scurried out, this one from NBC 6.

"Is it true there's a confession?" yelled Brennan, pushing closer, hoping it was his question that would get an answer, not one from the competition the next mike over.

"Was Jennifer raped?" shouted the newcomer.

"Are you seeking the death penalty?" yelled Brennan.

"Where the hell's your warrant? Where's your warrant?" the old man cried.

Another news van pulled up. Another reporter. More questions. It was chaos.

"Step back, sir," commanded Brill, hand on his Taser, as Alain moved closer to his

145

son. "I said step the fuck back! You, too Geraldo!" he yelled at Brennan.

"He's sick! He's sick!" pleaded the woman. Her face had turned ashen white matching her hair.

"Freedom of the press! We've got a right to be here!" shouted Brennan, thrusting his microphone at the woman and pressing close enough to Brill that Lat knew something really bad was gonna happen.

"David Marquette, you're under arrest for the murder of Jennifer, Emma, Daniel, and Sophie Marquette. You have the right to remain silent, and anything you say can and will be used against you in a court of law. You also have the right to an attorney, but you obviously know that one already. All right," Lat said to the uniform behind the wheelchair. "Let's go. Get him out of here."

That was when the woman fainted face-first onto the pavement, Brill Tasered a screaming Alain Marquette, and all hell broke loose in front of all those cameras.

Chapter 19

"This was nothing but an ambush, Your Honor!" an angry Mel Levenson shouted from the podium. His Hitchcock-sized jowls trembled. "Rather than call me to arrange for my client's surrender," he said, shaking a swollen finger in the direction of Rick Bellido, Lat, and a sulking Brill, "the Miami-Dade and Coral Gables Police Departments, with the blessing of the State, no doubt, set up a trap outside Jackson to nail my client as he rolled by in his wheelchair. But they don't just arrest the man with the oxygen tank and critical-care nurse at his side, because that would be sorry enough. No. Without any concern for the devastating emotional trauma Dr. Marquette's already been through — losing his entire family — or the life-threatening injuries he's just had surgery for, these detectives, in their quest for fifteen minutes of fame, manage to make sure the press is there, ready and waiting to get the whole thing on film! Although I guess it's a damn good thing they were because the entire world got to see these great detectives Taser — yes, Taser — Dr. Marquette's elderly father, a world-renowned neurological surgeon! It's outrageous!" Mel held up a copy of Friday's *Herald*. DOCTOR DAD ARRESTED WHILE ATTEMPTING TO FLEE!! was the headline. "In their mad scramble for some face time on CNN, the State's managed to prejudice every potential juror in South Florida against my client, Your Honor!" Mel wiped the spit flecks from his face and moved back from the podium, almost stepping on a cameraman.

Lat felt the rush of anger color his cheeks. He looked over at Bellido, waiting for him to be outraged and say something. To his right he could actually hear the knuckles in Brill's hand crack as he clenched his fists. Apparently he was waiting for the same thing.

Due to the sheer volume of people who tended to do more stupid things over the weekend than they normally did during the week, Monday in-custody bond hearings in Judge Irving Katz's claustrophobically small courtroom were always busy, but never packed. Except for the ASA, a PD, the judge, and the occasional private attorney, the courtroom was usually empty. Even the defendants didn't show up for court — at least not physically. They put in an appearance via closed-circuit TV from the jail across the street, so there was no need to actually bring them over.

"Great speech, Mr. Levenson, but your client's charged with murder. Four of them, to be exact. This is just the first appearance. All I get to decide now is if there was probable cause to arrest him," Judge Katz said, waving his copy of the pink arrest form in front of him. "And based on the facts cited in here, I sure do. Murder's nonbondable at this stage, so there's not a lot I can do about your complaints except listen to them, and frankly, I'm not Dear Abby. Besides which, if I'm reading this correctly, Dr. Marquette was wheeled off to Ward D, Mr. Levenson. He got his medical care. It's not like the detectives threw him in a cement cell with the rats."

"We all know Ward D is not like the rest of Jackson, Judge." Mel pointed to the TV screen. "Just look at the guy!"

Seated in a wheelchair next to the defendant's podium was David Marquette. Even Lat was a bit shocked at the figure he now saw on the TV monitor. The smooth-faced,

All-American-looking guy with the sheepish grin who in family pictures bore a striking resemblance to a young Robert Redford was gone. He was dressed in an orange jail jumpsuit, and his skin was pasty, his cheeks sallow. His strawberry-blond hair looked greasy and unkempt, and his facial stubble had practically grown into a straggly beard. Long, thin fingers awkwardly clutched the arms of the wheelchair in a death grip. He stared straight ahead of him at nothing and no one, and in the five minutes he'd been sitting there listening to everyone talk about him, Lat didn't think the man had ever blinked, much less moved. A long line of restless, tattoo-riddled defendants — some still dressed in the boxers they'd been arrested in — snaked its way behind him through the jail's peeling olive-green courtroom. The bored inmates began to chatter and the courtroom filled with noise.

"Keep them quiet over there!" yelled Katz to the corrections officer standing next to Marquette at the podium. He placed a hand over his ear. "I can't hear. If they don't wanna be quiet, then take whoever's yapping out and bring 'em back tomorrow."

The guard nodded into the camera. Then he turned around and yelled, "Shut up!"

"I could've done that," mumbled Katz

n disgust.

"He should be in a hospital bed right now," Levenson continued. "He never should've been released into the general population today."

"HMOs do it all the time," Katz said flatly.

"Mr. Levenson's client was apparently feeling well enough Thursday to try and flee the jurisdiction, Your Honor," Rick interjected.

"He was being transported to another hospital," protested Levenson.

"In Chicago," added Rick.

"I made those arrangements," said Alain Marquette, who stepped forward from the back of the room. "That's my hospital, and my son needs acute medical care."

"Your hospital?" asked the judge.

"This is Dr. Alain Marquette, Judge. He's the chief of Neurology at Chicago's Northwestern Memorial Hospital," Mel said.

"Ah, three sides to every story. Dr. Marquette, you have good counsel here, and as I'm sure that good counsel has told you, there's nothing more that can be done for your son at this point. Mr. Levenson will have another opportunity to seek bond at an Arthur hearing or before the trial judge when one's appointed, but there's nothing I can do for him today. He's gotta sit in jail.

151

As for what happened between you and the officers Thursday night, I'm sure Mr. Levenson would be more than happy to offer you counsel in that regard as well." Katz smiled slickly. "I understand he also does civil practice."

"This was unprofessional. It should've been handled differently," Levenson grumbled.

"If I had a nickel for each time I wished for something I didn't get, I'd be a rich man, Mr. Levenson. Instead, I'm just really old and really disappointed." Katz looked into the jail camera. "No bond," he yelled as if David Marquette were deaf. "Now, unless there's some other high-profile case that someone forgot to tell me was on my calendar this morning, you all can take this outside in the hallway so I can clear my courtroom. I imagine they're all with you Mr. Bellido," the judge added with a frown as he looked over at the mass of reporters who'd started to gather their cameras and hightail it for the door. Then he turned both his attention and his scowl back to the corrections officer on screen. "Bring the next one up, Sergeant! And keep the rest of them quiet over there!"

CHAPTER 20

Lat had been in media cases before, but this was Hollywood crazy. Flashes exploded as soon as the courtroom doors pushed open. A parade of reporters, cameras, and boom mikes trailed the Levenson camp to the escalators while another broke off to follow Team State as they headed for the elevators, all the while shouting dumb questions that they'd either just heard the answer to in court or weren't going to get an answer to anyway. At least not from him. Brill had wisely ducked into the men's room, having been warned in no uncertain terms by his department to keep his mug far, far away from anything with a lens.

At the elevators Rick addressed the crowd, selectively answering the stupider questions, such as "Will you ever agree to a bond?" with just the right amount of controlled outrage. Lat had watched Bellido work the cameras before on his other media-magnet cases and when he guested as a legal analyst on cable news shows. He had to admit they sure did love the guy, with his dark good looks, fancy suits, and silver tongue. But one thing was for certain, he thought as he spotted Eddie Brennan once again in a front-row seat — Bellido loved them right back. And if he had to bet a buck as to who the little birdie was that might've tipped of the press on Thursday night, he would put his money on one smooth-talking, well-dressed, tall, dark, and handsome prosecutor. Bellido didn't do anything on any of his cases without an audience. And that included a major arrest. If he couldn't be physically in the spotlight Thursday night, he'd make sure his case was.

Things hadn't always been bitter between the two men. Once upon a time they'd actually been friends. Then Bellido had fucked Lat on the stand without so much as blinking. Just like the Marquette family murders, the rape, abduction, and murder o nineteen-year-old Luisa Caballero by four teenaged boys had garnered a lot of media attention. The fingers had been pointing in a dozen different directions the second the scumbags had been taken into custody, and Bellido and Lat both knew that conviction were going to be made on DNA. The prob lem was that Luisa had had two boyfriends, both of whose DNA was also found by the ME during her autopsy. Lat had put that very important info into his reports, along with his interviews of both boyfriends, and had given the whole package to Bellido to presumably share with the defense during discovery. It wasn't until he was on the stand, being crossed at trial by one of the defendant's attorneys, that he found out that hadn't happened. And he quickly figured out that it hadn't happened on purpose. The rising star Major Crimes prosecutor did not like to lose. And he also didn't like to look bad doing it, so when the accusations of Brady violations and evidence being withheld started flying in the court-room, Bellido was one of the first to start throwing them around. The ensuing bullshit almost cost Lat his badge.

Just as the elevator doors opened on an empty car, Rick held up his hands like the pope at an audience. "That's all for now, folks. Right now our thoughts and prayers are with the family of the victims, and of course our concern is to ensure the safety of the community." Then he repeated the same thing in Spanish for the cute Tele-mundo reporter.

Lat could practically hear the sighs as

thousands of *abuelas* across Miami swooned in their easy chairs. "You sure can talk pretty," he said when the doors closed and they were alone.

"Thursday was a clusterfuck," Rick replied coolly. "Today was damage control."

"Damage control? At whose expense? What about controlling Levenson? What about making the detectives who're working this thing twenty-four/seven a priority? You know damn well it wasn't us that called in the press. That's what turned Thursday to shit. Your pals like Brennan, with their fucking microphones."

"You need to know how to work them, Lat. Don't let them work you."

"Thanks for the tip, but I don't need to learn shit on how to impress those assholes. I'm here to put a scumbag away — not to get face time on CNN. Got it? And I'm not gonna let you throw me under the bus again. Next time, pal, you're coming with me."

The door opened on 4, and there stood Julia. "I'm guessing I missed it," she said hesitantly, looking between the two men. She'd obviously just missed something else too. Tension poured out of the car like smoke.

"What happened to you this morning?"

Rick asked quickly.

"My DC happened. I was just heading up when she announced a new courtroom rule — every attorney in division stays through morning calendar."

"What? Does she know you're on Marquette?" Rick asked.

"I think that's why she made the rule."

"That'll be the last time that happens. I'll talk to her. Come on," he said with a wave. "Hop on. Let's get coffee."

"Hey, Lat," Julia said with a smile, stepping on the elevator.

"Hey, Counselor," he said, stepping off.

"You coming, John?" Rick asked, his voice strained.

"I'll let you fill her in," he called back without turning around as he walked down the hall. "I'm gonna catch up with Brill. Make some plans to head up to New Jersey."

"Good idea," replied Rick, but the detective was already long gone.

CHAPTER 21

"What happened?" she asked after the doors closed. Then added, "In court."

"No bond," Rick replied, hitting the lobby button. "Corrections wheeled him over from Ward D this morning."

"How'd he look?"

"Like death warmed over. His arraignment's set for Thursday, November second I'm going to the Grand Jury on the first That gives us a little over two weeks."

The important legal clock-ticking had officially kicked off. In Florida, formal charge had to be filed against a defendant within twenty-one days after an arrest. And while most crimes, including homicide, were formally charged by information — a sworn document signed off on by the prosecuto — capital murder had to be charged by grand-jury indictment. The penalty for missing deadline? The court could ROR Marquette — release him on his own recog nizance. That meant no bail, no bond, no house arrest. Just a heartfelt promise to come back to court.

She nodded. "Okay. What do you need from me?"

They stepped out of the elevator and waded through the thickening early-lunch crowd to the courthouse cafeteria. "I want you to handle the prefiles. We'll do the leads together, but you can take the peripheral players, like Crime Scene, the ME, and the responding officers, Colonna and Demos. I've already spoken with everyone on scene; you can make it formal. Besides, I wanna see how good your prefile skills are."

Even she saw through that last line. Prefiles were just witness interviews done under oath. To file a case formally, you had to have sworn statements from victims, witnesses, and cops to support the charges. Julia was a gofer, plain and simple — the price of admission for a prized seat at the State's table. But she was fine with that.

She finally asked the question: "Will you have a problem with the grand jury?"

"Because you rushed the arrest?"

She swallowed. "I was thinking more about the unidentified prints and stuff. . . ."

"Smeared footprints, lots of fingerprints, no fingerprints — that sort of crap's just nuisance facts that a defense attorney will try to make more out of than he should at trial. It's not evidence that tends to exonerate Marquette, so we have no obligation to bring it up. It's just me and twenty-four upstanding citizens in that locked courtroom. They hear what I want them to hear, and they leave when I tell them it's time to go. *Grand jury* only sounds intimidating. And as for moving up Marquette's arrest prematurely . . ." He paused. "You made the right call."

Whew. That had been on her mind the whole long weekend. He ordered two coffees, and they walked over to a quiet table in the back corner. She felt the eyes of several prosecutors and defense attorneys watching them as they passed.

"I've already arranged for my secretary to set the prefiles of the responding officers and Crime Scene techs with you. Just get with her on times," he said, sliding into a booth seat. "We'll do Lat and Brill together after they get back from Jersey."

"Who's in Jersey?"

"Jennifer was from Cherry Hill, New Jersey, on the outskirts of Philly. Her whole family's up there. That's where the funerals will be held."

"Have you spoken to the family?"

"Yeah. They're not much help, to be honest. 'David's a great guy' is all I heard. I'm hoping Lat will be able to get more from them."

"All right. I'd better head back, then," she said, reaching for her files.

"You're not gonna finish your coffee?"

She shrugged. "I've got a depo at eleven. I had three already today."

"Oh. How was your weekend?"

"Great," she answered with a smile. She hoped she didn't sound too enthusiastic. That would be a telltale sign she was lying. 'Busy running around. You know, before you realize it, it's Monday and you're nursing a hangover."

"Ouch. Sorry to hear that. I was going to call you Saturday, but I got caught up."

"I told you, it was a crazy weekend. And this, you know, *this,*" she said looking right at him but not actually saying the word most men didn't want to hear anyway, "it is what it is. I'm not expecting anything, so you don't have anything to explain."

It was going on two weeks since her wine-soaked lapse in judgment, and besides the sweet kiss in the car when they'd gone to the scene last Monday, there'd been nothing romantic between them since. Not even conversation. Any other man, and she probably would've written him off already. No, she definitely would have written him off. She didn't believe in one-night stands; she didn't want a trial partner with benefits. Mind games drove her nuts, and she hated herself for playing them with that stupid, juvenile hangover comment. But Rick was not most men, and this case . . . well, she couldn't just write him off as an asshole and never see the man again. This case would tie them together for at least a few months. But it was pretty obvious to her by now that hot and heavy one day didn't guarantee a steady Saturday-night date. Or even a freaking phone call. Maybe the rules changed when you hit forty. Maybe it was a casual screw and then everybody back to work.

"I went looking at nursing homes for my dad," he said, swirling the coffee in his cup. "That was my weekend." He shrugged. "Alzheimer's."

She hated being Irish. The guilt slammed her like a tsunami. "Oh, jeez, I'm sorry."

"Not to worry. That's life. Listen," he said, lowering his voice and leaning across the table. A finger found the back of her hand and subtly stroked it. "I'm sorry I haven't called. I'd like to do dinner again. That was nice. Maybe I shouldn't say this, and I know here's not the place, but I've missed you."

She felt her face grow hot. Don't roll over, Julia. Be strong.

"I'd like that," she said too quickly. *Ugh.* Then she shot him a smile that she knew gave away everything she'd hoped to hide. "Any word on who the trial judge is gonna be yet?" she asked, rising to leave with her files in hand.

He laughed and shook his head. He had the best smile, a toned-down Eric Estrada grin. "Oh, boy. I think you may need to sit back down, sweetheart."

From the look on his face, she already knew who it was. "Please tell me you're not gonna tell me what I think you're gonna tell me," she pleaded, sliding back down into the booth. "Tell me it's Henghold. Or Gibbons. Or anyone else you wouldn't want to get."

"No can do."

She sighed and slumped back in her chair, defeated. It had to be a Monday. It just had to be. "It's Farley, isn't it?"

He just smiled.

CHAPTER 22

"Look at me!" demanded little Emma with a squeal as she spun around the kitchen in her sparkly blue Cinderella gown. "Mommy! Look! Look at me!"

Julia stared at her television screen.

"Oh, my, don't you look pretty," purred Emma's mother off camera. The shot jumped across the room to the pretty, slight blond behind the island, a chocolate layer cake before her on a plate, a spatula full of frosting in hand. "Don't get it dirty, Em. We still have the parade at school and Halloween to get through. Oh, please, David," Jennifer said with a shake of her head when she spotted the camera, "point that thing at Emma."

The shot jumped back to Emma. "I can make it spin!" she shouted as she twirled, singing some tween pop song. Her long, honey-colored hair was done in a French braid, and it whipped about behind her.

The cranky cry of a newborn sounded. "Hush, now, Sophie. I'm getting it ready. Give Mommy a minute." Fatigue strained Jennifer's voice. She was still off camera.

A barefoot little boy suddenly streaked across the screen in a Superman t-shirt and droopy pull-up. "I'm *hungry!*"

The police had seized a bunch of videos from the Marquette home. At Julia's request, Investigations had made her copies to take home and watch. Normally she got to know the victims in her crimes when they came into her office. Of course that wasn't possible here. But she still wanted to get to know them, these small victims whose deaths she was now charged with avenging. So she'd watched video after video. She'd seen the babies come home from the hospital, one by one, bundled safely in their proud mother's arms. Smiled as Danny and Emma learn to sit and crawl and walk and swim. Watched as the dead breathed and giggled and smiled once more. The tapes were her only link to a family she'd never get to meet, a family she felt a desperate, compulsive need to know more about. A family that reminded her too much of her own.

The camera was back on Jennifer. "You just ate supper, young man. Maybe you should have some more carrots."

"Danny! I'm dancing! Go away," declared Emma with a pout, hands on her hips.

"I want cake," said Danny. His chestnut hair stuck to his sweaty forehead.

"Okay, everybody," Jennifer said. "We're going to sing now. Dave, are you ready? David?"

The picture bobbed up and down. The crowd sang, "Happy Birthday, dear Mommy," as Jennifer carried the chocolate-frosted cake over to the kitchen table, navigating her way through a bobbing sea of colorful balloons. She blew out the candles, and everyone clapped. Danny screamed, "I want some! I wanna big piece!"

"Watch me," Emma said, ignoring the cake. She stuck her face up close to the camera. "Look at me, Daddy!" she demanded. "Just look at me!"

Black-and-white fuzz filled Julia's television, like two armies of fighting ants.

Just like little Danny, Julia's older brother, Andrew, had loved cars as a kid. He'd carried a metal Matchbox fire engine around in his pocket wherever he went. In a department store one time, she remembered he'd gotten in trouble for something. Running off? Hiding? She couldn't recall why, but their mom sent him to stand in a corner by the fitting rooms. And there he was, forever embedded in her memory. Andrew. All of seven or eight, red truck in hand, standing stiffly next to a mannequin. Not a tear or so much as a defiant pout on his freckle-smattered, milky-smooth face, a mop of black curls spilling past his forehead over his dark eyes. When their mom turned her attention back to the salesgirl, he broke form, waved mischievously over at Julia, and poked his head into the ladies' fitting room behind him. With a hand over his mouth to stifle the giggle, he sent the truck careening underneath the row of stalls. . . .

Julia closed her eyes tight. It'd been a long time since she'd allowed herself to think of Andy. Even though he was five years older than she, when they got along, they'd been the best of friends. Her brother could make her do the goofiest things with just the flash of his lopsided grin and a double dare. Walk on the train tracks. Ring Mrs. Crick's doorbell on Halloween when everyone knew she was a witch and her creepy house with the caved-in roof was haunted. Eat the red squishy berries off the unknown bush by the garage. It was Andy she'd go running to when a thunderstorm woke her in the middle of the night, and he would let her come into his bed and under the covers, counting off the seconds between the thunder and the lightning. She could still smell his breath, sweet with mouthwash and the chocolate he'd sneaked after he'd brushed his teeth, as he whispered words in the dark to distract her.

"I hit a home run today at practice, Ju-Ju. Coach said I gotta work on my pitching, though. Said I'm the only one on the team that can throw a damn curve ball. He thinks I could even play JV next year. Imagine that, Ju-Ju. That would be so cool. . . ."

Planning for a future that would never be.

The rain pattered softly against her living room windows. She got up and hit the eject button on the DVD/VCR, and the last video ever shot of the seemingly happy Marquette family slowly popped out. With the back of her hand, she wiped away the tears and slipped the video into the sleeve marked "Mommy's Birthday 10/3/06." Then she put it back in the cardboard evidence box, along with all the others.

CHAPTER 23

Ten days after they were murdered, Jennifer Marquette and her children were flown up to Cherry Hill, New Jersey, and buried.

Hours after the funeral Lat and Brill sat in the plastic-slip-covered living room of Jennifer's parents, Renny and Michael Prowse, a stack of photo albums and two cups of coffee in front of them. An antique cuckoo clock ticked away the stagnant seconds.

Hummel figurines crowded the shelves of a curio cabinet, and a corner wall unit was filled with still-tagged Beanie Babies. On the mantel, tiny crystal figures had their own glass display case. *Obviously a family of collectors,* Lat thought, looking around. *A family that never liked to give anything away.* On top of a worn piano, a makeshift shrine to Jennifer and the Prowses' only grandchildren had been created, complete with pictures and burning candles and watched over by the outstretched arms of a crucified ceramic Jesus.

On the dining room table in the next room over, platters of food and casserole dishes were stacked on the long, formal table. The smell of lasagna, garlic, coffee, and sausage filled the house.

"It's been like this for a week now," Renny Prowse said absently, setting down a platterful of cookies and slices of apple cake on the coffee table. "People coming with dinners and stuff." A well-kept woman in her late fifties, Renny was dressed in a neat black suit, her blond hair pulled back in a clip. Lat noticed the band of gray roots that framed her face, the dark circles that sank her eyes. She'd put on makeup, but with no real purpose. Her round face was puffy, blotched red from days of crying. "People are kind. I just can't get over it. Some of them we don't even know, do we, Mike?"

"No," Jennifer's father said in a remote voice. "We don't even know them."

Jennifer's older sister, Laurel, sat next to her dad on the couch, her hand on his. Her younger sister, Randy, stood quietly by the door that led to the kitchen. Both women were blond and blue-eyed, like their mother. Laurel was only in her midthirties, but dressed in a matronly dress, with glasses

170

and no makeup, she was already forging full speed ahead into middle age. Of the three sisters, Laurel obviously had drawn the short end of the stick in the looks department. Randy, on the other hand, must've been the Prowses' late-in-life surprise. Lat guessed late teens, with an athletic, fit figure and a pretty face.

"Eat something, detectives. There's so much," Renny said, finally taking a seat on the other side of her husband. She licked her dry lips and clasped her hands together, obviously bracing herself for the conversation ahead.

Lat hated this part of the job. He could take the bodies and brutal crime scenes well enough, but it was meeting the next of kin that always got to him. Listening to their stories, seeing their hopelessness. At the end of every interview, a piece of him always seemed to have been gnawed away. After enough years and enough interviews, he figured his soul would eventually be picked over and eaten raw. That'd be the day he retired to a bottle of Jack and a log cabin somewhere in the mountains of Montana.

As a street cop in Miami, Lat had long ago learned how to distance himself from his job and the people he arrested. All cops did. The bad guys were no longer people but mopes, skells, perps, subjects, defendants. His ex-wife, Trish, was a psychologist. She'd once told him that labeling individuals with derogatory slang terms was a mental coping mechanism cops used to separate good from evil, their job from their everyday lives. "Us against them" helped a cop get through the shift and restore power to what was oftentimes a powerless situation, she'd theorized. When he had been assigned to homicide, Lat had taken that overanalysis one step further and learned how to distance himself from death, so that no matter how bad the scene, the bodies in it were not really people, either, but DBs, victims, stiffs. His job as detective was to simply solve the mystery of how they'd gotten that way. That was when Trish had finally stopped analyzing him. The papers had been filed six months later.

"We know this is a difficult time for you, Mr. and Mrs. Prowse, Randy, Laurel," Lat began softly. "But we're just trying to get background on your son-in-law."

Renny was shaking her head. "We don't know anything, Detective. Oh, God, David is — he seemed like such a good man. Such a good father." She buried her nose in a tissue.

"Jen met David in the emergency room at

Temple seven years ago," Laurel explained, taking over. "It was fate, really. She fell Rollerblading in the park, and David was doing an ER rotation. They dated for a few months and decided to get married. Everyone liked David. He was a doctor. He was handsome. He was . . ." She paused. "He was great. Jen was crazy about him."

"Crazy," murmured Michael Prowse.

"They got married at St. Mary's right before his residency was over. My parents invited the whole town, and everyone showed."

"Just like today," Renny said, almost proudly.

"Two weeks later they left for Miami. Last year they bought that house in Coral Gables. It was very expensive, you know."

"How often did you see them?" Brill asked, reaching for a cookie.

"Two or three times a year. Jen would try and come up for Christmas," Laurel said. "It was difficult for any of us to get down too often. We have to work, you know." Definite emphasis placed on the word *we*.

"When was the last time they were here?" asked Lat.

"Memorial Day. Mom and Dad had a barbecue."

"Were they getting along?" asked Lat.

"Oh, yes," said Laurel, nodding quickly. "They always got along. Always."

Lat already knew that David Marquette had completed his residency in October 1999. Emma's birthday was March 31, 2000. It wasn't hard to do the math. "Jennifer was pregnant when they got married."

Renny looked away, embarrassed. "Yes, she was," Laurel answered testily. "But it didn't matter. They were going to get married anyway. Emma was just a little earlier than planned."

Obviously a sore subject. Lat thought of the ceramic Jesus. "What about David? What can you tell us about his family?"

"Nothing," said Mike bitterly. "They didn't come to the wedding. No one came. No one."

"Did you think that was odd?" asked Brill.

"My father didn't talk to his own father for some years, Detective. It's not so odd," said Laurel in a voice that was both calm and patronizing. "Families fight. Not everyone can be the Brady Bunch. The point is, we all liked David. None of us can believe this has happened. None of us saw it coming, if that's what you're getting at."

"Did he have a temper? Did you ever see or hear them fight? Did Jennifer ever tell you about any fights?" asked Lat.

"That's just it, Detective. I was very close with my sister. They were the perfect couple. They never fought."

"Or she never told you," cautioned Brill.

"Or she never told me," conceded Laurel with some difficulty.

"When was the last time you spoke with Jennifer, Mrs. Prowse?" asked Lat.

"Two days before she was . . ." Renny's voice trailed off, and she bit her lip. "Murdered. We talked about two times a week. David was out of town, and she was taking Emma and Danny shoe shopping. No one ever heard from her again."

Laurel shook her head. "I talked to her a few days before that. She never mentioned any problems."

"And you?" Brill asked, turning to look at Randy.

Randy looked startled. "I don't know," she said, crossing her arms across her chest. "A couple of weeks before, maybe."

"Randy's still in college, Detective Brill," said Laurel sharply. "Syracuse. She had to come home for this. She's a very busy girl."

Lat sighed. This was not productive. Everything was too perfect, and no one saw shit. "Is there anything that any of you can think of that might be important for us to know? Anything at all," he prodded.

"There was one thing," began Jennifer's father.

"There was nothing," said Renny loudly, shaking her head, reaching for his hand. "Stop doing this to yourself, Mike. Please." She started to cry again.

"Damn it! I'm going to speak, Ren!" Michael said, his voice rising. He hesitated for a moment. "There was something about David." His eyes welled up, and he looked away to an unseen memory in the room.

The past ten days had probably aged Mike Prowse ten years. Lat knew the next six months would add another ten. The physical transformation of a murder victim's family from arrest to when a trial was finally held was unbelievably sad.

"There always was something not right," continued Mike. "Something I can't explain to you. It was like, when David looked at you, he never stopped looking. He never turned away. When he talked to you, he always listened very carefully. *Deliberately* is a better word. It was like he was studying you. And he always knew the right thing to say. The perfect thing."

"And?" Lat prodded.

Jennifer's dad finally looked at Lat. Tears ran down his cheeks, but he didn't bother wiping them away. "That was it. David was . . . perfect. It was as if he was too perfect. And he fooled us all."

CHAPTER 24

"Don't, Mike. No more. I don't want to hear it! I won't second-guess everything!" Renny said, crying full force now.

Lat shifted uncomfortably in his chair. "Do you want to take a moment, Mr. and Mrs. Prowse? We're almost done here."

Mike nodded and stood up. He looked around the room absently, as though trying to remember where he was. "Come on, hon. Let's take a break. This is too much," he said, leading his wife out of the room.

"Dad, I'll take her," said Laurel, getting up off the couch. The doorbell rang, and she looked at the detectives blankly. "I'd better get that. Give us all a minute or two, won't you?" Then she followed her parents out of the room.

Randy still stood by the kitchen door. An awkward silence settled in the room, broken only by the loud ticks of the grandfather clock.

"Hey, Randy, honey," Brill said with a wink when everyone was gone, "you think you could get some more of those cookies your mom set out? I didn't have any lunch."

"Sure," she said and shrugged, heading into the kitchen.

Lat looked at Steve Brill like he had three heads. "What the fuck is that?"

"She was porking the brother-in-law," he announced with a big smile.

"What?"

"The younger sis. College girl. Something's going on, boss-man. She knew something, saw something, heard something, did something. I ain't sure what, but my money's on the doc teaching her a private anatomy class."

Lat looked back toward the doorway Randy had just slipped through. "You think?"

"Female body language, brother. If there's anything I know, it's that — a pissed-off broad, or one that's hiding something. It sure as hell gave her away. Standing the polar opposite away from the Waltons. Arms crossed. Nibbling the corner of her pouty mouth. Scared-rabbit look. And the ugly older sister is the new matriarch now that Momma's breaking down. Ain't nobody gonna disparage the Prowse name. And that includes us. So your interview with the rest of the family, I'm afraid, is done, boss-man. They saw what they wanted to see when they wanted to see it. Even their hindsight ain't twenty-twenty."

Lat looked Brill up and down as if he were seeing a new person but somehow couldn't trust his own vision. "So you sent her for more cookies to tell me this?"

"No. I'm still hungry. I'd actually like to get my hands on some of that real food," Brill said, pointing to the dining room table and rubbing his stomach. "I just think it might be rude to ask. But you're good at this interrogation shit, Sherlock. I'm changing my mind about you. You have a way with people, I can tell."

Randy walked through the kitchen door with another platterful of cookies. "Do you want more coffee, too, Detective?"

"No. We want you to sit down, Randy," Lat said softly, but sternly. He hoped Brill's sixth sense was right or he was really going to feel like an asshole. "We think you have some information that you may want to share with us before everyone else returns."

Randy sat down slowly on the couch. "I . . . don't know anything," she said softly, looking around. Her blue eyes were large and scared.

"Were you sleeping with your brother-in-aw, or was your sister?" asked Brill, reach-ng for another cookie.

"Excuse me?" Randy asked. Her eyes nar-rowed, and she looked surprised, but what she didn't look was pissed off that Brill had asked the question in the first place.

The man had absolutely no tact. "That would be something we'd need to know, Randy," Lat said. "We're having a hard time with everyone telling us how wonderful the man was. If there was anything going on between you and David, it might help us make sense out of all this. And of course it would be better if we heard it from you first rather than learning about it from someone else later."

"He wasn't so wonderful," Randy said in a soft, shaky voice.

"When?" Lat asked.

"It was a mistake. I know that. It only hap-pened once." She lowered her voice to just above a whisper and looked back at the foyer. "Just once."

"When?" he repeated.

"In May. At the barbecue."

"Did Jennifer know?"

"Oh, God, I don't think so. But she saw him talking to me, and she got real upset. She heard him ask me to meet him at Skinny's, a local bar, after she went to bed."

"What did she do?"

"She ran into her room and cried, threw a tantrum. She was pregnant with Sophie. Everyone else thought it was the hormones. I never said anything to anyone."

"What did you do?"

"I met him at Skinny's, and, well, you know, we had a few drinks, and one thing led to another thing. The next day he went back to Miami without Jen, and I never heard from him again. Not even for my birthday." She grew quiet. "It wasn't the first time, either. With me, yes. But Jen knew about the others."

"There were other women?"

She nodded and sighed. "I don't know names or dates. They might've even been hookers for all Jen knew. But there were a couple of late nights and perfume-soaked shirts. I think she blamed Memorial Day or me, though. We stopped talking after that."

Finally. The perfect husband was not so perfect.

"Was she gonna leave him?" asked Brill. "Were we talking divorce here?"

She almost laughed and shook her head. "Don't take this the wrong way, detectives, but my sister, even though she was pretty, was always insecure. So when she met Da-

182

id, he became like an obsession for her. He was the guy she got but couldn't ever believe she really did. My parents, my sister, they never saw that. Only I did. I knew why he was hanging on so damn tight. David felt it, too."

"So the first pregnancy?"

Randy shrugged. "She never 'fessed to planning an 'unplanned' pregnancy. And she never would." She rose from the couch and looked nervously back at the foyer, lowering her voice again. "But you asked me if she was gonna leave him? Let me just say this. Jennifer was desperate-crazy about David. He could do anything to anyone, and she would never leave. Never. He couldn't get rid of her, even if he tried."

Brill looked at Lat. "Maybe that was the problem."

CHAPTER 25

"That is one fucked-up family," said Brill a[s] they climbed into the rental car. He lit [a] cigarette. "It's like a soap opera, but nobod[y] wants to admit to any drama. I'm sure a[s] hell happy my parents just beat my ass."

"Yeah. Just imagine how you might hav[e] turned out," Lat said as he started up th[e] car. "You know, they are in mourning."

"They're in denial, bro."

"Of course they're in denial. As we speak[,] Mom and Dad are sifting through ever[y] memory they ever made with their daught[er] and that bastard they called son-in-law t[o] see if any of them were real. They'll reliv[e] every word of every conversation for the la[st] seven years for the missing clue th[at] would've tipped them off that he was [a] psychopath. And then for the next seve[n] they'll get to blame themselves and eac[h] other for not seeing the telltale signs [of] catastrophe that, by the end of this case, th[e] prosecutors will have painted as obvious to everyone. So, yeah, they're still in denial. 'Cause if they deny it, then it didn't happen, got it? And then they're not the ones at fault for letting it."

Brill stared at Lat in amazement. Then he exhaled a thick plume of smoke. "Oh, shit. That's deep."

"That's the five stages of grief and an ex-wife who's a psychologist." He fanned his hand in front of him. The Marlboro sure smelled good. "Blow that shit out the window, man. I'm off the death sticks six months now."

"Christ, you've had it rough. An ex-wife who's a mindfucker. I take back most of the things I was thinking about you, Nitchy."

"That's Nietzsche, you idiot."

" 'If you gaze for long into an abyss, the abyss gazes also into you.' Watch who you call an idiot."

Now it was Lat's turn to stare.

"Why is she an ex?" Brill asked. "Ah, forget I asked."

Lat blew out a long breath. "It just wasn't in the cards. How about you? Exes? Wives? Kids?"

"An ex-wife and an ex-kid."

"That sucks."

"Only the ex-kid part. The ex-wife poisoned her, so she hates me, too. But she still loves my money. She's past eighteen now. Not supposed to be my problem anymore, but I still pay the tuition bill at college, and she still ignores me. I'm hoping when she moves out of Transylvania she'll see her bloodsucking mother is a fucking nut job. Maybe then she'll give her old man a call." He flicked his cigarette out the window. "Her name's Nicky. I haven't actually seen her in five years. That college girl reminded me of what she must look like now." He sighed. "Hey, this is a fuckin cheery convo we're having, bossman. Say, have you written up your will yet?"

"Well, at least we've got a motive now."

"Yeah. Banging your pregnant wife's younger sister would get the claws out of most women. And most lawyers. Maybe the denying relatives are wrong. Maybe she was gonna divorce his ass, and he wasn't havin no part of splitting everything he'd earned."

Lat nodded. "Especially if he was roped into a marriage to begin with and his career was just taking off. What did he pull in last year? A half million? With no prenup, that's a pretty pricey divorce."

"Forget alimony. I can tell you that 2 percent of my check went to child support each and every week for the past eleven years. If I got a raise, Nicky got one, too. So three kids and a wife who don't work . . . ouch. In Mr. Talented Surgeon's tax bracket, that's gotta be close to 35 percent."

"And Jennifer just gave birth to another annuity that will keep paying benefits for the next eighteen years," Lat finished with a whistle.

"What was the death benefit on Jennifer's MetLife policy?" Brill asked.

"Two million."

"There's another two million reasons to make it hurt."

"Yeah, but it's not such a crazy amount, given the guy's profession. The house is pretty pricey, and he had a hefty mortgage."

"Not anymore he wouldn't."

"True." Lat shook his head. "Damn. Even if money's the motive, even if he wanted out and didn't want to pay, even if he was a horn dog who hated his clingy wife, I still can't figure the kids. Jesus. A baby?"

Brill shrugged. "Maybe he wanted to wipe the slate clean. Maybe he wasn't the poppa type. Some aren't. Look at that freak in California who killed his nine kids last year with a bullet to the back of their heads. Or the dad who hated wifey so much he drove his two rug rats cross-country, killed 'em, and buried 'em in some state along the way, then offed himself so she'd never find their bodies. I don't need to tell you about all the fucking psychos in this world. Just pick up the paper." He paused for a second. "I hate doctors. Never go to 'em. Why? God complexes, every damn one. My dad goes to a doc — first time in twenty years he has a checkup. Walks in the door laughing and smiling, healthy as a goddamned horse. Then this idiot in a white coat straps him to a treadmill and makes him run like the devil's chasing him. Two hours later he's lying in a hospital bed. Two days after that he's dead. Can you believe that shit?"

Lat's cell phone rang. He looked at Brill and flipped it open. "Latarrino."

Brill lit another cigarette and turned to look out the window. He'd never been to Philly before. And now he knew why. With the naked, twisted trees, gray skies, and bleak rain, it was depressing. Plus, right now they were driving past what looked like a few hundred graffiti-stained chemical plants, all belching white smoke up into the rain, where it hung in the humidity like a giant poisonous cloud. Brill had lived in Florida long enough to be suffering withdrawal. He needed to see some green grass and white-haired golfers in plaid pants, and he needed to see them soon.

Two minutes later Lat snapped the cell closed. "Well, there goes a couple of possible theories. Rape kit's back. There was no lover, no sex-crazed intruder. She was clean."

Brill stared at him. "And you look pissed why?"

"I guess the guy didn't want to play daddy after all. The knife's a match."

CHAPTER 26

Aunt Nora and Uncle Jimmy's condo wa
sandwiched between two other high-rises a
the far end of a mile-long, overdevelope
stretch of Fort Lauderdale beach known a
the Galt Mile. Julia pulled her Honda into
spot that conspicuously warned, "GUEST:
ONLY!!" She turned off the engine, and sa
there listening to the crashing sound of th
ocean, hidden behind the building's elon
gated shadows, less than a hundred fee
away. The sun was beginning to set, and th
sky was a warm tangerine color, infuse
with fiery streaks of copper. The air smelle
and tasted of coconut oil and sea salt, lik
piña coladas and margaritas. It was Julia'
favorite time of day, the beach her favorit
place to spend it. And to top it off, it wa
finally a Friday. It'd been two weeks sinc
the murders, since her schedule had turne
upside down. She could feel the stress me
away with the sun as it slipped under th

horizon. She savored the quiet moment a little longer, then grabbed the Macy's bag off the front seat, along with the bottle of Uncle Jimmy's favorite Chianti, and headed across the parking lot.

During the recent real estate boom, big-name developers had snatched up a lot of the old condo and co-op buildings and weathered spring-break hotels that lined Fort Lauderdale beach. They'd either renovated the old with fabulous facades and chic lobbies or torn them down to construct opulent resorts. The much-needed facelift was helping reshape the city into a younger, edgier metropolis by the sea.

But not here on the Mile. Donald Trump and downtown might be looking for the young professional, but the Mile still had its sights set on the older, down-and-almost-out-of-here retiree, fifty-five and older with No Pets, No Renters, and definitely No Kids.

On her salary, Julia was lucky to afford a one-bedroom apartment that was just west of I-95. A place on the beach was definitely not happening without a little divine intervention from the Florida lottery. Her aunt and uncle, though, were two of the Mile's pioneering snowbirds; they'd bought their unit twenty years ago as a vacation home for next to nothing. After Julia had left home to go to law school and Uncle Jimmy had slipped a disc — painfully ending a thirty-year career with the Department of Sanitation — Nora and he had decided to make the move to Florida permanent.

Julia could still remember a time when the hallways didn't always smell like boiled meat, before the crimson flowers on the lobby wallpaper had faded to a dull pink. Her parents had combined their first visit to Aunt Nora's new vacation pad with her family's only trip to Disney. Just seven or eight at the time, she still remembered it vividly. The endless drive down from her house in Long Island in the family station wagon that, thanks to Andrew spilling an entire container of chocolate milk in the backseat, smelled like puke in the afternoon sun. Then there were the frequent stops on I-95 so her dad could collect cuttings from all sorts of strange plants he had no business disturbing. Fighting with Andy over who would get to rest his or her head on the console. Playing Jaws and Marco Polo in the motel pools. Clutching Andy's hand as the two of them anxiously waited to ride Space Mountain. But the clearest memory of all was the smiling face of her mother dressed in blue jeans and an orange t-shirt running down the aisle of McCrory's five-and-dime, clutching bunches of plastic flowers. "They're perfect, Nor!" she shouted as she ran. "Just perfect!"

McCrory's had long since closed, and her mom was dead now. Whenever Julia tried to picture her mother, that day was how she saw her. Young and happy, her long, dark hair flopping behind her, the lemony smell of Jean Naté on her skin, and bubble gum on her breath. The moment was framed forever in her mind like a brilliant picture, with one strange exception — she could never remember the color of the damn flowers her mother held in her hand. Strange because they were still sitting in Nora's bathroom.

She shook the memories out of her head as she walked through the musty lobby to the elevator, nodding at the ancient security guard who sat watching *The People's Court* on a portable TV set and couldn't have cared less if she'd been dressed in black and wearing a ski mask. A couple of tables of bridge were still going strong in the resident rec room, along with a few squabbles. For a Friday afternoon, the place was jumping.

She heard the blaring televisions as soon as she got off the elevator, shouting at her from behind every door. Oprah. Ellen.

Judge Judy. Today the fluorescent-lit, teal-carpeted corridor smelled like chicken soup and boiling eggs. Finally, outside 1052, she caught a whiff of sausage and garlic. Before she could knock, the door opened.

"Uncle Jimmy! Happy anniversary! How'd you know I was here?"

"Hey there, Munch," Jimmy said, sticking his head out the door and checking the hallway like he always did. For what, Julia never really knew. Maybe he was expecting her to bring along some more people. "Freddy called up."

Munch was short for Munchkin, which was really funny since in heels, Julia took her uncle by at least an inch. "Who's Freddy?"

"Freddy. The guard downstairs. He called up. Told us you were on your way."

Good thing she'd left that ski mask back in the car. "Where's Aunt Nora?" she asked, giving him a kiss. She walked into a mauve-and-gray living room that still looked like that day in 1985 when her dad had packed everyone back into the smelly wagon and headed for home.

As if on cue, Aunt Nora came out of the kitchen, swaddled in aprons and holding a spoon. "Well, there you are," she said, giving Julia what she called "a Sicilian hug" —

a squeeze with all her body and generous bosom, followed by a hard kiss on the cheek that was sure to leave a bruise. "We were getting worried about you."

Aunt Nora was her mom's older and only sister. Her only sibling, in fact. It was Aunt Nora and Uncle Jimmy whom Julia had gone to live with fifteen years ago when her parents had died. After her world had turned completely upside down. She'd been only thirteen — old enough, unfortunately, to understand what was happening to her and around her, and definitely old enough to know that she was being sent to live forever with her aunt and uncle in Staten Island.

They'd tried for years, but Nora and Jimmy couldn't have kids of their own. So Julia had become their daughter, and they'd raised her through the rest of adolescence into adulthood just that way — adored and sheltered and completely overprotected. The fragile porcelain doll they knew could easily shatter into a zillion pieces at any moment. But not everything was perfect. Crazy Aunt Nora had crazy rules. From the day Julia had walked through the door of their two-family house in Great Kills, Staten Island — her fuzzy purple overnight bag stuffed with clothes in one hand and a shoebox full of what were to become her most cherished possessions in the other — certain subjects were never spoken of again. Nor were certain people. Family pictures disappeared from Nora's clean white walls; treasured keepsakes were quietly put away, never to be seen again. Nora dealt with the pain of losing her only sister by simply ordering it from her house. Exiled mementos and the faces of the banished were replaced with new knickknacks and smiling photos of Julia and her mother, which were hung everywhere.

Hugs and kisses smothered in tomato sauce and cannoli cream were her aunt's well-intentioned cure-all for the emotional anguish that both of them knew never went away. Nora had replaced her mother. A stand-in. But time had only dulled the constant ache in Julia's heart. An ache that on occasion, like arthritis on a cold day, would flare up into the most debilitating physical pain, as if someone had torn a hole in her heart and then ripped the stitches out once again.

"Come in, come in," Aunt Nora finally said, taking her hand and leading her into the kitchen.

"I wanted to take you out," Julia tried. A ridiculous proposition. Nora thought no one in the world cooked as well as she, and she was right. Hence, no reason to go out.

"Where do you think you can get sausage 'n' peppa that's not dried out like shoe leather? Save your money, sweetie."

"Okay," Julia said, handing the package from Macy's to her. "I'm not gonna argue. Happy anniversary. Maybe you won't let me take you out, but I'm leaving the present. I thought it'd go with the kitchen. Don't you dare return it. And don't regift."

"Tell me you got it on sale."

"I got it on sale," Julia lied.

"Okay, then I'll keep it," Nora chirped.

Uncle Jimmy appeared behind her with a glass of wine. "So how's that big case Nora said you're working now?" he asked, handing it to her. "I don't see you on TV."

"He's been looking," piped in her aunt while cutting cucumbers for a salad big enough to feed the entire floor. "I told everyone at the pool my Julia's gonna be famous."

"I shouldn't even have said anything," Julia replied with a smile, shaking her head and reaching for a slice of cucumber. While she'd mentioned to Nora the other night over pork-loin sandwiches that she'd gotten assigned to a really big case, she hadn't gone into details. "But it's pretty exciting. It's my first murder, Uncle Jimmy. A prosecutor in Major Crimes asked me to try it with him. Can you believe that? I got to go to the crime scene, and I've been helping him get ready for the grand jury next week."

"What'd this guy do? What kind of murder are we talking?" asked Jimmy.

Julia took a long sip of wine. "It may even be a death-penalty case, y'know."

"Oh, my," said Nora with a frown.

"But what'd he do?" Jimmy asked again.

She hesitated and took another sip. "It's the doctor case, Uncle Jimmy. You know, the man who killed his family."

Aunt Nora stopped cutting.

"Are you gonna be on TV?" Jimmy asked, looking carefully over at his wife.

"Maybe, but I'm not the lead. I'm what they call second seat."

"Second string," Uncle Jimmy said absently, nodding at the TV that was mounted under a cabinet in the kitchen. Jimmy Rose was talking about Sunday's Dolphins game.

"Is that the man who was just in the paper?" Aunt Nora asked quietly. "The one with the wife from Jersey?"

"That's the one." Julia looked down into her wine and swirled it around.

"Mary, Mother of God," said her aunt, putting down the knife altogether and walking over to the sink. She put her hands across it and took a deep breath.

Julia nibbled her lip and turned back to her uncle. "Well, I'll be trying it with this Major Crimes prosecutor. His name's Rick Bellido. Maybe you could meet him sometime. I could have him over for Aunt Nora's sauce."

"I don't like you around these people, Julia. These . . . you shouldn't be around criminals. It's not good. It's not good for you."

"Criminals are not good for anyone, Aunt Nora. I'm not hanging out with them."

"Sounds like something serious," said Jimmy, eyes glued to the TV. After twenty-nine years of marriage, he knew enough to stay out of Nora's way; she'd get the job done herself. "Is this a boyfriend?"

"I don't know, Uncle Jimmy. Maybe. I hope so. I'm working on it."

"A boyfriend?" Nora asked, raising an eyebrow and her voice. Jimmy walked back into the living room.

"I said maybe." Julia held up her hands defensively. "We've gone out. That's all."

"I want to meet him."

"We'll get to that." Julia finished her wine. "Now, let's eat, okay? This stuff smells amazing." She picked up the salad bowl to move into the dining room and head off the rest of the conversation.

Aunt Nora grabbed her arm and held it fast. For such a little woman, she had quite a grip. "Listen to me, little one. Jimmy and I never wanted you doing these cases. I'll admit that. I don't know why you can't be a lawyer in an office with some nice people. Maybe make some money, find a good man. I worry about you. My God, do I worry. But you're a big girl, and I suppose you can pick what you want to do for a living." Her voice lowered to a harsh, commanding whisper. "But I don't want you on this case. I've read about it. It's too close, Julia. Please, I'm begging you to stay away. It can only bring . . ." She stumbled to find the right word. The word that could possibly describe a lifetime of tears and loneliness, nightmares and stolen memories. "It can only bring . . . despair."

Julia nodded and blinked back hot tears. Then she took the salad and walked into the dining room.

Aunt Nora had no idea how right she was.

CHAPTER 27

When the red digits on the bedroom clock changed from 3:59 to 4:00, Julia finally gave up the fight and climbed out of bed. Lying there with her eyes closed was useless; sleep would not come again tonight. She padded into the dark living room, twisting her long hair up into a clip as she looked out the window. Her skin was clammy from the night sweats. Her building's sprinklers had just turned on, lightly misting the lawn and the maze of deserted walkways that wove through and around the sprawling apartment complex. The sky was black, the streets empty. She put a kettle of water on in the kitchen for tea and flopped down on the couch to wait for it to whistle. Everything in the apartment was dark and still.

She hated waiting for morning to come, waiting for the world to finally wake up with her. It was the loneliest time of night. The first couple of years after she'd gone to live with her aunt and uncle had been the worst. If she was lucky, she'd get three or four hours of sleep a night. Most early hours, though, were spent staring out her bedroom window at the empty street outside, like a bird in a cage, watching neighbors either stumble home drunk or leave for work that started long before the sun came up. Watching, night after night, as winter turned to spring, spring to summer, summer to fall, fall back into winter. Watching as the world kept on turning and life marched speedily forward without once missing a beat. And every night she would wish she was any one of those neighbors, with a different life, full of different worries. Some nights, when the loneliness and pain proved overwhelming, she'd sneak out and defiantly wander the unfamiliar streets of Staten Island or hop the ferry into Manhattan, hoping some would-be robber or rapist or killer would find her and do her the favor of ending what she herself could not. But nothing bad ever happened.

She stared at the black television screen, absently rubbing her socks to keep her feet warm. Her nightmares lingered with her now in the darkness. She squeezed her eyes shut, struggling to hold back the tears and the memories that continued to force their way out anyway, like a rupturing infection from a blister.

"Julia? Julia? Sweetie? You have to get up."

She heard the words, but they were far away. She buried her head in the pillow.

"You have to get up now." Cold hands shook her shoulders.

Julia struggled to open her eyes, which felt like they had lead plates on them. It seemed like she'd just fallen asleep. The room was freezing. Outside the window, a bright moon lit the stripped, bare branches of an elm, which was still sprinkled with a crusty layer of last week's snowfall. What time was it? Tomorrow was Sunday, right? She didn't have to be home till ten. She blinked again and sat up, rubbing her eyes. She looked over at her best friend, Carly, who was already awake and sitting up in the other twin bed across the room, chewing on a strand of her brown hair. Carly stared at her, then looked away. She looked strange. Scared, maybe.

Mrs. Hogan, Carly's mom, was the one shaking her shoulders. Standing over Julia, she wore the same weird look on her face as her daughter. She clutched her pink velour robe closed by the bosom.

"What's the matter?" Julia asked. "Is everything okay?"

Mrs. Hogan hesitated and looked around

the room while searching for the right words. "There are detectives here, honey. Downstairs. Two of them. They want to speak with you." She spoke quietly, her voice just above a whisper, as though she feared waking up the rest of the house.

"Detectives?" Julia asked, reaching for the jeans and sweatshirt that Mrs. Hogan held out in front of her. She shook her head, letting the word roll around her brain like a pinball. Waiting for it to hit a memory or something and light it up. Her heart started to race, and a lump formed in her throat. She automatically felt guilty, even though she knew she hadn't done anything. She turned to her best friend again. Carly still had that awful look on her face, so Julia was the one who looked away this time. Her eyes trolled the bedroom while she pulled on her jeans. Carly had the coolest room. It was painted a freaky purple that was almost blue. Her mom had let her pick out the color and paint it herself. U2 posters hung on every wall, and neon-yellow and -pink butterfly mobiles dangled from the ceilings. And her mom let her have a phone in her room, too. Julia'd sometimes been just a little envious of Carly — of her cool room and her cool clothes and her cool mom — but never more so than at this very moment. Right now she just wanted to be Carly — the one who wasn't *in trouble — and she really wanted everyone to stop looking at her in that strange, scared, pathetic way.*

She pulled her sweatshirt on over her pajama top. "What do they want?" she finally asked, tying her sneakers. "I didn't do anything, Mrs. H. I swear."

Mrs. Hogan suddenly began to cry. "It's not you, Julia. It's nothing you've —" She stopped herself and reached over and hugged Julia tight. Then she wiped her cheeks with her hands and folded up the sleeping bag on the bed, tying it closed. She took a deep breath and handed the bag to her. "Something has happened, honey. You have to go now. You have to go home."

Julia opened her eyes with a sudden start and looked helplessly around her dark, still living room, her heart beating fast.

In the kitchen, the kettle had begun to shriek.

CHAPTER 28

It took the grand jury a little less than twenty minutes to return an indictment charging David Marquette with four counts of first-degree murder. Although everything about the grand jury was supposed to be kept secret — including the deliberations and the actual vote itself — Rick had it on good authority that the vote was unanimous. A bailiff with good ears had spilled the beans.

Marquette's arraignment was the following morning at nine, and the courthouse was jumping. On 3, Judge Flowers was trying a thirteen-year-old aspiring serial killer. On 5, Judge Macias was sentencing a young mom to life for drowning her newborn. Arson in 2-6, home invasion in 2-10, cocaine trafficking in 5-7. Pick a courtroom — any courtroom — and you'd be sure to be horrified. But as Julia hurried across the street — dodging raindrops and puddles the size of small lakes — she knew it was none of the above-named tragedies that had caused the pileup of news trucks in front of the courthouse, their monstrous satellite antennas towering fifty feet into the downpour. It was *State v. Marquette* that was drawing the crowd.

It was funny, she thought as she ran past them in her now ruined new suede Donald Pliners, you never knew what would make a headline. Like a sleeper of the year at the box office, or a best-selling novel from an unknown writer, you just couldn't predict what would strike the public's nerve. Some cases made a lot of noise in the beginning but faded to barely a mention in the local section as they made their way through the process and interest inexplicably petered out. Others never hit the paper at all. The aberrant exceptions — the Scott Petersons and OJ Simpsons — those were the defendants who grasped and held national attention, commandeering hours of legal discussion on *Nancy Grace* and *Hannity & Colmes.* Big-name cases that made and ruined careers and fixated a country of workaholics in front of their TVs in the middle of busy afternoons just to watch a verdict come in.

While David Marquette might not be making the headline desk over at CNN or

Good Morning America — at least not yet — there was no denying he held the fickle attention of the local press in Miami. And that was intimidating enough for Julia. She spotted the gaggle of cameras and the familiar faces she usually watched report the news as soon as she stepped off the escalator, all gathered in front of 4-10. Corrections had set up a search table, an additional metal detector, and roped stanchions. A crowd of curious onlookers lingered about, thickening the crush in the already congested hallway.

The butterflies in the pit of Julia's stomach fluttered furiously about. She'd never been a newsmonger or had a lifelong desire to "be on TV," so seeing the cameras and knowing they were here on her case made her anxious. It was still a few minutes before nine, and she knew she'd probably be the first to make an appearance for Team State through those doors. Rick was most likely still across the street flipping through the paper and finishing his coffee. He hated sitting around waiting for court to start, so he made sure to time it so he never did. She swallowed her fears about saying or doing the wrong thing and, with her shoulders confidently set back, walked past the cluster of cameras and into the courtroom.

She needn't have worried. No one even asked her for the time. A jabbering crowd filled every seat inside. Most were there for cases other than *State v. Marquette,* although Julia immediately spotted the cameras mounted on tripods in the corners of the room. She looked over at the box as she made her way up the aisle, but the in-custody defendants hadn't been brought over yet. Settling into a seat against the wall on the State's side, she spotted Karyn chatting with the C at the podium. Julia flashed her a smile, but all she got back was a cool nod. Things had definitely been strained between them since the first appearance. Karyn had never said whether Rick had talked to her, but the "everyone must attend" morning calendar rule was no longer enforced for Julia.

She glanced anxiously again at the box, which was still empty. Julia had seen killers in court before — chained and shackled and only steps away in a jury box or behind a defense table. In Miami courtrooms, they were not an uncommon sight. But whenever corrections brought in a murderer or one stepped up to the podium with his or her attorney, she had to look. Had to see the person who had taken someone else's life-blood with the pull of a trigger or the jab of a knife. She always expected those defendants to be somehow extraordinary — to look and sound different, to bear a sign or a notable disfigurement. Some mark that would immediately identify them as killers. But more often than not, it was frightening how completely normal they appeared.

Today it was her defendant she was anxious to get a look at. Outside, in the hallway, the press pounced on prey. Every head turned as the doors swung open and Dr Alain Marquette and his wife, Nina, hurried in, tailed by a flustered Mel Levenson. Insistent reporters, denied entry by Corrections, continued to shout out questions. Dr Marquette kept his arm protectively around his wife's shoulders as he ushered her to the front row of seats. Julia could see the yellowing bruises under her red-rimmed eyes and the butterfly bandage across her nose — long-lasting souvenirs, presumably, from her fall outside Ryder the night Marquette had been arrested. A statuesque woman, elegantly styled, she had strong facial features and squared shoulders. Julia suspected Nina Marquette dominated a room on most occasions. But not today. Today she looked frightened and overwhelmed, small for her size.

How did it feel to be the parents of a killer?

he wondered. Did the Marquettes feel any sense of responsibility for the sins of their son? Had there been warning signs during his adolescence that they'd chosen to ignore? Julia supposed it must be doubly hard for them — they'd violently lost their daughter-in-law and grandchildren. They had them to mourn, too. Now they stood to lose their son. Not to a prison cell, where they could maybe visit once a week — but to a needle that would stop his heart and kill him. And they would not be allowed to mourn him when he passed, either. They were just supposed to watch quietly with the rest of the witnesses when the warden pulled back the black curtain and the crowd outside the prison gates began to cheer. . . .

The door to the jury room opened, pulling her out of her thoughts. A human chain of defendants shuffled into the courtroom, chains rattling and mouths running as Corrections barked instructions. Fresh from the farm across the street, most looked mean and tough and somehow larger than life — no matter their physical stature — with their tattoos and piercings and gangsta attitudes. All except one. At the back of the line was a slight man, in physical comparison, wearing an orange jumpsuit, his head hung low, his face hidden from view. An electric murmur ran through the spectators.

The door to the judge's hall opened and Jefferson, the bailiff, stepped out. Before he could even open his mouth, the courtroom rose as Judge Farley rushed to the bench.

"All rise! No beepers, no cell phones. Court's now in session. The Honorable Judge Leonard Farley presiding. Be seated and be quiet!" Jefferson hesitantly shouted in one long stream. New to his job, he looked back at the judge for a nod of approval, but Farley was giving out none of that today.

The courtroom quickly settled into quiet as the judge stirred his coffee and surveyed his kingdom, seemingly oblivious to the cameras and the crowd presence. Even the defendants in the box shut up, as Farley's reputation for not taking shit stretched across the street, and upstate as well. Julia saw Lat and Brill slip into the back of the courtroom and move to a spot against the wall, next to Ileana, who'd popped in for support and to get a look at "the son of a bitch" herself. Lat smiled and gave a short wave. She smiled back. Allies, finally.

"All right," Farley began, studying the long line of attorneys that snaked behind the podiums. "We've got a full house today."

Let's get the party started. Who's first, Ivo-
ane?"

CHAPTER 29

Julia prayed that Rick would walk fast as Ivonne called calendar and the defense attorneys slowly worked their way one by one up to the podium. Farley hated passing cases for attorneys who weren't present, and she didn't want to be the first one to face his wrath. Just as Mel Levenson moved into the number-three position, the muffled shouts of the press started up in the hall once again. The courtroom door opened, the crowd hushed, and Rick strode in like a superhero, well dressed and ready to save the day.

"Mr. Bellido," Farley announced in a loud voice, cutting off the poor-schmo attorney at the podium who was in midsentence, "let me guess. You're here on —"

"*State versus David Marquette.* Page 9. Good morning, Your Honor," Rick answered back smoothly as he made his way up the aisle. "Ricardo Bellido for the State," he said

o the court reporter with just a hint of a
Spanish accent that Julia had not heard
before. Somehow he'd gotten to the head of
the line, and no one had complained.

"I heard this was coming my way," said
the judge, waving off the defense attorney
like a fly. Mel lumbered to the front of the
line.

"Good morning, Judge," he said gruffly.
His co-counsel headed over to stand next to
Marquette at the jury box. "Mel Levenson
and Stan Grossbach for the defendant, Dr.
David Marquette. I've already filed my ap-
pearance."

"Good to see you, Mel. I heard your office was handling this," Farley said. "Looks
like we've got quite a crowd." In between
careers as a prosecutor and then a defense
attorney, Mel Levenson had once been a
circuit court judge. In fact, he'd had the
courtroom down the hall from Farley. That
was a number of years ago, but the Good
Old Boys' Club offered lifetime member-
ships. The judge leaned back in his seat and
smiled smugly. "I'll tell you, gentlemen, this
is going to be some matchup. Tyson versus
Holyfield."

"Page 9, *State v. David Alain Marquette,*
felony case number F05-43254," Ivonne
said in a raspy monotone. "Today's the

twenty-first day."

"Is the defendant present?" asked the judge, looking at the box.

"He is," said Mel. "As are his parents Your Honor."

Farley didn't bother acknowledging them

Julia craned her neck, but Marquette's face was still obscured. Someone began sniffling loudly. It was Nina Marquette.

"Please stop that," said the judge, annoyed.

"The grand jury has returned an indictment against the defendant for four counts of first-degree murder. It should be in the court file," said Rick looking around the courtroom. His eyes caught Julia's, and he discreetly motioned with his head for her to come up beside him.

"I have a copy of the indictment. Waive formal reading, enter a plea of not guilty and demand discovery," responded Mel.

"Fifteen days." The judge slugged down a shot of coffee.

Julia took a breath and walked across the gallery to the podium as the clerk began tossing out dates. She felt Karyn and the other prosecutors watching her, some probably wondering what she was doing up there. Others perhaps jealous that she was.

Across the room, David Marquette finall

ooked up.

Julia sucked in a breath. He looked even worse than he had at his first appearance. He'd obviously lost a lot of weight, and his gray eyes were sunken, his cheeks drawn. Corrections had also sized his orange jumpsuit wrong — which the officers were known to do for child molesters and other particularly repugnant inmates — making him appear smaller and slighter than he had three weeks ago. His strawberry-blond hair was stringy and long, his face a thick carpet of gray-peppered stubble. He clenched the jury-box railing so hard that Julia could see the raised vein lines in his chained hand. His strange, light eyes stared out, vacant and lifeless, like the eyes of a mannequin in a department-store window. Watching everything but seeing nothing.

Stan stood next to him whispering in his ear, most likely explaining the proceedings and the charges in the indictment. But whatever Stan was saying — whatever Marquette was hearing — the words were having no effect. When Farley began to recite some of the grisly facts from the indictment after Mel requested a bond, the man didn't even blink. Julia finally had to look away. The whole strange scene reminded her of some late-century traveling circus that had finally unveiled the show's main attraction to the crowd — the hideous Human Monster, a freak chained and shackled to his stage. The terrified audience gaped in fear and disgust at the very sight of him.

"I'm not giving him a bond," the judge finished. "If you want an Arthur hearing take your arguments to Judge Glass. If she wants to give you one, I won't have a problem." Farley looked at Rick and winked. "Although I'm betting Mr. Bellido will."

"Correct, Judge," Rick replied coolly. He reached across the aisle and with a snap handed a piece of paper to Mel. "Especially as the State intends to seek the death penalty. I've already filed my written notice with the court."

"I've got it here," said Farley.

"This is a show," grumbled Mel.

"We'll be objecting strenuously to any release," said Rick.

Another electric murmur buzzed through the crowd. One of the defendants in the box cackled; another let out a "Whoo-wee! Free 'lectricity!" The judge shot them a testy look. "I think your client might need to find someone to take care of both his patients and his houseplants for a while longer, Mel. All right, let's set a date. Give me something quick, Ivonne. I don't want to die before

218

get to try this thing."

"February seventh for report. February twelfth for trial," replied Ivonne.

"Whose week is that?"

"That's a B week."

"Fine. February seventh for report."

"That only gives us three months," Mel said, exasperated.

"Let's see how we do, shall we, Mel? No need to drag this out if we can all be ready. In Texas they move their bad boys through the system like cattle to the table. Hundred and twenty days, arrest to trial."

Julia looked over at Rick. "Julia Vacanti for the State," she interposed, moving to the podium and clearing her throat. "Judge, excuse me, but that's my trial week. I would ask the court to set this matter down in an alternate week."

The eyebrows made a deep V. "Ms. Vacanti, this doesn't concern you. Step back."

Obviously the judge hadn't heard the news. How ironic was it that of all the criminal court judges in Miami, it was the Honorable Leonard Farley whom the computers had randomly spat out to hear this one? In a case that could catapult her career to another stratosphere, she'd beaten Las Vegas odds to get the one judge hell-bent on destroying it.

"Ms. Vacanti will be second-chairing this with me," Rick cut in. "Let's get a date that can accommodate her trial schedule, please."

The courtroom sat in silence for a long moment. She felt everyone staring at her. "Okay, Ivonne. Give me another date," Farley finally said. "One in an A week, please."

"February twenty-first for report. February twenty-sixth for trial."

"The twenty-first it is, people. I'll see you all then. Motions in thirty. And no delays." The judge peered menacingly over his glasses at Julia. "As I'm sure this young lady can tell all of you, I've got a very busy docket. And I don't like surprises."

CHAPTER 30

Charley Rifkin stuck his head in the door that led to the private office of the State Attorney. "I've got Rick Bellido with me," he announced.

Jerry Tigler, the State Attorney, sat behind a cherry desk, his slight body swallowed up by his leather executive chair. Behind him sheets of rain whipped against windows that looked out on the soggy Miami skyline. Across the room a flat-screen quietly broadcast the local news. "Good," he said absently. "Bring him in."

Rick followed Charley into the office suite, as he had a thousand times before in his long career as a prosecutor. Instinctively, though, he knew this time was different.

"Good to see you, son," Tigler said, shaking Rick's hand across the desk. "Watched you on the tube this morning. Good job."

"Thanks, Jerry," Rick said, taking a seat next to Rifkin.

"You announced today?" Tigler noted.

"There was no sense in waiting, Jerry. The facts on this are so outrageous. I've definitely got the aggravators. If anyone deserves the death penalty, it's this guy."

A crack of thunder sounded, and the skyline disappeared completely in a sudden deluge. "Can you believe this?" Tigler said, spinning his chair around to face the window. "I've been looking at rain for a month. Where the hell's the sun in the Sunshine State?"

"I think even my tan's fading," Rick said, looking down at his hand with a laugh.

"Now I know we're in trouble," Rifkin added with a chuckle.

Tigler turned back from the window. His plump pink face had deflated, as if the last of the laughter had been squeezed out of the tube. Tired lines sliced across his brow and pulled at the corners of his mouth. He looked every minute of his sixty-seven years. "I've got cancer," he said simply.

Rick stopped laughing. "What the hell?"

Rifkin stayed quiet. He'd obviously already heard the news.

"Prostate. Early stages. Real early, I'm hoping, but . . ." his voice trailed off. "No difference, boys. I'm done."

"That's it, then?" Rifkin said with a heavy

sigh. "You've decided?"

"I wasn't up to another campaign anyway, Charley. You knew that. The last one kicked my tired old ass, and frankly . . . I just don't want it anymore. It's time to enjoy life. Cancer's just the excuse to clear the calendar a little quicker." Tigler looked at Rick and smiled. "Which brings us to you, young fellow. You've done great work in this office, Rick. You're a close confidant, a good friend, a strong leader. As you know, I've offered to pass the reins to my golf partner here, but he doesn't want the target on his back."

Rifkin waved off his friend's proposal before he could offer it again. "My biggest challenge next year is gonna be to break 80 on my golf score. I've done my thirty, Jerry. I don't need the headaches; my kids still give me enough of those."

Rick felt the excitement bubble inside him, like when a jury was about to deliver a verdict. He knew just from the looks on their faces when it was guilty as charged. Now he was looking at Jerry Tigler's tired, sad face, and he knew the next words out of the State Attorney's mouth.

"You've been groomed for this job for years, Rick. I know you'll make a great State Attorney. I want to give you ample time in

223

my chair, though, before the November election. You'll be in for a fight for sure, but if you can rally your supporters and get the kids in the pits on board, there's not much likelihood of a mutiny come the fall."

"Thanks, Jerry. I appreciate your confidence," said Rick, drawing a deep breath.

Tigler nodded slowly. "I don't know when I'll make it official, though. A couple of months, maybe. That should get you up to speed. I'd like to get your name in the governor's ear now, though, since he has the actual say on my replacement. I'm having lunch with him next week in Tallahassee. What's your time frame on Marquette?"

"February, but it won't go then. If Me doesn't look for a continuance, Farley could push it, but I doubt it. Most likely the summer or fall."

"I don't want you juggling that and the responsibilities of this office at the same time. You'll have enough on your plate. Plea it, try it, or give it away to someone who can handle it. Consider this, though — winning Marquette would be a good note to start on. The case has garnered a lot of press attention. Free publicity will make you a household name quicker than any paid political advertisement."

The room stayed quiet for a moment, then Tigler stood up and walked back around the desk. "Congratulations, Rick."

"Thank you for this opportunity," Rick said, rising to shake Tigler's hand. "Of course you know I wish it were under different circumstances."

"Me, too, son," Tigler said softly as the rain continued to stream like tears off the windows behind him. "Me, too."

CHAPTER 31

He heard the gritty click of the guard's heels start up again, somewhere in this cold, putrid, green maze that he was trapped in. Slow and easy, they made their way down empty cement hallways, silencing all in their path.

Click, click, click.

Coming this way. Coming his way.

He cocked his head and listened so hard his brain began to hurt. There were two sets of footsteps now, walking almost in sync. The clicking slowed to a shuffle and then stopped. A jolt of adrenaline seized his chest; somewhere along the parade route the guards must have paused to observe one of the crazed animals they had caged.

He couldn't see them yet, but he could definitely picture his captors — peering through iron bars into squalid cells, shaking their utility belts for attention, black batons dangling from their sides like menacing third arms. Their eyes would be searching for a reason to call in an extraction team. He could hear their radios — chirping, squawking, blurting out strange codes they didn't want anyone else to understand. If they found something amiss, the screaming would begin, but he never knew why. He didn't want to know.

He closed his eyes.

The drugs they fed him made his head feel as if it were trapped in the spin of a crushing wave. Lucidity would be there one moment, then a sudden wall of water would buckle him at the knees and drag him under into murky, distorted blackness. Just above the surface was the world he'd slipped away from. He could see the watery shadows, the blurred faces laughing at him, talking about him, as he tumbled over himself, unable to find footing in the sandy muck. And as the wave pulled him further and further out to sea, he realized the screams of despair sounded only in his own head.

The creature in the cage one cell over began to shriek inconsolably. It was impossible to think, hear, feel, breathe in here with the screamers. He opened his eyes with a start and realized that the *click, click, click* had gotten much closer. Panic grabbed his throat. *Where are they now?*

The footsteps stopped. Keys jingle-jangled; the radio squawked. He felt eyes crawl over his person like roaches. He heard the heavy breathing of those watching.

"This him?" The voice was laced with revulsion.

"Yep. Yo, Marquette, get up. Let's go, Doc. Pisses me off. We just got him ready for court this morning, and now they want him out again."

"Where's his clothes?"

"Suicide watch," said the one jingling his keys. "No nooses on this floor. I guess you never worked 9 before."

"How's he supposed to make a noose out of a jumpsuit?"

"You wouldn't believe what they do up here. I once saw a guy stuff his own shit in his mouth, then choke to death on it. That's why they're here, man. That's why he don't have no clothes. We're saving him from himself. From choking on his panties!" Jingle laughed so hard he started to cough. Then he hawked back a wad of phlegm and spat it into the cell. It landed next to his foot. He watched it out of the corner of his eye, white and frothy as it oozed toward him. He felt the anger rise up, dark and ugly. When it touched his toe, he wanted to stand up and scream. He wanted to take

228

Jingle's fat, dumb neck in his hand and put his nose into his own spittle like he would a dog. Rub it around until it finally broke off.

But he didn't.

"Me?" Jingle continued, wiping his puffy, cracked lips with the back of his sleeve. "I say let him fucking kill himself. Guy offed a baby, man. His whole fuckin' family. Save the taxpayers' money and let him do it himself. But I ain't in charge."

"Thank God for that," said the other guard with a short laugh. "Well, he ain't coming downstairs like that. Is he violent? Do we need additional restraints?"

"Ain't given no one trouble. Yet. He don't say nothing. He don't do nothing. He just sits there like that." Jingle chuckled. "Freak."

"Well, let's get him dressed," the other guard said and looked at his watch. "He's got company, and I'm betting that his lawyers don't want to see him like this neither."

CHAPTER 32

Nina Marquette wished she had not worn her good jewelry today. Not to this place. The reception area of the Dade County Jail was filled with all sorts of sordid, dirty people. Every eye was now fixed on her, probably wondering what she was here for and how much money she had in her purse. She ran a finger over her nose. It was still bandaged where she'd broken it weeks before. Perhaps they thought her a crime victim.

Bulletproof glass separated the waiting area from the corrections officers on the other side. A sign warned that all weapons would be confiscated. Circled pictures of guns, knives, and bombs with black lines drawn through them illustrated what a weapon was for those who could not read. Although the jail was also filled with officers, Nina felt no safer. They watched her, too. She remembered what her father had once told her: *Never stare down an animal, Nina. They will get angry and bite.* So she pulled her sweater tighter around her shoulders and looked down at the dirty floor.

"Why's he still in here, Mr. Levenson?" Alain Marquette demanded angrily as they waited for Corrections to buzz them in. "That's my question. They won't bring him to visiting hours. He can't use the phone. Christ, I haven't spoken to him in weeks!"

"This is a jail, Alain. It's up to Corrections whether to allow an inmate visitors or use of the facilities," Mel replied patiently, wishing the door would buzz open and end the conversation already. "Your son hasn't been allowed. That's a problem, yes, but one I have no control over. I've been able to see him when I need to. That's what matters."

Mel was one of the best criminal defense attorneys in Miami. It wasn't shoplifters he represented unless the name was Winona Ryder. And it certainly wasn't the street-smart and destitute with a rap sheet a mile long that made up his clientele. But privilege and affluence came with their own type of ignorance — most of his clients had no experience with the criminal justice system before they walked through his door with a fat retainer check in hand. That almost always guaranteed a shocked and outraged relative at the end of the day. Indignant that Uncle Lou was actually strip-searched after he was arrested for securities fraud. Infuriated to learn that horrible jail conditions and toothless cellmates named Bubba really did exist. The system that had been falling apart in front of them their whole lives now had to be fixed yesterday. Usually Mel listened sympathetically while they complained. But today was different. Given what this client was charged with and the complete freak that the guy was, it was difficult to feign outrage because the man couldn't visit with Mom and Pop on a Sunday.

The steel outer door buzzed open, and Corrections waved them through. Painted arrows on green cinder-block walls directed them down a series of hallways. In front of another steel door with a square-foot wire-mesh window stood another CO. He ate a yawn and nodded at Mel. "He's in now," he said, unlocking the door with a key. "The buzzer's under the table. Hit it if you have a problem. We opened the mikes for ya."

A clear Plexiglas partition divided the small green room, splitting a metal interrogation table. Bolted to the floor in front of the table on each side were two chairs.

Fluorescent tube lights were caged to the gray ceiling.

David Marquette sat in his jumpsuit on the other side of the partition, his face drained of color by the bad lighting. Behind him was another steel door, which he must've been brought through. As at arraignment, he stared out in front of him at nothing.

Alain put his palms against the Plexiglas. "David?"

"It's only been a few days on the meds, Alain. The agitation is gone, which is good. . . ." Mel stopped himself. "Lawther's the jail doc. He says it could be weeks before the medication kicks in. Before we know what's the drugs or what's . . . him. They have him on Thorazine. A thousand milligrams."

"Jesus Christ!"

"They're still diagnosing him," Mel cautioned. "Remember, it's a jail, not a private hospital. He can't and won't have access to every drug under the sun."

"Thorazine? No wonder he's like this! They're making him a zombie!"

"Thorazine? Is that different than what Darrell —" Nina cautiously began to ask.

"Yes, Nina! Yes, it's different!" shouted Alain bitterly, cutting her off.

Nina bit her lip and turned away. She dabbed a crumpled tissue at her eyes, trying to remain as dignified as she could in this awful place. "I cannot do this, Alain. Don't ask me. Not again," she whispered.

He watched them all watching him. He felt his eyes roll in his head. Roll, roll, roll around the room as the wave smashed him from behind and submerged him once again in murky water. Their voices became garbled and thick.

"Enough!" Alain said finally, throwing his hands up. "This place is horrible. We need to get him out of here!"

"It's not that easy, Alain," Mel calmly replied. "This is very serious."

"That I do know. That prosecutor wants to kill my son." He held back tears. "Look at him," he said softly, placing his hands on the Plexiglas again. "David?" he shouted. "David! Do you know where you are? Do you know what you've done?"

As his father screamed at the man they called his attorney, his mother finally managed to pull her stare off her lap. On her black skirt was a pile of white shredded tissue pieces. She still clutched a few ragged strips in her fist, dabbing them gingerly at her eyes. Even through the heavy makeup, he could see that her face was swollen and disfigured. Fading bruises darkened the cruel saddlebags under her eyes.

Everything about her was always so refined, so picture-perfect. Even now she made the butterfly strapped across the bridge of her nose look fashionable. Not a hair out of place, no mascara running with all the tears. But beneath the cultured exterior, he knew she was squirming, itching to get out. Fretting about the vile germs she might be touching or inhaling right now, just by sitting here with the son she didn't want to look at.

"Then make them understand his condition, Mr. Levenson. I'm paying you enough."

"This isn't France, Alain."

Maybe it was curiosity. Maybe guilt. Maybe it was because not to look would be too obvious, but she finally did. Her deep blue eyes silently rolled over him like a lint brush, picking up all in their path, missing nothing. Finally they found his own. She squinted a little, her head tilted slightly, watching him as a tourist might study a monkey at the zoo.

"Let's go, Alain," she pleaded, rising from her seat suddenly, her face bleach-white. Shards of tissue fluttered to the floor. She turned and walked back to the door through which she'd come, her arms wrapped around herself as if she were incredibly cold.

"Just get him a bond, Mr. Levenson. I'll deal with the rest. I'll help him."

"Now!" Nina commanded. "I don't feel well, Alain. I want to leave now."

A few minutes passed before the guard came and let the three of them out of the room, but his mother never turned around again. Maybe she'd seen something in his eyes, or maybe it was nothing at all that she'd seen. Complete, vacant nothingness that had frightened the color from her face and made her want to run away. But it was clear that she could no longer bear to look at this man who was her son.

Or at what he had become.

Chapter 33

"Avon lady," Julia said with a shy smile when the door opened.

"I'll take it, whatever it is you're selling. In fact, I'll take two," Rick said, leaning against the doorframe of his apartment. "Come in. Please, come in. You look fabulous."

"Thank you," she said, stepping past him into a sleek, modern living room. She did a little twirl. "They're new. I wasn't sure where we were going, but I figured nice jeans are always a good call."

"Especially on you," he said. He came up and gave her a soft, sexy kiss, his hands moving over her hips. "Let me get us some wine," he said, pulling away after a moment and heading into the kitchen.

"Wow . . . this is really nice," she said, looking around. She'd never been to his apartment before. Black leather furniture, contemporary art, polished granite counters, gleaming stainless-steel appliances, an enormous flat-screen — the *GQ* Bachelor Pad special edition. She stepped through open sliding glass doors that led onto a balcony and a bewitching view of Miami Beach. "Are you sure you're employed by the same government agency I am?" she called out, thinking of her own cluttered one-bedroom — the one with the stunning parking-lot views. She hadn't made a bed since she'd moved in three years ago and had no idea which box the real plates were still packed in. Preframed posters from Kirkland's decorated her walls; Glade scented candles accessorized the mismatched furniture. Considering it was her bed that she and Rick had always ended up in, she couldn't help but wonder now what he thought of her when the lights were turned back on.

"I got into this building years ago, before real estate prices went nuts," he said as he stepped onto the patio, two glasses of chilled pinot gris in hand. "Before art deco was a hot phrase and South Beach was a cool place to be."

"There was a time when South Beach wasn't cool?" she mused.

"Very funny," he said, handing her a glass. "You know, I'm a native Miamian. Back in the day it was old Jewish men who lined Ocean Drive in their wheelchairs instead of rappers in their tricked-out Benzes. Rent *Scarface*, sweetheart. That was Miami Beach in the '80s. Domino games and ugly guayabera shirts and bales of pure-white snow falling from the heavens. A city that'd left its heyday back at the Fontainebleau with Sinatra and the rest of the Rat Pack. Ahhh," he said, sighing, "a time when you could actually get a parking spot on the beach."

"Hey, I like guayabera shirts," she said, sipping at her wine. She couldn't help herself. "Were hot dogs really a nickel back in the day?"

"You're a wiseass."

"You really are old."

"Don't tell anyone. And you really are young."

"Don't tell anyone," she returned.

He reached over and kissed her again. His tongue was cold and tasted like the pinot. "Are you kidding me?" he whispered. "I tell everyone. I'm very proud."

She thought about the ruthless gasoline trail at the State. "Not everyone, I hope," she said softly. It was one thing for people to wonder. It was another to confirm their suspicions that she'd slept her way into second chair.

His mouth moved over her ear, devouring an earring in its kiss. "Actually, I enjoy keeping this . . ." He paused, obviously searching for just the right word, "*secret* just between us. Neither one of us needs to handle personal PR during this case. It's not good for either of our careers. Besides," he added, flipping her long hair playfully off a shoulder and nibbling on her skin, "secrets can be an awful lot of fun, you know. Just like showers."

A light switched on in Julia's head, and she could suddenly see what was not there in front of her the whole time. Right then, she knew that their relationship was going nowhere. It might take a long, fun time to get to that destination, but in the end that was where it was headed. She was a secret to be kept hidden away from everyone who mattered, now and when the Marquette trial was finally over. And, like a mistress, random stolen nights and an occasional goodnight phone call were the best she could ever hope for, no matter how much she might wish for more. She knew she should probably just turn around at that moment and walk out — on him, on this case that had brought long-displaced, frightening memories back to life — outraged, insulted, saddened, disappointed. But his touch felt so amazing, his kiss so intoxicating. The devil on her shoulder quickly started his handiwork, with seductive, desperate whispers of "Well, maybe you don't *need* more than this. . . ." Simply put, Rick was like cheesecake — sinfully rich, luscious, and oh-so-bad for you. Indulging would bring nothing but heartache for a long time to come, yet, knowing this, she still ordered a slice whenever she saw it on the menu. The key to getting over the addiction was to stay the hell out of the restaurant. But for many complicated reasons, Julia just couldn't do that.

He moved behind her, running his hands through her hair, exposing the back of her neck. He traced the bowl of the cold wineglass over the soft curve of her throat. A chill electrified her spine, and she closed her eyes. A few droplets of wine splashed her skin, and he sensuously kissed them off with warm lips as they ran down her neck, disappearing into her silk shirt. She moaned as his tongue slowly worked its way up to her ear. His body pressed close to hers, he found the buttons on her blouse, undoing them one by one with his deft fingers. She felt him behind her, growing, pulsing. "No more talk," he whispered, unbuttoning the last button.

She arched her neck back into his lips, offering her throat to him. "I thought we were going out," she whispered.

He parted her shirt with the stem of the wineglass. A fading tan line disappeared into a sheer black lace bra. He moved the wet crystal over the lace, making her nipples hard. Running the bowl along the curve of her ample cleavage, with the stem he pushed the cup off one breast, exposing it. Then the other. They were on the fifth floor, but with the living room lights on, anyone on the beach or surrounding balconies could see. Then he poured the rest of the cold wine down her arched throat, letting it run over both breasts and down her new jeans.

He turned her around to face him, slipping the shirt off her shoulders. She stood there with her breasts exposed and the front of her jeans soaked with wine. He put down the wineglass and unbuttoned her jeans, pulling them down over her hips. They fell in a heap on the floor with her panties. He exhaled a deep breath as he looked at her. "I don't see any reason why we should go out tonight."

Then he picked her up and carried her into the bedroom.

CHAPTER 34

Wild, clandestine sex with your trial partner, a.k.a. boss, was one thing. Actually spending the night was another. Chalk it up to some weird *Pretty Woman* hang-up or some deep psychological loose screw, but by two Julia gave up the fight for sleep that she knew would never come in Rick's apartment, got dressed, and tiptoed out the door.

She didn't get home till almost three, finally nodded off at four, and completely missed the alarm when it beeped at six thirty. And again at seven. And again at seven thirty. It was Aunt Nora calling to leave some weird recipe on the answering machine that finally woke her up. She arrived at the Golden Glades interchange at precisely the same time as the other 2.3 million commuters headed into the city and managed to inch her car into the SAO parking lot just a smidge before nine. She raced across the lobby and up the stairs like FloJo,

grabbed the three boxes of files she'd
prepped the day before from her office, and
hopped the next elevator back down. All in
three-inch Joan and David patent mules and
a tailored pencil skirt. Because the only
thing worse than being late to Judge Leonard Farley's courtroom was being late on
your plea day. Today was her plea day.

Just as she pushed open the lobby doors
she heard her name.

"Is that her? Julia Vacanti?"

"That's her. Yup. Right there. The prosecutor, Vacanti."

The first voice she didn't recognize. The
second was that of Melba, her secretary. She
probably should've kept going, but instead
she stopped and turned to see Melba, a
Starbucks grande-something in one hand
pointing right at her with the other. She was
standing next to a well-dressed young guy
in a suit.

"Ms. Vacanti?" the man said, walking
toward her now. She spotted a manila
envelope in his hand. "Julia Vacanti?"

It just didn't feel like a Publisher's Clear-
inghouse moment. *Deny, deny, deny,* she
instinctively thought. "That's me," she said.
"Can I help you? I'm on my way to court."

"I have something for you," he said, holding out the envelope.

"You can just leave it with my secre-
ary. . . ."

"I'm an associate with the law offices of
Levenson & Grossbach. I was told to deliver
his to you this morning."

Levenson & Grossbach. The magic words.
"Okay," she said, taking the envelope.
Handsome Associate who probably made
hree times as much as she didn't move
iway, though. He just stood there, like he
vas waiting for her to open it. So she did.

Then she ran like hell for the elevators.

CHAPTER 35

"Hey there," Rick said with a surprised smile, looking up from his desk as Julia walked into his office. "What a coincidence. I was just thinking about last night. Mmmm . . ." He leaned back in his chair, coffee in hand. "I didn't hear you leave."

"I had to get home." She felt her face turning red, and she looked away. The morning-after angel with the oversized conscience was now whispering in her good ear, and she just didn't want to hear it.

"Too bad. I would love to have you wake me up in the morning. Breakfast could be quite filling. Come in, come in. You heading to court?"

"I was. It's my plea day. I was actually on my way out of the building when an associate from Levenson & Grossbach served me." She held up the envelope. "It's a change of plea."

"A change of plea?" He cocked an eye

row. "Is Mel throwing in the towel already? Saving the taxpayers the trouble of a trial with a guilty plea? How kind."

"It's a 3.216; he's pleading insanity," she replied, handing it to him.

"What the hell?" he asked, pulling the notice out of the envelope. He reached for his reading glasses. "You ever had a defendant plead insanity before, Julia?"

She shook her head.

"That's because insanity defenses don't work. Not in Florida. In twenty years I've seen maybe fifteen attempts. All but two have failed miserably. The two that did get a ticket to the state hospital in Chattahoochee, the guys were nuttier than fruitcakes and they weren't charged with murder, so I actually pled them both NGI."

NGI stood for not guilty by reason of insanity. At least she knew that much.

"I can't even remember the law on insanity in Florida," she said, hoping he wouldn't hold that against her. From her New York law school days she knew that each state had a different, convoluted test. And Rick was right — insanity was just not a commonly used defense. None of her friends in the pits had ever seen one, either.

He shot her a look that she couldn't quite read. "Florida follows the M'Naghten Rule, as about half the states do. Every person is presumed sane. To be found not guilty by reason of insanity, a defendant must prove that at the time of the criminal act he suffered from, quote, 'such a defect of reason from disease of the mind that he did not understand the nature of the act, or that it was wrong.' End quote.

"So unless Mel can come in and demonstrate that this guy had some mental disease that remarkably no one ever knew he had till now, and because of that condition he either (a) didn't know what the hell he was doing, or (b) he knew what he was doing but didn't know it was wrong, then he's legally sane. The emphasis is on cognition — the defendant's ability to discern right from wrong. An inability to control one's actions or rage doesn't matter as long as that person knew what he was doing. And being commanded to kill by God or Satan or Santa, or irresistible impulses of rage due to seeing your wife fornicate with the plumber, don't fly in the Sunshine State."

"Well Levenson certainly has the first part down," she commented, nodding at the notice in his hand.

"What first part?" he asked, frowning as he looked down and started to read.

"The 'mental disease or defect' part. Lev

enson's claiming David Marquette has
schizophrenia."

CHAPTER 36

They sat in silence while Rick finished read
ing. Then he picked up the phone and
dialed. "This is Bellido," he said in a con
trolled but angry voice. "I need you to cal
me in my office the second you get this. We
have a problem on Marquette."

Julia figured the call was made to John
Latarrino. And she also figured Lat had seen
who was calling him and let it go directly to
voice mail. Despite the fact that they had
displayed a unified front at yesterday's ar
raignment, things were uncomfortably tens
between the two men, although she had yet
to figure out why. This latest news was not
going to help relations. Lat was the lead
He'd conducted the interviews, asked the
questions, written the reports. And Rick
hated being caught unawares.

"He's a 'diagnosed schizophrenic'? He'
been 'hospitalized before'?" he shouted
waving the notice. "What the hell? The gu

was doing freaking surgery three weeks ago and giving speeches on how to protect the fallopian tubes from overstimulation. Insane, my ass. But why the hell am I just finding out about this now? That's what I want to know. This sort of shit should not come across my desk as a surprise filing!"

"Levenson says Marquette spent three weeks in a psych hospital when he was a teen, and it was under an alias. That's probably why Lat didn't know about it," Julia offered. "How could he? No one in Marquette's family's talking to us, and obviously no one in Jennifer's family knew he was sick. Maybe Jennifer didn't even know."

"Well we sure as hell know now," Rick barked. "Lat should've found it. At the very least, I'd have been prepared. And I wouldn't have let Doctor Death spend three long weeks on the ninth floor of DCJ learning the ropes on how to make an insanity claim stick from the loons and cons in residence. Jesus, I didn't even know he was on that floor! Corrections probably put him here initially on suicide watch, and now, with a little advice from his lawyers on the state of the law in Florida, I'm sure he's figured out his best chance at how to beat the system!"

"Okay. How do you want to handle it?"

she asked quietly when he'd calmed down.

"Like a bomb threat — as though it's real, but knowing that 99.9 percent of all calls are bullshit, which this most certainly is. Now we've got to catch him at it. First we get a court order, and we get those medical records from when he was locked down as a kid, along with any other psych or medical records he might have here in Miami. Then we interview every guard who works on 9 to see what Marquette's like when his lawyer's not around and the cameras aren't watching and the jail doc's not taking notes. And we research schizophrenia in the event the guy actually does have something wrong with him. But remember, a diagnosis is not a legal defense. Just because somebody's schizo, or bipolar, or whatever flavor-of-the-day mental illness might be out there, that doesn't give him a license to kill without responsibility. Especially not in Florida. And not with me."

He motioned to the *West's Florida Criminal Laws and Rules* that sat on top of her file boxes. "The competency and NGI laws are 3.210 and 3.211. Besides being insane, Mel's claiming Marquette's incompetent to proceed — which has nothing to do with his client's sanity on the night of the murders and everything to do with Marquette's bility to remain in the here and now during court proceedings. *Insanity*'s only a legal term, not a medical diagnosis. But before we get to have a trial to decide if he was legally insane, the judge will have to determine if he's competent. Does he understand the nature of the charges against him? Does he know what a lawyer is for? Will he sit in a chair at trial and assist his attorney, or will he scream for the mothership in his pajamas? This guy's educated, and he's bright, which makes him more dangerous than your average criminal. He's facing four murder counts and a death sentence, which makes him much more desperate. It behooves him to try to win a spot on the next bus going to Chattahoochee."

"What if he is sick?" Julia asked. "I'm just throwing it out there. We're planning three steps ahead, as if he's got to be faking, but what if he's not?" She couldn't forget those vacant gray eyes staring out at nothing in court yesterday. Dead eyes. The whole scene had creeped her out. If it wasn't the drugs that had him looking like a zombie, then he was a really good actor.

"I've seen everything from feces-throwing to devil-worshipping in a courtroom but only two real nuts in twenty years. Two. Forgive me if I'm skeptical when someone suddenly says they're crazy. Someone who, by all accounts until now, was just fine until he decided to Ginsu his wife and kids. And we simply can't afford to let the man take an extended vacation upstate to collect his thoughts while we work out our case. First, if he's found incompetent, it'll be another six months before he comes up on calendar for report and another eval. That's time spent in the loony bin perfecting the craft with the real loons, and time doesn't help a prosecutor. Witnesses forget, die, retire, relocate. Evidence gets lost and destroyed. Juries feel bad for defendants who've spent a long time locked away in a mental hospital. They tend to think there's really something wrong with them. They tend to think they're not responsible for their actions after all. They tend to acquit them. And what I'm sure Marquette knows by now is that an NGI is a walk. No matter if he killed four people or four hundred, he will walk out of Chattahoochee a free man the day the doctors say he's no longer a danger."

Rick pulled an accordion file from his file cabinet and rifled through it. "We need to set a competency hearing before Farley. The judge's gonna appoint at least two, possibly three, shrinks to evaluate Marquette. We want Christian Barakat. Levenson, or course, is gonna ask for Al Koletis because every defense attorney wants Koletis. He's useless — everyone's incompetent and we're all nuts. I could save him the paper."

Her cell phone buzzed. It was a 545 exchange — Farley. Oh, shit. Her plea day. She looked at her watch and her stomach dropped as if she'd rounded a blind curve on a roller coaster and saw the plunge just ahead. It was already ten thirty. They were all waiting for her across the street.

"Speaking of the devil, I've got to get to court," she said, rising. "I'm late. In fact, I'm more than late. I'm probably in contempt."

Rick grabbed his suit jacket and followed her to the door. "I'll walk you over. Let's see if I can't keep your incredibly cute ass out of the box and have Farley special-set the competency hearing. Maybe we can get it on for tomorrow morning."

"That's fast."

"Like the judge said, no need to drag this out if we can all be ready. From here on out, every second counts."

CHAPTER 37

— *Severe, debilitating mental illness*
— *Profound disruption in cognition and emotion*
— *Symptoms include:*
• *psychotic manifestations*
• *bizarre delusions*
• *assaultive, destructive, violent behavior*
• *auditory hallucinations — voices keeping
up a running commentary on a person'
behavior, or 2 or more voices conversing with
each other*
• *catatonia — state of minimal movemen
and responsiveness*
• *paranoia — an unwarranted feeling other.
are trying to harm you*
— *No lab test, CAT scan, brain imaging tes
(MRI), or clinical presentation can yield defini
tive diagnosis of schizophrenia*
— *Strikes young — average onset:*
• *Males — btw ages of 17 and 25*
• *Females — onset delayed 3–4 years*

developing usually btw 21 and 29
  — No cure

Julia rubbed her eyes and pushed herself back from the kitchen table, away from the pile of medical and legal treatises, psychology books, and case law on insanity she'd compiled. Her notes read like a jumble of thoughts from a twisted psychological thriller.

Schizophrenia. While she'd heard the word before, she'd never known more than what the media chose to print about the affliction in news stories about homicides or the scary symptoms that Hollywood selectively twisted into movie plots. What she had known for sure was that schizophrenia was *the* mental illness that defined the word "crazy." High-profile crazy like Van Gogh, Nobel laureate John Nash, would-be presidential assassin John Hinckley Jr., and serial killer Son of Sam. It was the condition that caused people to talk to themselves — or scream at themselves — as they walked down the street. The illness that statistically plagued the homeless, the affliction that made people see little green men, or God, or clandestine government agents.

The jumble of terrifying facts and statistics that she'd just learned spun inside her head. The mother of all mental illnesses, schizophrenia afflicted more than 1 percent of the world's population. With no known cause and no known cure, it struck seemingly at random, targeting young, healthy men and women in their late teens and early twenties — at the very beginning of their lives — crossing lines of color, culture, and social status without discrimination. As if in a real-life script from a horror movie, it robbed people of the most basic and fundamental of human instincts — reality. It made its victims see things that weren't there and hear voices that didn't speak, but it also changed the very way thoughts were processed and organized in the brain. A misfire somewhere in the circuitry made thoughts sound just fine in the schizophrenic's head, but once those thoughts were voiced aloud, made no sense to anyone hearing them. That was perhaps the saddest effect of the disease — the clinical symptom known as "decreased awareness of illness." To not know you were sick, to think you were completely normal while the rest of the world crossed the street just to avoid you, was incredibly tragic. No other medical condition could possibly be more socially alienating or more frightening.

Julia poured herself another glass of wine and looked out her kitchen window. The moon was full, hanging low in the sky — a funky, ethereal yellow color, dimpled with craters. She thought of her brother, Andy, and a conversation she'd had with him a lifetime ago. One of those innocuous exchanges she probably should never have recalled, like breakfast with your aunt and uncle on a Sunday morning . . .

"Andy, why does the moon shrink?"

"That's a stupid question." He sighed with annoyance. "It doesn't shrink, Ju-Ju. It's hiding."

Even though he'd practically just called her stupid, she still wanted the answer. "Okay, fine. Why does it want to hide?"

"So it can come back out and make everyone look again. Think about it," Andy said, looking up at a full yellow moon dancing in between whispery clouds right outside his bedroom window. It was so perfect, you almost expected a witch to fly past. "If it stayed fat and round all the time, no one would care. People wouldn't even notice it. Like the sun. No one pays attention to the sun until it disappears and rains for a few days. Then everyone wants it back."

"Ohhh . . ." It all made perfect sense now. Andy was so smart. He was going places, Mom always said. Julia hoped he'd take her with him when he did.

She blinked back tears, Aunt Nora's dire prophecy playing like a cold, detached voiceover to her bittersweet memories. *This case. It's too close, Julia. It can only bring . . . despair.*

Is this it? Is this despair, Aunt Nora? Or is this empty, hollow, dread-filled feeling just the beginning? A prelude to anguish . . .

She picked up the cordless and dialed.

"Hello?" said a sleepy voice on the second ring.

"Uncle Jimmy?" She looked over at the clock. Damn. It was past eleven.

"Julia? Honey? Waz'a matta?" Jimmy asked, his voice scratchy with sleep. She hung her head against the wall, mad at herself for not looking at the time before she dialed. While Nora would be up till three baking a calzone, Uncle Jimmy was often out cold by ten o'clock.

"I'm sorry. I just wanted to talk to Aunt Nora. I, uh, didn't realize it was so late. I'll just call tomorrow —"

"Is that Julia?" called her aunt in the background. "What's'a matter?"

"Hold on, Munch." Julia heard Jimmy say, "I dunno. She wants you," to her aunt as he passed the phone. "Yeah, she sounds okay. She didn't say nuttin' was wrong."

"What's'a matter?" Nora demanded when

she got on the phone.

"Nothing, Aunt Nora. I just wanted to ask you something, that's all."

"At eleven thirty at night? You feeling okay? You want me to come over there, honey? I can just get dressed —"

"No, no. I didn't mean to wake you."

"You didn't. I was in the dining room cutting out a couple of coupons; my ValPak came in the mail today. Jimmy got the phone first." She laughed, relieved. "At this hour, I thought maybe somebody died. That's how we found out about Jimmy's brother, y'know. The phone rang at four in the morning, and Jimmy just knew."

"I, uh, I just got done working on this case I've got."

"Oh." The laughter stopped. "The murder? I read the paper this morning. They're saying that man is insane."

"Don't believe everything you read," Julia replied and then closed her eyes. "I want to ask you some questions about Andrew."

There was silence on the other end of the line.

"Aunt Nora? You there?"

"Why you want to ask me about him?" Nora asked quietly.

This was so hard. Much harder than she'd imagined. "I've been thinking a lot about, um, not just that night but about the year before it happened. And how things were so different . . ."

The tears were back, slipping quietly down her cheeks. It was important that her desperation not show. "There's no one left that would've known him, Aunt Nora. You know, no other family or friends. I thought maybe my mom had talked to you about him," Julia continued. She pulled the hair back off her head, hoping to pull her thoughts together. "About what was going on with him after he left for college. And I thought —"

"No good can come of this, Julia," her aunt said in a firm, dismissive voice. "None. Leave the past in the past. For all of us. Please."

"What happened to Andy?" Julia finally demanded. "I think I need to know. I think I should know. I have a right, Aunt Nora —"

"I don't want to discuss this. I told you that case was too close. Remember what I said, Julia. You're not sleeping again, you're asking crazy questions, you're tired, and you're stressed." She paused. "You're drinking. Yes, I can hear that, too."

Julia quietly set the wineglass down on the counter.

"You're opening a box that you don't need opened," Nora continued. "One that Jimmy and I have worked very hard to keep closed for your sake. Walk away, Julia. Walk away now, and just let it be before any more people get hurt."

"I can't just walk away. I love you, but I have to know what happened!"

But Aunt Nora cut her off once again, her voice chipper and forced. "I don't think this Sunday's gonna work. We'll be in Jupiter at a bridge tournament, but we'll have to start talking about Christmas, I suppose, right? I'll make the lasagna. I don't know, maybe you can bring your boyfriend, the one you've been hiding. That'd be fine. But I don't want to talk about this no more. I have to go to bed now. I love you, but I've got to go," she finished with what sounded like a whimper. Julia could hear Uncle Jimmy asking her what was wrong before Nora hung up the phone and the line went dead.

She stared hard at the receiver in her hand. No matter how much she tried to keep them back, no matter how much she tried to concentrate on other things, the memories continued to creep forward. Ghosts kept knocking on her door, anywhere, anytime. All the time now.

Banging, banging, banging, just trying to get back in.

CHAPTER 38

"You have her?" squawked a raspy voice over the handheld.

"Yeah, she's in the car."

"ETA?"

"We're en route. We'll be there in two." The detective whose badge said "Potter" turned his head just a little and smiled a weak smile at the young girl who sat by herself in the backseat. Then he cast a silent look over at the driver before turning his attention back to the road. No one said anything.

Julia saw the mass of flashing blue-and-red lights as soon as the car made its painfully slow turn onto Maple from Hempstead Avenue. Her mouth went dry, and she nibbled on her lip, clutching the still-warm sleeping bag in her hand. She probably should have realized long before this moment that something was horribly wrong, but she hadn't. Or she hadn't wanted to. But now she suddenly got it, and she just as suddenly knew that she didn't want to see it yet. She turned to look out the side window and blinked hard, trying to force the leftover sleep from her eyes. Just ten minutes ago she'd been at her best friend's house, in the middle of a really good dream that she couldn't remember anymore. Now she was in the back of a cold police car that smelled like smoke and stale cologne and pee. She wondered what Carly was thinking right now. She tasted blood from where she had chewed her lip. What a difference ten minutes could make.

Most of the neighbors on the block had turned off their Christmas lights when they had gone to bed, but there were still a few colored lights twinkling through the night in the tall pines and plump evergreens. The car slipped into slow motion as it passed familiar houses and familiar lawns where familiar faces gathered in their pajamas and wool coats to see what all the commotion was about. They turned and pointed and squinted at the police car, straining to see the passenger in the backseat, and Julia buried her face in her sleeping bag. The car stopped in front of her house.

Potter turned around again. Red-and-blue lights spun across his face. No one said anything for a few long moments. "Something's happened, honey," the detective finally managed.

She nodded furiously, wanting him to stop talking. She couldn't look at him. Blood from her lip seemed to fill her mouth, and she was afraid to speak.

He paused and then sighed. Not an aggravated or impatient sigh, but one that was resigned and weary. "You wanna wait here for a minute, hon?" he asked, but it was more like a statement. She said nothing, and he opened his door, nodding at his partner. She watched as the two of them walked across the frozen brown lawn, dotted with gray patches of old snow, and then disappeared into her house.

Ten years earlier, her dad had hung his first and last strand of outdoor lights on the sagging two-story colonial, and more than a few of the oversized and now obsolete painted bulbs had blown. A glowing plastic Santa Claus waved at the middle-class neighbors and their fancy reindeers and glittering sleighs, the red on his coat and hat faded over the years to a dull pink. She had put out the decorations herself this season because no one else in the family had wanted to, and she couldn't imagine a Christmas without tinsel and lights and gaudy lawn figures, but all she had been able to find in the garage were the aging Santa and a weathered wreath.

Julia squeezed the sleeping bag tight against her chest and watched as faceless silhouettes moved through the upstairs rooms of her house. She could feel her heart pounding furiously — faster and faster, harder and harder — like a freight train out of control, barreling down open tracks. Any minute now it was going to jump the line.

Icy cold slowly began to seep back into the dark car, stealthily wrapping its invisible, wispy fingers around her body like the coils of a snake. She counted the ticks as the engine slowly cooled back to silence, and she wondered why she hadn't asked either Detective Potter or his partner what had happened or where her family was or why there were two ambulances just sitting there in her driveway. . . .

Something has happened to me — I do not know what. All that was my former self has crumbled and fallen together and a creature has emerged of whom I know nothing. She is a stranger to me — and has an egotism that makes the egotism that I had look like skimmed milk; and she thinks thoughts that are — heresies. Her name is insanity. She is the daughter of madness — and according to my doctor, they each had their genesis in my own brain.

LARA JEFFERSON,
THESE ARE MY SISTERS

CHAPTER 39

Julia looked up from the pile of dispos on her desk to see Brill standing in her doorway, wearing a Chicago Cubs cap and a half smile–half grimace on his face.

"No offense," he said, plopping into a chair, "but you look like shit, Jules. You want me to get you a coffee or something? Maybe a doctor?"

"You've got so much tact," said Lat as he walked in, a file box under his arm. "Someone needs to train him, Julia."

"Others much better-looking and far braver than you have tried and failed."

"Ignore him, Julia. I've learned to," he said, dropping the box at Brill's feet and flopping into a seat himself. His brow crinkled with concern. "You know I hate agreeing with him, but you do look a little tired, Counselor. You okay?"

"Thanks, guys," she replied, reaching for her glasses, suddenly self-conscious. "Gee, what a welcome. I'm fine, just not sleeping well. Farley's punishing me. I've been in trial for, like, two weeks straight, and it's getting to me." She smiled. "No big deal."

Actually, she was exhausted. It'd been weeks since she'd been able to just turn her brain off and go to sleep. And when she finally did manage to nod off, the nightmares would begin. She still had no answers to the questions she'd asked her aunt about Andy. As a prosecutor, she knew she had the power and resources to find them out herself, but there was a part of her that didn't want to run the computer checks or pick up the phone and call strangers in the Nassau County Police Department; there was a part of her that feared hearing the truth. She just needed Aunt Nora to tell her what she wanted to hear, and she'd be able to move on.

"That co-counsel of yours keeping you up late at night?" asked Brill.

She felt her face flush, and she looked down, pretending to pull out a drawer and search for a pen. She definitely didn't want Brill or Lat to know about Rick. Especially not Lat, given the strained status of their working relationship. "I'm just not a good sleeper. Never have been. Are you guys here to see him?"

"We've both decided that we'd much rather see you from now on. You're easier on the eyes, and you have a much better personality," Lat said, grabbing a bag from the file box and handing it to her. "Fresh from D'Amato's in Chicago. Pistachio cannolis."

"You know guys like girls with a little meat on their bones," Brill said matter-of-factly, wagging a finger at her. "That skinny shit might sell clothes, but it don't work for the boys. Eat a cannoli. Fill out them slacks."

She smiled. "Pistachio cannolis, huh? Thanks. Boy, my aunt would love you two."

"Vacanti I figured had to be Italian," Lat said. "A little taste of home."

"Like my new hat?" asked Brill.

"No," she replied. "I'm a Mets fan."

"Ouch! A New Yorker. I should have known. Now I know we'll be friends."

She smiled again. Lat was right — Brill was beginning to grow on her. He reminded her of an eleven-year-old boy entering adolescence, snapping the bra straps on the girl seated in front of him just to be annoying. "So what else did you bring me?"

Lat kicked the box. "Fun bedtime reading. And a copy of everything for the defense. I know you'll make sure they get it, Julia." He sat down. "So when's the competency hearing?"

"Not till the third week in December. The twentieth. The judge appointed Christian Barakat and Al Koletis. We're waiting on the psych evals, which will take a couple of weeks, I suppose. Rick will handle the hearing if it's a toss-up and the doctors don't agree. If they do see eye-to-eye, I suppose he'll stipulate to the reports. What have you been up to?"

"Well," Lat said, "we've pretty much interviewed everyone in Miami we could find who ever dealt with David Marquette as either a patient, employee, or colleague."

"And?"

"Intense media coverage always brings out the best in people, so some are remembering things a little differently than they did a few weeks ago. Everyone wants to be the first to say they saw the warning signs. Marquette was a loner. No friends, no family. Spent eighty hours a week at work. And he treated himself well. Spent tens of thousands on his clothes, Benz, five-star hotels, expensive dinners out. We're not sure how many of those dinners were with, or without, the wife. Jennifer's family, we can all agree, didn't know him. Hundreds of miles away and blinded by his success, they saw what they wanted to see. But the favorite son-in-law could actually be very difficult — so says the staff that had to work with him."

"Unless you were good-looking and female. Then he was sweet and smart and dedicated," noted Brill.

"Affairs?"

"Well, the sis-in-law was the doozy that we're thinking finally sent Jennifer to the web pages of MiamiDivorce.com and MiamiLaw.com, two recent searches we found on the family computer. No one at the law firms recommended through the site can confirm that either Marquette sought counsel, but someone was looking on that computer, and my bet's on Jennifer. As for other women, there were a bunch of one-nighters, we figure, but none will go on record. Everyone involved has a family to protect, *capisce,* Counselor? And we have not found any woman waiting in the wings to become Mrs. Marquette *numero dos,*" said Lat.

"What a dog. You're right. She was probably gonna take him for all he was worth. But I don't think the website stuff will be admissible. While it gives us a motive, it's inflammatory, and we have no way to prove it was Jennifer who visited the sites. Maybe we should call around to other divorce attorneys. Maybe she found somebody else to help her get a divorce."

"Good idea. Done."

"How was he difficult at work?" she asked

"God-complex difficult," replied Brill "He blew off appointments, missed two surgeries in the last couple of weeks that had to be rescheduled. 'His time is important to him, and no one else's is' sort o complaints. Cocky as a motherfu— ah," he said, catching himself, "as a . . . he wa. cocky in the operating room."

"He got into a screaming match with a nurse over something she said in the operating room a couple of weeks before the murders," Lat explained.

"Which was?" she asked.

"She says nothing. But he flipped, called her nasty names, and kicked her out of the OR."

She looked at the box. "That can't all be reports."

"Better. Medical records," Lat replied "We went back to Marquette's old stomping grounds in Kenilworth, a suburb or Chicago's North Shore."

"Nice 'hood," said Brill with a low whistle

"Interviewed a few former teachers, found a few old classmates, most of whom eithe didn't remember him or didn't care to."

"Even as a kid, the guy was a misfit," Brill said. "A Charley-in-the-box. Stuck to him self, no friends. Really bright but lazy and arrogant. Sailed through private elementary and middle — hit a huge snag in high school. Grades tanked till Pop built a wing or something, and then it was smooth sailing till young Davy went off to college at DePaul."

"Drugs?"

"That's what we're thinking," Lat replied. "Personality change coupled with a sudden drop in grades after the first year. But of course when we go near the Marquette compound to get their take on things, the curtains draw. Even the help avoids us. That's when Davy took his three-week vacation at Parker Hills Psych Hospital. He left DePaul right after, or DePaul booted him, as his GPA was below a 2. He started Loyola the following September. The few former acquaintances who we did find remember Marquette as either extremely charming or extremely manipulative. Self-assured or completely full of himself. No middle ground."

"I guess you have to be charming to be manipulative, don't you?" she asked.

"My ex sure wasn't," Brill commented.

"Grades were okay at Loyola, occasionally great. Looks like when our defendant likes something, he excels. He went to med school at Northwestern under his dad's watch, made the final walk to 'Pomp and Circumstance,' but by a hair."

"You know what they call the guy who graduates last in his class from med school?" Brill asked.

"What?"

"Doctor."

"Good point," Julia said. "And I think that's gonna be our biggest hurdle. We'll need to get a jury past the fact that he's a successful surgeon. I still need to get past it."

Lat tapped a finger on her desk. "We did find something very interesting, Counselor. An old arrest when young Davy was sixteen. Saw it referenced in the DePaul admission papers. A misdemeanor. Animal cruelty."

She raised her eyebrows. "Did you get the case file?"

"Nope. It's been expunged; that's why we didn't find it before on NCIC." NCIC was the National Crime Information Center, which maintained criminal histories from every state. "It's gone, and only the original charge is left in the computer, it was so long ago. Your guess's as good as mine what happened, but you know what I'm thinking."

She nodded. Cruelty to animals, particularly in childhood and adolescence, evidenced an alarming emotional detachment from living things — a classic warning sign of a budding psychopath. Many famous killers had experimented with animals long before they'd tried anything on humans. Jeffrey Dahmer had impaled dogs; Richard Allen Davis had set cats on fire. The list went on.

He tapped a finger to his temple. "Just tore it upstairs. He checked into Parker Hills right after he started his second year at DePaul. We faxed ahead with the subpoena, so they had the records ready for us. Like I said, some late-night reading. Maybe it'll help you sleep," he added with a soft smile.

"Is that when he was diagnosed schizophrenic?" Marquette would have been nineteen or twenty at the time — right smack-dab in the average onset for males.

Lat shook his head. "No. That was just Levenson being creative with the facts. The only thing the Parker Hills doctor wrote on his notes was 'Rule out schizophrenia,' but there's no reference to an actual diagnosis, or that it was ruled out. David was admitted involuntarily by his dad, apparently suffering hallucinations and for, and I'm quoting here, 'violent, combative, erratic behavior.' End quote. But the records upon admission only refer to a probable cocaine psychosis. By the time he was discharged, his 'psychosis' had been downplayed to a simple anxiety disorder. Probably at the request of his dad. Marquette's a real big name in Chicago."

"Cocaine psychosis? So this was a drug rehab?"

"That's what it looks like to my untrained eye. But I'm not a three-hundred-dollar-an-hour defense attorney grasping at straws. I'm sure that in a courtroom, anxiety disorder will become a misdiagnosed psychotic break. Make the illness fit the crime."

"Is the doc who treated him still there?"

"Hell, no. Left a year later. Died of a heart attack five years ago."

"And the violent behavior that he was admitted for?"

"He assaulted his mother with an iron."

"That was plugged in at the time," Bril added.

"Ouch. Was he arrested? Were the cops called?"

"Nope," Lat replied. "Looking at the admit remarks, Dad apparently dragged Junior's ass into the family Range Rover and drove him to Parker Hills, this exclusive Betty Ford–like rest stop. Under a different name. It was all very hush-hush, which i why you can tell Bellido we couldn't have found it even if we'd known where to look."

"This is a family that likes to keep secrets, Jules," Brill added. "Big ones. And, for you, we've saved the biggest for last."

Her eyes darted between the two of them. 'Why am I getting a bad feeling?"

"I don't know how this is gonna play out, and I don't know if it's gonna matter in the end, but it is pretty interesting — especially if psychotic behavior runs in the family and swims in the gene pool," Lat began.

She stared at him, waiting.

"Marquette had a brother," Lat finished. 'An identical-twin brother. His name was Darrell Armand Marquette, and he most definitely was a nut job."

CHAPTER 40

"Diagnosed schizophrenic when he was twenty-one," Lat said. "Had a breakdown two months after a new girlfriend dumped him and Grandma up and died. He was supposed to be up at MIT studying nuclear physics, but instead Wackenhut Security found him rearranging the lawn furniture o a high school buddy at three in the morning, preparing for the second coming o Christ with sixteen rolls of heavy-duty tinfoil and a few hundred yards of electrical tape. The family kept him hidden away a the homestead for a couple of years, but in '92 he was moved to South Oaks, a psychiatric hospital in the 'burbs. He never go out. He died there, some seven years later.'

Her head was spinning. An identical twin Every report and article she'd read had said Marquette was an only child. "How'd you find out about him?"

"That was tough. As Brill just said, this i

282

a family that likes to keep its secrets. We only found out this guy even existed after a couple of old teachers we interviewed asked us which Marquette boy we were referring to. That's when we discovered that even though Dave had an identical twin, not everything about the two of them was the same. Evidently Darrell was the one who stood out. He was the genius, one teacher told us. Our boy struggled in comparison. It was Darrell who was valedictorian, Darrell who jumped a year ahead in school, Darrell who won track meets, Darrell who dated the prom queen, Darrell who was accepted to MIT on a scholarship. Everyone we spoke to after that who remembered both boys all wondered what had become of Darrell. And so did we. Nothing came up on Autotrack or NCIC or with the locals. We got his Social from school recs and checked with the Bureau of Vital Statistics and found out he died in '99, but that was it. There was no work history, no marriage — nothing. It's like he just up and disappeared from sight fifteen years ago. Of course no one at the house would talk. So we found ourselves a former housekeeper who didn't mind chatting if we helped her out on a bench warrant for some unpaid moving violations. She gave us the name of the hospital. We used Mom's maiden name to figure out the alias Darrell Lamoreaux. Got a subpoena and looked at the records. They're in there, too. Darrell was pretty bad off. Had what the docs call hebephrenic schizophrenia, also known as the disorganized type."

"Who knew there were different types? I thought it was one size fits all." Brill chuckled.

Lat ignored him. "Didn't talk, arranged pencils all day. Lived in his own world. Looking at the daily activity logs from 1997, 1998, and 1999, Dad made daily stop-ins. Mom never stepped foot in the place. Our boy Dave would come by maybe once every couple of months. A couple of nurses who are still there remember his visits because they always caused a ruckus — the two of them looking exactly alike — when young Davy went to go home. In fact, it was on one of these brotherly get-togethers that poor Darrell met his demise. Drowned in a lake on hospital grounds while off with his bro on a stroll. Davy claimed Darrell ran off and he couldn't find him. Twenty minutes later security finds him floating face-down with the algae. Called it suicide in the death certificate. Two months later, guess who up and dies of lung cancer and leaves everything to the Brothers Grimm? Grandpa, all the way over in Paris. Since they were one Grimm short at the reading, our boy got the whole estate. An estimated three million in property, stocks, and holdings. Half when Gramps died and another half, interestingly enough, to be distributed ten years later. The ten-year anniversary of Grandpa's death is next May, 2008."

"Another small fortune that Jennifer, with the help of her new friends at MiamiLaw.com, would have stood to have included in her divorce settlement," noted Brill. "And not that I'm a cynic or nothing, but how fortuitous was it for Davy that his brother had to leave this good earth before terminally ill Gramps?"

"Holy . . ." Julia started.

"Shit," Brill finished for her, with a smile.

"The doc at South Oaks must've called Alain Marquette as soon as we hit the parking lot, 'cause the phone was ringing by the time our plane touched down at MIA. Levinson wanted to know exactly what we were doing over at Loony Land, who told us about it, and what we found out. It sounded like he might not know too much himself," Pat said.

"What'd you say?"

"I told him Nextel has a problem with

dropping calls. Then I hung up. It'll be interesting to hear what he decides to spill to the cameras."

"I knew his parents were holding out," Brill said gruffly. "Why not talk to the police? We're your friends."

"Unless you got something or someone to hide," answered Lat.

"They wouldn't be the first parents to want to distance themselves from their children," Julia said quietly. "Especially these kids."

Lat shook his head. "And now? The reversal of engines? The high-priced attorneys? Calling out the embassy? Holding press conferences?"

"Heading you off at the pass on the last one. If the story's inevitably coming out better to put their spin on it than ours. As far as backing this son," she shrugged "maybe they feel guilty for abandoning the other."

"Maybe. Wait a sec, you weren't a psych major, were you?" asked Lat.

"No. Why?"

"Just asking. So what do you think this twin thing means? Anything?"

"Maybe Dave's been taking notes all these years on how a nut's really supposed to act," Brill theorized.

286

"There's no known cause of schizophrenia, but it's thought that there is a genetic link," Julia said slowly. "The DNA of identical twins is the same. So if one twin has the disease, there is an increased risk of the other developing it. I think it's like almost a 30 percent chance or something like that. So yeah, this arguably might be very relevant. At least to the court-appointed psychiatrists. Is there any other family history of mental illness?"

"That's gonna be a problem," said Brill with a sigh. "And not just because Dad and Mom and the rest of the hired help don't wanna cooperate."

"Huh?" she asked.

"We told you this case was full of surprises," Lat said. "And they just keep on coming. There are no other blood relatives, Julia. Darrell and David were adopted."

CHAPTER 41

The same body, two completely different men. The same story, two completely different tales. Julia didn't need to tune in to Mel's press conference to hear how his closing argument was shaping up. She could spin the yarn herself for both sides.

She washed down the last bite of cannoli with a gulp of warm Diet Coke as she skimmed through the stacks of disturbing police reports, interviews, and medical records that covered her desk. Like a slow-developing photograph, the background of David Marquette's life was gradually beginning to emerge, the fine details being filled in, completing the picture of the strange man in the foreground, hidden in shadow. On paper those details read like a profiler's psychological composite of a psychopath. *White male, age twenty-five to forty-five, average to above-average intelligence, probably educated and in a high-risk profession. Has a problem relating to people — women in particular — with a controlling, domineering mother; a probable history of animal cruelty and substance abuse; and few, if any, friends.*

She spun her chair around and looked past the air handlers at DCJ. Somewhere behind the bars and steel-mesh windows sat her defendant, locked away from the general population and buried within the screaming corridors of the ninth floor. The Crazy Floor.

The same story, two completely different tales.

A boy who didn't fit in from day one. Strange. Odd. A loner. An underachiever. A misfit. A Charley-in-the-box with an identical twin who was anything but identical. In fact, he was perfect. Perfect grades, perfect personality. Wins track meets and scholarships and walks little old ladies across the street. Dates the cheerleaders and prom queens and makes Mom and Dad very proud. The Misfit Boy fits even less. He begins to act out. Hurts animals just to watch them suffer. Tries drugs. Flunks a couple of classes. If he can't be his brother, then he won't be his brother. As the Perfect Brother grows older and more perfect and his long list of accomplishments hits double digits, the Misfit's behavior gets worse.

Drug use intensifies. The violence reserved for animals escalates to humans; he focuses on the object of his rage and tries to kill his mother. He gets kicked out of school. Dad has to help him out of jam after jam. Dad has to clean up the verbal messes the Misfit leaves behind on arrest reports and admission papers so that no one gets "the wrong impression" about the family with the good name and deep pockets. It's Dad who pulls strings again to get the Misfit into another good school, buy him another chance. He is nothing like his brother. He is nothing but a scary, bitter disappointment. But then Perfect Brother gets sick. Comes down with the Mother of Bad Diseases. The most shameful: schizophrenia. Perfect Brother suddenly falls hard and fast from grace and becomes the son whom Mom and Dad now want to hide away somewhere. Dad pushes the Misfit into his new role as Number-One Son. Gets him through school, gets him a degree, gets him a prestigious job. The Misfit's given a license to practice medicine and officially stamped a success. Only he's really not. He's really a time bomb, ticking away in this new, uncomfortable, socially enviable role, with a clingy wife and three kids he didn't plan on having, until he finally, inevitably, just explodes. . . .

But the same facts could just as easily tell a different story; the same brush could paint a much more tragic picture — that of a boy who was always a little odd, who struggled to fit in but never could for a reason. Because deep inside his brain an insidious disease was taking hold and growing silent roots, as it had in his twin, destroying and disrupting communication pathways as it spread, seeding images and voices in his decaying mind like land mines — so incredibly real that his own brain was sure to be fooled. Layer by paper-thin layer, the disease slowly breaks the boy down from the inside out, leaving only his body intact as his frightened adoptive parents willfully misread all the warning signs, hoping their son's more and more obvious distress is anything but a mental illness. Anything but the horrible disease he is inevitably to be diagnosed with. And even then the diagnosis is unacceptable. It's changed, for the sake of the family name. When the boy's identical twin suffers the same fate, he's locked away in a psychiatric facility, never to be seen again. But brother Darrell's affliction is far worse, far more disabling, and so David must have recovered from whatever had ailed him in college. A bad case of nerves. Stress. *He's fine now,* the denying family rationalizes once again with a hushed whisper. Only he isn't fine. The boy with the unmentionable disease is sick. He was denied the help he needed all these years because of stigma and embarrassment — and now four people are dead.

The same body, two completely different men.

The pathetic Dr. Jekyll or the evil Mr. Hyde.

Who was David Alain Marquette?

CHAPTER 42

Business was obviously booming in Dr. Christian Barakat's private practice, Julia thought as she and Rick followed a tightly swathed receptionist in a Santa hat into an office that was a lot nicer than one would ever expect the office of a state psychiatrist to be. Faux-painted hunter-green walls, leather club chairs, expensive woodworking, and an address on ritzy Brickell Avenue. Forensic psychiatry was obviously the good doctor's side job.

"Look at this, a celebrity," quipped the tall, dark, and exceptionally handsome man who stepped out from behind a burnished oak desk. Dark hair, sculpted chin, big blue eyes. Christian Barakat, too, was far nicer-looking than one would expect any shrink to be. No wonder the desperate housewives were lining up to spill their secrets. "I was just reading about you, pal," he said with a wily smile, tapping the folded *Miami Herald* in his hand against the desk. Dimples end-capped a perfect grin. Behind him was a wall of awards and impressive diplomas. Julia spotted Johns Hopkins, Yale, University of Miami.

"Don't believe everything you hear," Rick grumbled, shaking Barakat's hand. "Chris, this is Julia Vacanti. She'll be trying this with me. Julia, Chris Barakat."

"Nice to meet you," the doctor said, leaning casually back against his desk. "Please, sit."

"Nice to meet you, too," Julia replied, taking a seat next to Rick in one of the club chairs.

"Where the hell's my report, bud?" Rick asked, anxiously running a hand through his hair. "I got this thing going Wednesday, you know. Nothing like waiting till the last minute."

"Ariana was about to messenger it. I only finished my interviews with this guy two days ago. It was a bitch to get to see him. He's been in lockdown a few times, and I had to reschedule."

"Yeah. Nice excuse," Rick bantered.

Barakat tapped Rick's shoulder playfully with the paper. "International protests? Wow. I'm impressed. They're cursing you in French now. That's big."

294

Seemingly overnight, David Marquette and the Gables Family Massacre, as it was known in Miami, had quantum-leaped from relative obscurity as a Local-section tragedy to a full-blown international incident. Organized protests in front of the U.S. Embassy in Paris and strong words by the French president condemning the American justice system as "barbaric" for trying to execute a mentally ill foreign national had grabbed headlines and ignited a bitter capital-punishment debate. Even the morning network talk shows, usually light on news and heavy on fluff, were calling the SAO for interviews and comments. Charley Rifkin's foreboding prediction about a media circus, uttered weeks back, was seemingly coming true. There'd even been talk of raffling off tickets to next Wednesday's hearing.

"So give me something to throw back at them. Get my face off dartboards. Tell me he's not a fruitcake, he's just French. The world can live with one less of those."

Dr. Barakat sighed and shook his head. "All that anger is no good for you, Ricky. What I can tell you is that, despite his very best efforts to convince me otherwise, he's competent."

Rick slapped his hand on the desk. "I

knew it. He's faking! Bastard!"

"Is there anything wrong with him at all?" asked Julia. "Is he schizophrenic?"

"I can't be official on a diagnosis until I do the full psych eval. This was just an eval to determine if he's competent to stand trial, which he is. But unofficially, let me say this: I don't think he's schizophrenic."

"Koletis found him incompetent, you know. He filed his report yesterday with the court," Rick griped. "I expected it the day Farley let Mel pick him. The old coot loves the drama. It makes his decision in front of all those cameras even more important."

"Don't go celebrating just yet, pal," Dr. Barakat cautioned, his blue eyes suddenly dark. "Word to the wise — you're gonna have a hard time with this guy. It's a tough call."

A chill ran down Julia's spine. She remembered the figure in the orange jumpsuit from arraignment. The Human Monster with his dead eyes and shackled hands.

"Here it comes. Another bleeding-heart excuse. He's not schizophrenic, but — let me guess — he's got emotional problems," Rick said sarcastically, leaning back in his chair.

"Psychiatry's not an exact science, you know, Mr. Hang-'Em-High Prosecutor," Dr.

Barakat scolded lightly. "There's no scan, no physical test, to detect mental illness. Only after taking a history and listening to the symptoms a patient claims to be experiencing in his head can you try and figure out his mental malady. The biggest challenge to a forensic psychiatrist is, of course, malingering — how to tell when someone's faking it to get a pass on a lifetime in jail or a visit to the execution chamber.

"Now, your average person thinks being 'crazy' means seeing little green men and shouting obscenities at the devil all day long. So that's exactly what a malingerer will do when trying to convince the world he's insane. But that's not an accurate portrayal of schizophrenia. While the disease afflicts people differently, many patients don't experience visual hallucinations at all. And it's not usually the devil yapping in their ear. You see, delusions are the hallmark symptom of schizophrenia — fixed false beliefs that defy logic and persist in spite of rational arguments or evidence to the contrary. From there, the audio — and only occasionally visual — hallucinations will spawn and then feed the delusion.

"Take Margaret Mary Ray, for instance, the schizophrenic known for stalking David Letterman. Ray believed she was Letterman's wife, despite being arrested multiple times and being told by everyone, including Letterman himself, that that was just not the case. But the delusion was her reality.

"Now, that's a difficult enough concept for someone in the mental health field to understand and treat and an almost impossible manifestation of the disease for someone to try and successfully imitate — twenty-four hours a day, seven days a week — if he or she's not actually in the throes of a delusion. For example, when Ray stole Letterman's Porsche from his driveway and, with her three-year-old kid in it, headed off to see him in New York, she really believed she was in *her* car with *his* child. Her actions followed, or furthered, the delusion. And that's just the sort of behavior — or lack thereof — that'll give a malingerer away. They'll steal the car and get caught at a chop shop. Or they'll present with questionable symptoms, like seeing the proverbial little green men. Or being symptomatic only at specific times, such as when they're in court. And they'll be fine at others, maybe when they're around other patients and feel no one's watching. Or perhaps they'll continue to claim they're having hallucinations or hearing voices long after the medication would've helped to subdue their symptoms because they're unaware of when and how a psychotropic drug actually works. These are all classic signs to watch for to detect malingering. Most of the time, though, as a psychiatrist, you just know ten minutes after meeting the person by the feeling in your gut whether or not he's faking it."

Dr. Barakat hesitated. "But then there's a different breed of malingerer. A different breed of human being, actually. This one's much more rare. Extremely smart, cunning, manipulative. Dangerous. He will convince those who want to be convinced of his illness, including professionals, and he will adapt to the tests they put upon him because he's a survivor. He feels no remorse for what he's done because he feels no empathy for others. He has no conscience, that internal Jiminy Cricket in all of us that keeps us on the straight and narrow and turns us away from evil. He's a psychopath, and I think that just might be your defendant."

Chapter 43

"A psychopath? Is that just your gut talking?" Rick asked.

"I spent a few hours with him at the jail," Barakat replied slowly. "He did present with some of the negative symptoms of schizophrenia: poor hygiene, blank expression, what's known as blunted affect or flat emotions. Zombie-like behavior. Most malingerers don't know enough about the disease to do that, as I said before. But again, this guy's not your everyday malingerer. He's got a degree in medicine. He's got a borderline brilliant IQ. He had a brother who was a hebephrenic schizophrenic. Now, it's difficult when someone's on a drug like Thorazine to distinguish what may be these 'negative' symptoms from what might be the effects of the medication. But, frankly, I don't think it's either."

He tapped his pen on his notepad. "Personally, if I was going to try and fake being nuts to beat a court case, I'd probably go the same route with the same symptoms. Why? The less said, the less for anyone — including a team of court-appointed psychiatrists — to interpret. It's the smart choice. It's perhaps not as egotistical as trying to verbally outwit the shrinks and nurses and cops, but it's much more controlled. Much more cunning, actually.

"So maybe I'm a bit skeptical, but in my hours with Dr. Marquette I was looking for certain bizarre behavior characteristics that are peculiar to catatonic schizophrenia — the type of schizophrenia he's demonstrating symptoms of. One of these characteristics is echopraxia, which is basically mimicking, or mirroring, the movements or speech patterns of another. Or inflexible muscle movement, where you'll move a catatonic's arm and it will stay in that exact position, sometimes for hours, even if it's suspended. These are characteristics even most medical professionals, such as Dr. Marquette, would not be familiar with unless they'd worked specifically and extensively with catatonics." He paused and added, "But I have. And I didn't observe any of those behaviors. When I raised his arm above his head, it fell to his side, carefully missing both his face and the table on its way back down.

"While we don't know exactly where a catatonic goes when he's in that state of extreme withdrawal, I feel pretty confident telling you that David Marquette is not in that place. He's right there in the room with you. Carefully watching you watch him with blank eyes. Waiting for your reaction to plan his. That's my gut talking."

"Did he speak?" Rick asked.

"Yes. Although for the most part he was mainly monosyllabic answering my questions. As I said before, I thought he was carefully reading my reaction, and I think he read that his act was clearly missing something."

"Did he talk about the murders?" Julia asked.

"Only in a limited capacity as it related to his competency. But he was oriented to time and place. He knows what he's been arrested for and what penalties he faces. He knows his entire family is dead. Bottom line in my opinion, with a medication adjustment, he's definitely competent."

"This brother of his," Rick said carefully. "You mentioned him. Where does he fit in?"

"That's an interesting twist," Dr. Baraka replied, frowning. "We don't know what causes schizophrenia, but we do know genetics definitely play a role in who gets it

His twin's illness will be a factor in his defense, and probably was in his evaluation."

"There's no known cause, but there have to be other factors besides genetics. . . ." Julia tried.

"For decades everyone thought schizophrenia was caused by bad parenting. More particularly, bad mothering. Obsessive, domineering mothers created stressed-out, psychotic kids who couldn't cope with reality. But bad mothering has been displaced by science. We know now that schizophrenia is an organic brain disease, in that the brain's structure is physically changed. As for suspected causes, they still range from viruses and food allergies, to neurochemical deficiencies, infectious agents, or physical trauma in utero, to a dysfunctional endocrine system."

Rick made a skeptical face but said nothing.

"Blame the cause on whatever you want," Dr. Barakat continued with another shrug, "but the genetic link can't be ignored. With each family member afflicted, the risk factor for fellow family members goes up. To put it in perspective, the worldwide general population, with no family history of schizophrenia, has about a 1 percent potluck chance of developing the disease. Now, take a parent with schizophrenia. His or her child is thirteen times more likely to develop it. If both parents have it the risk jumps to 36 percent. With identical twins the risk is close to 30 percent, even with twins separated at birth and raised in different households. And the risk is cumulative. So if Mom, Sis, and Grandma have it, Junior's at least twenty-six times more likely to develop the disease than, say, you or me.

"Since this guy's adopted, the argument, I'm sure, will be that his tree was loaded with bad fruit. We've seen whole families, unfortunately, afflicted with the disease. Margaret Mary Ray, who I was telling you about before, was a classic example. Two of her three siblings had schizophrenia, as did her father. All three kids committed suicide, including Margaret Mary, who knelt in front of a train in 1998. The identical Genain quadruplets from the '30s — all four girls developed schizophrenia before the age of twenty-four. Now, whether genetics cause the disease or merely predispose someone to it, no one knows. And no one's yet found a gene that causes schizophrenia. All that's clear is that it definitely runs in families."

Ariana came back in with the report. She

handed it to Rick with a coquettish smile. "Happy holidays," she said sweetly, flipping the ball of her Santa hat off her face.

"Thank you. You, too," Rick replied thoughtfully, matching her smile. He stood up and waved the report in his hand. "Good job, my man. I'll call you after I've digested all this, and you and I can go over your testimony. Dress nice and don't forget, nine thirty sharp. It's Len Farley, and he's unforgiving."

"Good luck with holiday shopping," Barakat said lightly in an inside-joke sort of voice.

Julia remained seated. Her brain was spinning, but not with worries of what Christian Barakat really meant with that last comment to Rick, or why Rick and Ariana seemed to have such a familiar relationship. "I have to ask you something, Dr. Barakat," she started. "If Marquette's not schizophrenic, if he's faking it like you're suggesting . . . well, I mean, without an obvious motive, what kind of person could murder his entire family in cold blood and then be devious enough to successfully fake the symptoms of schizophrenia to get away with it?"

Christian Barakat didn't hesitate. "For once that's an easy enough answer to give,

even for a psychiatrist," he answered coolly
"It would make him a monster."

CHAPTER 44

"He's competent," Julia said into the phone, slugging down the last of her cold coffee.

"That's not what I heard on the news at noon," Lat replied. "Says who?"

"Tune in at six," she warned, rummaging through her desk drawers for some quarters so she could go get another cup from the machine downstairs. She found three, buried in a forgotten paper-clip caddy. "Says Christian Barakat. Rick and I just now met with him. He thinks this catatonic-zombie act of Marquette's is just that — a well-rehearsed act. Says it could be a medication issue with all the psychotropics they have him on, but Barakat thinks the guy might be an actual psychopath. He needs to do the full psych eval to make that official, but the doctor scored high on this 'psychopathy checklist.'"

"A psychopath. That makes sense. Who the hell else breaks out the kitchen cutlery on their family in the middle of the night?"

She closed her eyes tight. *A monster, Lat. A monster.*

"That should make for an interesting hearing," he offered when she hadn't said anything.

"You'll be there, right?" she asked. She wiped away the tears she hadn't meant to shed with the back of her hand and rummaged through the bottom of her pocketbook with shaking fingers. She finally found another quarter, covered in lint and purse dirt.

"Definitely. I wonder if Levenson will put his client on the stand."

"I doubt it. He'd be crazy to." *Crazy.* The word sounded so strange on her tongue. It had such a different meaning now. She rolled the quarters around in her sweaty fist.

"Will you be handling the hearing?"

The idea was so funny that she actually laughed out loud. She had a better chance of winning Powerball than of getting Rick to let her handle an expert witness at a competency hearing. "I'll be sitting at the table," she said in a conciliatory voice.

"Too bad."

She wasn't sure if he meant that as a compliment or a slam against Rick, so she said nothing.

"Farley sure picked some week," Lat said. "Four days before Christmas."

"He did that on purpose. He does everything on purpose, and ruining holidays and vacations would be one of the things I imagine he does best."

Now it was Lat's turn to laugh. "Did he ruin yours? Family out of town?"

She felt the sudden pain stab her heart. She should've prepped herself for that question, but she hadn't. Julia hated this time of year. Hated it. Starting at Thanksgiving and lasting past New Year's, every day was a chore to get through, every night filled with bad 'memories and dread. She hated seeing everyone happy and together — in every commercial, in every print ad, on every box of cereal and can of Coke. She hated the intrusive, chipper questions that people seemed to ask without thought. *Are you going home for the holidays? Who are you spending Christmas with? Is Mom making the turkey this year? Does she let you help?* Nora and Jimmy and she always went through the motions of having a holiday dinner, complete with turkey and nonstop Christmas music, but Christmas at Aunt Nora's was like a bad wake with good food. There was nothing joyous about it, and no one could wait for it to be over. This year, Julia knew, would be especially difficult because she'd gone and brought up Andy.

Andy. Long-forgotten memories stormed her consciousness now without warning, striking her wherever and whenever they wanted, determined to show themselves after all these years buried in complete darkness. . . .

The box under the Christmas tree was wrapped so pretty, Julia knew it couldn't have been Andy who'd wrapped it. It must've been wrapped at the store — a fancy store. The ribbon was thick and tied into a bow that you only saw in department-store Christmas displays. A sparkling angel ornament hung from the pretty bow. "To Ju-Ju. Hope this makes it merry. Love, A.J.," read the tag. A.J. was the new nickname Andy had been trying to get everyone to call him.

She closed the door of the bathroom softly behind her, turned on the lights, and took a deep breath. There were only a couple of hours left to wait till Christmas morning, but she just couldn't help herself. The idea of a present under the tree with her name on it bugged her like an itch — there could be no relief until she knew what was in it. She moved the ribbon out of the way, slid a bread knife under the tape, and then unwrapped one end of the thick paper. She slid out the box careful to keep the shape of the wrap intact so she could just slide it back in when she was done peeking. No one would be the wiser.

When she saw that the box was from Cosby's Sporting Goods she stopped breathing. She took off the top and pulled back the folds of tissue paper. Shining under the lights of the overhead fixture was the white satin New York Rangers jacket she'd asked for, first for her birthday and again for Christmas. It was the only thing she wanted, but it was a hundred dollars, and her mom had said they couldn't afford it. Now, here it was — hers.

She couldn't help herself. She put the box on the sink and took the jacket out. She slipped it on over her pajamas, running her hands over the smooth satin. It felt soooo amazing . . .

"How does it fit?" came the voice on the other side of the door.

She froze, her arms wrapped around herself.

"Come on, Ju-Ju," Andy whispered. "How does it fit?"

"Julia?" Lat asked. "Did I lose you?"

"No," she said pushing the ghosts back once again. "I'm just going to my aunt and uncle's on Christmas Day. They live down here. And you?"

"Don't know yet. I might head over with a buddy to the Bahamas. He's got a fishing boat up in Fort Lauderdale and an ex-wife who gets the holiday with the kids this year."

"Christmas on the high seas? That sounds kind of nice."

"You're welcome anytime, Counselor," Lat offered.

Strangely enough, she and Rick had never even discussed the holidays. Thanksgiving had remarkably passed without comment and the most wonderful time of the year had not even been mentioned. It was less than a week off, yet she had no idea what he was doing for Christmas, and he hadn't asked what she was doing for New Year's. Considering her loathing of the whole holiday season, those glaring omissions in conversation really hadn't bothered her till this very second, but now it was as if someone had pointed out a tiny crack in her beautifully decorated wall. A crack hidden by a great paint job that she'd never even noticed before. But the defect was now so obvious, so ugly, so gaping, it made her wonder — how could she not have noticed? And how could it not have bothered her? Over the past couple of months she'd convinced herself that she was fine with things as they were between her and Rick. This was not the time in her life for a deep relationship; she didn't want or need a commitment. They saw each other almost daily in the office — add in a night or two here or there, and that was more than some married couples ever interacted. But now that Lat had gone and asked her about Christmas and invited her to spend it with him — whether or not he was kidding or just being nice — well, she feared that whenever she looked at Rick now, all she'd focus on was the crack.

She rolled the quarters in her fist. "Thanks for the invite. I might take you up on that one day."

"Eggnog's overrated. I'll stick a candy cane in your piña colada."

She was quiet for a moment, thinking about the other reason she'd decided to call Lat. "I have a favor I need to ask you, Lat," she said, twisting the phone cord around the fingers of one hand, crunching the quarters in the other. "Can you run an NCIC for me?"

It was actually a crime to run a criminal history without a legitimate law enforcement purpose. And since it was an NCIC she was asking for, it was technically a federal crime. Julia had never asked anyone to do something that was illegal for her before. She'd never done anything illegal herself. She felt guilty making Lat an accomplice, but she couldn't run one herself, and she didn't want anyone in her own office doing it.

"Sure. What's the name?" Lat asked without hesitating. If he sensed something was up, he said nothing.

Julia took a deep breath and closed her eyes. "Cirto," she said. "C-I-R-T-O. Andrew Joseph. Date of birth, March 14, 1972."

CHAPTER 45

"What is it you want, Mary? What do you want? You want the moon? Just say the word and I'll throw a lasso around it and pull it down."

Julia stared at the TV from her spot on her living room couch at three in the morning, watching, of all things, *It's a Wonderful Life!* on TBS. It had been her mother's all-time favorite movie. She used to let Julia stay up to watch it with her on Christmas Eve after midnight mass, when the rest of the house had gone off to sleep. They'd make popcorn and snuggle on the couch under the cotton-and-fleece pink blanket stolen off Julia's bed. Mom knew every line. Every single word, in fact. Sometimes she would say them along with the actors, with the same inflection, too. She'd had Jimmy Stewart down pat.

"Hey! That's a pretty good idea. I'll give you the moon, Mary."

They'd never had the chance to watch it that last Christmas. Christmas Eve that year had been spent in her new room at Aunt Nora's in Great Kills, far away from her living room in West Hempstead, far away from Carly and her friends and her school. Sitting on her new bed, with her new pink comforter and her new ruffled curtains, she'd watched out the window as carloads of well-dressed, smiling people had pulled up in front of her new neighbors' house, platters of food and bottles of wine in their hands, arms loaded with Christmas presents. She'd sat there for hours in the dark, her numb body trapped in place, watching the comings and goings of what was now to be her new life, reciting sad, cheesy lines from her mother's all-time favorite movie. Only, unlike a TV movie that you didn't want to watch anymore, she couldn't turn it off. Instead it just kept running, running, running as she sat at that window, until the entire film had played out in her mind. She'd spent the last fifteen years hating herself for taking those two hours and twelve minutes for granted every year. If she could go back and have one more moment with her mother, just one more, that would be it.

"Strange, isn't it? Each man's life touche

so many other lives," Clarence the Angel said to a sad and shocked George Bailey. "When he isn't around he leaves an awful hole, doesn't he?"

She mouthed the words along with Clarence and closed her eyes to stop the tears. She could still smell the damn fleece blanket — the one Aunt Nora had replaced — and the lilac-scented fabric softener her mom used to use. Since she'd moved into her own apartment she'd tried every brand known to man in the stores, but she'd still never found it. . . .

CHAPTER 46

Julia sat by herself at the State's table Wednesday morning and prayed. The judge tapped his pen against the bench in time with the second hand of the clock that hung in the back of the courtroom. It read nine forty-two. The jam-packed courtroom stayed eerily quiet.

"I think that's enough time, State," Farley finally said.

"Your Honor, if we could just wait a little longer. I'm sure Mr. Bellido will be here," she said anxiously, looking back at the courtroom doors. At that moment they opened, but it was John Latarrino who walked through them, not Rick. He shook his head, and her heart sank.

"Ms. Vacanti," the judge began with that all-too-familiar I'm-going-to-yell-at-you-now look, "I don't have the time —"

"Excuse me, Judge," interrupted Lat as he walked up to the State's table. "I apologize

out could I have a word with the prosecutor?"

Farley sighed loudly, threw the pen on the bench, and spun his chair around to face the wall, like a two-year-old having a temper tantrum. "Take as long as you need, Detective. It's not like we're waiting to start court or anything."

"Tell me something good, Lat," Julia whispered, hoping none of the cameras would pick up her words or her desperation. She could feel them focusing on her.

Lat shook his head again. "No can do, sweetheart. I just got a message. He was on his way back from Orlando, and he's had some kind of accident. Nothing bad. He wants you to reset it is all. Get a continuance."

"What?"

"Are you two done chitty-chatting?" Farley sniped. "Or do you think maybe we can resume court today?"

"Um," Julia began hesitantly, slowly turning back to the bench, "Detective Latarrino has just received word about Mr. Bellido, Your Honor. There's been an accident. It's nothing serious, but he is going to be delayed. He's requesting — the State is requesting — a continuance."

The judge looked around the courtroom.

"No," he said finally. An excited murmur buzzed through the crowd.

"No?" asked Julia in disbelief. Her hands began to sweat.

"Not that I mean to sound uncaring, but he's not dead, is he, Detective? He's not in the hospital? And even if he was," Farley explained, sweeping his hand at Julia, "he has a second seat handling this very important case for him. A handpicked second seat, I might add. That means MY time shouldn't be compromised because of some fender-bender or morning traffic on I-95. I have the reports of Drs. Barakat and Koletis in front of me — the experts are split on whether the defendant is competent. So I'm thinking that we're all here for a full hearing this morning. The defense is present and ready to go. Everyone's valuable time is ticking away while Mr. Bellido waits for a tow truck. I'm sure Ms. Vacanti is ready to proceed, lest only the defense present evidence today."

So much for the Good Old Boys' Club saving Rick's ass. Julia looked at a knot in the wood table. This was bad. Really bad. She might officially be second seat, but even she knew the title was only a warm-body position. Besides grunt work, the best she could've hoped for at trial was the direct exam of an insignificant witness. Now Farley was demanding that she handle a competency hearing by herself in a first-degree murder with news cameras rolling and the international press closely watching.

Ileana was seated in the front row next to the other ASAs who'd come to watch. She leaned over the railing and whispered calmly, "I'll call Legal. Don't do anything till they get here!" Julia nodded, and Ileana dashed out of the courtroom.

"Mr. Levenson, are you ready to proceed?" asked Farley.

"Yes," said Mel, rising. He was no fool. He smelled the chum that the judge had just tossed into the water. "We're ready to proceed. And due to my client's delicate mental condition and need for immediate treatment, I'd say that time is definitely of the essence and that we should conduct the hearing this morning without hesitation," he said, making sure he hit all the right appellate buzzwords. Mel motioned to his client, who sat between him and Stan Grossbach in the same orange jumpsuit and in pretty much the same condition as at the arraignment, except more overgrown. His hair hadn't been cut, and his carpet of facial hair was now a Una bomber beard. Shocking, yes, but Julia knew most defense attorneys would do anything to make their clients appear more sympathetic in court — from dressing them up in expensive suits to covering them in modest dresses when the case called for it. Tattoos were discreetly hidden, hair color changed, body piercings removed. In big-name cases, some lawyers went so far as to hire stylists and body-language consultants to help mold their clients into the defendants they ultimately wanted a jury to see. Image was everything in the courtroom, and if Marquette was going to try to play the role of a mentally incompetent, looking deranged certainly wouldn't hurt his cause. Once again he stared blankly out in front of him at nothing and no one.

"Wonderful," said the judge. "State? Are you ready to proceed? Or are you willing to stipulate to Dr. Koletis's report that the defendant's incompetent?"

"No, Judge, the State is not willing to stipulate. Dr. Barakat's report clearly states that the defendant is competent."

"Then let's go. Call your first witness."

"Your Honor, someone from the State's Legal Unit is on their way over —" she tried.

"Oh, no, Ms. Vacanti. You want to play with the big boys, then you're the one who's gonna play. Call your first witness."

"Judge, I believe the defendant is presumed competent under Florida law. The burden is with the defense to prove he's incompetent by a preponderance of the evidence," Julia protested, hoping that if Levenson was forced to put on his case first, that would buy some time for someone from Legal to show up. And everything would be okay.

"Nice try, Ms. Vacanti. But the federal courts have interpreted the United States Constitution as requiring the government to only bring competent individuals to trial. Particularly those they're trying to execute. So I believe the burden of proving the defendant actually knows what's going on in a courtroom falls on you, State." He smiled a devious smile. "As I was saying, honey, call your first witness."

CHAPTER 47

Time doesn't help a prosecutor, Julia. Witnesses forget, die, retire, relocate. . . .

There was no way she could just let David Marquette be found incompetent and sent off to Chattahoochee for the next few months — or years — while the case against him went to shit.

No matter what the reports said, ultimately a determination of competency was within the sole discretion of the trial judge. That meant Julia had to do whatever she could to prove to Farley that Marquette was competent, and she had to do it now. God knew her judge was vindictive enough to send the guy for treatment he didn't need just to burn her for not going forward.

"Then the State calls Dr. Christian Barakat to the stand," she said without even knowing whether Dr. Barakat was actually present. She heard the prosecutors behind her start to whisper among themselves like siblings who know that their little sister is *sooo* gonna get it when their dad gets home.

Jefferson stepped out into the hall, and less than ten seconds later Dr. Barakat, in a tailored charcoal suit and powder-blue dress shirt, strode to the witness stand to be sworn in by a blushing Ivonne. He settled into his seat, acknowledging Julia with a nod, but it was clear that he was more than a little puzzled to see her sitting at the State's table instead of Rick.

Julia had never put a psychiatrist on the stand before. Or any doctor, for that matter. As far as experts went, she'd qualified only a records custodian, fingerprint tech, and Breathalyzer maintenance tech. Before a witness was allowed to give expert testimony on a subject, counsel first had to establish to the court that he or she was in fact an expert on that subject. Important passages about qualifying medical experts from the Rules of Evidence flashed in her head, not staying long enough, unfortunately, for her to actually remember what they said. She opened her statute book and stared at the criteria for competence under Rule 3.211. Words that suddenly made no sense stared back at her, and she felt the room begin to spin.

"Look at me, Daddy! Look at me!" screamed

little Emma suddenly as she danced across the courtroom in her blood-soaked Cinderella ball gown, her French braid matted black with dried blood. Her little face looked like it did in her autopsy pictures — swollen to almost double its size, her lips blue, the whites of her eyes red where the blood vessels had burst. A twisted ringlet of thick black thread spooled from the neckline of her gown where the ME had neglected to cut the autopsy thread. "Look at me now, Daddy!" she demanded with a distorted pout as she spun around. "Look at what you've done to me!"

Julia closed her eyes tight. She was it. She was the only person who could make justice happen today. Who could make sure little Emma's father was held responsible for what he'd done. She was the only one who could make sure David Marquette didn't slip through the cracks of an unsympathetic system that was more than willing to forget its victims and move on to the next tragedy. She had to look past the mess at the defense table and do her job.

Lat leaned over the rail and touched her shoulder. "You can do this, Julia," he said softly. "You're better than Bellido. Trust me."

She nodded and took in a deep breath. *Here goes, Emma. Let's put this bastard away where he belongs.* Then she stood up, and for the next three hours, to the surprise of every single person in that courtroom, including herself, she proved John Latarrino right.

Chapter 48

He ran a finger slowly over the red dents that cut across his wrists where the steel handcuffs had dug into his flesh and pressed against the bone. A sharp pain radiated up through his right arm into his shoulder, but he resisted the urge to acknowledge it. He imagined that the lines were on someone else's wrist, the pain not in his body. He knew that the corrections officers made the cuffs extra tight on purpose because of who he was. Because of what he'd done. He'd watched them smile and heard them chuckle when they snapped the cuffs on behind his back, clicking them until they reached almost the very last notch.

But he'd never complained. Not even once.

. . . *He did present with some negative symptoms of schizophrenia, but, as I explained in my report, there were also no peculiar behavioral manifestations such as echopraxia. . . .*

He heard what they shouted at him in his cell and in the hallways as they shuffled him past the other inmates. *Baby Killer. Daddy Death. Dr. Death. Psycho.* He knew they spat in his food and tried to trip him in the halls. If they could, some of the animals in here would shank him or fuck him, or both, if they could just get close enough. That was probably the only good thing about the floor he was on. The crazies each had their own cell.

. . . Some symptoms can possibly be attributed to the medication that Dr. Marquette is taking; however, yes, to answer your question, Ms. Vacanti, it's my opinion he's malingering. . . .

He wondered what the chuckling guard would be like if he weren't in chains. If it were just the two of them, alone in a room. No batons. No radio. No cuffs. No buddies. He wondered how long it would be before Mr. Corrections Officer pissed himself when he looked into the eyes of madness. There was always safety in numbers. Take away the numbers . . .

. . . It's very possible that Dr. Marquette has what's known as a psychopathic personality disorder, referred to in the DSM-V as an antisocial personality disorder. . . .

Or any of the animals, really. Any of the caged zoo animals on the other floors. So big and tough with their gang colors and their tattoos. Again, take away their brothers, and they were nothing. And they underestimated him, which would be their downfall.

. . . probably the most dangerous of all mental disorders. In varying degrees, the psychopath is unable to actually feel emotion. He's like an empty shell. A machine. He doesn't know empathy, he doesn't feel love, he doesn't experience guilt. No one will change him, and nothing will affect him. He has learned, though, through watching society, what the appropriate emotional responses are, and he's learned to mimic those responses. So he's learned to cry at funerals, even though he doesn't actually feel sad, no matter who is in the casket. And he's learned to say "I love you" after sex, even though he really can't feel the emotion of love. . . .

He'd caught a couple of the big, bad ones looking at him in the box or in the halls, when the buddies weren't watching. He'd seen them send quick, nervous glances over in his direction. He knew they wondered what the hell went on in his head. It was one thing, after all, to kill a man because he owed you money. Or maybe take out a girlfriend because she cheated on you. But even the big and the bad had a code of conduct, a set of rules to live by. And when someone operated outside those rules, it frightened even the worst of them. As it should.

. . . Take Ted Bundy, for instance. Good-looking. Educated. A student at a top-ranked law school. Some speculate the number of women who fell prey to Bundy may have been close to one hundred. See, it's a common misconception people have that psychopaths somehow look different. That they sound different. That they're all drug dealers or unemployed roofers. Everyone thinks they'll spot the Charles Mansons right off when the truth is, we encounter psychopaths in everyday life and never know it, Ms. Vacanti. It was Scott Peterson's charm and good looks that were perhaps his most disarming weapon. They can be bankers and CEOs and basketball coaches. Of course not all psychopaths are murderers, and not all murderers are psychopaths. But the one textbook warning that does ring true is — especially, I believe, in this case — the smarter the psychopath, the more dangerous and destructive he will be. . . .

It was strange to sit in a room surrounded by people talking about him in the third person. Attempting to define him with tricky medical terminology. The cameras were a bit distracting. It was so important to listen right now, but so hard to focus. The medicine still clouded his brain. The waves still washed out their words sometimes. He swallowed a yawn.

. . . Like a chameleon, he will take on the persona he knows you want to see. He will say the words he knows you want to hear. That's what makes him so difficult to identify and almost impossible to catch. . . .

He looked over at the prosecutor. Vacanti. She was so pretty. *So young,* he thought. Younger than he. An apprentice, obviously. An ingenue. Was he her biggest case? Was this her biggest moment?

He watched as she walked around the courtroom with all those cameras trained on her. She was so sure of herself, but so . . . not. He caught her quick, awkward glances at him, studying him with her suspicious, yet curious pretty brown eyes, as if he were a specimen in a science lab. She looked at him with contempt but also with maybe . . . compassion? Even through the fog of drugs that made his tongue heavy and sometimes carried off his thoughts, he could tell she somehow doubted the confidence of her own questions. He had a thing with reading people. He always had. And he was never wrong. He could tell right then just by watching her that she was the one who would listen. Of all the people in the court-room, he knew she wanted to understand.

"Why?" she demanded, narrowing those chocolate-brown eyes and looking right at him. "Why would he do this, Dr. Barakat?"

Never ask a question you don't know the answer to. Even he knew that.

In not-so-clinical terms, Ms. Vacanti, he's a monster.

He needed to show her the real him. It was time to tell her what he knew she wanted to hear.

CHAPTER 49

Farley leaned back in his chair. "I've read the reports of both doctors. I've listened to their testimony here today, and I've had the opportunity to observe the defendant in court on several occasions. Let the record reflect this hearing is approaching its third hour now.

"The defendant hasn't been a disruption in court. He's able to conduct himself in front of a jury. Both psychiatrists have testified that he knows he's been charged with murder and knows the penalty he's facing. The defendant himself is a doctor. He's not mentally deficient. He's highly educated, and until the week before his arrest he was performing surgery down the block. While this court recognizes that intelligent people can be mentally ill, too, his intellect has to be considered as a factor when determining competency. And even though it might be sad that his twin suffered from schizophrenia, that's all it is — sad.

"I'm not going to get into whether the defendant's malingering. That's something for a jury to decide. The standard for competency is whether a defendant has the present ability to consult with counsel and whether he has a rational, as well as factual, understanding of the proceedings. Now, let me say this — no one and nobody's going to escape justice in my courtroom by faking a mental illness. Just refusing to answer questions, even when it's your own attorney or psychiatrist asking them, doesn't mean you're going to evade the long arm of the law. The defendant has a lot at stake in going forward to trial and a strong motivation to fabricate or exaggerate the symptoms of a mental illness. The law allows me to make sure he's medicated when he's in my courtroom so that he can remain competent during these proceedings, and that's what I intend to do. Based on the testimony presented here today —"

Hushed, heated whispers erupted at the defense table. Mel and Stan leaned across the defense table toward each other, their backs to the court, obscuring their client from view. It sounded at first as if the two of them were having an angry exchange.

"Is there a problem, Mr. Levenson?"

grumbled the judge.

"Don't," Mel whispered one final time. Then he reluctantly pulled back from the conversation to face the judge. He shook his big head angrily. "No, Your Honor."

"No, no, no," said a small voice. It was one Julia didn't recognize because she'd never heard it before. The courtroom fell completely silent as David Marquette stood. His waist irons jangled.

"David," said Stan forcefully, "sit down."

"No, no, no . . ." the voice continued. Marquette shook his head violently from side to side.

The judge waved off Stan. "Dr. Marquette, do you have something you'd like to say to this court? Something you think I should know?"

The courtroom fell silent. Marquette looked right at Julia. With his dead gray eyes locked on her, he finally spoke, his voice a broken, choked whisper.

"I saved them."

And with those words, the world as she knew it came suddenly and irreversibly crashing down around her as the protective firewalls in her mind slowly toppled, one by one by one, like dominoes, until, finally, only the frightening truth was left standing.

Like frenzied bats freed from a dark and

musty attic, the horrifying memories swarmed her. The ghosts had finally found their way back in.

CHAPTER 50

The car door opened, and Detective Potte. leaned into the backseat. His round face looked puffier in the yellow overhead dome light than it had at Carly's, his small eyes ever squintier. "Julie," he began with a sigh, and Julia smelled the cigarette smoke on his breath.

She breathed in the blast of cold night air Don't say it. Whatever you're going to say please don't, she thought. Let me have more time before you say something bad. More time before everything changes . . .

"Sorry to keep you waiting," he started with a sad smile, "but we needed to make —"

She stopped listening.

Her eyes suddenly caught on the two police officers in bulky dark-blue nylon coats who had stepped out her front door. They sand wiched a man dressed in a t-shirt and jeans She suddenly pushed past Detective Potte and out of the car, at first walking, then run

338

ning full speed across the lawn. She heard the shouts behind her calling to her to stop, but they didn't make sense.

"Andrew?" she shouted while running, the cold wind stinging her cheeks. "Andy?"

He turned to face her then, and she saw the bright-red splatters on his white undershirt, the smears on his face, the dark stains that soaked his jeans. At first she thought he was hurt; then her eyes fell on the handcuffs on his wrists, and she knew. Both of his hands were wrapped in white kitchen towels, like a boxer's, but blood had begun to seep through in spots. Her legs suddenly collapsed, refusing to hold her up any longer, and she fell to her knees next to the Santa.

"Oh, my God, what did you do? Andy! What did you do?" she screamed at him. "What did you do?"

The handsome young man who still had the face of a boy smiled. Tears spilled from his eyes. They met the smears of blood running down his cheeks in watery red streaks. "I saved them, Ju-Ju. I saved them. I had to. It had to be done." He thrust his hands up to the sky, creating a panic among the blue coats, who rushed to regain control. The kitchen towels fell away, and ribbons of bright-red blood streamed from his mangled hands. "Alleluia!"

She stayed on her knees, screaming, he *fists clutching at the frozen ground, the cold* *melting snow seeping into her jeans. Detec* *tive Potter and the other officers who had* *rushed to catch her on the lawn stopped and* *backed up slightly, awkwardly looking at each* *other, watching her as she rocked back and* *forth.*

The blue coats escorted the young man to *the back of a waiting cruiser, forcefully duck* *ing his head and placing him inside with a* *hard shove. He smiled softly at her once more* *out the window. Then he hung his head as* *the car drove off down the block.*

She never saw her big brother again.

CHAPTER 51

The courtroom stayed quiet for a few seconds, like the lull before the scream of a child who's skinned his knee — mouths hung open and contorted, but no sound escaped. Then the excited chatter started up, fast and furious, rising to an almost deafening crescendo.

"I'm ready to rule," Farley barked into the bench microphone — the one that had always been there but he'd never before needed to use. He looked around for something to slam on the bench and quiet the crowd, shooting an angry look over at his bailiff.

"Be seated and be quiet!" Jefferson nervously proclaimed. "No cell phones, no talking!"

The courtroom settled back down to whispers as the reporters ignored Jefferson and finished sending off text messages to their editors. When there was complete silence Farley began to speak. "I find the defendant competent to proceed. Now we need to know if he was sane. I'm extending the trial date by two weeks for you all to find out."

"Yes, Your Honor," Mel replied, rising.

"State?"

There was no response.

"Ms. Vacanti? Hello out there?"

How could it all be so clear now? Like physically stepping back in time and into a memory. She could suddenly smell the cold air, heavy with the snow that was expected by morning, the burning leaves, the pine trees and other evergreens, the cigarette smoke, the hint of Tsar cologne — strangely enough, her father's favorite — in the backseat of the police car. She could hear the squawking of the police radios, the crackle of the operator's voice erupting over a dozen handhelds at the same time, the frantic, excited, hushed whispers of her neighbors who stood on the sidewalk behind her, held back by crime-scene tape. She could taste the blood, warm and coppery in her mouth. And Andrew . . .

"Julia? Julia?"

She felt a hand on her shoulder again. It was Lat. "The judge," he whispered, nodding over at Farley. The courtroom sat in strange, excited silence, as if everyone in the room had collectively held their breath as they watched her. She looked around, dumbfounded. Lost.

"Penny Levine on behalf of the State," the chief of Legal said, rising from the front row and stepping purposefully up to the podium. "Mr. Bellido has asked that I assure the court that the State will be ready for trial on whatever date Your Honor sets."

The judge frowned at Julia but decided to move on. "Trial's reset for Monday, March sixth, then. Report date's Thursday the second. Short of one of the attorneys in this case actually dying next time, we're going on the sixth. I'm not letting this drag on for a year or so while we go back and forth squabbling with the experts. I'm appointing both Drs. Barakat and Koletis again under 3.216. If you're planning on using anyone else, let the other side know within thirty days. No surprise witnesses, and no last-minute additions or substitutions, so get your acts together. I won't tolerate delays. I hope you all heard me on that," he finished with one final, annoyed glance over at the State's table.

Then the judge sailed past Jefferson and off the bench as the courtroom erupted in chaos once again.

CHAPTER 52

It no longer really mattered whose distorted footprints had walked the halls of the Marquette house the night Jennifer and he children had died, whose fingerprints were all over the ledges of the fancy French windows, did it? David Marquette was a confessed murderer now.

A mob of State-side well-wishers spilled into the gallery. The very same prosecutor who'd gossiped just hours before about he uncertain career move all wanted to shake her hand now, including the chief of Legal It was, perhaps, a moment every trial lawye dreamed of but one only a rare few would ever experience — winning *the* case or *the* argument in a courtroom crowded with colleagues and cameras from around the world A moment others would surely bask in a they watched their careers soar on the NBC *Nightly News*. But not Julia. For her the mo ment felt frightening, claustrophobic, sick ning, exploitative. The old courtroom ooked the same as when she'd walked in ust hours before, but everything and everyone in it was completely different. She hought of the final scenes in *It's a Wonderful Life* when George stumbles upon his prother Harry's tombstone in the town cemetery and finally grasps the terrifying ruth that Clarence the Angel has been trying to tell him: George Bailey was never porn. The town, the homes, the buildings — even the faces — might physically look he same as George remembered them, but hey weren't. One fact had forever changed everything and everyone. One fact had changed history.

"Clarence! Clarence! Help me, Clarence. Get me back. Get me back. I don't care what happens to me. Get me back to my wife and kids. Help me, Clarence, please. Please! I want to live again! I want to live again."

Of course in the movie, George Bailey gets his wish. But Julia knew that no movie magic would happen here today. No matter how much she prayed, she could not undo he truth that, despite repeated warnings, she herself had gone searching for. There would be no Hollywood ending for her.

She quickly moved to gather her files, watching as Corrections fitted David Marquette — this shell of a man in his oversized jumpsuit — back into his frightening getup of iron shackles and steel handcuffs. He kept staring at her.

He's a monster. A psychopath. Like a chameleon, he will take on the persona he knows you want to see. He will say the words he knows you want to hear. That's what makes him so difficult to catch.

She looked away, not trusting her eyes anymore, and quickly finished packing up her briefcase. The noisy crowd of reporters seemed to have surreptitiously moved closer to the gallery while she had her back turned. She heard her name being called, mentioned, discussed in a dozen conversations, but all she wanted was to get the hell out of the courtroom.

A hand gently tapped her back. "I knew you were better than him." She turned to see Lat standing beside her. "Although you know Bellido's not gonna let you take any of the credit."

She tried to smile back. She tried to make everything look normal, but she wondered if that was even possible anymore. The mask she wore surely had cracks. Behind Lat, Corrections worked to clear the courtroom and move the reporters out into the hallway, where they would wait for her to come out

"Any word on how he is?" she asked.

"Except for the blown ego, I'm sure he'll be just fine."

She blew out a measured breath. "What a day. Thanks for before. I — I really . . ."

"You were great. Quite the shark. I was surprised. You always look so nice. And him . . ." he said, his voice trailing off as he looked over at Marquette. He shook his head but didn't finish the thought. "You know, Julia, nothing surprises me anymore. And that's not a good thing. Try not to take it home with you." He placed a manila folder on top of her statute book. "For you. Your NCIC. I also ran an Autotrack, which is in there, too."

"Thanks," she said quietly, looking down at the folder. "I've got to go," she managed.

"Well, let me know if you need anything else," he said as he turned to walk away.

She saw Brill standing in the back of the courtroom, talking with Charley Rifkin and Penny Levine and her DC. All four of them were looking at her. Brill was laughing, but the others weren't. Why was it that in a crowd full of people cheering your name, you could always hear the one or two small voices that weren't? Why were they always the loudest? She looked away before they could see what she was thinking, grabbed her briefcase, and headed for a quick escape down the judge's back staircase.

"Oh, yeah, Julia," Lat called out behind her. "I almost forgot." She turned to look back at him. "Merry Christmas!" he said with an easy smile when she did. "Have a good one."

CHAPTER 53

The air was so cold and dry, it felt as though she swallowed a dozen knives every time she breathed. She knew that everyone was watching her while she cried on the lawn, her world spinning like the red-and-blue police lights that lit the night sky — around and around and out of control. Blue coats and detectives, paramedics and neighbors had all begun to gather on the sidewalk, and she felt their eyes upon her, watching her as she writhed in pain on the frozen ground. Awkwardly fidgeting with the change in their pockets or adjusting the scarves around their mouths, they watched and waited for someone to do something to stop the scene in front of them, even though a part of them secretly hoped to see it play out to its natural conclusion. There was something fascinating, titillating, about watching bad things happen to other people's lives. Those who surrounded her were able to view the most excruciating emotional pain someone

could experience but not have to actually feel
it for themselves. They were macabre voyeurs, and they crawled over her lawn and
sidewalk and driveway, edging closer to get a
better look.

"Poor kid," one said.

"That sucks."

"Are they dead, Officer?"

"Oh, my God! Oh, my God! Oh, my God!"

"Is the news here? Will this be on the news?"

"Are they both dead, Officer?"

"What the hell happened in there?"

She wanted to curl into a ball right there on
the lawn, bury herself in a black hole, and cry.
Just cry and cry and cry until the earth swallowed her and she simply disappeared.
Strange, fragmented thoughts flew through
her head.

What did he do to them? Why was there so
much blood? They can't be dead. My parents
can't be dead. Please Lord, no. Where will I
go if they're dead? I have a Spanish test on
Monday. Why didn't I stay home tonight? What
would have happened if I did stay home? Why
was there so much blood? Where is Andrew
going? Will he be back? Do I have to get him
out of jail? Who should I call? Who will take
care of me? Why the hell was there so much
blood?

Then an instantly sobering, chilling

thought . . .

Maybe they're still alive.

She pulled herself up before the voyeurs could even gasp, and she ran as fast as her feet could take her. Faster than she'd ever run before. She heard Detective Potter again yelling for her to stop, but she just kept going. Across the brown, snow-patched lawn and past the blue coats smoking cigarettes on the broken walk and the EMTs chatting it up in the driveway.

Up the front steps and back into the decaying old house she'd once called home.

CHAPTER 54

Julia slammed on the brakes with a deafening screech, and the Honda fishtailed, skidding to a stop on I-95, missing the Lexus in front of her by only an inch. She blew out a breath and waved apologetically at the guy who was now angrily shaking both his head and his fist at her in his rearview. Drivers and passengers alike stared at her out their car windows in the stop-and-go early-afternoon rush-hour Miami traffic. She pulled over into the breakdown lane and with trembling hands reached over and picked her briefcase and purse off the passenger floorboard, where everything had flown when she'd hit the brakes. The folder from Lat lay faceup under the contents of her makeup case and the pack of Marlboros she'd picked up at the gas station. It was an impetuous purchase; she hadn't smoked in years. Now felt like a good time to start again.

"For Julia — Personal and Confidential" was scrawled across a sticky note in Lat's handwriting and stuck to the front of the folder. She hadn't opened it yet.

She sat up with a start.

Peeking out a corner was a black-and-white booking photo from the Nassau County Police Department. She knew the face in an instant, the soft dollop of curls, the wide brown eyes.

I saved them, Ju-Ju. I had to. It had to be done.

She leaned her head against the steering wheel and closed her eyes. Andrew. Her big brother. She saw him there on the front lawn, standing barefoot in the snow with their childhood house all ablaze in Christmas lights behind him. His handcuffed, butchered hands dangling in front of him like he was holding fistfuls of chopped meat, dripping bright-red blood on the blotches of white snow as if in some crazy horror movie. Smiling sadly, as if he knew it would be the last time they'd ever see each other . . .

Was it possible to hate someone in an instant? Someone whom you'd loved with all your being just seconds before? Could you turn it all off in a heartbeat? Could one horrific memory change the meaning of so many good ones? Should it? That night, as she sat alone in the cold interview room of the police precinct, she remembered it was Andy she still wanted. It was Andy she needed to hold her hand and hug her and tell her it would be all right, that this was all a crazy mistake. An accident. Because it had to be. It just had to be.

"No, no, no!" she shouted out loud in the empty car, banging the steering wheel angrily with her fist. She reached back down and pulled the picture out of Lat's file.

Cirto, Andrew Joseph. Nassau County Police Department, Division of Corrections #11970; 12-21-91.

Even in black-and-white, she could see the streaks of blood on his smooth cheeks, the sweat that matted his curls to his forehead, the pure fear in his wide eyes. The only pictures of Andrew that had survived these past fifteen years were the select few that remained in her mind. This was not one of them.

It was too much. Her brain threatened to revolt and shut down. Everything was going white; nothing was making sense anymore. But it couldn't, now, could it? How could any of this ever make sense? Maybe that was why she'd forgotten it all. Selective traumatic memory retention — the mind takes on only what it can handle and nothing more. Julia looked back down at the floorboard. The answers she'd been seeking all along were right there, only a foot or two from her grasp.

For Julia — Personal and Confidential

She cautiously picked up the file. Once she opened it, once her worst suspicions were confirmed, she knew there would be no turning back. That was what frightened her the most. This was it. Face the past or forever hold your peace.

She lit a cigarette with shaking fingers. The bad habit welcomed her back like an old friend. She didn't even cough. Then she took a deep breath and flipped open the folder.

The time had come for her to face what had destroyed her family fifteen years ago tonight.

CHAPTER 55

"In the matter of the petition for adoption of J. C., a minor, by Nora Clair Vacanti and her husband, James Anthony Vacanti. The parties are all present for a final hearing," the clerk called out to a nearly empty courtroom.

"Have the minor brought forward," called the judge as he read over paperwork and sipped a can of Diet Dr. Pepper.

A half-dozen or so people bustled about the small courtroom. The Staten Island Family Courthouse was so old that a permanent smoky yellow haze clung to windows that hadn't been washed in years, and fat dust particles danced in the stagnant air. Cardboard temporary file boxes were stacked to the ceiling in one corner, and papers covered the clerk's metal desk.

Julia stepped through the wooden pass-gate and into the cluttered gallery. The clerk directed her over to where Mr. Singh, Aunt Nora's attorney, stood.

"Mary Ellen Kelly appearing as guardian ad litem on behalf of the minor child," said the chubby woman with long gray hair who moved into the gallery behind her. Julia had met her once when she'd come to Aunt Nora's. She patted Julia's back. "We have no objection to the petition."

"What is the relationship between the minor —" the judge said, hesitating, then looking down at the file to read her name, "Julia Anne Cirto," he said slowly, "and the petitioners?" Only he said it as Cur-toe instead of Sir-toe. He looked at Julia for the first time. "She's how old?"

"Julia will be fourteen at the end of the month," answered Mr. Singh. "She's the petitioners' niece, Judge. The daughter of Mrs. Vacanti's deceased sister, Irene Cirto."

"Where is the father?"

"Dead as well."

"There's no other family?"

Ms. Kelly shook her head. "No, Your Honor," she said into the microphone, then cleared her throat. "There's no one else. Everyone's gone. Her aunt and uncle are all this girl has left in the world now."

"Okay, there's no objection, so the petition is granted. The legal name of the minor shall be changed to Julia Anne Vacanti," the judge said, signing the last of the papers in front of

357

him and pushing the pile toward the clerk. "Best of luck to all of you." With a swift level of the gavel and an official stamp from the clerk's office, the past was officially erased.

"You know, you don't have to call me Mom or anything like that," Aunt Nora said quietly as she and Julia stepped inside the court-house elevator that stank of coffee and body odor. Uncle Jimmy had gone ahead to get the car. "This," she said, shaking the rolled-up stack of legal papers in her hand, "this is just, you know, to protect you and other nonsense." The small elevator lurched with a loud creak and then started down. "It's what your mother would've wanted," she added when Julia still hadn't said anything.

Her aunt must've aged a dozen years just since the morning car ride to the courthouse. Today was the final chapter in a bad book that the two of them both knew there'd never be a happy ending to. Tears rolled down Nora's cheeks, but she didn't wipe them away. She just looked at the elevator doors in front of her, tapping the rolled-up legal papers against her leg.

"Where is Andrew?" Julia asked quietly.

Nora looked at her, her wet eyes instantly filled with hate, and Julia wished she'd never asked the question. The forbidden question. "He's in hell," Aunt Nora said flatly just as the *doors opened onto the lobby. "Where he be-longs."*

CHAPTER 56

FYI. Andrew Joseph Cirto is currently being held at Kirby, Ward's Island, NYC. Veri-
fied 12/20 by telephone with M. Zlocki in
records.

The sticky note was stuck to the top sheet
of the NCIC. Julia sucked in a sharp breath.
He's alive. Jesus Christ, he's still alive . . .
Lat had highlighted the criminal history
for her. It was out of New York. The date of
arrest was December 22, 1991. The charge
was two counts of first-degree murder. Her
eyes searched the print-out as they had millions of times before in court, skipping past
entries that detailed every court hearing —
from arraignment to case status — to find
the final disposition. Lat had highlighted
that for her, too.

08/12/1992. Judge: R. Deverna. Disp: Adju-
dicated not responsible by mental disease/
defect.

She stared at the words on the paper — relieved to know he was still alive, yet sick to her stomach at the same time. She hung her head between her legs, but it wasn't enough. She opened the car door and threw up her lunch on the side of I-95 as drivers watched curiously from the passing traffic. The tears rushed out soon after, like a broken water main. Counting to ten or thirty or a million wasn't going to work anymore.

He was supposed to be dead. Dead and gone from her life and her memories. But he never really had been, had he? Maybe it had just been easier all these years to assume Andy was dead than to deal with the responsibility of knowing he wasn't. Maybe not looking was the same as not seeing. But now she knew the truth. And there was no more running, no more hiding from it.

After her parents' funeral, they'd never spoken of Andrew again in Nora's house. Ever. Mention of even his name was strictly forbidden. Uncle Jimmy stopped getting the paper for six months, maybe longer, and the news was never permitted to be on, to prevent her, she supposed, from hearing about the case. So how could she have known what had happened to him? For fifteen years Julia had rationalized her own ignorance. Her indifference. She had only been thirteen, after all. A kid, right? There was no one else — no other family, no friends — she could've confided in or gotten information from. There was no way for her to bum a ride to the courthouse on Long Island or to the prison or hospital — hell, she didn't even know where Andrew was. The day after the murders she'd moved away physically from her home while everyone she knew had moved away from her emotionally. And they didn't just gradually move on — they ran. Carly included. So Jimmy and Nora and Great Kills had become her world. In her heart she knew Nora had done what she thought was best, but she also knew that her aunt would never get past her own anger at losing her sister and best friend. There was no such thing as therapy — Jimmy wouldn't allow that. Families solved their own problems. As the years passed, Julia learned to deal with the pain and isolation in the only way she knew how — by simply pushing it all out of her mind, as Nora had taught her.

Now that responsibility was all hers. She couldn't blame her aunt or uncle any longer, or excuse herself because she was thirteen and without a mode of transportation or access to a paper. For better or for worse,

Pandora had opened the box.

She took her chances on the HOV lane and sped home as fast as she could. She flipped on the computer in the kitchen, poured herself a glass of wine, and with the NCIC report in front of her typed the words into Google's search box: "Kirby Wards Island New York."

In 0.4 seconds, she had 673,000 hits. The very first one was headed *Kirby Forensic Psychiatric Center.* She clicked on the site. She could hear her heart beating in her head, feel it pulse in her temples.

. . . maximum-security hospital . . . provides secure treatment . . . forensic patients and courts of New York City and Long Island . . .

Julia leaned back against the refrigerator and closed her eyes. She knew exactly what Kirby was. It was the state hospital in New York for the criminally insane.

And her big brother was still a patient there.

CHAPTER 57

Julia stood outside apartment 1052, her hand poised over the bell for a few seconds while she tried to gather her thoughts. Before she could actually hit it, the door opened.

"What's this?" Nora demanded with a big smile that quickly melted into a concerned frown. "A Friday afternoon? You didn't get fired, did you?"

"No, I didn't get fired," Julia replied quietly. "I wanted to talk to you and Uncle Jimmy."

Her aunt raised an eyebrow. "You just wanted to talk to us? Hmmm . . . that doesn't sound good." She reached out and took Julia's hand and brought her inside, giving her a big kiss on the cheek. "Come in, come in. Jimmy's at the track, though." She started for the kitchen. "So, what time you want to come over on Sunday? Do you want me to make a *panettone* this year?"

"If you want."

"Is this about that man you're dating? You're not engaged, are you? He better know to see Jimmy first," Nora called out behind her as Julia followed her into the kitchen.

"I don't think you need to be worrying about that."

Nora turned to face her. "Pregnant?"

"Aunt Nora . . ."

"Just checking," she replied with a smile. "You know, that wouldn't be the worst thing. Not that I'm pushing, but you're not getting younger, and I want grandchildren." She flipped on the kitchen light. "Is he coming on Sunday?"

"No."

"Hmmm . . . all right, we'll talk. Come. Have something to eat before we talk about a subject serious enough to take you away from your criminals."

For two days, all Julia had been able to think about was how to have this conversation. She'd rehearsed her thoughts again and again, reducing them to carefully constructed sentences, like she would an opening, but somewhere between the elevator ride up and the walk down the hall, she'd forgotten them all. She wished Uncle Jimmy were here to keep things calm, like he always did, but she couldn't wait any longer. "I've been doing research on my murder case," she started.

"I saw you on the news. Why didn't you call me? Deb Casalli had to tell me you were on." She turned her face away, pretending to wipe invisible crumbs off the counter, but Julia heard the warning in her voice. The subtle signal to stop right there. *Leave the past in the past.*

Julia's eyes fell on the happy picture of her aunt and her mom hamming it up in front of the Hamilton House, a catering hall in Bayridge, Brooklyn, the day of her mom's high school graduation. They were both dressed in white patent-leather boots and '60s psychedelic minidresses. The photo had been taken two years before her mom had met her father. "I've been thinking about what happened with," she said, taking a deep breath, ". . . with my family."

Aunt Nora stopped wiping and watched her carefully for a long moment, then headed over to the refrigerator. "I could make you a sandwich. I made Jimmy meatballs last night. I have some semolina. How 'bout a hero?"

"I found him."

Nora hesitated, her head still in the fridge. But she said nothing.

"Andrew. He's in a mental hospital, Aunt Nora. In New York City. It's a hospital for the criminally insane. He's been there for fifteen years now."

"He might as well be dead," Nora said quietly, closing the refrigerator door.

"Aunt Nora . . ."

"You have no business looking for him. He's a murderer."

"I got a copy of the court file yesterday. He has schizophrenia, Aunt Nora. He's sick."

"Call it what you want to," Nora snapped, her blue eyes suddenly igniting with anger. "G'head, give it a label! To me, he's the devil. What he did to your mother, to your father. He's a monster, a —" A choked sob cut off the rest of her words, and Nora turned away to face the cabinets. Her aunt was such a strong person. It was hard to be the one doing this to her after all she and Uncle Jimmy had done for her, after all they'd sacrificed to give her a normal life. Nora slapped her hands hard against the counter. The anger was back. "You have no place looking for him now. None. You owe it to your mother to stop this craziness and move on with your life. Let him rot with his. I hope they never let him out. They should've executed him. They should've given him the goddamned death penalty. That's who it's there for. Animals like him."

"He's my brother. My brother . . ."

"And she was your mother!" Nora shouted, spinning around. "And she was my sister! My baby sister! You and Jimmy and your *forgiveness . . .*" She spat the word out as if it was battery acid corroding her tongue. Her cranberry-red lips folded in on each other. "It's so easy to forgive when you're the one who wasn't home that night, Julia! Don't you kid yourself, now. If you'd been there, warm in your pretty little pink bed, he would've dragged you out, too. He would've carved you up, gutted you like a pumpkin. He would've taken that hunting knife and butchered you, too, while you begged him for your life!"

Julia felt like she was going to be sick. The room began to spin. She put her hands over her ears. More than once she'd wished she had been in that house that night. She'd wished she had died. It would have been so much easier.

"You," Nora said, pointing her finger, "she gave birth to you, Julia. You were her everything. The little girl Irene always dreamed of. Do you remember her at all? Anything you wanted, Reenie would see you had. She oved you more than anyone could love a child!"

"She was a great mom, Aunt Nora. I do remember . . . I never forget . . . I never forgot." Julia cried as the words stumbled out. "How could you say that?"

Nora turned away, her hands in the air.

"And I miss her." She grabbed Nora's shoulder, trying to get her to listen. "So much that it physically hurts. Sometimes it feels like my chest, my head — they're going to explode!"

Nora shrugged off her touch. "For you to betray her . . ."

"I'm not betraying her." Julia ran her hands through her hair, trying to pull her thoughts back together. They were starting to get jumbled with her emotions, and things were not making sense like they should — like they had when she'd rehearsed them. "I lost everyone that night, not just Mom. I lost Daddy, too. And I lost Andy. My whole family!"

Her aunt looked bewildered. "Jesus, Mary, and Joseph, Julia! He was the one who took your family from you! Don't you see that? Can't you get it?"

"He was sick, Aunt Nora. I remember him being sick when he came home early from UNC. Mom said he was tired and stressed,

369

that it was all the pressure from college, bu
he was a different person than when he left
And now I know what it was. This case I'm
working has made me see the signs. They
were all there, even before Andy went to
school in North Carolina, Aunt Nora. He
wasn't right. He was distant and, well, no
there sometimes. We used to be so close. He
wasn't just my brother — we, we were
friends. But then he just, he just wen
somewhere. He would hide in his room, and
he wouldn't . . . he wouldn't let me come
in. . . ."

Her aunt stared at Julia as if she were a
stranger, babbling in an odd foreign language.

"Maybe . . . maybe it wasn't his fault
Maybe he had no choice. Because it's a sickness," Julia continued, trying to explain it to
herself as well. "In his brain, eating it away
Maybe it wasn't his fault."

Nora finally spoke. Her voice was cold and
detached. "You're right, little one. It wasn'
all Andrew's fault. As much as I hate your
brother for what he's done, you go ahead
and place the blame where it really belongs.
On who it really belongs. But he's not here
anymore, either, so I don't see much poin
in that."

Julia felt as if someone had taken the

oxygen from the air and she was waiting for it to be put back in before she inhaled the poison she knew would kill her. "What are you talking about?" she whispered. But down deep the bells had begun to ring, the alarms had sounded. She knew the answer, but she willed her aunt not to speak the words.

Nora studied her for a long moment. The anger that had fired her eyes before was gone now. She looked defeated. "Your father, Julia," she said quietly. "Don't you see now, little one? It was your father who brought this crazy sickness, like you call it, into your house, who gave it to his own son. Your father had it, too."

CHAPTER 58

It all started to make sense. The pieces of her childhood that had never seemed to fit before now slid deliberately into place, like hidden walls in an old house that led to a labyrinth of caves and secrets; each wall opened another and then another, forcing her to plunge further and further into the darkness of the unknown.

For the first thirteen years of Julia's life, her mother had obviously done her very best to create the illusion of a normal family. For the last fifteen, Nora and Jimmy had tried hard to keep up the charade. To protect her, they'd simply pretended the past had never happened. And Julia had let them. Partly because she had no choice. Partly because it was much less painful — a new house, a new name, a new identity, and no questions to be answered. She'd taken the name Vacanti so she wouldn't be teased or ostracized at her new school, on the

372

remote chance some parent figured out the familial connection from the newspapers and told their kid, "That new girl in class has a psycho brother who killed their parents! Stay away from her!" The second they'd returned home from the funerals, her aunt had taken down all pictures of her brother and thrown them away. Then she'd gone into her room and cried. When she finally came out two days later, the subject was never spoken of again. Julia was the niece from upstate whose parents had been killed in a terrible car crash. Andrew had never even existed.

Julia sat down at Nora's kitchen table. She stared at the picture of her mom and Nora on Irene's graduation day. Her mom was so young then, so pretty, with long, dark, wavy hair that went down to her butt and saucer-sized light-brown eyes. Creamy skin and full lips the color of rubies. Snow White, Daddy used to call her. She took in every stray dog, nursed every homeless baby bird. She'd sing along to *The Phantom of the Opera* as she cleaned and cooked. When Julia was growing up, everyone would say that she looked just like her mom, down to the splash of paint freckles across her nose.

"When?" she asked quietly.

"I've said enough. You were raised right, is

all. Reenie was a saint. She did the work o
both parents."

"When, Aunt Nora? When?" she demanded.

Nora turned away again, her lips pursec
tight.

Up until the night of the murders, her
family had seemed as normal as the Muse-
meci family and their twelve kids down the
block. But normal is always a relative term
— it depends on who's doing the judging
and who your competition is. Through the
crime victims she'd dealt with, Julia had
learned some hard truths, one of which wa:
that when you're in a dysfunctional family
it's hard to see it the way others do because
to you, it's just life. And it's the only life
you've ever known. A battered woman
thinks all men beat their wives; a sexually
abused child accepts a father slipping into
her bed at night. It's only when you get ou
and examine your life from the outside look
ing back in that you see it for what it really
is — sick and different.

It was as though someone had suddenly
placed a silk screen over her memories, al
lowing her to see behind the scenes while
the actors changed places and clothes and
the sets moved. She remembered when
she'd been sent with Andy to live at he

Nana's tree farm up in Hunter Mountain. She couldn't have been more than six, Andy must've been ten. She didn't know exactly how long they were gone, but she remembered they'd gone to school there for a while. Her mom said Daddy had broken his arm climbing a painting ladder in the living room and needed to recuperate, but when they finally came back home, nothing in the house had been painted, and her father didn't have a cast. And his arm looked fine from a distance. But they were never allowed too close to him after that because . . . why? She couldn't remember the reason. For months after they'd come back, she couldn't remember seeing Daddy much outside of his room. When she did, he was always in pajamas. Soft, blue-striped pants and a white undershirt.

Was that the break? Was it the first one? Why hadn't she been able to see it all before?

Her mother began to work a lot after that. She waitressed at Pompeii, the Italian restaurant down the block, and cashiered on Saturdays at Pearl Paint — but Julia couldn't remember a time after the farm when she or Andrew had been left alone with their father. There were always friends' houses, or, on occasion, they would go to the restaurant with their mom and sit outside on the steps that led to the parking lot reading comics or playing handball until she got off. Funny how she'd never thought that odd until this very moment.

Julia tried to remember her dad — the handsome man with a quirky temper who took her sometimes to fly kites at the playground. Who got crazy mad when a single pencil went missing from his desk but belly-laughed when Peanut the dog ran away. Then there was the time he bought her an ice cream off the Mister Softee truck when she hadn't even known he was outside. Or when he let her steer his car as she sat in his lap and rode around the block more times than she could count. The memories were there, but they were different. Her mother was like a continuous stream of good memories assembled into a person. Her father was a person whom she had a few good memories of.

"Why didn't anyone tell me?" she said softly. The tears still fell, even though she would've sworn there were no more left to shed. "Why didn't I know about Andy?"

"Because she didn't want you to know," Nora replied, pulling a paper towel off the roll and handing it to her. "We didn't want you to know. You were only a kid. It was for your own good, Julia. You've got to know that."

"But why?" Julia pleaded. But then she just as quickly answered the question herself. The last piece had slid into its place; the final wall had opened into the darkness. She looked down at her lap. "Because everyone thought I might get it, too."

CHAPTER 59

The genetic link can't be ignored. With each family member afflicted with the disease, the risk factor for fellow family members goes up dramatically.

Dr. Barakat's words played over and over in her head, with the same inflection and reflective pause as when he'd said them in his office a week ago. She saw herself in that room, admiring his faux painting and leather chairs, never once thinking he was talking about her.

And the risk is, unfortunately, cumulative. So if you've got a mother, a sister, and a grandma with schizophrenia, you're at least twenty-six times more likely to develop the disease than, say, you or me.

Than, say, you or me.

We're different was what he meant. *We don't have mental illnesses like the defendants do. We wouldn't get that dirty disease.*

And in the courtroom just two days ago,

casually discussing the cause-and-effect relationship of schizophrenia with the experts, she'd been right up there at center stage, asking the dramatic questions and secretly relieved to be part of the club. The Majority Club. A part of the Than, Say, You or Me crowd. At that moment she was an intellectual, able to discuss and examine the clinical causes and frightening symptoms from an objective perspective in a court-room full of other intellectuals. Now that was all gone. She was a percentage now — a statistic waiting to be realized. And just the word alone sounded repulsive and dirty and terrifying. *Schizophrenia.* Schizo.

She wiped the tears with the back of her hand, but it was no use. She'd been unable to stop crying for two days. Rain poured off her windshield in heavy sheets. Even with headlights, it was impossible to see more than a few feet in front of the car, and traffic on I-95 had slowed to a crawl. She should've called the airport before she'd left her apartment to see if her flight had been delayed or canceled, but she hadn't. After finding a seat on the last Jet Blue flight of the day, she'd quickly thrown some clothes into a duffel bag and hurried to the airport. She had to keep packing, moving, going, hurrying — or else risk stopping to think.

And right now that was just too dangerous. Because she didn't really know what she was going to do when she got off that plane in New York, including finding a place to sleep. She turned the radio up, hoping someone could sing loudly enough to stop the troubling thoughts that were running through her head. She exhaled a plume of smoke and wondered, then, if the voices did come for her, would she know they weren't real? Would she know the difference between a DJ on the radio and a phantom?

She felt incredibly alone, with shameful secrets no one could ever know. No one wanted to be friends with the girl whose parents had been murdered. The girl whose brother was a murderer. Old friends had stopped calling right after the funerals. New friends wanted no part of someone so different. So she made sure she wasn't. She buried her past in lies that she told everyone — friends, boyfriends, teachers, professors, bosses. Her parents had died in a terrible car crash. She had been raised by her aunt and uncle. She was an only child. She'd told the same story for so long that on occasion even she had thought it sounded right. And every once in a while even she would forget what it felt like to be so damn different.

Andrew's mischievous face flashed before

her, with his milky skin, dark, curly hair, and crater-sized dimples. Bobby Brady, her mom thought he looked like. He'd never looked evil to Julia, even that night when he'd pulled away in the police car, covered in the blood of their parents. A boy of barely eighteen. That was all he'd been. A boy. Ten years younger than she was now. She'd abandoned him all this time while he'd sat alone, going through a cold, indifferent justice system that she knew he didn't understand and that didn't understand him.

She chewed her thumbnail till it started to bleed, staring straight into the blurred red brake lights of the Mazda in front of her. Now there was one more horrible secret to bury from friends and coworkers and boy-friends. She squeezed her eyes shut. Only this one she might not be able to keep all to herself.

"Schizo," she said aloud in the empty car. Then she opened her window and spat the dirty, scary word out into the rain.

CHAPTER 60

"Whoa, little lady. I know you don't want to be in here," said the deep voice of a blue coat whose large body blocked the foyer. His broad arms grabbed her and held her tight.

Julia screamed something, anything. And she punched out at him, hoping to distract him with a claw to the face. Make him flinch so she could run past. It was her house, damn it!

Maybe they were still alive.

It was no use. Her small body was no match against Burly Man. "I have to go in," she pleaded. *"Please! Please! You don't understand! I have to go in!"*

"No, you don't, honey. No, you don't," he said in a voice that was too calm. Too soothing. As if to say, *"There is no emergency anymore; there's no need to be rushing."*

"They're my parents! I have to see them!"

"No, honey. You don't want to see them this way. Trust me. Where's Potter?" Burly yelled

to one of the other blue coats in the living room behind him. "Have him get a psych out here, will you? Get me one of those EMTs!"

"That's my mother! My mother!" she screamed. "Mommy! Oh, God, Mommy!"

Through Burly Man's legs she could see the puddle of bright-red blood that stained the cream living room rug behind him. It looked like it ran up the walls. Her eyes caught on the bright-yellow rosebuds and pink ribbon that trimmed the sleeve of her mother's new nightgown, sticking out from behind the couch. Long, slender fingers still held a bloody phone in their frozen grasp, the nails painted a dainty, soft pink. Julia's legs began to shake uncontrollably.

Detective Potter ran in the front door. He was more than a few pounds overweight, and the run across the lawn had left him red-faced and wheezy. "Julie, you need to come with me."

"No! I want to see them! I have to see them!"

"Julie, it's very bad," said Potter.

She turned and screamed the words at him. "My name is Julia, you asshole! J-U-L-I-A. And that's my parents in there! That's my mom! I want to see her! You can't not let me see her!" She began to cry again, and she felt her body weaken with exhaustion against Burly Man. There was little fight left. The blue coats and *cheap suits in the living room had all stopped what they were doing to watch.*

"Get me Disick," Potter said into his hand-held, running a palm through his sweaty hair. "Have him meet us down at the precinct in thirty."

Julia had seen enough movies. She knew from Detective Potter's tone just who Disick was, and she slumped down, defeated, on the floor. It must be a dream. This must all be a dream. Life couldn't change this fast.

"Take her outside," said Burly Man to Potter. "Let them finish up in here."

"We need to find your family, Julia," said Potter softly, stooping down to her eye level. "Do you have any other family, honey?"

Any other family. Hers was all gone now. She stared blankly at the pinprick-sized spot of grease on the detective's tie.

He reached over and gently lifted her up by the arm. "Come on, Julia. Let's go. There'll be someone down at the station you can talk to while we try to find your relatives."

Potter's voice finally tapered off. She could tell from his moving mouth that he was still speaking, saying something, but she couldn't hear him. She couldn't hear anything any more. Sound had suddenly been sucked up into a vacuum, replaced by an intense, deafening pressure inside her head, and she thought she might pass out. She watched as the different characters slowly came back to life all around her, busying themselves once again in her living room and moving across her lawn and her driveway. Burly nodded grimly at her before turning his attention back to the officer behind him, giving him directions with animated hands.

And just like that, the world went on.

She let Potter lead her back through the foyer with the fake-brick linoleum that her mother had always wanted to replace and out the front door into the cold night air. Yellow crime-scene tape held back the growing crowd of pajama-clad neighbors. When she reached the cement walkway that led down to the sidewalk, she stopped, turning to look back for one long last second at the house she'd lived in for thirteen years. She knew she would never see it again. Every room, including hers, was ablaze with lights, crawling with silhouetted strangers. Through the living room window she could see the technicians and photographers and detectives do their handiwork right alongside the Christmas tree that she and her mom had decorated last week.

No one had thought to unplug it yet.

CHAPTER 61

The taxi ride from the hotel at LaGuardia Airport over to Ward's Island took only about twenty minutes on a Saturday morning. It was strange, Julia thought, staring out the window of the cab as it turned off the Grand Central and followed insignificant green-and-white highway signs for Randall's and Ward's Islands, she'd grown up in New York, but until three days ago she'd never even heard of Ward's Island. She'd volunteered summers at the Bronx Zoo, spent countless weekends at the Seaport or in Greenwich Village clubs, gone to concerts in Washington Square and Central Park, and she'd memorized the NYC subway system like a treasure map, but she'd never known that she was only a short taxi ride away from her brother.

The road twisted around what was, by NYC standards, a forest of tall oaks, sycamores, and maples as it wound down a hill and under the Triborough Bridge. Through the barren branches, the million-dollar-and-counting view was breathtaking. The skyline of Manhattan loomed less than a mile to the west, over the churning waters of the East River. But there were no homes here to appreciate the vista. No office buildings, restaurants, gas stations, or so much as a park to play in.

The taxi pulled up to the gate of a stone guardhouse. A small sign read, "Manhattan Psychiatric Center."

Julia lowered her window. "Kirby?"

"Name and picture ID," said the guard, holding a pen and clipboard in front of him.

"Vacanti." She held out her State Attorney's badge, hoping it would work the same powerful magic in New York as it did in Miami.

It did. The guard nodded and pointed, dropping the clipboard to his side. The fact that she'd come by taxi instead of in a marked police unit didn't seem to bother him at all. "Take this straight ahead."

"Which building is it?"

He looked at her quizzically. "Trust me, lady, you ain't gonna miss it."

She sat back in her seat as the taxi pulled away from the gatehouse. She already knew from researching the Internet that Manhattan Psychiatric was made up of three build-ings — Meyer, Dunlop, and Kirby — built in the '50s to house New York City's over-whelming number of mentally ill residents. Twenty-eight thousand at one point. But after the first generation of antipsychotics was discovered in the '60s and institutional-ization fell out of public favor, the number of committed patients fell to just a few hundred. Dunlop and Kirby closed their doors, leaving Meyer as the center's only operating facility for years. Eventually Dun-lop reopened to house administrative of-fices, but Kirby stayed shuttered and aban-doned, until 1985, when it opened its doors again as a maximum-security forensic psy-chiatric hospital. An asylum for the crimi-nally insane. Julia watched out the cab's cloudy window, already caked with winter, as the taxi made its way through the hills and past the first two buildings. It was near freezing out, but she spotted a few green scrubs and white uniforms seated outside at bolted-down picnic tables, sipping coffee or smoking cigarettes or simply staring off into the trees. Given what they did for a living and where they had to do it, it was easy to see why they would take their break as far away from their day as possible, no matter the weather.

As the taxi rounded the turn, she saw it. Kirby. As the guard had said, it was impossible to miss. A double chain-link fence climbed forty feet off the ground, wrapping around the perimeter of the twelve-story, steel-barred building. Thick rolls of barbed wire topped both fences. Julia paid the driver and watched as he turned around and took off through the parking lot. She fought the sudden urge to run after him, scream for him to stop, pull out another twenty, and demand that he take her back to the airport. Back to Miami. Back to where everything was a mess, but at least it was safe and familiar.

But her feet didn't move. And she said nothing as the cab disappeared from sight behind the trees. She lit a cigarette with cold, shaking fingers, watching as the cab's trail of white exhaust fumes floated off into the sky and disappeared. She knew she couldn't just go back. Nothing in her past was real anymore. Nothing was truly safe, or secure, or even familiar. It was as if she were standing on a dangerous precipice with one foot dangling over. One more step in the wrong direction and she'd surely free-fall out of control. But what was the right direction anymore? Inside the building behind her was not just the past she'd never known she had but also the future she might not want to ever meet. Backward or forward, the ground was unsettled.

She finally turned to face the dirty gray institution that loomed behind her. The black steel-mesh windows stared back at her like cold, vacant eyes; rolls of prickly barbed wire formed a twisted smile of razor-sharp teeth. She wondered how many faces might be watching her at that moment from behind those windows and through the checkered links of the fence. Watching her hesitate. Watching her deliberate. The faces of murderers and rapists. The faces of the criminally insane. Were any of them Andrew? Would he know her if he saw her? Had he been waiting all these years for her to come? Every Saturday and Sunday and holiday for the past fourteen years?

She sucked in the final puff of smoke and made her decision. She stepped forward off the ledge and into the darkness of an unknown future, not sure if anything would hold her up when she did. And as she made her way along the concrete walkway, past the razor wire and the abandoned picnic tables, through the double security doors and metal detectors, one last question burned in the back of her brain.

Did he still wait?

CHAPTER 62

"Who you here to see?" asked the guard behind the bulletproof window as he examined her driver's license and badge. Behind him, a half-dozen other uniforms milled about in the small room, eating doughnuts and drinking coffee. Saturday-morning cartoons played on a small portable TV. On the foldout table next to the metal detector, another officer went through her purse looking for weapons.

"Cirto. Andrew Cirto," she said.

"Cirto, huh? That's a first. You a detective?" he asked with a thick New York accent, fingering her badge. Under where it read, "State Attorney's Office," a red enamel sun rose over a green palm tree and blue water. Even she had thought it looked fake the first time she'd seen it.

"No. I'm a prosecutor. In Miami."

"You seeing him for a case? You know, he's been locked up as long as I been here."

She cleared her throat. "It's personal." She looked around the empty screening and waiting room. On a table in the corner a fake silver Christmas tree flashed on and off. She knew from Corrections that visiting day in prison could get pretty busy. Obviously that was not the case here. Not even on Christmas Eve.

"Well, they got to call up to the ward and bring him down to the visiting room. It may take a while. Have a seat."

"Okay." She nodded, turning away. Then she thought of something and turned back. "Do they tell him who's here to see him?"

"I think so."

"Make sure they tell him it's Ju-Ju," she said quietly, taking a seat on a ripped vinyl bench. A stack of outdated *People* magazines gathered dust on a chipped end table.

She pretended to flip through a magazine and tried to imagine the conversation she wanted to have with Andrew. But past "Hello," she still didn't have a clue.

Maybe a half hour later, the door to the waiting room opened. A slight, balding man in a dark suit and white doctor's lab jacket came in. A frown sliced across his wide forehead. He didn't look happy. "Ms. Vacanti?"

"Yes," she said, rising.

"I'm Dr. Harry Mynkus, the director of psychiatric services here. I'm one of Andrew Cirto's doctors."

She nodded. There was an awkward pause.

"The SHTA told me that someone was here to see Andrew. I'm sorry, I don't recognize the name Vacanti."

"I didn't know you were supposed to," she replied. "What's that, an SHTA?"

"That's one of our Secure Hospital Treatment Assistants. An aide on the ward. He called me to say that Andrew has a visitor." He paused, obviously waiting for her to say something. "I've been the director here at Kirby for eight years, Ms. Vacanti," he continued when she didn't, "and, well, to be honest with you, that's never happened before. In fact, since I'm quite familiar with Andrew's records, I can tell you that in all his years at this facility, he's never had a single visitor. That's why I took an interest in meeting you. I wanted to speak with you before you actually met with him today." He nodded at the uniform in the booth, who buzzed the door. "Can you accompany me to my office so we can go over a few things?" Dr. Mynkus asked, holding the door open for her.

Julia swallowed hard and nodded, following him into a deserted hallway that looked a lot like the basement of the science lab in her high school — windowless and clinical. "These are just administrative offices," he said, watching her. "The wards are on the upper floors. Visitors are not permitted up there.

"I have to ask," he said when they'd arrived at his office door. He held it open and motioned her in. "All the way from the Miami State Attorney's Office. Who are you?"

Julia looked around the sparsely furnished room, her eyes hoping to land on anything besides Dr. Mynkus's disarming stare. A degree from the Medical College of Wisconsin hung behind the desk, as did one from Cornell. "I'm his sister," she said after a moment, finally taking a seat. "Andrew's my older brother."

"Oh," he replied, seating himself behind the desk.

"I just want to see him again. I didn't know he was here. I just found out. I thought he was . . . well, I thought he was dead," she said carefully. "I just want to see him again, Dr. Mynkus." She probably didn't have to tell him anything, but there you go — he was a psychiatrist, and although it wasn't a couch, she was sitting in his office.

"Andrew murdered your —"

She nodded and cut him off with a deliberate wave of her hand. "Yes. I, uh — I know he was sick now. I didn't know that before." She shifted in her seat.

"Oh." But she could tell he didn't believe her. "He's better, Ms. Vacanti. Since I've been director here, he's been a model patient. Are you familiar with his history?"

"I've read the court file. I know he has schizophrenia."

"And you didn't know that before? Were you living with him when he was diagnosed?"

"I was very young at the time. What medication is he on?"

He shook his head. "I can't discuss that with you. HIPAA privacy rules."

"I've read the plea transcript. I know he's paranoid, Dr. Mynkus. I know from those transcripts what he thought that night. What he was thinking," she cleared her throat, "about the CIA. About my father. I know what the voices told him to do to them." She took a deep breath.

"The murders were very brutal."

"I'd rather not discuss that night."

There was a long, difficult pause. "I don't know how much you know about the disease itself, but schizophrenia doesn't go away,

Ms. Vacanti. So I don't know what you're expecting to find today. With paranoids, some hold on to the same delusion or auditory hallucination their whole lives; others may develop different delusions, or perhaps hear new or different voices. Medication can do wonders for some patients — completely quieting the voices they hear, or dulling those voices to whispers. In others, we unfortunately have limited success. There are some who will always exist in a foreign world that no one, and no medicine, can ever reach. I can tell you that your brother is one of the lucky ones. But since he hasn't seen you in so long, without divulging any privileged information, I have to suggest that you show him your hands before you sit down. Palms up. Let him inspect them, so he doesn't become agitated."

She stared at him. Goose bumps erupted on her arms.

"He needs to look at your hands to make sure they have no implants," he explained. "To make sure you're not a robot or a CIA spy. Medication successfully helps your brother learn to live with his illness. To him, though, his delusion and the people in it can still seem as real as you or me. Without medication, he'd bet his life on it. And yours."

"I know there are privacy rules," she said quietly, rubbing her hands together, "but, well, how is he now?"

"You can see for yourself in just a moment. He's waiting in the visiting room upstairs."

"Does he know I'm here? Does he know it's me?"

"Yes. Yes, he does."

The doctor's face gave away nothing. She still didn't think he liked her.

"Thank you for speaking with me," he said, rising. "I was just curious to meet you. You know, fourteen years in here and no one. Not even a phone call. Now, just weeks before his release, he gets his first visitor. It couldn't just be coincidence, I thought. I wanted to make sure you weren't with the press, trying to stir up some reaction in the community. From what I understand, his case did receive a fair deal of coverage in the news at the time."

"Released?" she asked, startled.

"Yes," Dr. Mynkus said as he opened the door. He studied her with that same suspicious frown. "Andrew just had his two-year review. The Forensic Committee met and reviewed the report of the ward psychiatrist, the staff psychologist, and the OMH social worker and this time recommended that he be released to a less secure, civil psychiatric facility. He's being sent to Rockland Psychiatric within the next ninety days or so, as soon as there's a bed available. The hope, of course, is that from there he can eventually be released back into society."

CHAPTER 63

The stairwell that led to the visitor's room smelled like fresh paint, but the steel-gray walls looked as if they were about to shed, bubbling and flecking in many places. The ceiling, the air ducts, the pipes, the railings — everything was painted the same color. Caged fluorescent tubes buzzed overhead, bathing the hall in a ghoulish purple tint.

Julia walked up the center of the steps with her hands in her pockets, her nose buried in her turtleneck. She didn't want to touch anything; she didn't want to even breathe in the air. She remembered the first time she'd gone to DCJ as a brand-new C to take an inmate's statement. The stench had hit her the second the steel door had slammed shut behind her in the interrogation room. The air had smelled of urine, shit, and old paint, but it had also smelled dirty. Like the rancid men in the holding cells next to her and the catwalks overhead,

399

who leered and cackled and coughed and breathed back into the same air she had to inhale. Today it was not so much dirty as the smell of sickness. Like the stink of a hospital. The smell disinfectant never washed away. She held her breath for as long as she could, breathing in and out through her mouth only, wishing she were outside under the trees in the freezing weather with the aides and nurses, sucking in the icy air. Far away from this peeling, probably asbestos-filled building where she breathed in the panicked breaths of sick, crazy people.

A handwritten sign on the second-floor landing read, "Visitors," and an arrow pointed toward a door at the end of a short hall. Above that door the face of a guard peered through a security window, watching her. The door below him buzzed. Julia quickly moved to grasp the knob in her sweaty palm, pushing it in before it could lock again. She hesitated for just a second longer, then walked into the room.

In here administration had picked powder blue for the walls. Round press-wood tables and mismatched chairs were scattered about the large room, but there was no one seated at any of them. Another fake Christmas tree blinked in the corner. Cardboard dreidels hung on the wall.

Sunlight streamed in from the wall of security metal-mesh windows that over-looked an empty exercise yard, casting diamond-shaped shadows across the tables and on the white floor. A few orange easy chairs that had likely been left in storage when the building had originally closed in '75 sat empty, too, in front of a console TV. Two guards sat like DJs in an open booth that was mounted against the wall, ten feet above the room. A young, muscular black man in a white polo shirt stood in front of the booth, arms folded across his chest, watching her intently. Probably one of those SHTAs. No one said anything when she walked in. In fact, the only noise in the room was from the boom box on the ledge of the booth that played soft Christmas music. She looked around her again. Then she saw him. The heavyset man at a table in the far corner. Dressed in a tan plaid shirt and brown pants, he practically blended in with the dull furniture and the barren landscape that could be seen out the win-dow behind him.

His face was cast down at the table, his fingers folded neatly in front of him. The first thing she noticed was the tousled mop of thinning black curls on his head. She knew right away that it was Andrew, although just last week she probably couldn't have picked him out of a line at the supermarket.

Julia walked slowly across the stretching room, her heels clicking on the polished floor. She felt the eyes of everyone in the room following her. All except one. "Andrew?" she heard herself ask, standing in front of his table. "Andrew, it's me. It's Julia."

The man seated in the chair slowly looked up. His large, light-brown eyes found hers. A long, terrible moment passed.

It was Julia who looked away. "Can I sit?" she asked, pulling out a chair. "Do you mind if I sit down?"

He said nothing.

So she sat, and she waited. Waited for any one of the million sentences rushing through her brain to just come out. Waited for him to say something. Waited for the SHTA to say something. And she tried not to stare at her big brother, the person she'd idolized from the time she could walk. The person who'd taught her how to play guitar and climb a tree. Who'd held her hand every morning on the walk to the bus stop, even when their mother wasn't looking. The person who'd introduced her to Led Zep-

)elin and Pink Floyd, when everyone else vas singing along with Madonna.

Andrew was only five years older than she,)ut he easily could've been twenty. He had)nce been lean and fit, but she guessed he vas about forty or fifty pounds overweight 10w, and his dark curls were already pep-)ered with gray. In high school, he'd been he varsity starting quarterback and captain)f the baseball team, earning a full athletic :cholarship to UNC Charlotte. Every girl 1ad wanted to date him; every guy had vanted to be him. It'd obviously been years ;ince he'd done more than a short walk hrough an exercise yard. Deprived of :unshine, his face was pale, his skin blotchy,)robably from all the medicine he took. But t wasn't so much the dramatic change in 1is physical appearance that made her fidget 'or something in her purse. It was his eyes. Not just ordinary brown, Andrew's light- :hocolate eyes had sparkled and fizzed when he light hit them. Now they were flat and 1ull. Devoid of light. Devoid of life.

She finally broke the silence. "It's been so ong, Andrew. I came today because I vanted to see you," she whispered, her voice :racking. "I didn't know you were . . . well, 1ere."

"I understand," he answered, nodding.

His voice sounded exactly as she remem
bered it. The clock ticked off a few mor
tense moments. "How are you?" he asked.

She smiled hesitantly. "Okay. I live ir
Miami now. I moved from New York a few
years ago. I work on my tan when I'm no
actually working. As you can see, I'm in the
office a lot," she babbled with a short
desperate laugh, holding out her arm.

"What do you do in Miami?" he asked
his eyes on her hands.

"I'm a lawyer. I work for — I'm a tria
lawyer." There was no need to get into
details. "How about you? What's it like ir
here? Are the people nice?"

He shrugged. "It's okay. It's better than i
was. It wasn't so good when I first got here
It was . . ." He paused for a moment, a:
though remembering something. "It wa:
hard. We watch TV and see movies. We have
computers to use, and someone comes ir
and teaches some of us how to use the In
ternet. I like to read the paper. The *Times*
when they let me." He smiled again. "You
see, I'm a Republican now."

"Maybe you do belong in here," she said
laughing.

He laughed, too. "It's a good thing I can'
vote, right?" Then his face grew dark and
he scratched at the back of his head. "

404

don't like the screamers, though."

The goose bumps were back. "The screamers? What are they?"

Andrew quickly shook his head back and forth. He blinked a few times and looked back down. "Are you married?"

"No, no. I date people — I'm dating someone, but that's it right now." Given where she was and what Andrew had been diagnosed with, part of her wanted to speak to him as if he were an imbecile or a little kid: in short, loud, and carefully enunciated Dick-and-Jane sentences. But he obviously didn't need that. She felt herself gently slipping into a conversation instead of just sentences.

"Any kids?"

"I'd like to try marriage first. We'll see about kids after that. I don't see me as a mom."

"You probably have your pick of boyfriends. You're a pretty woman, Julia. Not just a little sister anymore. Your hair, it's so long. And you got tall. You look so different from the pictures I have in my head. Wow. Good, I mean."

"Thank you. The height's an illusion, though." She stuck out her foot and pointed. "Three-inch heels. You look good, too, Andy."

He shook his head again. "Nah. No more baseball for me. Only on TV. The medicine makes you gain a lot of weight. It used to make me real tired, and it does other things, too." But he didn't say what those other things were.

"What are you taking?"

"I think its Risper-something. I'm not so sure of the name. I've been on a few. I don't like when they change them, though." He blinked a few more times and rolled his tongue about the inside of his cheeks. She heard his foot moving underneath the table.

"I think you look good. I hear you're gonna be released soon. You must be excited."

"Can I see your hands, please?" he asked suddenly with a frown, blinking fast. "I'm sorry, but I just need to — I really would like to see your hands. Can I see them?"

She swallowed hard. She'd totally forgotten what Dr. Mynkus had said. She nodded and put her hands out on the table, palms up. Andrew had grown very intense very quickly. She could hear both feet tapping away under the table as if he were running a marathon in place.

He moved his rough, lumpy fingers over hers, and she felt an electric jolt run through her. The thumb on his left hand was twisted nward, flopping uselessly at the wrist; his other digits were strangely deformed. They were the hands of her brother but yet the hands of a murderer — the very hands that had brutally taken their parents' lives. She could see the raised red scars and white lines that haphazardly sliced across the palms, dissecting his fingers into tiny pieces like a ripped-up piece of paper that someone had tried to glue back together. She fought the urge to pull away while he probed, carefully feeling every knuckle, every joint, every line. Her hands began to sweat, and she wondered if he would think that meant she was hiding something. Then she went one step further and wondered what he might do if he did think that, which made them sweat even more. Suddenly he grasped both her wrists in his hands. He was strong, very strong. "Where have you been?" he demanded, his eyes black stones, his face dark.

She could feel her heart thumping in her chest, so fast and so hard that it felt like it might push through her shirt, as if she were some love-demented cartoon character. The adrenaline instantly tensed every muscle; fear froze her where she sat. But, strangely enough, she didn't try to pull her hands back, or scream for the SHTA, or even stand up and run out. Rather, she looked into those sad, questioning eyes and knew Andrew wasn't angry or even dangerous. He was scared. And he was pleading with her for an answer. An answer she'd owed him for fifteen years. It was at that moment that she knew it was the scarred, broken hands of her brother that held her fast, and that he was no murderer.

"I'm so sorry, Andy," she whispered. " never should've left you." She felt his grip relax, and he looked down at the table again, defeated. She could've pulled away then, gotten up and walked out on shaky knees, promising to come back but not meaning it. But instead she squeezed his hands lightly. "I'm here now, Andy. And won't go away again. I promise."

The moment stayed there, held in suspension. Andrew closed his eyes. "I'm sorry, Ju Ju. Sorry, sorry, sorry," he rambled, over and over again. "I didn't mean for you to hate me. I know what I've done, and I wish I didn't do it. I wish I could go back. I wish I wasn't born. I wish, I wish, I wish . . ." He squeezed her hands and started to weep. So did she.

They sat together like that for hours, holding hands across the table, talking and crying until the light faded from the winter sky.

behind them and the SHTA named Samuel came to tell them visiting hours were over.

Anxiety:
like metal on metal in my brain
Paranoia: it is making me run
away, away, away
and back again quickly
to see if I've been caught
or lied to
or laughed at
Ha ha ha. The Ferris wheel
in Looney Land is not so funny.
— A PARANOID
SCHIZOPHRENIC PATIENT

CHAPTER 64

Dr. Christian Barakat stepped into the small, sparsely furnished attorney's interview room at DCJ, as he had dozens of times before on dozens of different cases.

"He's all yours, guy," the CO snorted as he turned and walked out. "Call when you're done." Then he closed the steel door behind him with a clang.

Christian heard the rattle of keys, the screech of metal on metal as the dead bolts slid into place and he was officially locked in. Even though the guard was supposed to wait right outside the door, Christian knew he wouldn't. The COs hated court-appointed psychiatrists. They viewed them as excuse givers, quacks, mindfuckers. So they did their collective damnedest to make things as uncomfortable and time-consuming for psych evals as possible. That included hour-long waits in a holding-cell area before gaining access to the inmate —

if the eval wasn't canceled outright for some bullshit excuse. And when Corrections did finally give the green light, it was to throw the doc into a locked room with a potentially psychotic inmate — who just might've inadvertently missed his meds that morning — and walk off for coffee in the hopes that things might get a little crazy in the cement box.

Christian readied himself mentally. In fellowship he'd been taught to prepare himself for situations such as this, when he knew help might be a long time in coming, if it ever came at all.

David Marquette sat in a metal chair in a corner of the vomit-green, cement-block room, dressed in his orange jumpsuit, his wrists cuffed in front of him. He was bare foot, but his dirty feet were notably unrestrained. He was pale and very slim, his crepe-paper skin the color of skim milk — almost translucent with a bluish tint. It hung off his bones like a wet towel on a doorknob. Deprived of sunlight, his strawberry-blond hair had become more of a dark red, streaked with gray and, while still long, was now slicked back off his face. The Unabomber beard was gone, but random red cuts — probably compliments of whoever had shaved him — pockmarked his pallid skin. Some were scabbing, others raw and open. It looked as if someone had tried to claw his face off. *Given where the guy was and what he'd been charged with,* Christian thought, *that observation might be closer to the truth than a dull razor.*

"How've you been, David?" Christian asked, pulling a metal chair up to the interrogation table. He noted that neither the chairs nor the table were bolted to the floor.

David shrugged. His bulging, light-gray, almost albino-like eyes didn't blink.

"I hear you've been doing much better on the Loxitane. Is that true?"

He nodded slowly.

"Your trial's coming up soon. Do you think you'll be okay to go to court?"

He shrugged again.

"Are you nervous?"

"No."

"Okay. Well, do you know why I'm here today?"

"To see what's inside of me," he said softly, licking his dry, cracked lips.

"Not exactly. You've been charged with murdering your wife and children. Your lawyer has told the court that you were insane when you did it. That you were not responsible for your actions. I'm here to talk to you about that."

David shook his head as his eyes welled up. Then he put his face into his cuffed hands and started to cry uncontrollably, his shoulders heaving up and down.

It would be hard for most people to not feel pity for the man, breaking down, both physically and emotionally, right before them. A brilliant doctor, the victim of a devastating disease, his whole family gone by what he was seemingly just realizing was his own hand.

But Christian Barakat didn't feel pity. He felt cold. Like he was watching a great performance in a tragic play, but the role had been miscast. It threw everything off. Instead of getting absorbed in the story, it made him watch and wait for the slightest flub. Some great *aha!* moment that would make it apparent to all the raving critics that the performance was flawed.

Christian let David cry for a few more minutes. Then he pulled some tissues out of his sports jacket and pushed them across the table, which he was careful to keep between them at all times.

"I think it's time we talked about that night, David," he said in an easy, nonjudgmental tone when the sobs finally subsided. "I think it's time you tell me exactly what happened."

CHAPTER 65

"Excuse me, miss? Miss?"

Julia opened her eyes.

"We're preparing to land," said the flight attendant with a pretty pink smile. "Can you raise your tray table?"

"Oh, yeah, sure." Julia flipped up her tray table and turned to face the window, wiping the sleep from her mouth with the back of her sleeve. Below the thinning clouds, she could already see the urban sprawl of western Broward County, the kidney-shaped blue dots in everyone's backyards. She looked at her watch. It was already nine. She had a final pretrial conference on the Marquette case in an hour at the SAO, with everyone from Investigations on up to the State Attorney himself. The Coral Gables Family Massacre, a.k.a. The Trial of the Century, as it was now being called in the press, was set to begin tomorrow.

"Early flights are ungodly," said the thirty-something woman in Bermuda shorts and a Minnie Mouse sweatshirt seated next to her, stretching out the word *god*. "Especially on a Sunday. You hope the pilots aren't too hungover. Although I guess it's not too bad if you're going on vacation." She waved an empty mini-Stoli bottle at Julia and grinned. "It's never too early to start that."

Julia smiled and dug in her purse for a mirror and some concealer. The dark circles that'd been growing under her eyes since her sleepless nights had begun last October were sure to be darker. The latest weekend trip to see her brother — a harried, stressful event to begin with — had been reduced to a thirty-hour whirlwind because of the trial. She probably shouldn't have gone at all, but Dr. Mynkus was going to tell Andy on Saturday about his transfer to Rockland — which was, of all times, set to happen in three weeks. He'd asked that she be there. There was no way she couldn't go — she'd made a promise to her brother that she wouldn't leave him again, and she intended to keep that promise. So she'd hopped a late-Friday-night plane, spent the whole of Saturday at Kirby, and then turned around on an ungodly six thirty Sunday-morning flight, right back to the madness in Miami. In the past two days she might've gotten six hours of sleep, the bulk of which had been on airplanes.

She could feel the woman look her up and down. Dressed in a fitted black skirt and her old Michael Kors pumps, Julia obviously wasn't headed off to spring break when the plane set down, like most of the other passengers. "You from New York?" she asked suspiciously.

"I was. I live in Florida now."

"Lucky! I'm from Rochester. We've been snowed in since November, I kid you not. Global warming? My ass. Right about now I'm so done with the white stuff. I need sun. My friends and I are cruising the Caribbean for a week. I'm so excited!"

"You picked a nice time of year. No hurricanes."

"Yeah, tell me about it. Eighty degrees and piña coladas in February, woo-hoo! So what in the world are you doing leaving that to go to New York? I can see Christmas. I can see the summer, spring, or fall, maybe, but I can't see February. Were you working or something?"

Julia smiled again. "I was visiting my brother. He still lives there. I fly up on weekends to see him." It was strange saying that. Julia hadn't told anyone about Andrew. No one but the folks at AmEx and Jet Blue knew she flew to NYC every other Friday and back again Sunday night. "I was visiting my brother" actually sounded normal, when the truth was anything but.

"What part?"

"Hmmm?"

"What part of New York does he live in?"

"Manhattan."

"Ooh, well, if he lives in Manhattan, he must be doing pretty good for himself. New York's not so bad then, even in February. Broadway shows, fancy dinners, museum-hopping."

Julia almost laughed. *The accommodations aren't exactly five-star,* she wanted to tell the woman. *And the food's definitely not gourmet.* But they were together. She finally had a part of her family back. She had her brother back. It wasn't easy; conversation was not always possible, and Andrew was by no means "normal" all the time. But the old Andy, the brother she remembered, would shine on occasion with a joke or a childhood memory, and that made the effort and the sacrifice worthwhile.

They had never discussed the night their parents had died, but she'd rationalized that maybe they'd never have to. Maybe their future could just go forward from here. She didn't want to know details. She didn't want o hear any more apologies, or read any more transcripts. She understood Andy's illness now. She understood what it had done to him. And she knew she could forgive him. That was enough, wasn't it?

"That's a lot of traveling," said the woman.

"It's not so bad, really. Only a couple of hours in the air."

"Any plans on moving back to the Big Apple?"

That was an interesting question. Julia found herself nodding. "Maybe. My brother, he's moving in a couple of weeks and I'm going to help him get settled. But not the city. Someplace a little more quiet."

"Where's he moving to?"

"Rockland. Rockland County."

It was hard to believe Andy would be getting out of Kirby in only a matter of weeks. Although it was still a lockdown facility, Rockland wasn't maximum security, and the rules were much more relaxed. Now, instead of her visiting for just a few hours a week under strict supervision, Andy would eventually be able to leave for the day, or leave with her on a weekend pass. That would be weird, for sure. For both of them. The man hadn't been on the other side of razor wire and barred windows in fifteen years. He hadn't been able to sleep past seven or stay up after ten or make it through the night without bed checks every thirty minutes. He hadn't picked what he wanted to eat or when he wanted to eat it. He hadn't played in a park, eaten in a restaurant, or set foot in a grocery store. What would freedom feel like for him? What would it sound like, taste like, look like? She thought of the hundreds of defendants that she'd pled to lengthy prison sentences without much thought at all. For a prosecutor, after a while, years just became numbers. The defendants just names on a calendar.

"Wow. You sound close. I don't even talk to my brothers or sisters. I wish we were that close sometimes. It's always a fight at the Thanksgiving table."

"Well, he's my big brother. He's all I have," Julia answered softly. She still needed to explain it to herself sometimes.

"The only sibling?"

"Yeah."

"What about your parents? Are they in Florida?"

She shook her head. "No, they're gone. It's just us. And he's . . . he's disabled, so he needs my help." The sad reality was, Andy really was all she had anymore. It'd been two months since she'd spoken with Nora or Jimmy, since that night before Christmas when everything had changed. She'd tried calling, but after leaving too many messages that were never returned, it had become all too clear that they weren't going to be home for her again. She hadn't wanted to make a choice between them and Andrew, but she obviously had. Aunt Nora, she knew, could not forgive her for making that choice. As for Jimmy, he was more rational, but it was Nora whom he went to bed with at night and Nora he would grow old with. Julia couldn't expect him to give that up for her. After all, Nora was the bloodline.

"Oh, I'm sorry," said the woman.

"No, no. It's okay. He's doing fine. I'm really proud of him. He's come real far."

"Welcome to Fort Lauderdale International Airport," the stewardess announced sweetly over the intercom. The passengers all stood at once. Julia was glad the conversation hadn't started until the last five minutes of the trip. She hadn't meant to be so chatty. Imagine what she would've said if it had gone on for three hours. . . .

"Well, it was really nice meeting you . . . ?"

"Julia."

"Julia. I'm Sharon. Sharon Dell."

"It was nice meeting you, too, Sharon. Have a great cruise," Julia replied, grabbing her carry-on from the overhead.

"You know, I've been thinking the whole trip — you look so familiar, Julia. I was actually wondering if we've met before?"

"I don't think so," Julia answered, wishing the line would move a little faster.

"It's been bugging me all morning. Have you ever been to Rochester?"

"No." She could see that the line had stopped moving near the exit. A heavyset woman completely blocked the aisle, struggling with the overhead bin a few rows up.

"What do you do?"

"Hmmm?"

"What do you — oh, that's it! I got it now!" the woman said excitedly. "You're the woman in that crazy-doctor case! The attorney! The prosecutor! I've seen you on TV!"

Julia shook her head. Every eye still on the plane turned toward her.

"I knew it! Oh, shit! I just sat next to somebody famous!" Sharon proudly exclaimed.

"Fry him!" someone shouted out in the back of the plane. Most people just stared.

The line again began to move. A clean-shaven young man with a buzz cut stepped out into the aisle right in front of Julia. "That guy is sick," he said angrily, spinning his index finger next to his temple, his blue eyes wide. "He's a sicko. But if you put him to death, that makes you no better than him. That makes you a murderer. And God will exact his revenge on *you,* then."

Whispers erupted all around her.

"Blessed are the merciful," hissed the man as she pushed past. "For they shall be shown mercy! The rest of you will go to hell."

CHAPTER 66

"He says the voices began right after the baby was born," Dr. Barakat explained to the crowd seated around the SAO cherry conference table as they stirred their coffees and finished up their donuts. Julia sat next to Lat and Brill. At the helm Charley Rifkin and Rick flanked a small, tired-looking Jerry Tigler. The Coral Gables police chief, the MDPD director, and Penny Levine, the chief of Legal, filled in the rest of the seats along with various lieutenants and sergeants from both agencies whom Julia had never met before. Three senior investigators from the SAO Investigations Unit held up the back wall. Everyone wanted a preview of what the world would be tuning in to watch for the next couple of weeks.

"Medical records confirm that Sophie Marquette had what's known as a strawberry hemangioma above the left eyebrow," Barakat continued. "It's a noncancerous, vascular tumor that looks like the lump on a cartoon character's head after he's been hit with a frying pan. As is typical with hemangiomas, the bump grew and became more discolored in the weeks after birth. Dr. Marquette says he noticed it then began to take the shape of a horn."

"A horn?" asked the State Attorney with a skeptical frown.

"Like the devil, Jerry," scoffed Rick, holding his two index fingers up behind his ears. The room tittered.

"He claims Jennifer began to act strange immediately after Sophie's birth," Barakat continued. "She stopped going to Sunday mass and praying at night with the kids. He says she wouldn't even drive by the church anymore, going out of her way just to avoid it. Emma and Danny had each gotten a Bible when they were baptized, but he couldn't find either in the house. Same with rosary beads, crucifixes. Not even a dried palm from Palm Sunday. He claims all religious artifacts had been mysteriously removed from the home. Although their other two kids had had lavish christenings, Jennifer refused to even discuss baptizing Sophie, and he says he became concerned that something was fundamentally very wrong."

"Who is this guy? Jimmy Swaggart?" asked Rifkin. "Who the hell keeps tabs on where the little woman's been stashing the family Bibles and palm fronds?"

"Delusions with religious undertones or themes are experienced in almost half of all people with schizophrenia," Dr. Barakat explained. "Most organized religions require a person to believe in things they can't see, taste, hear, smell, feel. Biblical stories speak of heaven and hell, damnation and the devil, God revealing Himself to Moses through a burning bush. It's acceptable in society to believe such things in the name of religion, so when you think about it, it's really not so far a leap for a delusional person to light the hemlocks up in an attempt to open a dialogue with Jesus."

"Nobody we interviewed described Marquette as a zealot," Lat said.

"Well, let's make sure we go back and talk with some parishioners at that church he and the missus were regulars at," Rick replied, "just in case you missed something."

Lat caught the use of the pronouns, as he was sure everyone else did, and his blood boiled. "Maybe you want to handle it, Bellido. If you're afraid we're not giving you enough, feel free to get the job done yourself. But just make sure you supply a copy to the defense so we don't end up doing all this all over again."

"Yo, John, that's enough," snapped one of the MDPD brass.

Rick smiled and held up his hands, as if to show the room he wasn't hurt. "It's all good."

Dr. Barakat eyed the two men carefully. "It was around this time he says the voices started up, followed by visual disturbances," he continued. "He claims to have heard angry voices, sometimes speaking in rhymes, graphically explaining what was happening to his family, the changes that were taking place in their souls and in their bodies. He claims demons had possessed his family, living like tapeworms feeding off a host, sucking the life out of each of them from the inside out, so that eventually, as Dr. Marquette continually stressed, they were no longer human. Just hard shells that would wither and crumble when the demons finally left, like the shed exoskeleton of an insect."

"So he had no intent to kill a 'human being' as it's defined in the homicide statute," Penny remarked, leaning back in her chair. "Very clever."

"That was my thought."

"This guy has all the right answers," said

Rick. "He's smart as hell."

"School records place his IQ at 149," Dr. Barakat replied. "He's a genius."

"Don't be too impressed," Rick replied. "So was the thrill killer Nathan Leopold of Leopold and Loeb fame. And the serial killer Ed Kemper."

"The voices would tell him when to look at just the right moment to see his children in their *real* forms," Dr. Barakat continued, "so he'd know the voices weren't lying to him. That was when he'd catch the flash of a yellow smile on his son. Glowing red eyes, gone with a blink, on Emma. Fangs on his wife."

"I'm sorry, but I had a wife like that," Brill piped in. "Sucked the life right out of me, too." The room laughed.

"So *he's* not possessed, it was the wife and kids?" Lat asked. "Is that it?"

"Yes."

"Usually we hear it the other way around. But that doesn't work in court, and our boy knows that," Rick said. "And of course he didn't tell anyone he was thinking these thoughts, did he, Chris? That he was married to the devil's spawn? That his mansion was haunted?"

"I would've been surprised if he did. He says he couldn't discuss his suspicions with anyone because he knew no one would believe him. He reports hearing his thoughts broadcast over all the radios in the house whenever he was home — night, day, whenever, whether the radio was on or not. Sometimes at work, too. That was why he wouldn't allow any music in the OR. These demons were always listening to him. It was a form of intimidation to keep him subservient, to torture him and make sure he didn't tell anyone what was happening."

"Anybody got him acting loony, agitated, speaking to the empty chair next to him?" Rifkin asked.

"The week before the murders he missed two surgeries and fired that nurse, Doris Hobbs. But nobody has him speaking in tongues," Lat replied. "That confrontation was nothing more than a demigod versus a subordinate who dared question him in the OR."

"She's on their witness list," said Penny. "Guaranteed Mel's gonna use her to support his argument Marquette was losing it."

"That's bullshit!" Brill groused. "You can't believe this crap story might actually work?"

"I haven't met a jury yet that I trusted to do the right thing. Make sure when you cross her, Rick, that you play up her incompetence," Rifkin said.

"I might let Julia handle her; she's got a soft touch."

Rifkin started to reply but then caught himself, sat back in his seat, and said nothing.

"How does he explain being the only one in his family not possessed?" asked Julia.

"Good question. He says he was spared for one reason only — to save the souls of his family. Their bodies were already devoured on the inside — all that was left was an empty skin shell. He says he had to intervene or their souls would be damned for all eternity, like vampires. A fate worse than the mortal death they'd already suffered. And 'the presence,' as he called it, these demons . . . well, they would move on to feast on others."

"So he killed them and saved the rest of society." Elias Vasquez, the chief of Coral Gables, sniffed. "We should give him a medal."

Barakat shook his head. "That's the interesting part — he doesn't actually admit to the murders. He stops short of describing what happened that night by claiming he can't remember. He says he can't even remember driving down from Orlando."

"That I still don't get. Why would he say

he can't remember when he's already admitted it by pleading insanity as the reason he did it?" Lat asked.

"Two lines of thinking," Barakat offered. "Three, actually. One is he's truly schizophrenic, and his brain can't actually face what he's done yet. The psychotic break from reality has effectively enabled him to stay in a deluded state of denial about the actual murders themselves."

"Or?"

"He's a psychopath and doesn't want to take responsibility. He's playing a game with you. He knows he's in check, but not checkmate, and he doesn't want to give up on a way out. Once he admits to certain facts, the jig's up and he's locked into a story. Ted Bundy, a classic sociopath, played that game with detectives for years, frustrating them with promises of confessions that never materialized."

"Obviously you're choosing what's behind door number two," said Rick.

Dr. Barakat slid his notes into his briefcase. "He was sane when he murdered his family. And I think this very involved, legally clever story of his only bolsters my position that the man's a sociopath. Don't you have Pat Hindlin also on this?"

"Yeah," Rick said. "He's sane, and he's

psycho. The score's tied two-all. Levenson has Koletis and some woman out of California no one's heard of, Margaret Hayes. But everyone knows that for twenty grand a pop, Levenson & Grossbach can buy whatever opinion it wants a jury to hear."

"So you really think it's going tomorrow?" Barakat asked. "You think you'll seat a jury?"

"Farley's already denied Mel's request for a continuance, right after he denied his motion for a change of venue," Rick replied. "So I'd say it's going, and it's going here in Miami. Jury selection should take us about a week, if not more. It's going to be interesting trying to find twelve people who've been living in a cave for the past four months."

"Who's opening?" asked the State Attorney.

"Julia. I'll handle closing," Rick replied in a voice that said the subject was not up for discussion.

Julia turned to Dr. Barakat as he rose to leave. "I'm sorry, Dr. Barakat. And the third?"

He looked at her, puzzled.

"You said there were three possible reasons why Dr. Marquette wouldn't give specifics on the killings."

"Well, that one's rather obvious, isn't it?"

Dr. Barakat smiled. "He didn't do it."

The room fell completely silent.

"I'm not saying that's the case, people. I'm just advising you what you all probably already know. Mentally ill people make false confessions in criminal cases all the time. Statistically, schizophrenics top that list. If he was schizophrenic, it would be a possibility."

"Defense attorneys are pieces of shit," Brill said with a bewildered shake of his head. "So let me ask ya. This 'devil made me do it' crap might actually let this guy walk free?"

"Could be another angle Mel's gonna spring later, Ricky," Rifkin said. "Two theories of the case. The jury can pick and choose their sympathy verdict: He didn't do it; it was somebody else. But if you think he did, then he was sick and didn't know what he was doing."

"That's what I'm prepping for, Charley," Rick said as he tossed his pencil into the middle of the table. " 'The devil made me do it.' I wonder if we'll have to name him in the conspiracy. . . ."

CHAPTER 67

"Where are you rushing off to?" Lat asked Julia when the meeting finally broke at three thirty. "Don't try and hide 'em now, Counselor. I see the car keys in your hand."

Conversations cluttered the room and clogged the doorway, preventing a quick escape. She wanted to go, but she didn't want to be remembered as the first one out the door. "I flew in this morning from New York," she explained, "and haven't had a chance to go home. I have so much stuff to do before tomorrow, and I want to get in a good run before the sun goes down."

"A good run, as in jog?"

"Yup. It helps me think." Actually, the opposite was true. Running helped her not think about much at all. That was what made it so therapeutic.

"I'm impressed. New York? What were you doing there? A marathon?"

"That's next year," she replied with a

smile. Then added, "Just seeing family."

"And you came straight here?" He let out a low whistle. "No wonder you're Bellido's favorite. Tell me, where do you go running?"

"Hollywood Beach. It's old Florida. A boardwalk, mom-and-pop motels, pizza by the slice. I love that."

"You must be an AMC girl."

"You must be an AMC guy to know what AMC is."

"I like the oldies. No age cracks, please. I have a birthday coming up."

"Ooh. How old?"

"The big three-seven."

"Happy birthday in advance. You know, no one in movies today can hold a candle to Audrey Hepburn. *Breakfast at Tiffany's* is still one of my favorites."

"Hmmm . . . You do kind of look like her. So what are you up to after your run?"

Rick walked up before she could answer. "Hey there," he said with a smile, his hand casually pressed on the small of her back. "We're gonna grab some grub at La Palma. You want to join us, Julia?"

She figured the "us" meant sitting sandwiched between Charley Rifkin and Bob Biondilillo, the MDPD director, who were both looking across the room at them. Reason enough to pass on osso buco for a

PB&J. She'd also had enough talk of psychopaths and murder. The morning's unexpected confrontation on the plane had rattled her all day, and she knew that for the next couple of weeks practically every thought and conversation would be consumed by David Marquette. "Thanks, but like I was telling Lat," she started, turning her attention back to the detective to find that he'd already walked off, "I need to get home. I've got laundry to do," she finished softly.

Rick lowered his voice and looked around to make sure no one was within listening distance. "Maybe I could come by and help you with your clothes tonight? Or you could come try out my new washing machine. . . ."

She laughed. "That's it? That's your best line?"

"That's all I got on short notice." He smiled. She felt his thumb gently rub her back, the tingle involuntarily run up her spine. "It's been a while. . . ."

It had been a while. Visiting Andy had left only every other weekend open for romance, something Rick had an unpredictable track record with anyway. But she was still there whenever he did call. She hadn't fixed that yet. And with so many upheavals and changes in her life, she didn't know when or if she ever would. She was coming to understand that casual sex and companionship had their benefits. At least you weren't alone. "Call me later," she replied. Then she said her good-byes and slipped past the conversations. She looked for Lat, but he was nowhere to be found.

The Broadwalk at Hollywood Beach, as it was called, was still bustling when she finally pulled up an hour later. Joggers, Rollerbladers, and a lot of sunburned Canadians offered a distracting, eclectic mix to get lost in. She made her way through the sticky perfume of coconut-scented sunscreen and frying funnel cakes over to an empty bench in front of the landmark Hollywood Beach Resort, a onetime haunt of Al Capone's. The boardwalk was one of the reasons she'd chosen Hollywood to live in. The eclectic t-shirt shops and fast-food stands, mom-and-pop restaurants, and seaside motels that still hung out vacancy signs. Like she'd told Lat, it was a place you just knew had once been great, where you could picture Annette Funicello partying beachside with Sandra Dee and Dolores Hart, because it hadn't changed. Yet. Of course, like South Beach twenty years ago, Hollywood was in the process of rediscovering itself. As the architects made their way down Johnson

Street, Julia knew it was only a matter o
time before the new and shiny resurfaced a
small slice of history.

Against the backdrop of the tired iconic
hotel, the setting sun shot ethereal beams o
light out from behind puffy white clouds
bathing everything in a golden hue. Even by
Florida sunset standards, it was breathtak
ing. The air felt alive, buzzing with people
and music. So different from yesterday, she
thought while she stretched, when she and
Andy had watched the bleak winter twiligh
descend upon the concrete Manhattar
skyline from the visitor's room at Kirby. She
wondered if her brother remembered a
sunset any other way but through dirty glas
and checkered steel. If it was ever truly
beautiful in his mind. Maybe one day, she
thought, she could show him this. . . .

David Marquette suddenly invaded he
thoughts once again, and she saw him a
clearly as if he were standing right in fron
of her, sitting in his squalid cell at DCJ
perhaps listening to the shrieks of the
screamers right now, his hands over his ears
But there were no windows in his cell. There
were no windows at all on the Crazy Floor
And there were no cells with a view or
Florida's Death Row, either. There would
be no more breathtaking sunsets for him.

Blessed are the merciful, for they will be shown mercy.

She took a deep breath, put her earbuds on, turned up the music, and ran, shutting out everything and everyone from her brain. When she got back to her car a couple of hours and a lot of miles later, it was dark. The parking lot was almost empty, the sunbathers and arepa carts retired for the night. She climbed into the Honda and picked up her cell. She didn't want to be alone tonight. She didn't want time to herself to think anymore.

"Hey there," she said when Rick answered. "Wanna do some laundry?"

Chapter 68

The potted palms on Rick's patio blew about in the gusty breeze. Julia lay in the dark, watching the violent dance their shadows created on the bedroom ceiling. Rick lay next to her under the covers, his body pressed against hers. She could tell by the sound of his breathing that he was almost asleep.

"What if he really is insane?" she whispered.

There it was. She'd finally said it. Hours before she was to pick a jury in the most important case of her career, she'd finally said aloud what had been gnawing at the back of every thought since Marquette had pled NGI. Since Andy had come back into her life. Since she'd looked into the eyes of her brother and witnessed firsthand the effects of an insidious disease that caused nice, gentle people to do horrible deeds. A disease no one seemed to really understand including the very doctors who treated it.

Or diagnosed it.

For Julia, Marquette's sanity just wasn't as cut-and-dried as Christian Barakat, Pat Hindlin, and Rick made it out to be. Four different forensic psychiatrists had delivered two radically different, irreconcilable diagnoses of the same man. And it would soon be up to a jury of twelve ordinary men and women to decide: Was David Marquette a brilliant psychopath or a paranoid schizophrenic? Brutal killer or selfless savior? Dr. Jekyll or Mr. Hyde?

That didn't mean the responsibility was out of her hands. Because those jurors would look to the State to help guide them to the right decision, to present the evidence that David Marquette was the cold, calculating killer they had charged him with being. And even if it was her trial partner who discredited the contrary opinions of other psychiatrists, the jury would still look to Julia because she sat at that table. They would rely on her word, her arguments, her questions. And that was the problem. That was what kept her up all night, whispering in the dark. You could only play for one team, and the sides had long ago been chosen. Julia Vacanti was on Team State.

"You're kidding me, right?" Rick asked. "I

guess not," he said with a sigh when she didn't respond.

"What if we're wrong? I mean, what if he really is sick?" Julia asked. "Haven't you ever just once wondered that?"

"Julia, you've been to the depos. You've read the reports. You've talked to the shrinks. What's there to wonder about? You've also been a lawyer long enough to know that for enough money, you can find an expert to say just about anything for you. And that's just what Mel has bought himself — a different opinion. Listen, babe, I've been at this job for a long time, and I've seen some sick crimes and some sick people. But what I've mostly seen is bad people pretending to be sick."

She stayed quiet for a moment. "You think most people fake it?"

He almost laughed. "In the criminal justice system? Yes, I think most people fake it. Wouldn't you? Look at what the man has to lose here."

"But do you believe some people are mentally ill?" She felt her stomach flip-flop. *Never ask a question you don't want to know the answer to.* Number-one rule taught in law school.

"Jesus," he said with a yawn, looking over at the clock, "most women like to cuddle

444

after making love, Julia. Not cross-examine."

She said nothing.

"Okay, I'll bite." He propped himself up against the headboard and tried to look at her in the darkness. "Yes, I do think that some people have mental problems. Serious ones, like schizophrenia and manic-depression and maybe even postpartum psychosis. And I think that many of those who do end up, unfortunately, spinning through the revolving doors of the system. It's just a sad fact of life.

"And I feel bad for those people. It must really suck to have something wrong with your head. But I don't believe in the 'devil made me do it' crap, Julia. I think even the mentally ill can control themselves. And if you do hear voices, I believe you also know it's wrong and against the law to drown your five children in the family tub, no matter who's telling you to do it.

"Now, before you count me in with the Tom Cruise 'psychiatry's a fraud and there's no such thing as a chemical imbalance' crowd, let me just say this: While I may be sympathetic to someone who's mentally ill, most brutal killers know exactly what they're doing when they're doing it. Just because the crime is sick or repulsive or heinous doesn't mean the person who committed it is legally insane, or for that matter mentally ill. People — even prosecutors sometimes — tend to look at those acts, at the crime itself, and think, 'Jesus, there must be a reason someone turned out this way. He must be insane to burn someone alive or lock his own kids in a cage and starve them to death.' Then come the psychiatrists, parading about with their DSMs and medical jargon, half of whom are bleeding hearts who want to believe everyone has something wrong with them. But the truth is, Julia, the BTK killer knew exactly what he was doing when he broke into women's houses, tied them up, and tortured them for hours before killing them. Just listen to his *Dateline* interview if you're not so sure. Same goes for Cupid, when he drugged and raped and slaughtered those women, and the Menendez brothers when they blew their parents away to get a head start on spending their inheritance. The list goes on, since the beginning of time. Pick up a paper anywhere in the damn country on any day of the week and you'll read about some crime that defies moral comprehension. The crimes are sick, yes, but these are not sick people. They're evil. A psychiatrist may give them a medical diagnosis and tell them that they have an antisocial personality or are bipolar or maybe are even schizophrenic, but we certainly shouldn't give them an excuse."

She nodded. "No excuses," she said softly.

He sighed again. "You're having pretrial jitters. It's totally normal. We're picking a jury tomorrow. The past few months have been draining for both of us, and the press coverage has been intense. A million voices on the TV every night — half of whom don't have the wits to comment on the weather, much less a complicated legal case — helping you second-guess your decisions. It's your first homicide, and it's an insanity case, and we're seeking the death penalty. I wouldn't have thrown all three at you your first time up at bat, but there's no undoing it now." He paused for a moment before looking over at her. "Unless you want off."

"No," she replied quietly, still watching the shadows dance.

"I hope not. It's kind of late for that. Besides, I'm looking forward to hearing your opening." He rearranged the pillows underneath his head and lay back down, his hand finding her shoulder under the covers. "Look at it this way. Maybe they do hear voices, and maybe those voices are mean and tell them to do horrible things, but that doesn't give someone the legal excuse to go out and butcher their family." He yawned again. "If I told you to go out and kill your mom right now, would you do it? Hell, no. I'm just as real a voice. The point is, you still have to make the decision to do the crime, honey. That's why it's not insanity. It's murder."

Julia bit her cheek hard. For what seemed like an eternity she watched the shadows and waited until Rick finally rolled over on his side and she could tell by the sounds of his deep breathing that he'd fallen asleep. Then she got out of bed, locked herself in his bathroom, and in the darkness, where she was sure he could not hear her, began to cry.

CHAPTER 69

John Latarrino was so conditioned to his phone ringing in the middle of the night that he sometimes thought he heard it before it actually rang. This was one of those times. He reached over Lilly, his snoring eighty-pound golden retriever who'd sneaked up onto the bed again, and grabbed the cell off the nightstand. He didn't recognize the number. He looked at the clock and rubbed his eyes. It was three in the morning. Maybe it was one of his snitches.

"Hello?" he asked, his voice scratchy with sleep.

"Lat?"

He knew immediately who it was, and he sat up with a start. "Julia?"

"I'm sorry to bother you —" she started.

Maybe it was the connection, but her voice sounded so small and unsure. Vulnerable. Distracted. Lat felt a strange panic, and his chest grew tight. Something was wrong. He knew it. "No, no, that's fine. I didn't recognize the number is all."

"I'm at a pay phone."

"A pay phone? I didn't even think they made those anymore." Now he was out of bed, parting the blinds and looking out the window. Looking for her, somewhere out there. He watched as the palms whipped about under the streetlights. A couple of his neighbors' garbage cans had toppled and tumbled out into the street, where they aimlessly rolled about. The wind was nasty tonight. Judging from the small puddles that dotted the sidewalk and the smattering of drops on the window, it'd rained, too. He must've been in a pretty deep sleep not to have heard it. "What's wrong? Are you okay?"

She hesitated. "I'm okay, but I need another favor, Lat. I . . . I went for a run, and I lost track of where I was."

"A run? Like jogging?"

"Yeah, yeah. I'm in North Beach, at a gas station, but I don't think it's a very safe area," she said rather breathlessly. "I'm scared, Lat. I . . . I have to get back to my car. I have to get back. I was hoping maybe you could help me."

CHAPTER 70

He threw on a pair of jeans and a t-shirt, grabbed his gun, and ran out. North Beach? What the hell? The intersection where she'd said she was, 86th and Harding, was the middle of a creepy area of Miami Beach called Open Space Park. Even he wouldn't venture into that part of Miami at three in the morning without a badge, a gun, and a warrant. He sped out of his complex and onto US1 and then 95. Thankfully, the roads were empty at this hour.

Fifteen minutes later, as he pulled up to 86th, he spotted her. Standing there in the Citgo gas station parking lot next to the bullet-proof booth. Dressed in a t-shirt, a pair of shorts, and sneakers, her long, black hair pulled back into a ponytail. Her arms were wrapped around her as if she was incredibly cold, and even though she tried her best to fake it and look tough, he could see that she was scared. She paced the length of the booth, back and forth, her brown eyes darting everywhere. He spotted the unsavory characters, like giddy hyenas hunting prey, in the shadows all around — behind the liquor store, in the empty lot, under the overhang of the dilapidated efficiency motel next door — slowly moving closer, smelling her fear, trapping her from at least a couple of angles. A loud purple car full of hollering teenagers pulled up next to her as the attendant locked in the booth just watched. "Come on, Mami, get in," shouted one, hanging out the window with no shirt and a chest full of tattoos. He waved a beer in one hand and beckoned her closer with the other. "It ain't safe here. You need to come with us!"

The rest of the car laughed. "She gonna be safe all right!" someone squealed.

Lat turned on his lights and siren and pulled in. The loud purple car pulled out. The rest of the hyenas backed off, slithering back into the shadows where they lived, their smiles gone.

He opened the door and got out. "Are you okay?" he asked, looking around. "How the hell did you end up here?"

"I don't know. I don't . . ." she said, her voice small. "I just went running. But I have to get home now. I have to get home."

"Damn straight you do," he said, shaking his head and trying hard not to think about what might have happened if he hadn't heard the phone. He led her to the passenger door. "Hop in."

"Thank you . . . for coming." She turned her head toward the window. "My car's down on South Beach. Um . . . 2nd and Collins."

He stared at her. "You ran all the way up here from 2nd? That's like six miles. . . ."

"I . . ." she stammered in a small voice, "I just needed — I lost track of where I was."

"I'll say. This is a shit 'hood, honey. What were you doing down on South Beach? Do you live there?"

She shook her head. "I was just out, that's all. Tomorrow's a big day."

She looked so small, so fragile, like a little girl. Hunched up against the window, chewing on a fingernail. When he'd first gotten the call, he'd wondered if maybe she'd gotten stung in a drug deal or was out at the wrong party with the wrong people. Just because she was a prosecutor didn't mean it couldn't happen. Cops got busted all the time for doing shit they weren't supposed to, including drugs and prostitutes. Just because someone had a law degree or a badge didn't make him or her immune to addictions or bad circumstances. But once he'd seen her, standing there in her running shorts and sneakers, still sweating either from the run or the fear, he knew it wasn't drugs or bad people she was running from. It was something else. She was in a different kind of trouble. And she didn't want any help getting out of it yet.

"Are you okay with tomorrow?" he tried after a few minutes.

"Yeah, yeah. I'm fine. I just have a hard time sleeping. I don't sleep that much."

"That's not good. Where do you live?"

"That's it, right there," she said, pointing to her Honda, which was parked on a side street.

"Where are your keys?"

"Right here. I have them." She pulled a car key out of her fist. "Thanks," she said as she opened the door.

"Listen, Julia, whatever's going on you can always talk —" He stopped himself. She was shaking her head. "It's a really bad idea to go running at night, Ms. Marathon Girl. No matter how stress-relieving it might be," he admonished as she got out of the car.

"I know, I know, I know," she said quickly, looking around the deserted street. She leaned back in. "Look, Lat, I'm really embarrassed. I . . . hope that . . ."

"This stays between us," he finished. "No worries."

He watched her climb into her car and wave at him that she was okay. That he was free to leave. Crisis averted. He drove away with a short wave of his own. At the end of the corner he pulled in behind a truck, turned off his lights, and sat there, watching her in his rearview. His brain was still racing, thinking about what might've been tomorrow morning's headline.

When she finally pulled out a few minutes later, he followed her from a safe distance all the way home.

CHAPTER 71

News vans and satellite antennas lined 14th Street in front of the Richard Gerstein Justice Building by eight thirty in the morning. Even though Rick was still the main player whom everyone wanted to score an interview with, Julia took no chances on getting burned by the spotlight. She slipped across the street to the service entrance of the courthouse, where the judges' parking garage was, and took the back elevator up. She made it through the doors just as Jefferson started the morning royal proclamations and Farley whooshed to the bench.

After the competency hearing debacle, Rick no longer took chances with timing a perfect entrance. He was already seated at the State's table. She hurried up the aisle and slid into the co-counsel seat beside him. He didn't even look over.

"Good morning," said the judge. "I do believe we are picking a jury this morning.

Are there any matters that we need to address before we get started?"

"Good morning, Your Honor," said Mel, rising. "First off, I'm renewing my motion for a change of venue. It's impossible for my client —"

"Denied. Next thing on your mind, Mr. Levenson."

"Since you're denying my motion to change the location of this trial, I move for a continuance —"

"Denied."

Mel sighed loudly. "— so that I may file an appeal."

"Denied, denied, denied. No changes, no continuances, no delays. I warned you all. Everyone in the world has heard about this case, unless they've been living under a rock, in which case they're too stupid and ignorant to sit on a jury anyway. Miami is just as fair a location for trial as Jacksonville. Now, look, my blood pressure's already up; let's get this thing tried before I drop." The courtroom tittered. He shot a look at the court reporter, who obediently deleted that last sentence. "Let's move on. Jefferson, what's the pool downstairs?"

"Four hundred, I think."

"Just on this?"

"Yeah, the clerk did a special seating to

make sure we had enough. We have them separated from the rest of the jurors, Your Honor. They're all just for you."

"All right," sighed Farley, with a smug smile he tried to hide. It was unheard of for a judge to hoard four hundred jurors for just one case. Even the serial killer Cupid's pool had been less than that. "Mr. Levenson, are you waiving your client's right to be present during selection?"

"No."

"Can someone tell me then why the defendant is not here yet? Corrections, this better not be a preview of how well you all do your job. Get Dr. Marquette in here. And Jefferson, bring the first fifty up. Let's see what we can get through today. Call me when everyone's here and they're all quiet. I have to make a call," said the judge. Then he disappeared off the bench, slamming the door behind him.

Most of the room figured that left at least enough time for a ciggie, coffee, or potty break, and the gallery slowly emptied, until just the clerk and a few spectators remained.

"What happened to you last night?" Rick asked coolly, as he jotted down some notes. He still hadn't looked at her.

"I went home."

"No shit."

"Do you want me to make up the juror cards?"

Now he turned to face her. He was definitely angry. "Nice to tell me that before I wake up at four in the morning to see that you're gone, but your clothes are still strewn on my floor, your purse is on my counter, and my front door's unlocked."

"I went for a jog on the beach. I needed to think. There was just —"

He cut her off with a shake of his head. "A jog? I thought you were kidnapped or had an accident or jumped off the freaking balcony!"

"I'm sorry."

"I race downstairs only to see that your car is gone."

"I just needed to —"

"Your clothes are still at my house," he said flatly.

She could feel herself getting defensive. "I'll have to pick them up."

"And your —"

Now it was her turn. "Purse," she finished. "You said. I'll have to pick that up, too."

"No. It's in my office."

"Well, thanks. I'll get it later."

"I was about to call the police, you know. What a nightmare that would've been. And of all times, the night before this fucking trial. Wouldn't that have been great?" He stared at her as if she were a stranger. A chill ran through her, and she wondered if he remembered that only hours ago he'd made love to her in his bed. "Julia, if you can't handle this, then I think maybe now's the time to get out."

She said nothing, wondering exactly what he meant by "this." She looked around the empty courtroom, at the abandoned tripod-mounted cameras and Court TV boom mikes. At the circus that had moved into town. Maybe Rick was right. Maybe she couldn't handle this anymore. Maybe there was nothing at all for her here in Miami anymore. Andrew was in New York, and he wasn't getting out anytime in the foreseeable future. Her relationship with her aunt and uncle was over. Even if Aunt Nora ever did start to pick up the phone when Julia was on the other end, it would be impossible to get back to the way things used to be. There were too many secrets to navigate through. Too many lies to forget. And forgive. As for a career, judging by the look in Rick's eyes, that was looking shakier by the minute, as was their romance.

The question was hanging out there. The choice was hers.

She shook her head and bit back the tears.

"No. I can handle it just fine," she quietly replied, not sure what question she'd answered.

Then the courtroom doors swung open once again, as Jefferson walked in with the first fifty potential jurors.

CHAPTER 72

Five days later they had a jury.

As Mel had argued, it was unrealistic to think they could find fourteen people who hadn't heard the name David Marquette. And they didn't. What they did find was five men and nine women who said they hadn't yet formed an opinion on the case, could put aside everything that they had heard, could render a verdict based solely on the evidence presented to them in court, and could vote for the death penalty. At four fifteen on Friday afternoon the panel, which included a firefighter, a retired librarian, and a "Cowboys for Christ" self-ordained preacher, was sworn in. Opening statements were set for Monday.

"Farley swore them all in a couple of hours ago," Julia said into the phone, swallowing a yawn. Outside her window, she saw that the enormous floodlights that lit every dark crevice of DCJ had just been flicked on as night descended on a deserted down-town.

"I just heard on the news," Lat replied. "You sound tired."

"It's been a long week." She tapped her pencil absently on the desk. He had not brought up last Sunday's midnight rescue mission, and neither had she. "Where are you?"

"At the Alibi." Tucked away in the lobby of an unassuming Travelodge, the Alibi Lounge was a favorite haunt of the Miami criminal bar. Conveniently located within walking distance of the courthouse, SAO, PD offices, and the jail, it was also far removed from the sunburned tourists and overpriced cocktails of South Beach. A down-and-out Cheers.

"Rick said in court that he wants to go over your testimony. Can you come back over?"

"It's six thirty on a Friday night. I'm off the clock. If Bellido wants me, he can go over what he wants me to say here while I have a cold one and enjoy the NCAA finals." His voice softened. "Better idea. Why don't you join us for a beer, Julia? Forget Bellido. You can interview me. I'll tell you anything you want to hear." Then he yelled out, "Whoa. That's a bullshit call!"

Presumably at the TV.

"I've got to finish things up here."

"Like what?"

"My opening. But I'll try and buy you some time till tomorrow at least. Enjoy the game."

"Don't work too hard," he warned.

"Too late," she replied and hung up the phone.

Julia's bone for being second seat was the opening. Most legal experts extolled the closing summation as the most important part of a trial, as it wrapped up all the facts that had come out at trial, and wove them into a neat and easy-to-understand story for the jury. But the opening was not without impact.

Opening statements were the first opportunity for both sides to stand up and tell the jurors exactly what their case was about — what evidence was going to be presented, what witnesses would be called, and most importantly what they intended to prove. With all the juicy, gory, never-before-told details thrown in. It was the first time jurors actually heard from the attorneys, outside of being asked questions during voir dire — jury selection. Julia had tried enough cases to know that first impressions were lasting ones. It was perhaps fundamentally unfair, but convictions and acquittals often came down to personality contests between the attorneys. If the jury liked you, if they felt for your story, if they trusted you — then you had them at hello, and they would extend that trust to your victim and witnesses as they would a personal reference from a respected friend. With one caveat: If you told them that you were going to prove something, then you'd better damn well prove it, because back in that jury room, like a scorned girlfriend, those jurors would remember everything you didn't do but said you would, and the trust you'd worked so hard to build would be gone. Then, in their eyes, you'd be nothing but a well-dressed liar.

Since the moment Rick had first pulled his Beamer up to the pretty yellow house on Sorolla Avenue, Julia had been crafting her opening. It was a prosecutorial habit. As soon as you were assigned a case, skimmed through an A form, prefiled a witness, you began to piece together the way you were going to tell the story — what facts and what witnesses brought it to life or moved you to tears. She'd imagined time and again how she would bring a jury back to the night of October eighth with just words, how she would walk them through bloodstained dark hallways, how she would make them feel the fear and horror that had brought veteran officers to their knees. As the facts had developed and the case had come together, piece by circumstantial piece, she'd continued to develop and polish her opening.

But now, as she sat alone in her office, a legal pad full of notes before her, hands poised above her laptop keys, the pieces weren't fitting as perfectly as they once had. The facts were jumbled like the colored squares of a Rubik's cube, and no matter how she worked them, she couldn't get all of the sides to align at once, even though everyone else who toyed with it seemed to have no trouble. The questions that she kept remanding to the corners of her mind bobbed back to the surface, and she felt an overwhelming, almost debilitating pressure squeezing her head like a vise. A pressure to please, a pressure to succeed, a pressure to do the right thing, when she wasn't sure just what that was anymore. A pressure that seemed to be growing more intense every day as they drew closer to showtime.

She stared at her notes. The ones from last Sunday's pretrial.

One is he's truly schizophrenic, and his brain can't actually face what he's done yet.

The psychotic break from reality has effectively enabled him to stay in a deluded state of denial. . . . I'm just advising you what you all probably already know. Mentally ill people make false confessions in criminal cases all the time. Statistically, schizophrenics top that list.

Julia had read enough mental health treatises, articles, and books to know all about the bizarre phenomenon of false confessions. Some studies placed the number made in criminal cases as high as 22 percent. Almost every high-profile murder case attracted a number of false confessions. Charles Lindbergh Jr., JonBenet Ramsey, Elizabeth Short — the "Black Dahlia."

She sat back at her desk, chewing on a pencil tip. What if David Marquette really was schizophrenic? What if his shrinks were right and the State's were wrong? What if the delusion that he'd killed his family had seemed real in his mind, but he *hadn't* actually done it? What if someone else had been in that house, attacked his family, and, after being surprised to find Marquette there when he was supposed to be out of town, stabbed him, too? What if he was a victim of bizarre circumstance, like Sam Sheppard?

It was a crazy thought, but . . .

She grabbed the 911 tape from the Marquette file box and popped it into her boom box.

"Police and fire. What's your emergency?"

She fast-forwarded to the end of the call.

"Hello? Is there someone on the line? Is there anyone there? This is the emergency operator. . . ."

"No, no . . . Oh, no, no!"

The muffled sound of silence, then the tape enhanced.

"Emma?"

"No, Daddy!"

It could go either way. Emma never said on the tape that it was her father stabbing her. She only said, "Daddy." Maybe she was calling out *for* him, not naming her attacker!

Maybe there was someone else in the house. . . .

It was definitely bizarre, but stranger things had happened. The walls of the PD's office and the Innocence Project were filled with pictures of the mentally ill who'd been wrongfully convicted. Marquette had never gone into detail with all the psychiatrists about exactly what had happened that night, stopping short of actually describing the murders. Drs. Barakat and Hindlin had called that "blame deflection," a psychopathic character trait. Even when admitting something, the psychopath won't ever take full responsibility. *I didn't do it. Nobody saw me do it. And if you did see me do something, it wasn't my fault.* But what if David Marquette couldn't describe the murders because he didn't commit them? Then there were the unidentified fingerprints around the windows, the unidentified footprints down the halls, the lack of real motive other than potential financial gain . . .

Whoa. Slow down, Julia. She pulled her hands through her hair. She felt embarrassed to be thinking like this. It must be nerves because she was quite sure no one else was thinking such thoughts. No one else was grasping at straws. For everyone but her it had always been an open-and-shut case. She was the only one who'd never seen the picture, who dragged her doubts and what-ifs around with her like baggage. And now Andy and her own past had caught back up to the present, and all she could see was him, fifteen years ago, possibly facing a prosecutor who didn't want to understand, who only saw a conviction.

Aunt Nora had been right all along. This case was too close. Much too close. What was happening to her?

She stood up and paced the office. She needed to talk to someone. She needed to step back and see the forest through the trees again. She needed it all to make sense. She needed to be the confident, sure prosecutor she'd always been. She was reaching for excuses because of Andy, wasn't she? This past week had just been so bad, and she was under crazy stress and had had no sleep. She thought of Rick and Sunday night. How hurt and worried and angry he'd been when she'd walked out in the middle of the night. Things had been cool between them ever since. He didn't deserve that, did he? He'd given her a shot with this case. He hadn't given up on her. He was letting her do the opening, which was huge. And this was how she repaid him? She'd been blaming him all these months for not wanting a relationship when the truth was she was the one who couldn't stay the night. She was the one who couldn't commit. . . .

She grabbed her purse and briefcase and hurried out. It felt as if a weight had been lifted from her shoulders. Admitting you have a problem is the first step to solving it. He would convince her that she was grasping at straws. He would make her feel okay again. Confident. And this time she would listen. She would really listen. . . .

The offices were dark, the halls deserted. On Fridays the SAO cleared out at five. By seven the only souls still left hanging around were pushing a vacuum.

On 2 she slid her security badge through the access doors and walked down the black hallway. She passed the empty secretarial maze and stopped at Rick's door. For some reason she hesitated, her hand barely touching the handle. Her eyes focused on a crack in the door.

She heard the rushed, heavy breathing inside. The familiar, intimate sounds that only a few days earlier she herself had been making in his arms. She saw the blur of body parts through the sliver of open door but couldn't place who was inside or what exactly they were doing.

No, that was crazy. She knew what they were doing. She knew just who was in there.

She closed her eyes and let go of the handle, backing away. Then she turned and walked back down the hall.

Chapter 73

Even as she walked through the lobby of the Travelodge she wondered why she was here. Why she hadn't just gone home to a bad movie, a bottle of wine, and a good cry.

"Hey there," Lat shouted to her from his spot at the bar next to Brill. He motioned her over. Then he turned to Brill. "Go get another chair, man."

"What the fuck do I look like?" Brill barked.

"Be gracious for once in your life," Lat said as Julia walked up. "The lady needs a seat."

"Give her yours," Brill grumbled. Then he looked at Julia and sighed. "Ah, for you, Jules, I'll do it. But I ain't getting one for your trial partner. He can sit on the floor," he yelled out as he stomped off.

"Speaking of the devil," Lat said, looking back at the door. "Where's Bellido?"

"He's not coming."

"Why not?"

"I didn't get a chance to actually ask him."
She looked straight at the bar, focusing on a
bottle of Hennessy on the top shelf.

"What?"

"He's busy. Or he was. I suspect he's done
now."

"What the —" he started to say, then he
finally found her eyes, which picked that
moment to swell with tears. "Oh, shit."

She hung her head. "I think I need a
drink," she said quietly, her voice catching.
She never should've come here tonight.

"It wouldn't be the first time," Lat said
after a moment.

"No?"

"Ricardo's got quite the reputation with
the ladies. Most of it of his own making,
though. I haven't heard too many impressive tales from the other side."

"How did you know?" she finally asked.

"Julia, please. Everyone knew about you
two. If it makes you feel any better, everyone
also knows he's an asshole."

She said nothing.

"Who was it?" he asked.

"My DC, I think. It was hard to tell. I
never saw her naked before."

Lat shook his head.

"I feel like a fool. An idiot." She looked

helplessly around the room. "And I don't know why I'm here. . . ."

He pushed himself back from the bar. "Stop. Enough. Let's go."

"What?"

"We'll get you that drink, love, but somewhere else." The bar and pool tables were crowded with private defense attorneys, PDs, corrections officers, and cops. Odds were that the Travelodge guest list included a few reporters as well. "There's too many people here who would love to see you cry, Julia, and then spend the next hour or two wondering why. Let's go. I'm out back."

Brill walked up, bar stool in hand.

"No need, brother. We're out of here," Lat said, grabbing his leather jacket from a hook on the wall. He slapped Brill on the back. "Thanks."

"Where we going?" Brill called out.

"I'll call you in the morning," Lat yelled back.

Julia quietly followed Lat past the pool table and through a back door that led directly to the parking lot. To her surprise, he walked past the police cruisers and black Tauruses over to a polished red-and-silver Harley.

"Technically, today's my day off. And this is what I ride on my day off. Here," he said, unsnapping a helmet off the back and handing it to her.

She stayed where she was. "A motorcycle?" she asked hesitantly.

"I wear one. I'm no idiot."

"I . . . I don't ride motorcycles," she stammered.

He stared at her. "Why not?"

She hesitated again. "My mother always told me not to. Told me I'd crack my head open." She anxiously rubbed her thumbs on the helmet's smooth surface.

He climbed on the bike and smiled at her. "Is your momma here now?"

"Well, no," she said. Then added, "She's dead."

"That sucks. I'm sorry," he replied, and the smile instantly disappeared, replaced with somber silence. "Have you ever ridden one?" he asked when she still hadn't said anything.

"No."

"There's nothing to be worried about. You're in good hands."

She looked about the lot. Her car was parked on the other side of the motel.

"You could always follow me, I suppose," he said with a shrug, starting the engine. The bike rumbled to life.

She said nothing. But she didn't move.

"Come on, Julia," he said over the engine, "get on the bike. You've had a real shitty day, and mine hasn't been much better. Let's go for a ride." He held out his hand.

She bit her lip, then nodded slowly and took it, climbing on the back. Good thing she'd picked a pantsuit today. She strapped on the helmet.

"Ready?"

She wrapped her arms around his waist and nodded, her head against his back, her eyes shut tight.

"Hold on," he said. Then he hit the gas, and the bike sped out of the Alibi with a loud roar, past the courthouse and the State Attorney's Office, onto the ramp for I-95, and out of Miami.

Chapter 74

The wind whipped at the exposed skin on her hands and neck as they raced north. She finally opened her eyes and watched as cars and trucks moved beside them at seventy miles an hour — so close she could maybe reach out and touch them — yet she couldn't hear anything over the roar of the bike, which was probably a good thing. The noise and the fear prevented her from thinking.

She wrapped her arms tighter around Lat's waist and buried her face in his leather jacket. Her palms began to sweat, and she feared her fingers might slip through one another and cause her to lose her grip. She had a frightening but funny thought that she might blow off the back of the motorcycle like a cartoon character and smack straight into the path of a semi, her body splayed like da Vinci's Vitruvian Man across the grill.

Traffic was light. They sped over the fly-over at the Golden Glades — the concrete clog of ramps and overpasses that connected Miami's four main expressways — and into Broward County. She had no idea where they were going, but as exits streaked by in blurs of green and white — including her own — she found that she didn't care. The cold wind was invigorating, the deafening roar of the bike strangely soothing. She could feel the distance stretching between her and Rick — physically, emotionally, metaphorically — with every mile marker Lat passed, and she didn't want him to stop. She wanted him to keep going until she just couldn't think anymore.

At I-595, he headed east toward signs for the Fort Lauderdale/Hollywood International Airport and the beach. When the interstate finally ended he turned north onto a quiet, almost deserted stretch of three-lane highway. Closed, no-name car-rental agencies and auto-repair shops lined the road that led toward downtown Fort Lauderdale. Just to the east Julia spotted the smokestacks of Port Everglades, where massive cruise ships from all around the world dropped anchor. She'd been to Fort Lauderdale countless times to see Nora and Jimmy but had never been this way before.

He pulled up to a light, and the engine quieted a bit. Lat turned his head to look at her. "You okay back there?"

She nodded. Her ears were ringing like she'd just stepped out of a rock concert.

He reached down and took her hands in his. Her fingers felt like blocks of ice. "Cold?"

She nodded again.

He rubbed her fingers gently, and she felt a tingle run up her spine. When the light turned green, he moved her hands up underneath his jacket, pressing them back together against his stomach, a signal for her to hold on again.

Her fingers began to defrost, and she could feel the rise and fall of his chest under them as he breathed, his strong muscles tightening against her hands through his shirt as he leaned his body into the bike. It was a strangely intimate moment. Lat and she had definitely developed a friendship over the past few months, but Julia suddenly felt embarrassed to be this close to him, her arms wrapped around his waist, her face buried against his back, smelling the leather of his jacket. Embarrassed to be feeling the way she was now feeling.

As they got closer to downtown, fast-food restaurants and drugstores popped up next to Blockbusters and nail salons, and the traffic got a little heavier. He turned down a side street into what at first looked like a quiet residential neighborhood, but a block or so up, in a small strip mall, Julia spotted a dive shop and a yacht-uniform outfitter next to what looked like an unassuming restaurant. The Southport Raw Bar. Hand-painted sea creatures swam across nautical blue walls.

Lat pulled the bike past the cars that packed the lot, creating a spot next to the front door. A sign above the entrance read, "Eat Fish — Live Longer. Eat Oysters — Love Longer. Eat Clams — Last Longer."

She pulled off her helmet as the sound of silence slowly filled her head again. "Where are we?" she asked, looking around.

"We're getting you that drink." He helped her off and then watched with a grin as she walked carefully to the door. "You okay, Counselor?"

"Just a little stiff," she replied with a grimace. "Thanks for breaking me in slowly."

"I kept it under ninety," he said, laughing as he held the door.

They'd taken maybe two steps inside when a tall guy in retro horn-rimmed glasses wearing an apron and a mop of curly brown hair strode up and slapped Lat hard on the back.

"John-John! What the hell are you doing up here?"

"Hey, Buddy!" Lat said to his friend, shaking his hand hard. "Just in the 'hood. Thought I'd bring you a new customer. Julia, this is Buddy. Buddy's the owner of this fine establishment and the maker of the best chowder in town. Julia's the prosecutor on a case I'm working."

"I thought you looked familiar," was all Buddy said, and for that Julia was relieved. "This guy's gonna single-handedly double my business this year," he added with a smile.

"Look at this." Lat gestured around the packed restaurant and bar. TVs blared basketball and hockey games from every corner. "He's turning them away. Speaking of which, you got a table?"

"Are you kidding me?" Buddy led them outside to a crowded waterfront patio. Boats bobbed up against the dock slips, and the air smelled like fish and beer. Two minutes later they were sitting at a picnic table nursing their own Budweisers.

"A Harley, huh? I never figured you the type," Julia said after the waitress had taken their order of chowder and Old Bay shrimp.

"There's a life lesson for you. Never judge a book by its cover. Guys who ride Harleys aren't all outlaws, you know."

"Obviously," she said with a smile. She sipped her beer and looked around the deck. "We sure are a long way from Kansas, Auntie Em. Do you live around here?"

"Nah. My friend's got a boat off one of the canals, and we take it out fishing sometimes. I got an apartment in the Grove, but I wish I was here. I like Fort Lauderdale. It's quiet, more laid-back. I just don't want to do the commute yet."

"The Grove's nice. Real nice."

"I can't complain," Lat said with a shrug. "I'm not home too much anyway."

There was a strained silence. "Thanks for . . ." she hesitated, struggling to say just the right words but not much more, ". . . this." She looked around the restaurant with a smile. "This place is great." Colorful Budweiser and St. Pauli Girl umbrellas dotted the tables, and in the center of each was a roll of paper towels, a few well-used plastic menus, and a Corona bottle with a single flower in it. "And with real flowers, too," she said absently, gently fingering the petals. "I love peonies. The cheap man's rose, my mom used to say. But they're still my favorite." She shook a thought out of her head. "And the ride was . . ."

"Scary?"

She smiled. "A little."

"I thought you were gonna take out a rib."

"Sorry," she said, turning red. "It was only scary at first, though. You're a good driver."

"I'm glad I didn't crack your head open. I would have hated to prove your mother right about us outlaws. I'm sorry, by the way."

She shook her head, not understanding.

"About your mom. I'm sorry. When did she die?"

Julia swallowed the lump in her throat with a long sip of beer. "A long time ago," she said finally. "It's been fifteen years." It was funny. She'd never even shared that information with Rick. Why had she told Lat her mother was dead?

"What happened?"

The question took her by surprise. "It was an accident. Her and my father."

"You must have been young. Damn . . . I'm sorry."

"It's okay. You didn't do anything."

"Do you have any brothers and sisters?"

"No," she answered quickly and took another sip of beer. "There's just me." She suddenly remembered the biblical passage between Jesus and Simon Peter at the

Mount of Olives before Judas's betrayal. *I tell you, Peter, the cock will not crow this day, until you have denied three times that you know me.* She looked away, feeling ashamed.

"Who raised you, then?"

"My aunt." She tried to change the subject. "So are you from Florida?"

"Is anybody actually from Florida? L.A. I came to Miami because I learned Spanish in high school and I knew I didn't want to work in the movies. My family's still out there. A mom and two brothers. One's great, the other not so great."

"Why?"

"Drugs, gangs. Same house, three different results: a lawyer, a cop, and a criminal. At least we're all in related professions. And it definitely makes for some lively conversation when we do get together." He shrugged again. "So how'd you end up with Bellido?"

"I don't know." She looked out at the water. "Six months later and I still don't know."

"Six months. Woo-hoo . . ."

"Is that a long time?"

"Not for me. I've had some go into the home stretch."

That same stab of pain jabbed her chest. The one the fast motorcycle ride had let her forget. "It was off and on. I wouldn't say we were always together. I mean, tonight shouldn't have been a surprise. I'm sure, as you said, there were others." She looked off at the water again. God, she didn't want to have this conversation. She didn't want it to smart so much, and she didn't want everyone to have seen it coming. Everyone but her. "I guess I'm a fool. He was there whenever he wanted to be, and I was there whenever he wanted me to be. It was a destructive cycle. Now we have to finish this case."

"Do you love him?"

"Jeesh," she said, looking at him. It was easy to see now how he could work a subject in his custody. "No. I can't say I love him," she answered, twisting the edge of the paper towel on her lap. "I want to say I did, but I can't. It never even came up between us. I guess that's strange. But I wanted him to want me. I wanted him to love me, I guess. I wanted him to say it. . . . Why am I telling you this? I need more liquor to justify telling you this stuff. A lot more." She finished her beer. "Tell me something, John Latarrino. Please. Something I can use against you later on if I need to. I am so embarrassed right now."

"I'm an insomniac, and I don't clean my bathroom."

She laughed. "That's helpful. Tell me, why do you pace the floors at night, Detective?" The waiter picked that moment to drop off two more beers, the bowls of chowder, and platters of fried seafood, extra obviously sent over by Buddy.

Lat turned and waved a thank-you to his friend, who stood by the door. Then he looked back at Julia and smiled. " 'Cause I haven't found the right woman yet to keep me in bed."

Her cheeks went hot. "Oh."

"I was married once. Right after I came to Homicide from Robbery. It lasted a year. It never should have happened, but it did. Thankfully, there were no kids. We never had time to make any, which, according to her, was the root of my problem."

"Was the divorce amicable?"

"I'd say so. She wound up marrying her attorney. Now they have three kids. I got the dog. Lilly. An overweight, neurotic, really cute golden retriever."

"Ouch. And you . . . now?"

"Like I said, now I pace the floors at night. Just like you."

As Lat had promised, the food was great, but the company was even better. They slipped into lighter conversation that, over the course of the next two hours, covered every topic from politics to U2. Buddy joined them for a drink and a Lat story before hopping off to another table. It had been a long while since Julia could remember belly-laughing.

Through the palms, a yellow moon sliced ribbons of light across black, motionless water. It was late. The restaurant had emptied; most of the boaters had left. Southport sat at the dead end of a long canal, but T-boning the other end was another waterway. Julia could see an elaborate yacht zigzag by in the distance, all lit up. "Is that the Atlantic?" she asked.

"Nope. That's the Intracoastal," he answered. Then he looked at her. "Were you close?"

She stared at him. "What?"

He picked the peony out of the Corona bottle and handed it to her. "To your mom. Were you close?"

The tears started to spill before she could even think to hold them back.

"Oh, shit," Lat said, startled. He began pulling off sheets of paper towels and shoving them across the table at her.

She nodded, her face buried in her hands. She felt like such a moron. "I'm sorry. I'm okay."

He stood up and slapped money on the

table. "I'm the one who should be sorry. I didn't mean to get you upset." He looked around the restaurant, then reached down and took her by the hand. "Come on, Julia. Let's get you out of here."

Chapter 75

Neither of them said anything as he led her by the hand down the dock, around the back of the restaurant, and through the empty parking lot. He took off his jacket as they came to the bike. "Put this on," he said. "I think it's gotten colder."

She slipped into it without a word. He hopped on the bike, started it up, and offered her his hand. Without another word she climbed on behind him, hesitantly wrapping her arms around his waist. The past two hours had been so good; now everything felt awkward and clumsy. Almost as if he'd read her mind, Lat reached down and took her hands once again in his own, rubbing them with his fingers before tucking them up under his shirt, like he had before. Only this time it was his bare chest that she felt under her fingertips. She closed her eyes and rested her head against his back, unsure again what to make of her feelings — or his

— as the bike rumbled out of the parking lot.

Instead of heading back down to Miami, he passed 595 and the airport, turning finally on the deserted Dania Beach Boulevard toward the beach and A1A. It was well past midnight, and the sleepy highway, normally packed with tourists, was empty, the beachfront restaurants and t-shirt shops all closed up for the night. If she'd been with anyone else, even Rick, she would've felt a bit anxious — on a remote part of the beach, not knowing exactly where she was or where they were going — but not with Lat. "Trust me, Julia," he'd said to her that day in court months back. And she did.

The same moon followed them as they drove along the beach, past seaside motels and the occasional high-rise. She inhaled the salty sea air, watching the black waves break white against the shore. She could almost hear them calling her. She closed her eyes and thought of Andrew.

"Can I help?" Julia asked.

Andy looked up at her from his trench in the sand, his eyes squinting against the sun.

"Mom said to tell you I can help."

He shrugged, but only because he had no choice and he knew it. "If you want."

"What'cha making? A hotel?" she asked.

"The Colosseum."

"The what?"

"The Colosseum. It's in Italy. It's like a stadium, like a really old baseball stadium."

Wow. She could see it now. A stadium. That was so cool. "Can I make the concessions?"

"No," he sighed. He thought for a moment while she stood there pouting. Then he motioned for her to come into the trench with him. He took her hands in his and carefully guided her to where he was carving the seats. "You have little fingers, Ju-Ju. You make the tunnels. . . ."

Why had she denied him?

They said nothing along the ride, even at the lights. But the awkwardness was gone now, replaced by this silent, scary, electric energy between them. She didn't let go of his waist, even when she could have, and he didn't move away. She could feel his heart beating under her fingers. When he suddenly turned off A1A onto Stirling, she knew where he was going even before he pulled into the parking lot.

He shut off the engine and stepped off the bike. She stared at him. "How did you know where I live?"

He smiled. "I'm a cop, remember?"

"My car . . ." she started to say.

"I'll take you in the morning. I don't want

you to have to drive tonight. It's real late, and it's a long way to Miami, Toto, so don't even think of putting on your running shoes. It's my bad that you ended up all the way up here anyway." He held his hand out to help her off.

There was no point in arguing with him. And the truth was, she didn't want to. She nodded and, with her hand in his, climbed off the bike.

They walked in silence up the stairs of her building to the second floor, their fingertips still lightly locked. "Do you want to come in?" she asked quietly, looking down at the doorknob after she'd slid the key in. This was how it had started with Rick. The ill-thought-out invitation. But she'd never felt like this when Rick had touched her.

"I'd love to," he said.

She turned and looked back at him in surprise. Her heart pounded furiously.

". . . but I'd better not."

"Oh," she said, hoping she didn't sound disappointed. Hoping he couldn't read her thoughts but knowing he probably already had. She felt so exposed with him. He was standing close to her, just inches away. She could smell the faint scent of his cologne.

"Look, I'm sorry about before —" he started to say.

She shook her head. "Don't be. Thanks again for dinner." She slipped off his jacket and reached over to kiss him good-bye on the cheek, but hesitated, her mouth lingering for a moment against his skin, and neither of them moved. His five o'clock shadow felt like fine sandpaper under her lips. She stepped closer, her body touching his, as her lips softly brushed his face, finding his mouth. She felt his warm hands on her shoulders, pulling her even closer, his fingers pressing into her back. His lips were very soft; his tongue tasted like beer. She remembered how her fingers had felt against his chest, how it had felt to touch his heartbeat. The kiss lasted just a few seconds before he pulled away.

"Whoa," he said, backing up slightly. He ran a hand through his hair. "I don't do rebounds, Julia. They never work out in my favor."

She didn't know exactly how to feel right then, but if she could use one word, it would probably be empty. She watched him walk off down the stairs and wished once again that she could do the impossible: that she could undo time. She listened to his motorcycle start up across the parking lot and then fade away as he drove off. Then she went inside her apartment and cried. But it wasn't over Rick.

When she woke up the next morning, her car was parked in the lot downstairs, and Lat was nowhere to be found.

CHAPTER 76

"I wish I could be there, Andy," Julia said into the phone as she poured herself a mug of coffee. From her kitchen window she looked out onto the complex's deserted pool area. Beer cans and liquor bottles overflowed from one of the garbage receptacles; discarded pizza boxes were stacked on a lounge chair. Someone must have had one heck of a party last night.

Andy hummed for a few seconds. It was a sign, she'd learned, that he was nervous. "Me, too," he finally said.

"I'm going to buy you a new suitcase," she declared cheerfully. "I'll bring it the next time I'm up. What color would you like? Black? Red? Tweed? Maybe a backpack instead?"

More humming.

"Andy?" She sighed. "Andy, I'm sorry. I wanted to come. Next week for sure, though."

More humming.

"Did you watch anything good on TV last night?" she tried.

"Black," he replied simply.

"What?"

"I'd like a black suitcase, I think. One with a lot of zippers and pockets."

"Sure. I can do that. I'll go shopping tomorrow."

"Can I keep it here?" he asked.

"Well, you can use it when you go to Rockland. I bet they'll let you keep it there."

More humming. He didn't like to talk about Rockland. She lit a cigarette and blew smoke out the window. She wondered if it was just coincidence that her brother liked to smoke the same brand. If it was just coincidence that he took two sugars and cream in his coffee, too. Or hated tomatoes, but loved pizza. Pepperoni pizza with pineapple. The same mystery authors. The same quirky habit of chewing food thirty times before swallowing. Invisible, innocuous ties that over the past couple of months she'd learned they shared. Julia couldn't help but wonder, with a bit of unease sometimes, just how many more of those ties there might be. . . .

"Why can't you come today?" he asked.

She rubbed her eyes and tried to figure

out what to say. A modified version of the truth was the safest bet. "Like I told you, I — I'm a lawyer. I have this big case that I'm going to court for on Monday. I can't come up this weekend because I have to prepare my opening."

"Oh." More humming. "What's that? What's an opening?"

"The opening statement is the beginning part of the trial, where I get to tell the court what my case is about. It's a speech, sort of. I'm nervous, though," she added.

"Really? You?"

"Oh, yeah. It's a big case, and I want to do a good job. I have to do a good job. I don't want to screw up. I don't want to get fired." An image of Karyn and Rick rolling around on top of his desk Friday night suddenly popped into her head, and she shook it out. "Although maybe that wouldn't be the worst thing."

"You'll do good. You're really smart, Ju-Ju," Andy said softly.

"Thanks."

"Uh-oh. The nurse is pointing at the clock. I can't talk anymore."

"I'll call you during the week, Andy, okay?" she said quickly.

"Okay."

"I love you, Andy," she said, but he'd

already hung up.

She listened to the dead hum of the dial tone for a second before clicking the *end* button. Outside, her eyes fell on a lone foam noodle that drifted slowly across the blue water. She thought of the kiddie toys that floated in the still pool in back of the Marquette house, the elaborate swing set in the yard. The quaint brick path lined with marigolds that led to the house that Norman Rockwell had painted.

But things were never as they seemed, were they? Up the perfect walk, behind the perfect door, was a house of horrors that was anything but perfect. Behind the boyish grin of an accomplished surgeon, father, and husband lurked a dark and disturbed monster.

"It's not about what you believe," her Crim Pro professor at Fordham had said, "it's about what you can get a jury to believe. At the end of the day — at the end of deliberations — that's the only thing that's gonna matter."

Maybe that was the key, she thought as she ran her cigarette under the tap. Maybe the sides of the puzzle that were turned away from the audience didn't need to align, didn't need to make sense, because no one was going to see them anyway. She looked over at her computer.

Maybe the jury didn't need to hear the whole story. . . .

CHAPTER 77

"Ladies and gentlemen," Julia began, slowly rising from her seat, "the opening statement is the State's opportunity to tell you about their case. To tell you what witnesses will be called to the stand during this trial and what those witnesses will say; what evidence will be presented and what that evidence tends to show." She paused. Abandoning her legal pad and index cards at the State's table, she walked past the podium and the cameras and over to the jury box. "It's like reading a comprehensive review of a true-crime novel before you flip open the cover. The opening is a detailed synopsis of the real-life thriller you are about to hear, complete with a description of the characters you will meet and a breakdown of the plot. It's an opportunity for me, ladies and gentlemen, to tell you a story. A story of rage, deception, and brutal, premeditated murder. A story of a crime so violent, so seemingly senseless, that it defies comprehension. A story that will shock you, horrify you, terrify you, haunt you, as it has me. A story that will bring the strongest among you to tears."

The twelve jurors and two alternates watched her every move, following her with their eyes as she casually ambled in front of the jury box. She caught several of them nodding absently as she spoke while others glanced uneasily over at the defendant, trying to connect her words to the well-dressed, slight man sitting calmly at the defense table. Trying to place him in the horrific tale that she was telling.

Flanked by his attorneys, the shackles and cuffs removed, David Marquette was now clean-shaven, his hair cut short and swept youthfully to the side, his fingernails clean and clipped. As he had during all of last week's jury selection, he stared out before him at nothing and no one — "the thousand-yard stare," Dr. Barakat called it. But apart from his vacant expression, he looked nothing like the scary Human Monster who had been on display eight weeks ago at his competency hearing. Of course his attorneys' goal had been different then. Rather than having to convince one theoretically learned judge that their client was incompetent to stand trial, Marquette's team now had to persuade twelve not-so-learned citizens that he had been legally insane at a particular moment in time. More important than the fine legal distinctions, it was a completely different audience. An audience that would swiftly convict a man who scared them with his deranged and disheveled looks. For Marquette's attorneys it was a fine, very dangerous line to walk. They had to present a man who was tragically ill, but not frightening. A man who, but for his sudden and severe mental illness, the jury would find likable, trustworthy. A person physically more akin to Mr. Rogers than Charles Manson.

". . . and you will hear Officer Colonna tell you that as he approached the master bedroom, as he turned the knob, he closed his eyes, and he prayed. Prayed that the carnage he had found in the children's rooms had not come here. Prayed that if it had, he would not be too late. But his prayers went unanswered. And he will tell you that he fell to his knees at the sight of young, pretty Jennifer Marquette, splayed lifeless on her bed, the white walls and ceiling of her bedroom splattered red with her blood. . . ."

Julia watched as the jurors' expressions changed from curiosity to disgust; as the characters in her story slowly came to life in their minds through just her words; as little Emma danced in the courtroom in her princess gown and Danny played with his Matchbox cars and Jennifer baked birthday cakes. But all the while it felt as though she were watching an operation from the spectator seats high above the operating room — she was present, but she wasn't really there, removed somehow from the ugliness of it all while the guy at the defense table below flatlined right in front of her.

" '. . . he's coming,' Emma whispered in the dark to the 911 operator, just as the last person she would ever see on this earth suddenly flicked on the lights. And you will hear little Emma's scared voice, ladies and gentlemen, at the very moment when her killer finally found her secret hiding spot. You will see the box of Barbie dolls and the Hello Kitty chair that she hid behind. You will hear her whimpers as he came for her, moving the box out of the way, tossing the chair aside, finding her huddled in her Cinderella princess gown in the corner, her knees drawn to her chest. You will listen to that moment. The precise moment Emma knew she would die. 'Oh, no, no, no, no!' you will hear her cry out to her killer as he fell upon her with his knife." Julia paused deliberately and looked over at David Mar-quette. " 'No, Daddy!' "

If her argument had lost its emotion or conviction over the past few weeks, that was apparently not what the jury saw, heard, or felt. Some jurors broke down in tears while others turned red with anger, gasping and shaking their heads in revulsion. And when she finally finished, an hour and forty-five minutes after she'd started, it was no longer curiosity or even disgust with which they stared at David Marquette. It was pure contempt. She had done her job well. And they hated him for it.

"You nailed it!" Rick whispered excitedly when she sat down. He clasped his hand over hers. "You really freaking nailed it. I don't think I've ever gotten jurors to cry in opening!"

Julia nodded, staring at his fingers on hers. She hadn't discussed her doubts with him again. She hadn't shared her thought about the possibility of another killer. She hadn't reasoned with him about the statistical likelihood of a false confession. There was no point. She knew that now. The lights were on, the curtain was up, and it was on with the show.

Although she wanted to scream at him to not touch her again, she didn't. There was no point in confronting him with what she'd seen Friday night. Their romance was over, and she didn't want it back. He was weeks away from officially ascending the throne of State Attorney, and no matter how brilliant her opening, he would probably use even the perception of jealousy as an excuse to boot her off the case if he had to. The case that was supposed to make her career, she thought bitterly. Now that career teetered precariously on the brink of self-destruction as she grappled with the truth and everyone else's perception of it.

Farley broke for lunch, and the gallery slowly emptied. Rick left to speak to an officer, Corrections escorted the defendant back to his holding cell, and the bailiff led the jurors back to the jury room. Julia turned to look around the courtroom, which somehow looked different than when she'd walked into it this morning. There, in the back, chatting with a lone reporter by the courtroom doors, she spotted her DC and Charley Rifkin. Karyn picked that moment to turn her perfectly coiffed blond head in Julia's direction. Their eyes caught, and then her DC did something that Julia hadn't seen her do in months. She smiled. A big, toothy grin.

Like they were the very best of friends.

CHAPTER 78

"Rohr, Cirto, Grubb, Morales." Nurse Lonnie's voice crackled to life over the intercom.

Andy looked up from the picture he was drawing.

"Please report to the nurses' station."

Outside, the light was almost gone; the skyline of Manhattan was beginning to glow. It was six o'clock. Meds time.

He tucked his sketch pad and his pencils into the footlocker next to his bed, under the stack of polo shirts Julia had given him. Nothing was allowed to actually be locked up at Kirby, and things were known to "disappear" if measures weren't taken to hide them. His sketch pad was his camera, and he didn't want his pictures to go missing again. Especially this one.

Meds were dispensed from a rolling cart in front of the nurses' station — a Plexiglas-enclosed island strategically placed right where the TV room, dining area, open dorms, and semiprivate dorm hallway connected so that the nurses and SHTAs could watch everyone all the time. Andy joined the end of a long line of men that had started to snake its way down the hall. Even though many of them had been locked in here as long as he, he had no friends. No one really had friends in here. None that you could trust.

". . . A story that will shock you, horrify you, terrify you, haunt you, as it has me. A story that will bring the strongest among you to tears."

Andy froze. Just down the hall on the big-screen TV in the rec room, there she was. Julia. On the news. In a blue suit and wearing stylish chrome glasses, her long hair in a soft, pretty bun. What was she doing? She was walking around a courtroom. Then it clicked. Her big case. The reason she couldn't come see him this weekend! This was it.

". . . Assistant State Attorney Julia Vacanti started off the case for the government this morning in a packed Miami courtroom by doing exactly what she promised — bringing many of the jurors to tears," the reporter said. "Today some of the more gruesome details of the case were revealed as the prosecutor described just how the bodies of the children were first discovered in the home on . . ."

For the government? Wait . . . Julia worked for the government?

"Isn't that the woman who was here last Saturday? The one who came to see Cirto?" Nurse Lonnie asked the other nurse, who was filling out med sheets and putting pills in dispensing cups.

The door to the nurses' station was open. He could see them through the thick, scratched plastic. He could hear them as they worked. The guy in front of him, whose name was Snaps, turned and stared at him.

". . . attorney Mel Levenson, in his opening, told the jury that his client is a paranoid schizophrenic who is not responsible for the deaths of his wife and children," the reporter continued.

"Sure looks like her," replied the new nurse, whose name Andy didn't know.

"Yeah. That's his sister," Samuel the SHTA said quietly, glancing up from his chart.

"No friggin' way. I didn't know Cirto even had family left," said the new nurse. "Thought he whacked 'em all."

"Guess he missed one," Samuel replied dryly. "She's been here a lot lately. Last couple of months. You just don't work enough weekends is all, Barbara," he added with a grin and a teasing nudge of his clipboard.

"I don't need to work any more than I already do in this place, thank you very much."

"What's her business on that doctor case?" Nurse Lonnie asked.

"I think she's the prosecutor," Samuel replied.

"The prosecutor? No friggin' way!"

"Again with the friggin' . . ." Nurse Lonnie sighed.

"So what's she doing showing up here all of a sudden?" Nurse Barbara asked as she looked out into the rec room, her eyes scanning the crowd of inmates. "Research?"

He knew they didn't see him standing there on line. Or maybe they did and just didn't care if he heard them. If anybody heard them. After all, the men in here were not human anyway. Snaps continued to watch him, his head cocked sideways. He had yet to blink.

Andrew stepped off the line and into the rec room. He watched as his little sister walked into a waiting crowd of photographers, like a movie star. Her briefcase in hand, she looked so smart, so confident. So important.

A somebody.

He remembered her better than she remembered him. Maybe because he was older and had had more time to make memories before the bad thoughts came and changed everything. But all the bad never erased the good that he had stored up in his head. No matter what they'd done to him in here, no matter what they did to him anywhere, nobody could take those memories. . . .

Julia stood on the bed in her pajamas, a pink-striped scarf wrapped dramatically around her neck, a pair of mismatched mittens on her hands. When she jumped, her long, black hair seemed to just float on the air, spreading out around her like a huge parachute. "I don't want to be a vet anymore, Andy," she said with unflinching conviction in between jumps. "I'm gonna be an actress. I want to be in movies and on TV."

"That's a stupid idea," he said, watching her.

"No, it's not."

"Yes, it is. Do you know how hard it is to be an actress?"

"So? I can do it if I want."

"Fine. Go ahead. You have to take your clothes off if you want to be famous, though, you know. All famous actresses do."

The jumping slowed. "Nuh-uh."

"Yup. Just watch R movies. The girls are all naked. And they curse, too."

She was silent for a long time, and he suddenly felt bad for trying to pop her balloon. But before he could apologize she sullenly asked, "What are you gonna do? Play baseball? Duh."

"I'm gonna be famous, but you got to have a plan to get there, Ju-Ju."

"Give me a break." The jumping resumed full speed.

"Dad says Little League's full of dreamers. You gotta be special." He looked down at his right hand and wiggled his index and middle fingers. "This is the secret weapon. This hand's gonna take me places, Ju-Ju. I'm gonna work on my split till I can get it up to maybe ninety-five. Coach Rich says I have it, too. I got the stuff. If I can throw a split faster than ninety, I'll definitely make the Bigs one day. You gotta have something nobody else has. Ain't nobody gonna have a split-finger like mine."

Andy looked down at his maimed hands, the ones that were supposed to take him places. On his pitching hand, his thumb flopped listlessly back toward the wrist. He couldn't wrap his fingers around a baseball anymore. Deep pink scars sliced his palms all the way up to his fingertips. That was where the government had implanted the chip so many years ago. Rusted and rotting now, its wires probably frayed and poisonous, he knew it was still in there somewhere.

He could feel it.

Then he hung his head and started to cry.

CHAPTER 79

"The knife was placed almost straight into the umbilicus. There was no tearing, ripping, or pulling of the surrounding tissue, like you would expect to find if there was a struggle or if the target was moving about when stabbed. The tissue below the navel is not vital unless the blade were to puncture the loop of small intestines, which, as I testified before, didn't happen."

Dr. Larry Price, the trauma surgeon who'd operated on David Marquette, sat on the very edge of the witness chair, his face hovering less than an inch above the microphone. He'd been in that seat for over an hour — on direct, then cross, and now back on redirect, and his nerves were beginning to show. He shifted, wiped the sweat from his upper lip, and cleared his throat. A twang of feedback blasted the courtroom. Judge Farley rubbed his ear.

"And, again, if the intestines had been

punctured, Dr. Price?" Rick asked.

"I would've had to repair it. And of course there's a risk, you know, of infection from spillage of the intestinal fluids into the abdominal cavity. Can it be serious? Yeah. But if you know what you're doing, if you're a doctor, you know there is no vital, life-sustaining organ in that area." He looked over at the jury, his eyes finding one of the jurors in the front row. "That's why when the Japanese samurai would commit *seppuku* — a ritualistic form of suicide, known to the Western world as *hara-kiri* — they would actually disembowel themselves by digging the knife in and then dragging it across their belly," he explained, standing up and gesturing with his own hand on his stomach. He leaned back over the microphone again. "And then they'd pull sharply upward at the end. More than a knife wound, it pretty much ensured death in the event they didn't have an assistant to cut off their heads and finish the job," he finished with a smile.

"Objection," said Mel, standing. "Inflammatory and irrelevant."

"Definitely sustained," said Farley. "Are you done with redirect, Mr. Bellido? I think we all get your point. It didn't look like a suicide attempt to Dr. Price. Let's move this along."

"Thank you, Doctor," said Rick. "I have nothing further."

"Mr. Levenson? Tell me you're done with this witness, please."

"Yes, Judge. Nothing further," Mel replied.

Dr. Price practically ran for the courtroom doors.

"All right, State. Who's next?"

Rick leaned over and conferred with Julia. The courtroom hung on his pregnant, very deliberate pause. Then he rose and straightened his suit. "The State rests, Your Honor."

A loud murmur broke out. To the surprise, maybe, of some of the reporters and commentators who were expecting the fourteen-week marathon of a Michael Jackson trial, it had taken just five days to put on the State's case-in-chief. But it was far from over. In a criminal case, the burden of proving the defendant's guilt — beyond and to the exclusion of every reasonable doubt — fell on the State. A defendant was under no obligation to prove anything and in fact was under no obligation to even present a case, make an argument, or call a single witness to the stand. And on rare occasions defense lawyers didn't — choosing to gamble their client's freedom on the argument that the government simply hadn't done its job. But insanity cases were different. The law in Florida presumed that every man was sane when he committed a criminal act. As such, a plea of insanity was an affirmative defense. That shifted the burden of raising the defense of insanity and then proving it by "clear and convincing evidence." So while the State still had to prove that a murder had been committed and that the defendant was the one who'd committed it, the defendant then had to prove that he wasn't responsible because he had been legally insane at the time of the crime. Then the burden fell back on the State to prove that he had been sane. It was a confusing game of legal semantics, but the end result was that Dr. Barakat and Co. would not actually get put on the stand until the defense directly placed the defendant's sanity in issue with its own psychiatrists. The trial was far from over.

"All right, then, Mel," said Farley after he'd dismissed the jury for the weekend. "Who's on for Monday, and what's your time frame?"

"I've got several defense witnesses, Judge," Mel replied carefully.

Farley looked over at the defense table.

"Does your client plan on testifying?" he asked skeptically.

Mel shrugged. There was no way he was going to give away his hand in front of opposing counsel and a courtroom still filled with cameras, but based on the odd behavior of his client, it wasn't just Farley who was obviously doubting whether Marquette would take the stand. Through five days of graphic testimony, Marquette had sat expressionless, tapping his foot under the table and staring out into space, rolling his tongue about the inside of his mouth.

"I want to go to closing by next Friday. Is that going to happen?"

"I know you have a schedule, Judge —" began Mel.

"No. I have a cruise," replied Farley, cutting him off as he climbed off the bench. "It's the thirtieth anniversary of my wife putting up with me. It cost too much, and we're in the no-more-refunds zone. I have no intention of missing it," he said flatly as he walked through the door that Jefferson held open for him. The door closed with a thud.

"I've been thinking," Rick said in a low voice as he and Julia packed up their files and the courtroom emptied out. "I want you to handle Christian when we put him on." He stopped what he was doing, leaned back against the table, and looked at her. "You did well at the competency hearing. You handled your witnesses, and your opening blew everyone away."

She just stared at her briefcase.

"You've really stepped up to the plate, Julia. I know you had some reservations at times, but you've been a team player. I thought I should tell you that. I think there are a lot of things I should tell you. . . ." A long moment passed, and she still said nothing. "I know it's been . . . well, difficult between us, but you've handled it. It hasn't been easy. I know it hasn't been on me, at least," he said with a sad smile when he finally found her eyes.

She wondered just what Rick meant by that, considering he still didn't know she knew about Karyn. Julia certainly wouldn't put it past him to work the two of them if he could. She thought of the intimate moments in his apartment, in his bed — his hands on her body — and she wanted to cringe.

"From a strategic standpoint, I think the jury needs to see you take on this issue," he continued. "We've made our case, and the only problem I see is going to be how believable Marquette's shrinks are. A couple of liberals, unfortunately, got through in jury selection. So I'll do the cross of Koletis and Hayes, but I think it's a good idea for the jury to see you dismantle the defense with our own psychiatrist. I might have you handle Pat Hindlin, too, so be prepared. It's getting your face in front of that jury again before we close that I want. That's one of the reasons I asked you to second-seat in the first place — your demeanor with them. Your presence. You have a knack, no doubt. A talent. The jury can identify with you, and through you with our victims."

One of the reasons. The other was over now.

"Are you okay with this?" he asked when she didn't reply. He rubbed her arm gently.

"Yes," she heard herself say. "I'll do it."

"Let's get together this weekend and go over your questions, hmmm?" he said as he closed up his briefcase. "We'll have dinner, maybe. I'll call you." He started down the aisle. Outside in the hall, a mob of reporters still lingered, hoping for a sound bite to go with the six o'clock news. "Because they like you," he called out, his hand on the doors. "The jury really likes you. And more importantly, they trust you. That I can definitely tell."

Then he pushed open the doors and

greeted the waiting crowd with a confident smile.

CHAPTER 80

When Julia finally got back to her office there were three new cases on her desk, a dozen phone messages on her voice mail, and thirty-two e-mails in her inbox. She might be a prosecutor in the murder trial of the century, but in the pits of the SAO that didn't mean shit. The chief felony assistants who handed out the new cases didn't care that she already had 102 of them, and Karyn, of course, didn't want to know how Julia prepped her calendar as long as it was prepped.

She felt so overloaded, so out of touch with everything and everyone. This double life that she'd been leading was no doubt catching up to her. The pressure was all around, pushing her from every direction, and no matter how hard she tried to get it all done, no matter how much she withdrew, she couldn't seem to distance herself from it.

Rick. Karyn. Charley Rifkin. Judge Farley. There was no one in the office to trust anymore. Even her detractors wore smiles. And there were Aunt Nora and Uncle Jimmy. God, how she missed them. She missed having a family, even if it was a dysfunctional mess. But she, like Andrew, was an outcast now. A misfit. A Charley-in-the-box.

She put her head in her hands and rubbed her temples. This case. The hidden political agendas, the leaks to the media, the press-op photos. The underhandedness of it all. She'd always thought that prosecutors were above all that. That they sought justice, not just convictions. She'd heard every sleazy-lawyer joke in the book, but they were never about prosecutors. That was what had taken her by surprise the most. Maybe she should've seen Rick and Karyn coming. Or Rick and any other woman, for that matter. Maybe that was her mistake. But she never would've thought he'd manipulate a case for his own political benefit.

It must be like this for other prosecutors who tried high-profile cases, she told herself, like Marcia Clark or Linda Fairstein. Launched out of obscurity, everyone watched your every move, hairdo, outfit. You were constantly in the spotlight, yet you had never asked to be a celebrity. The pressure-cooker feeling was to be expected. She just had to get a grip, that was all. It would all be over soon enough.

It was almost eight by the time she cleared her desk. Once again the building was empty except for her. She checked out the window for signs of Karyn's or Rick's cars because the last thing she needed was to catch an elevator down with the two of them.

Her eyes caught on the Dade County Jail. While South Beach was just getting the party started when nighttime descended, this part of the city definitely emptied at the stroke of five. Especially on a Friday. Law firms, medical offices, the courthouse, the PD's office, the SAO — all lifeless till Monday morning. That was when you couldn't find a parking spot if your appointment depended on it. All except for DCJ. Like at a Motel 6, the warden always left the lights on for you. She stared at the ninth floor. The Crazy Floor. She could almost hear their shrieks. . . .

The screamers.

The phone rang, pulling her out of her thoughts. The only people who'd call her this late at the office on a Friday were Lat, Rick, or a reporter trying to hunt down a quotation for tomorrow's headlines. Considering she didn't want to talk to two out of the three, the odds were already against her when she picked up the phone.

"State Attorney's. Vacanti," she answered, pulling her car keys out of her purse.

There was silence.

"Hello? Can I help you?" she tried.

"Julia Vacanti?"

It was a male voice. Deep and scratchy, yet muffled. There was something familiar about it. Julia tried to place where she'd heard it before. Maybe it was that reporter from the *Post* who'd called yesterday.

"Yes?" she asked.

"Julia Cirto Vacanti?" he repeated. "The prosecutor?"

"Yes? This is she." A strange, uncomfortable feeling washed over her as she listened to his labored breathing. "Can I help you with something, sir?"

"It wasn't him," he whispered. "Are you listening now, Ms. Prosecutor? Do I have your attention now? He didn't do it."

Then he laughed, and the line went dead.

CHAPTER 81

Maybe it was a prank.

Julia pushed open the glass doors of the SAO and hurried across the deserted parking lot to her car. She threw her file box and purse into the backseat, climbed in behind the wheel, and locked the doors, breathless. She looked around her. Hers was the only car left in the lot.

Maybe it was a reporter. Or a protester. That had to be it. A right-to-lifer messing with her. Reporters had found the direct line to her office and had been calling her for weeks. They were like cockroaches, waiting for her everywhere. Outside her office. Outside her apartment. On the beach when she jogged, she'd spotted a few. And now the protesters who yelled nasty things at her on her way into court had obviously found her, too. They would say anything, she knew. Anything to draw attention to their cause. Anything to get rid of the death penalty.

She sped out of the lot and onto the ramp for SR836 and I-95. That had to be it. But why would they call her and not Rick? He was the lead. Maybe they had, and he'd dismissed it. Or maybe he didn't really care if someone else had done it as long as David Marquette paid for the crime and he became State Attorney. She thought back to when Marquette had said those three words to her at his competency hearing: *I saved them.* The only words he'd ever said in court, and they had been said to her. It was almost as if he knew what she was thinking. It was as if he knew about her past. About Andrew.

And how did they know she was still in her office tonight? Court had gotten out hours ago. Was someone watching her car? Her office window? Was someone watching her right now? Ready to jump out of the bushes with his creepy breathing and anti-death-penalty poster and scare her half to death when she opened the car door at the curb?

She thought of something funny Andrew had said to her once at Kirby. *Just because you're paranoid doesn't mean someone's not following you.* She was definitely paranoid now, but with good reason. And she was taking no chances. So she got off a couple of exits before Stirling and took the back roads home, careful to keep checking her rearview mirror to make sure she wasn't being followed. She didn't park in her spot, instead parking in the complex across the street and ducking through the walkways of the buildings adjacent to her own.

She wanted to call Lat. She wanted to tell him what had happened, what she'd found out. What the protesters knew now. She wanted him to come check her apartment for her. She wanted to hear his voice tell her it would be okay. But she couldn't. He'd made it clear what their relationship was, and she'd have to accept that.

She locked her apartment door, turned off all the lights, and closed the blinds in every room. *It was a protester,* she told herself as she locked her bedroom door and slumped down on the floor in the dark with her back against it, both the cordless phone and her cell phone between her legs. *That was all it was.*

There was no reason to be afraid.

CHAPTER 82

"I'm sorry, Ms. Cirto, but he won't come to the phone. He's being uncooperative."

Julia sat on the couch in her living room, peeking out through the blind at the parking lot below. A few bikini-clad teenagers ambled through the gate that led to the complex pool. A man with a Packers cap worked the bushes with a hedger. She nibbled on a fingernail. "Did you tell him it's me, though?" She cleared her throat. "It's Ju-Ju?"

"I did, but again, he doesn't want to come to the phone," the nurse replied. "To be honest with you, he's been very difficult, and I'm just not going to deal with difficult today. You can try back again tomorrow between the call-in hours ten and twelve and I'll make another go at it, but today's not gonna happen."

"He's upset because of Rockland," Julia insisted, "because he's moving to Rockland next Saturday."

There was silence on the other end.

"That's probably it," she continued. "It's gotta be Rockland. He's probably really nervous. Has he been humming a lot?"

The nurse sighed. "I don't know why any of them get upset in here, Ms. Cirto. It's a pretty nice life, considering. And, no offense, but I really don't care, to be honest, if their feelings are hurt or they're a little anxious. This is a state criminal forensic hospital. I just do my job, and I get paid. But I don't get paid to figure out why one of them doesn't feel up to taking a phone call, so with all due respect, I will tell him you called —"

"And that I'll definitely be there next Saturday," Julia quickly added.

"And that you'll be here Saturday."

"And that I'm sorry. I couldn't help it. I couldn't come up." She peered out the slats once again. The teenagers were gone, but the man with the Packers hat was still there. The clippers were gone, and he stared at her window. She closed the slats and sat back on the couch. "I can't leave here right now."

"I'll give him the message."

"And that —" Julia started to say, but the nurse had already hung up.

CHAPTER 83

"It's as if a cataclysmic earthquake has happened inside David's head."

The Monday-morning crowd stayed quiet as Dr. Al Koletis took a long sip of water and looked up from the notes. His reading glasses sat precariously perched on the tip of his long, hooked nose. "That's how I explain schizophrenia to the parents or loved ones of patients I've diagnosed, Mr. Levenson," he continued. "In the simplest terms I know how. Here we have a normal person. Everything is fine. He or she has friends, a job; they've developed normal, loving relationships. They're functioning, thriving, well-adjusted members of society, oftentimes headed for a bright future, perhaps preparing to leave for college, as the disease tends to historically strike young men in their late teens, women a few years after that. But far below the surface, undetectable seismic changes deep within the brain's structure have already begun. These changes then cause — let's call it a preexisting fault line — a genetic weakness or genetic predisposition, perhaps, far below that surface to collapse and catastrophically fail. Suddenly and seemingly without warning. Like an earthquake.

"Now, sometimes earthquakes can just jolt you out of bed or knock a few paintings off the walls. But other times they can have a far greater effect. They can change the integrity of the structure so that it might appear fine at first glance, but one look inside the walls and you'll see how fragile they are, how they can fail at a moment's notice. And sometimes an earthquake of a great enough magnitude can change the entire landscape, leveling mountains and relocating seas.

"That's the disease of schizophrenia. The period of this gradual buildup of stress factors and seismic changes in the brain is called the prodromal stage. Looking back on that stage, you might be able to see subtle early-warning signs that something was not right. Depression. Withdrawal. Changes in sleep patterns. The earthquake itself is acute psychosis — when reality has collapsed and catastrophically failed. That is when the hallucinations and paranoia begin.

And the aftermath is called, appropriately enough, the recovery period.

"Like an earthquake, the disease strikes every person differently. Some come through psychosis and do fine on medication. Some even without. The very lucky few are fortunate enough to never experience another psychotic episode. But then there are the ones who live on the fault line and are in constant danger of aftershocks and more quakes. These are the victims of the disease who might look fine on the surface — with two arms and two legs and a college degree — and yet they can't live by themselves. Their foundation is unstable, and their walls are cracked. And, finally, there are those whose whole landscape has changed. They are the ones who go into a hospital and don't really ever come out. They cannot function in society. They are almost a completely different person because of their illness.

"David was living on a fault line," he continued, taking off his glasses and thoughtfully chewing on the tip. "He had experienced a psychotic break at the age of nineteen. It was a matter of time before he had another, especially since he was not taking preventive medication. It's perhaps a miracle that he did as well as he did until that point. But outside stress factors — like the distant forces that work to destabilize the earth in and around a fault zone — such as, perhaps, his new baby and pressures at work and within his marriage, caused that fault line to break once again. This time with truly catastrophic results."

"You've testified that David is a paranoid schizophrenic," Mel began. "You and Dr. Hayes have both testified that on the night of October eighth, David was psychotic, hearing voices and experiencing visual hallucinations that told him his family was possessed by demonic spirits —"

"Objection!" Rick yelled. "Is there a question in there somewhere? Or is counsel making his closing argument?"

"Don't be picky, Mr. Bellido. I gave you leeway, too," cautioned Farley. "Move this along into a question please, Mr. Levenson. *Tempus fugit.*"

Mel shrugged. "Due to this mental infirmity, this disease of schizophrenia, did David know his actions were wrong? Was he able to distinguish right from wrong at the time the crimes were committed?"

Mel was careful not to label his own client a killer or a murderer. It was a delicate dance with words. He needed to match the language of the law that Farley would instruct the jury on before they headed in for deliberations without further alienating them from his client. He also, obviously, wanted to leave his options open for a second argument, if necessary.

"Objection. Leading."

Farley shot Rick another dark look.

Dr. Koletis didn't wait for a ruling. "In my opinion, David was indeed legally insane the night his family was killed. He was acutely psychotic and delusional. He still cannot and will not discuss his actions in detail, other than to say he saved his family, because he fears reprisals. From whom he refuses to say, but I suspect it is the demon spirits he rid his family of. He has buried those intimate facts because they are too difficult and frightening for him to deal with, given his fragile state of mind. But he saw fangs on his three-year-old, and his daughter's eyes glowed yellow. His baby daughter sprouted a horn. He believed these spirits were hypnotizing him with subliminal messages broadcast over the radio. These visual hallucinations were corroborated by audio hallucinations that continued to tell David his family was not human. That continued to tell David that his own life was in danger, and that if he, too, became consumed by the devil, there would be no one left who could save his family from damnation. Don't you see?" he asked, looking over at the jury, demanding their attention. "He didn't kill his family, because he knew they were already dead. What he did was save their souls from eternal damnation by ridding their bodies of the demonic spirit that had murdered them. It was all part of the paranoid delusion he was suffering from." Only one juror nodded. The others looked away. Dr. Koletis turned back to Mel. "To answer your question — no, he did not know that what he was doing was wrong."

"And now?" asked Mel.

Dr. Koletis paused and looked over at the defense table, where David Marquette still stared blankly out in front of him, rolling his tongue and tapping his foot.

"Sadly enough," he finished, "in his mind he still thinks he's done nothing wrong."

CHAPTER 84

The man with the stringy long hair and gladiator sandals sat in the rain on the courthouse steps, dressed in a straitjacket and shorts. Taped to his chest was a sign that read, "Don't Medicate Me Just to Kill Me." The rain had gotten the sign wet, and the words had started to run.

Obscured from view by her oversized umbrella, Julia hustled into the courthouse past him and the large, strange crowd of protesters, reporters, and trial watchers. The garage had been closed off, so she had no choice but to use the main entrance. She moved along with the restless herd of criminals, witnesses, cops, and attorneys through the lobby metal detectors and onto the escalator. At ten minutes to nine, waiting for a spot on an elevator might take hours. She could feel people pressed up against her, touching her with their wet clothes and umbrellas, breathing on her.

She buried her face in the lapel of her coat and tried not to breathe it all in.

"Hey there," a voice whispered in her ear. "Where've you been hiding?" She jumped in her skin and turned around to see Lat, dressed in slacks and a sports jacket dotted with raindrops, standing one step below her.

Mel had invoked the rule of sequestration when the jury had been sworn in. Better known simply as "the Rule," it excluded all prospective witnesses from the courtroom during trial so their testimony wouldn't be influenced by listening to someone else tell a different version of the facts. Lat had testified last week, but since he might be called back in rebuttal, he was still barred. Julia hadn't seen him in over a week.

"I stopped by your apartment Saturday," he began. "But you weren't in. I thought maybe you'd want to take a Sunday-afternoon spin with an outlaw." His smile melted into a concerned frown. "Are you okay?" he asked in a low voice, gently grabbing her elbow as they stepped off the escalator and into utter bedlam.

She nodded but pulled away, disappearing quickly into the sea of cameras and strangers that waited outside 4-10. A sea held back by corrections officers, cops, and metal stanchions. With her head down and eyes averted, she made her way through the crowd and onto the line behind those lucky enough to have won a seat in the courtroom lottery. A few signs bobbed up and down in the hallway, as they did in front of the courthouse. Some had been handmade by angry people with Magic Markers and time on their hands; others had been supplied and waved by volunteers from the National Mental Health Association (NMHA), the National Alliance for the Mentally Ill (NAMI), Human Rights Watch, Amnesty International, and the ACLU. Someone stuck a sign that read, "The Death Penalty IS Murder!" in her face. "You know, you'll be going to hell, too!" its holder sneered, so close Julia could feel the spray of his spittle on her skin.

"Back off!" she heard Lat shout. "Take your shit outside. Yo, Lewis! Nobody should be touching her!"

"Freedom of speech! I can say what I want! Does it make you feel good to put an insane man to death, lady? Does it make you feel important?" was the last thing she heard as the courtroom doors closed behind her.

Until this past Monday, the focus of the trial had remained on the murders and the cold, calculated brutality with which they had been executed. Jennifer and David's marriage had been microscopically examined, David's multiple affairs exposed, his financial motives speculated upon. Stroke by careful stroke, the portrait had been painted of David Marquette as a cunning, treacherous psychopath. A secretive man who wore two very different faces — one for the world of doctors, patients, and colleagues and a very different one at home behind closed doors.

But Mel Levenson had changed that focus. At least temporarily. For the past three days the defense had put on its case. Psychiatrists Al Koletis and Margaret Hayes had told the jury about David's bizarre delusions, about the world he'd supposedly lived in since he was a teenager — the voices he heard and the twisted faces he saw. Witnesses and doctors had dissected his childhood, his family life, his marriage, and his deceased schizophrenic twin with an eye on the subtle signs of mental illness that had been missed or willfully ignored. Now the topic du jour around water coolers everywhere was insanity. What it meant legally. What it was medically. Legal commentators now debated the morality and constitutionality of medicating the mentally ill so that they could stand trial or be executed, while famous criminal cases of those who'd pled insanity were discussed ad nauseam during prime time as the video reels of their trials ran over and over again. Most of those defendants, the commentators noted, had failed miserably. Berkowitz. Dahmer. Bundy. Sirhan Sirhan. Henry Lee Lucas. Charles Manson. John Wayne Gacy. Andrea Yates. Spitting out statistics alongside mug shots, analysts pointed out that insanity was offered as a defense in less than 1 percent of all criminal proceedings and was actually successful in only a quarter of those cases where it was pled.

This morning it was Julia's turn with the state psychiatrists as the State began rebuttal. It had taken all her energy every day to come back to the circus. After Friday night's bizarre phone call she'd spent the weekend holed up in her apartment, afraid to venture out even to get the paper for fear that a reporter might pop out of the bushes, snap her picture, and put it on the front page. Then the protesters might be able to find out where she lived. The invisible pressure in her head made it feel as if it were about to explode, and she willed herself not to turn around and look at the strange faces filling the courtroom seats behind her. She knew he could be out there right now, the protester. In the rain. In the hallway. In the courtroom. Right behind her with his labored breathing and creepy laugh, a Packers hat stuffed in his pocket.

The door to the back hallway opened, and in walked her defendant, flanked by corrections officers. After the ME had testified, the jail had gotten so many death threats that, in addition to the standard metal accessories, he now sported an armed entourage and wore a bulletproof vest whenever he set foot out of his holding cell lest some nut try to take him out.

That was so ironic it was funny, Julia thought as Farley took the bench in his usual huff and Jefferson commanded everyone to rise. The State would risk the lives of five other men just to keep this one alive long enough so it could kill him itself. Even Jay Leno had made a joke of it last night on *The Tonight Show.*

What a laugh.

CHAPTER 85

"State?" Judge Farley gestured to the witness stand, where Ivonne had just sworn in Christian Barakat. The doctor looked dapper and distinguished in a tailored charcoal suit and silk tie. The female jurors sat attentively in their seats.

The courtroom sat in silence for maybe thirty seconds, which was thirty seconds too long for Farley. He sat up in his chair and leaned into the bench. "Hello? Ms. Vacanti, do you want to actually question this witness, or are we just supposed to look at him all day?"

Julia stared at the notes in front of her. Her well-rehearsed lines. She bit the inside of her lip and slowly rose, walking over to the podium without them. She felt the jurors' eyes on her, watching her every move. One even smiled at her.

The jury likes you. They trust you.

"Good morning, Doctor. Please state your

name and occupation for the record."

"Christian Barakat. I'm a board-certified forensic psychiatrist in private practice here in Miami. I have an office over on Brickell in downtown."

"How long have you been practicing psychiatry?"

"Sixteen years."

"Please tell the court about your professional qualifications and experience."

Barakat was a seasoned witness. He'd testified in dozens of high-profile cases, and he knew exactly what information he needed to get out on the stand to establish himself as an expert. His impressive list of professional accomplishments alone, including an undergraduate degree from Yale, an MD from Johns Hopkins Medical School, and a prestigious fellowship in forensic psychiatry at the University of Miami, took almost ten minutes to rattle off.

"Have you had an opportunity to examine the defendant in this case, David Marquette?" she asked.

"I have."

"When was that and under what circumstances?"

"I interviewed Dr. David Marquette on two separate occasions," Barakat replied, taking out his notes and leafing through them. "The first time was December fif-teenth, 2006, pursuant to a court order to determine the defendant's competency to stand trial. I then examined him again on January twenty-fourth and twenty-fifth to determine whether he met the legal defini-tion of insanity when he murdered his wife and three children."

"Objection!" Mel said, rising. "The wit-ness is drawing a legal conclusion."

"Sustained," said Farley. "Let's let the jury decide if the defendant's a murderer, okay?"

Julia looked over at David Marquette, small and unsure, staring vacantly out from his spot at the defense table, oblivious yet again that people were labeling him a murderer. It was as if he were in his own little world, a million miles away from the courtroom.

"This case. Remember my words, Julia. It can only bring . . . despair."

"It wasn't him. Are you listening now, Ms. Prosecutor?"

"I saved them, Ju-Ju. I saved them. I had to."

She shook the rambling thoughts out of her head and delivered another well-rehearsed line. "Please tell the court about your most recent evaluation of the defen-dant this past January."

What was he thinking in that world? Was he frightened? Did he really know that he was facing death? Did he understand yet that he had done something horribly wrong? Would he be terrified when reality finally came knocking on his door, demanding entry, like Andy said might happen? Would he be able to live with himself when he discovered the truth?

"It's like you lived this whole other life, Ju-Ju, and then someone pulls the curtain back and says, 'Ha! No you didn't! This is your life!' But you don't even recognize it. And there you are, left with what you've done, and it doesn't even make sense. That's when you realize you'd be better off if you'd just stayed crazy. Because you hate yourself, too. Just like everybody else."

She suddenly saw Andrew in that chair. Fifteen years ago, in a courtroom filled with photographers and prosecutors and judges pointing at him. Condemning him. A frightened boy whose mind was trapped in a very different, terrifying world, all alone in a courtroom full of people who hated him. A courtroom full of strangers who didn't understand, who didn't want to understand. At least David still had his parents sitting in the row behind him. Family that had stuck by his side. Family that recognized what this disease could do. She tried in vain to blink back the tears. There had been no one sitting there for Andrew.

"State? Hello? Is there another question you want to ask the nice doctor, or are we done here?" asked Farley, irritated.

She looked around the courtroom. All eyes were on her. Waiting for her next question. She had no idea what Barakat had just said. Or how long he'd been talking. Or how long the court had been waiting on her. But it didn't matter anymore.

She took a deep breath. "Doctor, psychiatry isn't an exact science, is it?"

Barakat looked surprised by the question. "No, it's not," he answered.

"I mean, there's no test, no physical test, that can determine if someone is actually suffering from a mental illness, is there?" she asked. "Like there is for cancer or heart disease?"

"No, there's no blood test or X-ray or MRI used to diagnose mental illness, if that's what you're asking. By its very name mental illness refers to a sickness in the mind, Ms. Vacanti. Disturbances in one's thought processes or emotions that are not measurable in a blood or urine sample."

"So how is mental illness diagnosed, Doctor? More particularly, how is schizophrenia diagnosed?"

"By listening to the patient's complaints, observing their symptoms and their behavior."

"Basically by listening to what a patient tells you is happening inside their head?"

"Basically, yes."

She could feel Rick trying to catch her attention from behind her at the State's table, but she ignored him. "Schizophrenia presents itself with different symptoms in different patients, right, Dr. Barakat? I mean, no two people will ever experience the same exact paranoid delusion?"

"That is correct."

"And no two people will experience the disease in the same way, right? For instance, some might have visual hallucinations, others might hear voices, and others might even smell weird smells or have other sensory distortions. Some might withdraw into catatonia. Some might demonstrate a combination of these symptoms. Correct?"

Barakat looked over at Rick. These were leading questions with the confrontational undertone of a cross-examination. Technically, Mel could object because leading questions were not allowed on direct, but he certainly wasn't going to do that. The courtroom sat in tense, excited silence. "Yes.

It can be a difficult disease to correctly diagnose and treat, but there are hallmark symptoms that a psychiatrist looks for."

"Did David Marquette have any of those hallmark symptoms?"

"Yes," Barakat replied slowly. "Again, he said he did. He claimed to be hearing voices and having visual hallucinations as part of the paranoid delusion that his family was possessed."

"But you don't believe he's telling the truth about his experiences?"

"That is correct. I believe he is malingering. As I testified before, I believe he's manufacturing the symptoms of schizophrenia to avoid criminal responsibility."

"But his case, this was a tough call for you, wasn't it?" she asked.

Dr. Barakat stared at her for a long moment, but Julia didn't even blink. He'd suddenly figured out what she was doing and where she was going. "Pardon me?"

"Even though the defendant presented with all of the hallmark symptoms of schizophrenia, symptoms that you have previously admitted are not readily faked or manufactured by most malingerers — blunted affect, flattening of emotions, catatonia, severe withdrawal — in the end it was simply your gut that told you he must be malingering, correct?"

There was no way to escape his own words, and he knew it. Dr. Barakat shifted in his chair. "Yes, sometimes as a psychiatrist I must rely on my instincts."

"And if those instincts are wrong?"

"I don't believe they are."

"You don't believe they are, but there's no medical test to confirm that, now, is there? Let me ask you, Doctor, if David Marquette is a paranoid schizophrenic, if he did suffer the persecutory delusion exactly as he claims to have suffered it, if he did actually believe his family was already dead when he stabbed them and bludgeoned them, if your gut instinct was wrong, would he be criminally responsible for the murders of his wife and children?"

"Objection!" Rick finally sprang to his feet.

Farley looked at him, his brow furrowed. "You can't object to your own witness, Mr. Bellido. This is direct examination." He raised his eyebrows and with the hint of a smile added, "Maybe you forgot, but Ms. Vacanti is your co-counsel. She's on your side."

Julia pressed on. "Yes or no, Dr. Barakat? If David Marquette suffered this delusion, if it was all real in his head, would you say he was insane under the definition of Florida law?"

Barakat looked at Rick and then over at the judge, as if he didn't want to say what Julia was about to make him say.

Farley shrugged his shoulders. "Answer the question, please."

Barakat sighed. "Yes. I would have to say that if Dr. Marquette did in fact act under the delusion he reported, he would have been unable to discern right from wrong at the time. He would be considered legally insane."

A frenzied murmur swelled in the crowd, threatening to explode. Julia finally looked over at Rick and met his icy stare with one of her own.

"I have nothing further," she said flatly.

CHAPTER 86

She held up her hand before her and moved quickly past the press that tried to block her exit. Their lights blinded her; their questions made her head spin. She just wanted her fifteen minutes of fame to finally be over.

"Do you believe that Dr. Marquette's being wrongly prosecuted?"

"Is David insane? Do you believe he really is insane?"

"Is this a political persecution?"

"Murderer!" someone shouted out, but Julia didn't turn to see who it was. "He's a murderer! A butcher! You're the one responsible! You're letting him get away with murder!"

"How could you do this?" another cackled. "He's the devil!"

"Order! I want order in this court!" Farley bellowed.

She pushed open the courtroom doors

and hurried into the hallway. The doors slammed shut behind her with a dull thud, silencing the questions and the shouts, but only for a moment. Her eyes darted about for a quick escape, but the hallway suddenly looked unfamiliar. Like in Wonderland, the many doors that sprouted off were all the same now, and she couldn't remember which one led to where.

Liaison had moved the morning crowd outside, but people still milled about in front of the courtrooms, rocking baby strollers and waiting for their lawyers on graffiti-laden benches. They eyed her strangely as she ran to the escalator on shaking legs. At the far end of the hall she spotted a cameraman who threw down his coffee and reached for his camera, quickly figuring out that he must've missed something.

She felt physically ill. She would probably lose her job today. No, she would definitely lose her job. That was a given. She probably would never get another job as a lawyer in this city — Rick and Karyn and Charley Rifkin would make sure of that. She ran her hands through her hair. Or any other city, for that matter.

Even with the impending crash and burn of her career, it was a sense of calm that settled her when she reached the escalator.

"I didn't raise you to go along with the crowd," her mother had said to her once after she'd skipped class in junior high. "I raised you to do what's right. Listen to the voice inside your head and you'll know just what that is." Julia closed her eyes. Even if a jury chose to ignore all that they'd just heard, she'd done what she knew was right today.

"Julia! Wait up!"

She heard Lat call out her name, and she moved quicker, pushing past people down the escalator. She couldn't look at anyone right now. She couldn't face their questions or their disappointment. Especially his. She got off on 2 to grab an elevator down to the basement and head off the press, who she knew had their satellite trucks waiting outside. They were probably looking for her right now as news spread about what she'd just done.

The cell phone in her purse rang. She reached down and grabbed it with trembling hands. Maybe it was Rick, calling her to fire her himself before she even cleared the building. Or Lat looking to see where she'd gone. Or Friday night's protester calling to comment on what a fine job she'd just done. Or the hecklers to call her a murderer. But it was a 212 exchange.

"Hello?" she whispered as she waited with the crowd, looking over her shoulder.

"Ms. Vacanti? It's Mary Zlocki at Kirby Forensic."

"Mary, I'm just getting out of court." She moved onto the elevator and hit the B button.

"It's about your brother," Mary continued.

"I'm coming up on Saturday for his transfer." The line grew thick with static as a bunch of people got off on 1. Julia pressed herself up against the far side of the car, out of the direct line of sight of anyone looking for her in the lobby. "I'm in an elevator, Mary. I may lose you."

The people around her shot her an annoyed look as the doors closed again. Everyone had a cell phone nowadays, but no one seemed to like it when you actually used yours in public.

"I need to speak with you about Andrew," Mary repeated. Then there was dead silence.

Shit. "Mary? Mary? Are you there?" The doors opened into the dark basement garage, and Julia stepped out alone. The car closed behind her. "Mary?"

"Ms. Vacanti?" said a voice over the line that Julia immediately recognized. She walked toward the ramp that led to 13th.

"This is Dr. Mynkus. I have to speak with you about Andrew."

"I just told Mary, Dr. Mynkus. I'll definitely be there Saturday. My plane comes —"

"Ms. Vacanti," the doctor interrupted in a soft, but firm voice, "Andrew is dead."

Julia dropped the phone, watching it shatter on the garage floor. And beneath the circus that was David Marquette's lynching, she began to scream.

CHAPTER 87

Julia sat on the same ripped vinyl bench staring at the same *People* magazine that she had almost three months before. She looked around the empty waiting room.

The guards in the booth wouldn't even look at her once they'd figured out why she was here. "That's Cirto's sister," had quickly spread among the Mental Health police like the panic of an infectious disease. And she was the leper.

The door next to the booth opened, and Dr. Mynkus appeared. Julia gathered her purse and rose to follow him back to his office, but he stepped into the reception area, letting the door close behind him this time. In his hand he held a large brown paper bag, like one that you might get at a supermarket.

"Ms. Vacanti," he began in the same cold, impersonal voice he'd used on the phone, "on behalf of the staff here at Kirby, allow me to say that we are sorry for your loss. This is a tragedy, and of course we'll be looking into all the circumstances surrounding your brother's death." He handed her the bag. "The nurses on Andrew's ward thought you'd like to have this. These were his belongings. Most of it's just clothing, but there are some drawings he was keeping as well as a journal he was writing, his wallet, and a high school graduation ring. All the things he came to Kirby with."

Dr. Mynkus's words were spoken so quickly and matter-of-factly that Julia knew he didn't mean them. He didn't mean any of them. For him, Andrew's death wasn't a tragedy, it was a statistic. An unfortunate statistic that had unfortunately happened on his watch. To him, Andy was a patient number, an inmate — a murderer — and his death was insignificant.

She took the bag, which felt too light to contain all of someone's worldly belongings, and stood there for a few moments, not sure what to do. Not ready to leave. Not ready for any of this to be real. "What happened?" she finally managed in a squeaky voice that sounded nothing like her own as she looked around the waiting room. She felt the guards watching them. She saw that one of them was laughing.

Dr. Mynkus didn't even blink. "Suicide. Like I told you on the phone yesterday."

She didn't look away. She didn't nod. She didn't shake her head. She just stood there with that profoundly blank look on her face until he finished.

"He hung himself. In the shower," he finally added. He looked at his watch. "Look, once again, I am sorry for your loss, but depression is a by-product — for lack of a better word — of schizophrenia. Your brother had come to terms with his illness and, eventually, the crimes that he'd committed. That was one of the reasons he was being transferred to Rockland. Sometimes, unfortunately, those realizations are just too overwhelming for a person to handle. Once the medication has worked its magic and the hallucinations, especially in paranoids, are brought under control — once reality's restored, many patients cannot deal emotionally with the crimes they committed when they were ill. And then with all the recent changes in Andrew's life . . ." His voice trailed off. He held up his hand in front of him. "I am not saying that's the reason Andrew took his own life. There was no note, and he told no one what he was going to do, so this is all, of course, conjecture."

There was nothing left to say. Dr. Mynkus had said it all without saying a thing. Julia had been the recent change in Andrew's life. The reminder from his past that he could not cope with.

"Now, if you'll excuse me," he started to say, but she didn't hear the rest. With all of Andrew's belongings clutched tightly in her hand, she'd already headed back out the security doors and into the cold New York City sunshine.

Chapter 88

She stood next to her rental car in the empty parking lot of the Barnes & Sorrentino Funeral Home, staring at the quaint-looking house with the yellow aluminum siding and white shutters and flowerpots on the front porch. Flanked by a gas station and a strip mall on a busy two-lane road, it had always looked out of place to her when she'd been growing up. It wasn't until her parents were waked there that she'd discovered it was actually a funeral home.

A light drizzle had begun to fall, but Julia stood where she was. It'd been fifteen long years since she'd been back to West Hempstead. The gas station had closed, and the businesses in the strip mall had turned over, but the beauty-supply store was still open down the block, and the Venus Café was still doing lunches across the street. Julia remembered how her dad would take the family to the Venus for pancakes after church some Sundays. The last time she'd been there was in between the afternoon and evening services for her parents, when Aunt Nora and Uncle Jimmy had taken her out for something to eat.

"Come on, Julia, honey. We can't be late getting back. People will be waiting."

"Can I help you?" asked the older woman with yellow-white hair who answered the door on the first ring.

"I'm . . . my name is Julia Cirto. I called yesterday about my brother, Andrew Cirto."

"Oh, yes," the woman said, opening the door. "I'm terribly sorry for your loss. I'm Evelyn. Won't you come in?"

Julia followed Evelyn through a dark, drab lobby with a regal red carpet and into a small office. "We received the body today from the Medical Examiner's Office in New York County," Evelyn began, pulling out a notepad. "We just needed to meet with you to . . . well, go over a few things. We have a catalog that you can look through, or —"

"I can't afford much, Evelyn," Julia interrupted with a shake of her head. She held up her hand. "There's no insurance. My brother didn't have any money. But I want him to have something nice. I can spend about five thousand dollars. So can you pick something nice for me?" She didn't want to see all the prettier caskets she could have picked or all the extras she could have had. Just take her money and get this done.

Evelyn nodded. "Of course. We'll handle everything, then, but I'm curious. You're from Florida, and your brother died in Manhattan. Why'd you choose Barnes & Sorrentino? Are there other relatives here in West Hempstead? Is there any church bulletin you'd like us to notify?"

Julia looked past Evelyn out the window. The rain was coming down hard now. She remembered trick-or-treating with Andy down McKinley Street, walking to Echo Park Pool. Memories rushed her from every direction. "I used to live in West Hempstead," she said absently. "My brother and I did. We grew up here, a few blocks away, on Maple. It was the only funeral home I knew." She looked at Evelyn. "My parents had their services here."

"Oh, my," answered Evelyn with a sad shake of her head. "When was that?"

"A long time ago."

"Well, we'll make sure everything is taken care of. Now, about the wake. When would you like to have the services, over one day or two?"

"No wake. There's just me," she replied quickly, her voice small. "There won't be

562

anyone else. No one here knows my brother anymore."

"Oh." Evelyn looked out the door down the hall. "I'm not so sure about that. We did get a flower delivery today. We put them in Chapel A."

"That's mine." She bit her lip. "Everyone deserves flowers, Evelyn."

"Okay," replied Evelyn slowly. She rose from her seat. "Let me show you the room for the service, then, in case you decide to have it here."

Julia nodded, and together they walked down the hall in silence. Outside the room designated "Chapel A," a black magnetic board encased in glass read, "Andrew J. Cirto" in small white letters.

"You don't have to look, Munch. The casket will be closed. You don't want to remember her that way," Uncle Jimmy whispered as they came upon the room.

"As you can see, it was a rather large delivery. We had to put them all in here," Evelyn started as she opened the double door.

Julia gasped. The room was filled with hundreds of white peonies.

CHAPTER 89

The patter of rain slapping against the stained-glass windows echoed through the empty church late Monday morning. The white peonies from the funeral home filled the simple marble altar. Julia sat by herself in the front pew, a few feet away from where Andrew's casket rested on a metal gurney, draped in a white cloth and the funeral spray of roses and calla lilies she'd ordered. She hoped Evelyn had selected a nice casket. She hoped it was lined with satin and maybe a soft pillow. She hoped he looked peaceful inside.

St. Thomas the Apostle Church had been their church growing up. Both she and Andy had gone to the elementary school next door. They'd both been baptized here, received First Holy Communion here, made their Confirmations on that altar. It was the church where her parents had had their funerals, and it was the last church that Julia had set foot in.

The door to the sacristy opened, and a young priest walked out, his heels softly clicking on the polished marble floor. He fashioned a long stole around his neck and kissed it, genuflecting in front of the altar. He looked down the center aisle. The two pallbearers from Barnes & Sorrentino stood in the far back by the doors that led to a side hall. "Do you want me to wait a little bit longer?" Father Tom asked softly.

Julia shook her head. She didn't look behind her. She didn't need to. "No, Father."

Aunt Nora had hung up on her last night the second she'd mentioned Andy's name. She hadn't even gotten to tell her he'd died. There was no one else to call. There would be no one else who even cared.

In her hand she held the folded-up drawing that Andrew had almost finished sketching. She'd found it in the paper bag of belongings from Kirby. It was a picture of her. Sitting at the table in the visitor's room, smiling, framed by stars and moons.

"Okay, then, I suppose this will be very intimate," Father Tom began gently. Instead of moving behind the pulpit, he stepped down off the altar and slid into the pew beside her. To her surprise, he took her hand in his. "We are here today to say good-bye to Andrew Cirto, a loving son and brother," he started in a mild voice that matched his smile and his touch. "A lost soul who will be missed by all who knew him, by his family, and most of all by his sister."

Julia didn't correct him. She bowed her head and listened while Father Tom held her hand and went on for ten minutes about all the things Julia had told him last night when they'd met at the rectory. About ice-skating with Andy in Hall's Pond Park and movie nights at the Elmont Theater with their mom. About how it was Andrew who had always held her head over the toilet when she threw up and who'd shared his sandwich at school when she'd forgotten hers — even though that meant being made fun of by the older kids. About how he'd shoved the first boy who'd said something nasty to her. About how he would wait for her when she missed the bus at school so they could walk home together. About what a great listener and great friend he'd been. All about the gentle, misunderstood man with the sheepish grin of a boy whom she'd just come to know again after too long an absence. She was relieved that Father Tom never once mentioned that Andrew had been a murderer. Or a crazy. Or sick.

"Let us now pray," Father Tom said, and Julia got down on her knees and prayed hard to a God she thought was cruel sometimes. A God she had long ago stopped believing in. A God who now beckoned her back with soft whispers. She closed her eyes and saw Andrew's face as she wanted to always remember it, before the sickness had sucked the life out of him. Swinging a baseball bat with a smile at sixteen. The tears slipped out of her eyes as Father Tom led an empty church in prayer.

"Hail Mary, full of Grace," he began softly. "The Lord is with thee. Blessed art thou amongst women, and blessed is the fruit of thy womb, Jesus."

"Holy Mary, Mother of God, pray for us sinners," Julia said, joining him. "Now and at the hour of our death." She cast her eyes up to the crucifix suspended above the altar. She saw Jesus smile down at her. He was whispering the words along with her.

"Amen," she whispered back.

CHAPTER 90

A "Home Sweet Home" mat greeted visitors outside her front door; a wreath of dried flowers blocked the peephole. He'd have to talk to her about that. It wasn't safe. Lat rang the bell again and waited, slapping his palm impatiently against the door.

"Julia," he said in a quiet voice, "it's me, Lat. Come on, I know you're home."

Still no answer. Then he started to knock. Hard. Dried petals fluttered to the ground. "I saw your car across the street, so I know you're in. I need to talk to you. Come on, open up."

Still nothing. He walked back down the stairs to see the window that faced the parking lot. He didn't see any lights on whatsoever. That was when Lat started to worry. He'd checked Jet Blue and knew she'd come back this afternoon. Her car was parked across the street in another complex's lot, but she wasn't answering her phone, and she wasn't answering her door. She'd been acting so strange lately, and after what he'd found out this past week, he knew anything was possible. Even the worst anything.

To hell with her neighbors. He banged on the door with his fist. "Julia!" He hoped his voice sounded steady, devoid of the raw fear that gripped his belly. "I'm gonna take the goddamn door if you —" he started, but the knob suddenly twisted in his hand.

She stood in the foyer of her pitch-black apartment. Moonlight filtered in through the living room windows, backlighting her petite frame. He couldn't make out the features of her face. "You scared me," he said.

She said nothing, and she didn't move.

He ignored her body language and moved past her into the dark apartment, looking around the living room. He could make out the shadows of clothes and boxes that were strewn everywhere. "Are you okay?" he asked, reaching out to touch her shoulder.

She shrank away. "You checked up on me."

God, he wished he could see her eyes. Did she hate him? Maybe he shouldn't have sent the flowers. . . . "Yes. I checked up on you," he said finally, because there was nothing else he could say. He looked around the hall for a light switch. "Why are you sitting in the dark? Where are the lights in this place? 'Cause we have to talk —"

"I don't want the lights on, and I don't want to talk. I want you to go. That's what I want."

"Julia, I'm sorry about your brother. I'm really sorry. I wish you'd told me —"

"Told you what?"

"Told me about him."

"I don't know exactly what you know, Lat, so I don't know what it is you wish I'd told you. That my brother was a murderer, but he couldn't help himself? That he was just sick, and inside he was really a great person who was misunderstood by everyone, including me?" She turned her head away, crying.

"I want to see you, Julia. Where the hell are the lights?" That feeling of panic was grabbing at his throat once again.

"No, just go, please," she pleaded.

He grasped her hand in his and moved her further into the apartment with him, closing the door behind him with his foot. He felt along the wall until his fingers finally found a switch. A living room light snapped on.

She had her head down, her long, dark hair draped over her face. Her whole body was shaking, and he knew she was trying to control the sobs. He didn't know what to say, but he knew bullshit wouldn't work.

"Listen, Julia, I've read the newspaper articles. I talked to the DA in New York. I know what happened to your mom and dad." He stopped himself, wondering how far he should go. He wasn't very good at these things. He sucked at funerals and awkward moments. "Dr. Mynkus told me about Andy. And I'm sorry, Julia. I'm so sorry for your loss — your losses. You were acting really strange. Things weren't adding up, and then, well, you burned Dr. Barakat in court, and . . . you just took off in the middle of trial. And you haven't been back. It all makes sense now. Why didn't you tell me? Maybe I could've done something."

She turned again toward the wall, wiping her eyes with the palms of her hands. "What is it you wanted me to tell you? And when? Maybe over a ride on your Harley I could whisper in your ear that my brother's a schizophrenic? Oh, and by the way, he killed my family one night while I was at a sleep-over? What do you really think you would've done with that information, Lat? But that's not all. There's more to the story," she said, her voice rising. "See, it wasn't actually his fault because he was made that way."

"What're you talking about?"

"That wasn't in the court file? It must've been. 'Cause it turns out my dad, he was sick, too. And my grandfather, we think. We think, 'cause nobody wants to talk about these things. No one should've ever thought about having a kid. They knew what it was like. My mom knew, too. She watched him struggle with it. They both knew hell, right here on earth. My dad lived it." Julia struggled to find her breath. "They knew the odds — that we could get it. They knew they could give it to us. But they did it anyway. They still had us, Lat. It was the most selfish thing in the world they could've done — to bring us into it. But they did it anyway!"

He moved toward her. "Julia . . ."

But she held up her arms in front of her, keeping him away. "I don't want your pity, John. I don't want anyone's pity. No, no, no, no. No pity."

"Is that why you never said anything?" he demanded, his voice rising in frustration. "You're so damn strong you think you can handle all this alone? You're gonna prove yourself to everyone watching? That you can take on bad judges, and you can take on the criminals, and you can take on the system? This case — Marquette — it's so close . . . I can see that. It's unreasonable to think it wouldn't get to you. That it wouldn't get inside your head."

"I read the paper this morning on the plane," she said softly. "The *New York Post.* A little girl watched her mom's boyfriend kill her, then turn the gun on himself. Then this little girl, she sat in the house for two days next to the bodies before someone finally came and rang the bell and found her. And I felt bad, Lat. I felt pity for her — for what her life is now and for what it will be like for her growing up, so different from everyone else. But tomorrow there'll be another tragedy to read about. Maybe it will even be worse. And in a week or two I'll forget all about the little girl who was found with the dead bodies. Right? I mean, we all do. We forget about the tragedies that are bad enough to make the paper. There're too many of them, and they always seem to happen to someone else, don't they?

"But the headline-makers, you know, they grow up, Lat. They ride the bus next to you, they work in the next cubicle over. They're people whose tragedies define who they are to everyone who meets them. You're not the nice girl in algebra anymore — you're the girl whose parents were murdered by her crazy brother. You're not the secretary with the terrific laugh — you're the chick whose family died in a car crash. And I'm . . . I'm just so tired of being defined. I'm tired of being different. Of being the girl in the headlines."

"Julia . . ."

"So I don't tell anyone, and maybe I do try and prove myself every day. Maybe I have to. Prove that I can get through life, that I won't be swallowed up by my tragedy, by memories that never, ever go away, no matter how much I wish them to, or lie about them."

He was next to her now, his arms wrapped around her shaking body. She tried to break out, but he just held her until the fight was gone and she collapsed against his chest. He smoothed her hair back off her face, his fingers running against her wet cheek.

A long, long while passed before he finally spoke. "I still think you're the hot prosecutor with the great laugh and the nice chest," he whispered softly in her ear.

He felt her body shake, and he knew she was laughing. He moved his hand gently under her chin. She tried to move away. "Sshh," he said, bringing her face up toward his.

Her soft brown eyes were red and swollen. She must've been crying for days. He wiped her cheeks with his thumbs. She looked so beautiful. So defiant. So vulnerable. So scared. He bent down, close to her face.

"You said no rebounds," she whispered.

"This," he said, pulling her even closer, "this is no rebound." Then he did what his body and soul had ached to do for so long, and he kissed her.

I felt a Cleaving in my Mind —
As if my Brain had split —
I tried to match it — Seam by Seam —
But could not make them fit
The thought behind I strove to join
Unto the thought before —
But sequence raveled out of Sound
Like balls — upon a Floor
                    — EMILY DICKINSON

CHAPTER 91

"Are you ready to proceed with closing, Mr. Bellido?" Farley grumbled as he swept to the bench Tuesday morning. Jefferson had, once again, missed his cue, but the judge waved him off and motioned for the packed courtroom to sit. The antics of the past few days had worn him thin. Last Thursday's *Matlock* melodrama with that Vacanti girl had set off a flurry of motions and hearings that had ruined his weekend and seriously threatened to derail his vacation, and he was none too happy.

"I am, Your Honor," said Rick.

"Then let's get on with it."

Rick rose from his seat at the State's table. "David Marquette is a murderer," he began calmly. "He took a baseball bat and smashed in his wife, Jennifer's, head while she slept. He ripped her pajama top to make it look like a rape attempt, and then, using a boning knife he'd taken from the kitchen, he stabbed her not once, but thirty-seven times, with such force that the knife went through her and into the mattress. When his wife was dead, he went down the hall to his three-year-old son's room. He intentionally struck his son upside the head with that same baseball bat and stabbed him nine times. He then walked into his newborn's room, intentionally placed a pillow over his daughter's little head, and suffocated her. Then he went into his six-year-old daughter, Emma's, room, found her hiding in a corner, and stabbed her twenty-six times. Make no mistake, ladies and gentlemen, David Marquette is a murderer."

Rick walked over to where sixteen-by-twenty-inch portraits of the victims had been mounted on easels across from the jury box. Beside each portrait was a graphic montage of crime-scene photos. The jury hated looking at the crime-scene pictures; they'd cringed when he'd first introduced them at trial. The female jurors in particular wanted to turn away. But he wouldn't let them. Like a skilled hypnotist, he held them there, fast in their seats, while he took them back in time.

"Cold, intentional, premeditated first-degree murder. The only issue for you to decide really is whether the man was insane.

For that we turn to the facts. We know that on the night Jennifer, Danny, Sophie, and Emma were murdered, David Marquette was a registered guest at the Marriott World Center in Orlando. We know that on the morning of October eighth he was slated to give a speech on reproductive endocrinology at that same hotel before five hundred members of the AMA. Cell records tell us that sometime after ten P.M. on the night of the seventh, the defendant sneaked out of his hotel and drove 225 miles back to his home in Coral Gables. We know that sometime before four thirty A.M. the defendant sneaked back into his house and began to execute his carefully planned exit strategy. An exit from the marriage he felt roped into and the three little kids who were keeping him from the life he wanted. A life free of financial and emotional responsibilities. The plan, folks, was to clean up, get in the car by five, drive back to Orlando, teach his conference at nine thirty, and wait for the phone to ring to tell him the devastating news that his family was dead.

"Now, if all had gone according to plan, we probably wouldn't be sitting here. The Coral Gables Family Massacre would likely have been just another unsolved homicide. Dr. Marquette would've collected his condolences and insurance money and moved on with his bachelor life. But something did go wrong. Something the defendant hadn't anticipated. Emma woke up. What woke her we'll never know — maybe it was the baby, or her brother whimpered, or her momma screamed — but she woke up, and she sneaked the phone into her room, and she called 911. And when her hiding spot was discovered it was with Emma's final, brave breath that she told the operator exactly who was coming at her with his knife. She named her murderer, and we all heard her, right here in this courtroom. 'Oh, no, no, no!' she cried. 'No, Daddy!' "

Rick looked at the defendant and let the words sink in. The courtroom stayed perfectly still, as if everyone was afraid to breathe lest they miss something.

"That's when the plans changed, folks. That's when David Marquette realized there would be no escape back to a comfy hotel room in Disney. That's when he needed to think of a Plan B. Of a way out. And he needed to think fast because he knew that within minutes the police would be knocking on his front door.

"Perhaps he first thought he could blame the carnage on an intruder. A madman who'd climbed through a window, tried to rape his wife, killed his children, and then, surprised to find our defendant home, slipped a knife into his gut as he stepped out of the shower. A skilled surgeon, David Marquette would know just how to deliver a horrible, dramatic knife wound to back up that story. A serious, potentially life-threatening wound that had amazingly missed every single vital organ but would bleed a lot and require quick medical attention — medical attention he already knew was on its way. Not bad for on-the-spot thinking. Not bad for someone who had minutes to rinse off all the blood of his wife and kids in the shower and then delicately perform surgery on himself with the very same knife. Not bad at all. In fact, some might say thought processes made under such pressure were brilliant, not disorganized. Cunning, not illogical.

"Or perhaps David Marquette did try to kill himself, knowing he was boxed into a corner, and it was simple fate that guided the blade past all those vital organs."

Rick stared at the defense table. "Or perhaps, folks, as is much more likely the case, as soon as David Marquette heard his daughter scream his name at that operator, he knew he was in an impossible situation for which only one solution existed that would enable him to walk away from what he'd just done. Only one. You've seen it in movies. You've watched it develop in soap-opera plots. You've heard it used in the most outrageous and infamous of court cases. The only legal excuse that could keep him off Death Row and out of prison and eventually, one day, ensure his freedom. A plea of insanity."

"Objection!" Mel shouted. He could smell it in the courtroom, the change in the air. He had to break the spell. "This is all conjecture, Your Honor."

"This is closing argument. Overruled," said Farley, motioning Mel to sit back down.

"Schizophrenia," Rick continued confidently. "It was the only disease that could offer an explanation for the unimaginable carnage David Marquette could no longer deny he'd committed. A disease he himself was all too familiar with. The disease that had confined his brilliant identical twin to a mental institution and ultimately caused that brother to take his own life. For David Marquette, a skilled doctor who'd done a rotation on a psych ward, mimicking the bizarre symptoms he had watched unfold in a mirror image of himself over the years would not be that difficult. Let's face it, folks, the defendant knew the symptoms to manifest, the voices to offer up to the psychiatrists. He knew enough not to claim it was little green men he saw but the devil. He knew enough to flatten his emotions, to feign catatonia. He even knew how to compensate for the physical and mental effects of the antipsychotic drugs they'd be sure to give him. The stint he'd done in a private rehab facility for cocaine psychosis during his second year in college could now be considered his first misdiagnosed 'psychotic break.' The young man whom a caseworker had noted during that very stay as, and I quote, 'manipulative and deceitful, superficial in thought and speech, with grandiose ideas that are not grounded in current reality.' The man who had demonstrated, as far back as fifteen years ago, evidence of a psychopathic personality was really a misdiagnosed schizophrenic. Just like his twin.

"It was this disease that had corrupted his brain with sick thoughts. That had made him believe his family would be damned if he didn't save their souls. That had made him try to commit suicide to save himself from possession, too. That knife wound was a half-hearted attempt at *hara-kiri,* he wants us to believe. A failed attempt to join his family in the hereafter.

"Don't buy it, folks. Don't believe any of it. Dr. Barakat, a forensic psychiatrist with sixteen years of experience, didn't. Neither did Dr. Hindlin. See the cunning pattern of behavior. See the brilliant thought processes that are involved here."

Rick waited until all of the jurors' eyes were focused back on him. Even the criers. "The defendant has fooled some people with his story and his act, but he hasn't fooled us all. The facts are the facts. They speak for themselves, and he can't get out of them. He hasn't fooled the seasoned homicide detectives or the State's psychiatrists, and he hasn't fooled me. Don't let him fool you. He's not a man whose illness manipulated him to commit murder; he's a man who's using an illness to manipulate the system. He's not a schizophrenic, ladies and gentlemen. He's a cold-blooded psychopath. And he needs to pay for what he's done."

Chapter 92

Rick sat down by himself at the State's table, which had a conspicuously empty seat at it. Julia's absence this morning had been the talk of all the papers, tabloids, talk shows, news programs. All morning, all over the world.

As soon as the silence broke into excited chatter, Farley declared it was time for lunch and recessed court till two P.M.

Julia sat on her living room couch in her pajamas and slippers, chewing on what remained of her thumbnail. She stared blankly at the TV as the commentators quickly took to the air to analyze what Rick Bellido had said, and what it meant, and what the jury must be thinking, and what this must mean for the defense. The consensus, she saw as she flipped through the channels, was that the State had delivered a brilliant closing.

As she watched, one by one, the parade of

smiling, well-coiffed analysts disparaged her name, seemingly disregarding everything that had transpired just last week. Rick had exacted his revenge on her. He had discredited her and her direct exam of Dr. Barakat as much as he could without discrediting his case. She was the inexperienced, naive fool.

She finally walked into the kitchen and made herself a pot of coffee for lunch. She opened another pack of cigarettes and sat at the kitchen table, her head buried in her hands.

And she didn't answer the phone, no matter how many times it rang.

CHAPTER 93

At sixty-one years of age, six foot two and 310 pounds, Mel Levenson might not be a match for Rick Bellido's looks or his suave Spanish charm, but he certainly had more experience with a jury. Thirty-six years' worth. And that was a hell of a lot more than Bellido and his Cupcake of the Month had. He rose slowly from his seat and lumbered over to the jury. He could tell from the jurors' faces — those who would look at him, anyway — that he was down a point or two. So he'd better make every word count if there was any hope of keeping his client off Death Row.

"I've been doing this a long time, folks," Mel began with a smile, his tone friendly. "A long time. And I always like to remind the jury that whatever the prosecutor or I say in closing is not evidence. No matter how we say it, no matter what we say, and no matter how convinced we may look while

589

we're saying it. Closing arguments are just an opportunity for the State and the defense to sum up the case and what they think the evidence showed during the trial. But it's not evidence. That's not always easy to remember when you have someone as well dressed and good-looking as Mr. Bellido up here telling you how you should see things," he said, throwing his smile in the direction of the State's table. The courtroom tittered, and a couple of female jurors looked sheepishly down at their shoes.

"Mr. Bellido has offered us, to use his own term, a 'brilliant' theory of the case. But it's his theory, and it's just that — a theory. It's what he thinks the evidence showed, not what it did. And Mr. Bellido has a very active imagination. He has concocted a convoluted tale — three different tales, actually — of what he says my client really meant to do that night. But he's no psychic, no mind reader. And none of this theory he's expounded is grounded in any facts we heard during this trial. He's built you a big castle out of nothing but buckets of sloppy mud, but it has no factual foundation, so it doesn't stand up. His story doesn't work.

"The law in Florida is this: If, at the time he committed the crime charged, the defendant suffered from a mental infirmity or disease, and because of this condition either he didn't know what he was doing, or he didn't know what he was doing was wrong, then he's legally insane. That's it. It doesn't matter if he was sane last year or last night, or even if he's sane right now as we look at him — what matters is if he was legally sane at the moment when he committed the crime.

"Mr. Bellido doesn't want you to believe David is a paranoid schizophrenic. He doesn't want you to believe he hears voices, or that he has disorganized thoughts or suffers from paranoid delusions. He doesn't want you to believe that the voices — which, as Dr. Koletis and Dr. Hayes both testified, never let up — told David his family was possessed by demonic spirits. He doesn't want you to believe that these voices told him he was not killing his wife and children but that he was saving their souls. Saving their souls from a damned eternal existence in hell. Mr. Bellido doesn't want you to believe that in David's mind — in David's reality — he didn't know that what he was doing was wrong because in this reality his wife and children were already dead. He wasn't killing them — he was exorcising the devil that possessed the shells of their dead bodies. The devil that was soon to consume his own soul as well. And no matter what a prosecutor or a seasoned homicide detective or even his own attorney might tell him, David knows this was true. There is absolutely no reasoning with him, even if you could reach him, because that is his reality. And he knows he did the right thing. And I'll tell you this much, folks — in his reality, he did do the right thing!" Mel slapped the railing and turned to face the rest of the courtroom. It was as if he were addressing not just the panel, but the world.

"It's easy to not believe, isn't it? It's easy to question how someone could actually think these crazy things. So, folks, I want you to imagine for a moment that you are in the delusion David was living with. And then I want you to imagine that it's really happening. I want you to imagine what it's like to constantly hear different voices chattering and screaming and whispering away in your head. Voices that sound just as real to you as I do, or Judge Farley, or Mr. Bellido. Voices that talk to you constantly, even when you're sleeping. And you don't know that you're ill, folks. You can't recognize something's wrong because that's part of the disease, after all. So close your eyes and imagine the terror that David lives with every day."

"Objection!" Rick was on his feet as the jurors closed their eyes. "It's a Golden Rule violation. He's asking the jury to place themselves in the position of the defendant!"

"I'm asking them to step into a delusion and imagine that that is real. I'm not asking them to imagine they are the defendant," responded Mel.

"Mr. Levenson is splitting hairs," barked Rick.

Farley raised an eyebrow. "Maybe. But he makes a good argument. Overruled."

"The voices whispered to him — all day, all night, every day, every night — that his children were slowly being possessed by Satan. He saw the signs of possession — the mark of the beast in the growths on their skin and heads. He saw the signs of the devil's presence in the way they chewed their food and grasped at their toys. He saw the signs when his wife cut her finger, but it didn't bleed. It was these signs that confirmed what the voices had been saying all along.

"So David knows now that he's not paranoid — he's right. The voices can truly be trusted. And these voices that have befriended him with their prophetic whispers tell him that his children's souls will be consumed — forever condemned to burn in hell if they are not saved by the father who spawned them. He looks at his children from across the breakfast table and now he suddenly sees the red flash of demon eyes before they look away, or the dark yellow teeth when they smile at him. When he kisses his wife, he feels a piece of rotting skin slip off her cheek. The devil has just shown his face to David. And the voices are right once again. Satan is in his house, he has possessed his family, and only David knows it. Only David can see it. Only he can stop it. Think about it. It's like being trapped in a horror movie, but for David, there's no theater to run out of. No one to tell him, 'It's only a movie!' There's no escape. Because for him, this is reality.

"I ask you, folks, to put yourself into the delusion and imagine that that is your reality now. This is what you see, smell, taste, hear, believe. And maybe now you can imagine the frightening hell that is David's everyday existence. That's the disease of schizophrenia.

"Sure, it would make us feel better to blame someone," Mel continued, looking over at Rick. "It would be neater to wrap it all up and call David an evil SOB. A cold-hearted psychopath, as Mr. Bellido contends, who didn't care about his family and only wanted a carefree life to spend his new-found millions. But that's not what the facts show. We heard from many different witnesses, including Jennifer's own family, who told us that David was a great father and husband. Yes, he had a couple of affairs, but that doesn't mean he wanted to kill his wife. It doesn't mean he wanted to kill his children. And the State has offered no witness to testify that he did, or that he even wanted to leave them. But the prosecutor knows that calling David a psychopath actually makes the whole brutal crime easier to explain to the voters of Miami."

"Objection!" Rick said, jumping defiantly to his feet once again.

"Sustained," Farley said, looking down over his glasses with a coy smile. "Try not to characterize Mr. Bellido as pandering to the good people of Miami in hopes of getting them to vote for him in his election bid next November."

The courtroom tittered again. Rick sank back in his seat, red-faced.

Mel smiled. "Let's face it. It would be easier for us all to hate David if he is a psychopath. There would be no pity then, only loathing. And it would be a lot less frightening than the truth — that a debilitating mental illness could actually drive a once brilliant surgeon, a loving father, a wonderful husband, to commit the crime of murder without any provocation. It would be a lot less frightening than finding out that there's no one we can blame.

"Schizophrenics — as every doctor who testified up here explained — don't all suffer from the same delusion. They don't all hear the same voices or see the same hallucinations. As with any mental illness, the disease affects each victim in a unique way, so there's no standard psychiatric litmus test, no MRI, no rash, no wayward cell that can be examined under a microscope to identify it. Christian Barakat, the State's own psychiatrist, called David a malingerer. A liar, basically. And yet we all heard Dr. Barakat in this courtroom last week when he finally conceded to the Assistant State Attorney herself that he cannot say with any medical certainty that David does not suffer from schizophrenia. We all heard Mr. Bellido try to object and prevent his own witness from speaking the truth. We all heard the State's doctor testify that if the delusion David reported to him was in fact accurate — if that was what David saw, heard, believed, thought when he picked up that knife and that bat and killed the devil —

then David is not legally responsible for his actions. That he is, in fact, insane. Even the State agrees.

"One final thought. We've become a society of 'I'll believe it when I see it' people. Church attendance around the world has fallen off, people are suing to have 'In God We Trust' removed from our dollar bills." Mel held up his hands defensively. "Don't get me wrong — this is not about religion, folks. I'm only making a point. Which is — we know schizophrenia is a real disease, even though we can't 'see' it on a microscope slide or in a blood test. We know that it makes people who have it suffer from auditory hallucinations, terrifying paranoia, and sometimes even vivid visions that can make them legally incapable of distinguishing right from wrong. We know that inside the brain of a schizophrenic, reality as we all know it is actually seen differently. We know this even though we ourselves cannot see it. Even though we cannot hear it. In this instance we can only close our eyes, and — thank God, or whoever else you want — we can only imagine.

"My job's been to prove to you that David was legally insane at the time when he committed those murders. I've done that. The only way Mr. Bellido's theory works —

the only way that David can be found guilty of murder — is if you do not accept that he suffers from schizophrenia."

Mel looked over at the defense table, but his client just stared down, rolling his tongue around in his mouth. It was as if he'd been in another room with a set of earphones on and hadn't heard what everyone had just been saying about him. His eyes remained as ghostly gray and lifeless as they had the day he'd first set foot in a courtroom.

"He's already been sentenced to a lifetime in hell. Please don't sentence him to death."

CHAPTER 94

The damage was done before Rick's feet found the floor. "Objection! The jury's only determining guilt at this phase of the proceedings, Your Honor. Mr. Levenson's comment leads them to believe that if they find the defendant guilty he's going to be sentenced to death!"

The wiry eyebrow went up again. "That is the penalty the State is seeking, right?" asked Farley.

"Sentencing's separate and apart from a finding of guilt," Rick protested. "That's determined after the penalty phase. In any event, sentencing's imposed by Your Honor, not the jury."

"But you are seeking the death penalty, right, Mr. Bellido?" Judge Farley was clearly annoyed. He hated being challenged, especially in front of cameras. "Isn't that correct?"

Rick gritted his teeth. "Yes, Judge, but —"

"I thought so," Farley snapped. Then he looked over at the jury. "If you find the defendant guilty, then we'll proceed to the penalty phase, where you will get to decide if the defendant should be put to death. However, I'll be the one who actually sentences him." He turned back to Rick, his eyes narrowed. "Anything further, Mr. Levenson?"

Mel settled in his seat again and patted his client's back. "No, Your Honor. I think we're done here." The courtroom was quiet, but there was a charge in the air. The end was near.

"Mr. Bellido, will you be giving rebuttal?" asked Farley.

Rick thought for a moment. The judge was obviously pissed at him, and, knowing how vindictive Farley could be, he knew that that fact would be communicated to the jury should he give another closing. He looked at the men and women in the jury box and saw that they were getting restless. It had been a long couple of weeks and a draining day. Giving a rebuttal meant risking boring the jury, further confusing them with psychiatric terms, or worse — pissing them off. And that could translate into unintended sympathy for the defense. The biggest problem most lawyers had was not knowing when to shut up and sit back down. As he watched the jury, he was thankful to see that no one on the panel was looking at the defendant, which was a good sign. An inability to make eye contact with either Marquette or his attorney meant they were siding with the State. It meant they felt guilty for condemning him.

There was no reason to push it just because he could. "No, Your Honor," Rick said finally. "The State will rely on its closing and the jury's own recollection of the evidence."

"All right, folks, that concludes closing arguments," Farley announced. "Let's break here. I'm going to release the alternates and charge the panel on the law in the morning. They should be ready to go into deliberations around lunchtime tomorrow." Then he climbed down off the bench and stormed into the hallway, letting the door slam behind him.

"All rise!" barked Jefferson, once again just seconds too late.

CHAPTER 95

The phone call came maybe an hour or so after court had recessed for the day. She knew right away from the 305 area code and the 547 exchange on the caller ID that it was the State Attorney's Office. The last four digits told her it was Major Crimes.

Julia didn't bother picking up the phone and hearing the news that she was being fired directly, so she just let the answering machine get it while she sat on her kitchen counter, listening with her eyes closed. She didn't want to have to defend herself or argue about what had happened in court last week. She didn't want to explain what had happened with her brother or why she'd suddenly disappeared from sight for the last five days. She knew that a desperate attempt to try to save her job at the last minute would sound like just that — desperate. And she didn't want to give anyone, especially not Rick Bellido, if it were he on the other end of the line, the satisfaction of hearing her cry or break down over the phone.

"Please leave a message after the tone."

"Ms. Vacanti, this is Charley Rifkin over at the State Attorney's Office. I was hoping to speak with you this evening. I have Colleen Kay from Human Resources in my office. . . . Your behavior in trial last week was completely inappropriate, rising to the level of insubordination . . . unprofessional and unbecoming . . . in such a hostile and aggressive manner . . . I am shocked and discouraged . . . Mr. Bellido has commented that . . . Further, your failure to show up . . . necessary to terminate your employment . . . it is expected that your office will be cleaned out within the next forty-eight hours. . . ."

At some point she just turned off the machine. When she flipped it back on again, she hit the delete button. She'd heard all she needed to hear. She'd been fired over her answering machine. And if that wasn't bad enough, Rifkin hadn't even bothered to take her off speaker-phone while he did it. She knew Rick was there, probably snickering with his buddy over what a good bang she'd been and how right Rifkin had been about her from the beginning.

She'd expected the call, she supposed, but it was still a blow. Being a prosecutor was the only thing she knew. And it was over. Her entire career had just crashed and burned, and she'd piloted the plane. She wiped away the tears and looked around her messy kitchen. She couldn't stay in this stifling apartment a second longer or she'd go crazy. She'd retreated into her tiny cave to lick her wounds, but now they'd found her and were shooting their bullets in here, too. She could feel the walls moving in, crushing her, and in the living room the TV beckoned her to come back in and watch as the commentators talked about her in a dozen different languages. She hurried into the bedroom and threw on a pair of running shorts and a t-shirt, pulled her hair back into a ponytail, and headed out the front door.

She'd done her job. The protesters wouldn't even be looking for her anymore. She blasted her MP3 player as she ran, hoping to drown out the voices of her detractors. Everyone who'd wanted to see her fall now had a front-row seat on national television. As the miles dragged on and she hit her runner's high, she saw Andrew sitting in the visiting room at Kirby, waiting for her to come see him, his carved, bloody hands outstretched across the chipped press-board table, his lips blue and swollen.

"And with all the recent changes in Andrew's life . . ."

She thought of all the ways she could have saved him from himself. All the things she should have done. All the ways she'd failed him.

"Look at me now, Ju-Ju! Look at what you've done to me!"

She thought about David Marquette and how she'd failed him, too, not recognizing his sickness from the beginning. How she'd helped bring him to this point. How she would be responsible when they stuck the needle in his arm. The tears slipped from her eyes, trickling past her temples as she ran faster, brushed off course by the wind in her face like a raindrop on a windshield. She ran and ran until they stopped coming. Until she didn't see Andy anymore. Until it was just the music that she heard in her head. Then she turned around and ran back home. It took over ten miles today to clear her head, and she wondered if there would come a point when she couldn't outrun the demons anymore. She wondered if that would be the end or if, like Andrew and David Marquette, she wouldn't even realize it.

She slowed to a walk as she approached her parking lot. The first thing she noticed was the red-and-silver Harley in guest parking.

"Hey there!" Lat called across the lot. He sat on the stairs that led up to her apartment. He got up and started toward her.

She hadn't expected to see him today. Deep down she supposed part of her hadn't expected to see John Latarrino ever again. She'd spent the day preparing for that reality by not allowing herself to even think about what had happened last night. And now here he was, waiting for her.

"You look like you need someone to take you to dinner," he said with a smile.

"Yeah?"

"Yeah." He waited while she caught her breath. "I tried to call first, but you didn't seem to want to pick up the phone. So I figured I'd come over and make the invitation in person."

She felt her cheeks go hot. She hoped her face was still red from running so he wouldn't notice. There were so many thoughts running through her head, so many things he'd heard her say last night. She hated feeling so exposed. No matter how intimate she'd been with Rick, there was always a part of herself that she'd held back. And after all that had happened, after how he had betrayed her, she was thankful that she had exercised that emotional discretion. But last night . . . she'd been so damn vulnerable. So needy when Lat had shown up at her door unannounced. So she'd said things — too many things. He knew everything about her now. Everything.

Tangled against his body, his heartbeat pulsing in her ears, his touch had made her quiver in a way Rick's never could. When he'd finally kissed her, there had been a completion of this connection that she'd not felt before with any man, and she'd just let herself give in completely. For fifteen years she'd been hiding behind a made-up past of well-spun lies — lies that sometimes even she believed were true — and now, for the very first time since her parents had been murdered, someone finally knew what her life really was all about. And he hadn't run away in fright. That was what was so beautiful. So peaceful. He hadn't judged her. He hadn't judged Andrew. He knew who she was, and it was like an enormous burden had been lifted off her shoulders, carried with someone else's help.

He'd made love to her for hours, slow and sweet and incredibly gentle, but their first kiss had never ended. His mouth had never left hers. It was as if John was as hungry for her as she was for him, and neither could bear to let the connection go for even a split second for fear it might end. So he'd moved with her into the bedroom, his body pressed tightly against hers on the bed, as they danced and writhed as one to soundless, frenzied music — but he'd never once broken the kiss. When he'd moaned, it was with her. Even their voice was as one. Afterward they'd lain facing each other for the longest time, their mouths only a few inches apart, so that she breathed his breath and he hers. That was when she'd told him things she never should've told him. And he'd listened until she was finally empty. His soft blue eyes had never looked away. Not even for a second. She hadn't wanted to fall asleep for fear of losing the moment, because she knew she would. As any drunk knows, daylight changes everything. And even through the sweet, euphoric stupor she was in, she knew that when the sun rose she'd probably come to regret too many moments from this night.

He was gone when she woke up.

She finally looked up from the asphalt. "Dinner, huh? I guess a burger would be nice."

"A burger?" he replied incredulously, heading back with her across the parking lot. "You are a cheap date. I was going to suggest stone crabs and a bottle of wine. Oh, well." He shrugged, kicking a stone. "A burger and a beer it is, then. My type of woman. I know just the place."

"Stone crabs? Wow. You do know how to impress a girl. Uh-oh, what have I done?"

"Only the best, sweetheart." He reached out and gently touched her hand as she stepped onto the staircase. He hesitated before he asked his question. "You doing okay today?"

Maybe he already knew from Rick that she'd been fired. Maybe that was why he was here, to pick her up yet again after she'd tripped and fallen on her face. Poor, fragile Julia with the awful past had just had another bad day. But there was no way she was going to lean on him again. She would not allow herself to be a pity call, or worse, a pity fuck. She'd rather be alone with the demons.

"Yesterday was . . ." she began, her voice trailing off. "Look, I'm sorry about last night, Lat," she said flatly.

"Don't be sorry."

"I said some things —" she started.

"That I hope you meant."

"And I did some things —"

"That I also hope you meant." He smiled. She pictured his warm body pressed on top of hers, his hands moving over her, and she looked away to a spot of peeling paint on the staircase railing. "I'm so embarrassed right now," she said softly.

"Don't be. If it was too heavy, Julia, I wouldn't be here."

"Okay," she finally said, nodding. "Let me just go change." She started up the stairs.

"I was called out at seven or else I wouldn't have left," he said.

She didn't turn around. "Good," was all she said before disappearing inside her apartment.

Chapter 96

Dinner was just that — cheeseburgers and coffee and hours of conversation in an empty all-night diner. The night ended with a lingering kiss at her door, but she didn't invite him in, and he didn't press for an invitation.

Sleep did not come at all after that. Even so, she spent most of the next morning buried under the covers, toying with the idea of just staying put until after the jury came back with a verdict and the Marquette case finally disappeared from the headlines. Until she figured out what to do with the rest of her life, where she was going to do it, and who might be in it. Charley Rifkin's foreboding cleanout deadline kept ticking away in her head. While she definitely didn't want to go down to the SAO, she feared putting off picking up her things lest she have to consider reordering her diploma from the microfiche archives of

Fordham. She certainly wouldn't put it past Rick or Charley Rifkin to order everything but the furniture in her office to be tossed out in the Dumpster. Just the thought of Rick going through her things and touching them made her cringe with anger and revulsion. She thought of calling Ileana, but their relationship had slipped over the past few months, and she didn't want to get her involved. At the end of the day Ileana still had a career to worry about.

Just after five Julia pulled her Honda into the lot at Kristy House across the street from the SAO and watched from a distance as the secretaries, investigators, witness counselors, and ASAs hurried to their cars or to catch the Metro. People she'd known for years, friends whom she'd fondly once thought of as her second family, were strangers to her now. Strangers she suspected she'd never see or hear from again.

A half hour later she headed in. While she would've preferred doing this at two in the morning when no one was around, the first thing Personnel had probably done was deactivate her security card. As it was, she figured she'd probably have to endure the embarrassment of an escort from Investigations standing over her while she cleaned out her desk, making sure she didn't slip an extra paper clip into her moving box. Best there be as few witnesses to that as possible.

But the lobby was practically empty, and no one paid any attention to her when she stepped through the glass doors, including the guard who motioned her through the metal detectors. She was dressed down in a t-shirt, jeans, and sneakers, her hair pulled into a ponytail and hidden under a ball cap, and recognizing her out of a suit and heels would probably require a double-take. With the cardboard boxes she'd picked up from Publix tucked under her arm, she ducked into the stairwell and took the stairs up to 3. Most of the support staff was long gone. As for prosecutors, she could only hope that most of them were either heading home via the elevator right now or were otherwise buried under mounds of paperwork in their caves.

The hallway was clear, and as she slid her card through the security access, she prayed that neither Colleen Kay in Personnel nor Charley Rifkin was as smart as she gave them credit for. They weren't. When she heard the familiar click, she let out the breath she'd been holding and headed for the last time down the hall to her office.

She felt the eyes of a few prosecutors still working in their offices look up as she passed. She could feel the walls buzz around her — they were probably all picking up their phones right now and calling each other to whisper about her. The hallway stretched before her like the passage through a funhouse, and she held her breath until she finally reached her office and shut the door.

She was the talk of the office, no doubt — getting fired was about as rare for a state employee as a solar eclipse. She imagined the crowd of curious coworkers waiting all day to hear through the grapevine that she'd finally shown up to collect her things. Then they could come down and take a peek and watch her get escorted back out by Security, discreetly checking to make sure she left the screws in the wall when she took down her diplomas.

She wiped her eyes with the back of her hand. Thoughts like this were unproductive, especially now that there was work to be done. The walls were thin. She didn't want to listen to them gossiping about her. She switched on the portable TV on top of her file cabinet for company and started to dump her drawers into her Publix boxes. The six o'clock news was on, and she was grateful that they were not talking about the trial. The world was still waiting on a verdict, but since Farley had not sent the jury in to deliberate until almost two, no one was expecting anything till the morning, and maybe not until after the weekend. The complicated jury instructions alone had taken almost three hours to get through. Judge Farley would probably miss his cruise. Good.

Julia sifted through old files and old messages that at one time had been important. Her eyes caught on the date on one of them. Friday, January 12, 2007. She'd gone up to see Andy that day. She'd brought him Dunkin' Donuts that Saturday morning. His first real cup of coffee and Boston Kreme in fifteen years. He'd been so happy. He'd sucked out the cream like a little kid, his nose dotted with chocolate icing. She closed her eyes and tried to stop the memories. There was no time for this.

"Now we'll go live to the courtroom."

"This was completely unexpected, Tony!" the reporter on TV shouted excitedly. "Completely unexpected. The judge is waiting on David Marquette to be brought back over from the Dade County Jail, which may take anywhere from a few minutes to an hour, we're told."

A sudden rush of excited voices sounded in the hall. Footsteps hurried past her door.

She looked over at the TV. Channel 6's Tim Sweeney was standing outside courtroom 4-8. A news prompt ran underneath him: THE JURY HAS REACHED A VERDICT IN THE CORAL GABLES FAMILY MASSACRE.

CHAPTER 97

She rushed to the window. TV trucks from every station lined the streets and circled the block. MDPD and City of Miami cruisers blocked off 14th Street, and more were busy setting up a perimeter around the building, their blue-and-red lights spinning. On the court house steps a large, frenzied crowd of reporters swarmed around Rick Bellido as he tried to make his way into the building. Rick never took the entrance under the courthouse. And he never turned down an opportunity for a press conference. She heard his voice on the TV as she watched him out her window.

". . . we are a bit surprised that a verdict came so soon. That just means the jury did not have much to talk about in deliberations. It proves the evidence was pretty clear."

She looked at her watch. It was only five fifty. The jury had been officially out for less than four hours. A verdict this quick wasn't good for the defense in an insanity case, not with all the issues the jurors had had to consider. She paced her office. Now would be a good time to throw the rest of the contents of her desk into a box. Take her diplomas and her Bic pens and hightail it out of Dodge while everyone was busy looking the other way.

But she couldn't.

She looked out her window and across the street again. The steps of the courthouse were empty. Everyone had gone in.

This was her case. Her last verdict. She wanted to take that walk across the street one last time to hear it. And she wanted to see the faces of the jury she'd picked. She wanted to look in their eyes and know what they were going to do before the clerk announced it to the world. And, perhaps most importantly, she wanted those three men and nine women to see her there, too. She wanted them all to know it was not just another case for her. It never had been. She left her boxes on her desk and headed across the street.

No one paid any attention as she slid into the very back of the packed courtroom because every eye and every camera were trained on the somber-faced jury that was already filing into the box. None of the jurors looked out at the crowd. None looked over at the defendant.

Lat came from somewhere and stood next to her in the back of the courtroom. Without a word his hand found hers, grasping a pinky and rubbing it gently. Her palms were drenched in perspiration.

"Ladies and gentlemen of the jury, I understand you've reached a verdict," said Judge Farley, folding up the verdict form he'd just read to himself. He passed it back to the clerk.

"We have, Your Honor," said the red-faced foreman, swallowing the back half of his words as he finally looked up and spotted the wall of cameras trained on him.

"Will the defendant please rise," said Farley.

"Wanna get out of here?" Lat whispered in her ear. "We don't have to stay. . . ."

"I want to hear," she whispered back. She swallowed hard. "I want to hear them say it." She never took her eyes off the foreman.

A somber-faced Mel leaned in and said something into his client's ear before they both stood. Mel straightened his jacket and buttoned it, but David stared straight ahead, his hands held behind him. Julia noticed they were shaking ever so slightly.

"Will the clerk please publish the verdict . . ." said the judge.

Ivonne nodded and stood. She put on her reading glasses and opened the verdict form. "We the jury, in the county of Miami-Dade, Florida, on this the twenty-second day of March, two thousand and seven, as to count one of the indictment, to wit, the death of Jennifer Leigh Marquette, find the defendant, David Alain Marquette —"

Ivonne gasped just a little as her eyes rolled over the words before her mouth spoke them. She looked up into the cameras, her eyes wide. She finally stammered out what the entire world was waiting to hear.

"Not guilty by reason of insanity."

Chapter 98

The courtroom exploded as a stunned Ivonne continued to read all four verdicts. One after the other, Not guilty by reason of insanity. Judge Farley had known what was coming, and he'd wisely hit the Liaison security button under the bench as soon as he'd handed the form over to Ivonne. A few armed plainclothes officers stood in the back to help the judge maintain order.

"Oh, my God!" shouted one reporter into a camera, breaking the courtroom code of conduct. "Not guilty! He's not guilty! All counts!" That started the rest of them as Farley's rules were quickly discarded. Reporters began to air directly from the courtroom, not wanting to be beaten in the ratings department by competing with the shouts and screams of the competition out in the hall.

Farley was yelling at Jefferson. Jefferson was yelling, "Be quiet! Court is still in session!" at everyone. And no one was paying any attention.

Rick sat alone at the State's table, literally stunned, staring at the jury, who were now unable to look at him. Reporters snapped pictures and shoved microphones in his face over the gallery railing, demanding comment. For once he had nothing to say.

David Marquette hung his head on the table as Mel slapped his back. Alain pushed his way up to the railing and hugged his son's attorney, tears streaming down his face. Julia scanned the crowd for David's mother, but she wasn't at her husband's side, where she had been every day since the start of trial. She finally spotted her, further back in the crowd. While the whole room surged forward to the gallery, Nina Marquette slipped further and further back toward the door. Reporters shouted questions at her, but she held up her hand, turned, and walked out of the courtroom. Her eyes met Julia's for a simple moment as she pushed open the doors, but Julia could see that she wasn't crying today. And she wasn't smiling. She was shaking. Her skin was the color of ash, and she looked physically ill.

A reporter finally noticed Julia. With his microphone pointed at her, like a scene from *Invasion of the Body Snatchers,* he began to scream her name. An army of cameras spun in her direction, their lights blinding her. She pulled her hand away.

"Ms. Vacanti, are you happy with the verdict?"

"Was justice done?"

"Have you spoken to David Marquette?"

"Can you confirm that you've been fired?"

"Were you prepared to testify for the defense in the penalty phase?"

Another set fell on Lat.

"Detective, are you angry with the State?"

"Do you believe Ms. Vacanti is responsible for the verdict?"

The questions came so fast, it was almost as if the reporters shouting them didn't really want answers. Julia just kept shaking her head as the world began to spin and the cameras and faces closed in on her. She didn't know how she should feel, what she should say. Part of her, she supposed, felt vindicated — the jury had heard her, and they'd listened. They'd placed the blame where it should be — on the disease, not the man. Part of her felt guilt and sorrow for Jennifer, Danny, Sophie, and especially Emma, who'd known only terror in the final minutes of her life and would never understand why. Julia hoped that in their eyes, she'd done right by them. They were all consequential victims of madness. Finally, part of her felt ashamed — as if she'd betrayed her office and her prosecutorial oath. Justice was never as black-and-white as it seemed in case law and statutes.

The judge finally found something heavy to slam on his desk and with the help of Liaison brought the courtroom back under control. He was done making nice with the cameras. The love affair was over; let them write what they wanted. "So help me, I will find everyone in this courtroom in contempt if I don't get quiet! The defendant might be the only one here who I don't sentence to jail tonight." Farley's eyes caught on the reporters in the back. And then on Julia. "And there will be no interviews in my courtroom; I don't care who they're with! Now, let's get this over with."

He turned to the jury. His face and body language instantly told them he was not pleased. "Ladies and gentlemen, thank you for your service; it's no longer needed. The bailiff will show you out. If you want to speak with the press, you can; God knows they want to speak with you. If you don't, you can remain in the jury room, and Jefferson will eventually escort you to your cars, although I can't guarantee when that will be."

As Jefferson began to usher the jury back into the jury room, Julia saw some of the men and women cast a final halting glance over at the defense table. The expression on their faces was one she'd seen before, but not here in a courtroom. It was the same look strangers would afford some disheveled, babbling bum on a street corner that they'd reluctantly just given a dollar to. It was a look of pity. Of contempt. And of unmistakable fright. But there was a flicker of something else, too. As they dashed to safety on the other side of the street, as they filed back into the comfortable security of their jury room, it was the look of self-righteous pride that Julia recognized. Pride at their own generosity and understanding.

As soon as the jury was gone, Judge Farley turned to the defendant. "Mr. Marquette, the jury has found you not guilty by reason of insanity on all counts of the indictment. I think we can agree — Mr. Levenson, Mr. Bellido — that you are indeed mentally ill, and further, that you are manifestly dangerous to yourself and to others. Can we dispense then with the need for an evidentiary hearing on that issue?"

Both Rick and Mel nodded. "Yes, Your Honor," said a visibly emotional Mel. It was clear that even he had not expected the jury's verdict. Rick's "Yes" was almost inaudible.

"As such, pursuant to section 916.15 of the Florida Statutes and any applicable sections of the Florida Rules of Criminal Procedure, I find that the defendant most definitely meets the criteria for involuntary commitment and as such am hereby committing him to the custody of the Department of Children and Families. The department will decide what the appropriate state facility is that the defendant shall be sent to for treatment, but this court will continue to retain jurisdiction. Ivonne, set this down for report status in six months. At that time, Mr. Levenson, I will review the hospital's report on your client's progress and we will proceed from there with any further extended commitment that I may then order." Farley looked at the gaggle of press as he stepped down. "That's it; court's concluded. We're done here." He disappeared for the last time into the judge's hallway.

Lat attempted to lead Julia toward the doors, his hand pressed protectively against the small of her back, as the questions and shouts started back up again. The crowd around her had thinned somewhat; some of the reporters had already hurried into the hallway to grab the jurors before they left the building, and others had gone to hunt down Rick, who'd apparently ducked out after the judge. Julia turned to look one last time around the courtroom where her career had abruptly, unfortunately ended. It was not lost on her that she might never be in another one again.

In the gallery David Marquette held his hands out patiently in front of him for Corrections to cuff them. Another CO knelt at his feet, locking the shackles that chained his ankles. She watched him, his shoulders slumped, his arms and legs bound, as the remaining spectators talked excitedly about him. That was when David Marquette suddenly turned his head and looked behind him.

Maybe he was searching for his father to say good-bye. Or maybe his mother. Maybe he was even searching for her. Or maybe, she would come to wonder later, he was actually looking for the cameras that filmed him. Whatever the reason, in a courtroom full of people, his ghostly gray eyes found hers once again, just like at the competency hearing.

She couldn't look away. She couldn't move, even with Lat and the press that surrounded them pushing her gently to the door. Sound swirled in a vacuum. Everyone, everything moved in slow motion, as if time was suspended. And as Corrections finally began to lead David Marquette across the gallery to the door that would take him to the bridge and DCJ, he did something Julia had never seen him do before. Not even once. Something that made her heart stop and her blood turn cold.

He smiled at her.

CHAPTER 99

"Ladies and gentlemen of the jury, I understand you've reached a verdict."

The judge's words sounded thick, as if they'd been dipped in molasses. All around him time had slowed to a virtual stop. Seconds stretched into minutes, like a bad movie with too much slow motion in its direction. He heard the restless crowd suck in a collective breath and then hold it as the judge spoke. The moment seemed so fragile, as if he'd just watched someone drop an expensive vase and was just waiting for it to shatter into a thousand pieces. He imagined, as he looked straight ahead at nothing, that if they did sentence him to die, this might be what his final moments alive would feel like. The last few hours lasting as long as days, final seconds becoming an eternity, until, he suspected, there'd come a point when he'd actually be anxious for it to just end. His body was tingling from both terror and excitement. The prickly feeling was at once euphoric and insatiably itchy and uncomfortable, and he resisted the urge to claw himself out of his restless skin. It was imperative that he remain here, in the moment. The end was almost here.

"Will the defendant please rise."

His eyes took in the room without ever moving. He knew they were all here for him. Not for his brilliant father or his society mother or his tragedy of a dead brother. This time it was for him. The masses had traveled from all around the world to see him. To hear him. To watch him with their cameras. And as he sat there, waiting to rise and hear his fate, suspended in this fragile instant, he knew that in dozens of countries millions of people were talking about, and shedding tears over, him. The attention had never been his intention, yet he couldn't help but find it funny how things worked out sometimes. And he couldn't help but be more than a bit proud of himself. At how far he'd come with this, how far he'd made it. But of course it was not time for smugness. The vase was still out there in midair.

His attorney gripped his arm and leaned into his ear. "David, David, listen to me," he whispered sternly, hoping to get through. "If the verdict is guilty, say nothing. Do nothing. Everything you say and do can be used against you. I'll come see you across the street as soon as they complete the booking, and I'll try to have you placed back on 9 so you can continue your meds. The penalty phase will not be for a few weeks, probably." Mel lifted him by the elbow, encouraging him to stand up now. "So say nothing; that's very important to remember."

He stood.

"Will the clerk please publish the verdict."

The judge kept up his commanding, stoic stare as the clerk rose, unfolded the paper, and finally put on her reading glasses. Sitting up stiffly in his seat, the judge moved closer to the bench, surveying his courtroom with a suspicious, anxious stare.

And that was when he saw the judge blink. It happened so fast, he was sure no one else had noticed. But he'd played enough poker in his life to know a tell when he saw one. Judge Farley, with the flicker of panic in his angry eyes, had just choked and given away his hand. He'd reached under the bench. And under the bench was the magic button that would send the troops a-running to help keep the upcoming pandemonium in check. In that brief, fragile instant, he knew exactly what the clerk was about to say. He felt everything inside him relax, and he bit his cheeks hard to keep from smiling.

"We find the defendant not guilty by reason of insanity. . . ."

He wanted to scream. Or jump. Even hug his attorney back. He wanted to reach over the gallery rail behind him and hug his crying father, too, before he finally smacked that pitiful look of despair and disappointment off the old man's face. It was the same familiar look his face had slipped into whenever he'd gotten within ten feet of Darrell after he'd been diagnosed. That was why he wanted to remove it. His mother had always been far more discreet, reserving her looks of shame for more private moments, when the cameras were off and the guests had gone home, but there was no need to look behind him to know that she was long gone. There was no way she could handle the failure of being the mother of two schizo sons — the mother of an insane murderer — no matter how well she'd played the supportive role these past few months.

The cameras were still set upon him; the men and women who judged him were still sitting in the box, shifting uncomfortably in their seats, so of course he didn't slap his father. Or yell at his mother's shadow. And he didn't hug anyone. He didn't do anything. He just swallowed the blood from the chewed wall of his cheek and stared straight ahead as the cheers of those who had made him their cause erupted around him. He was the Pro-Life poster boy. The champion of the Treat People with Mental Illness in a Fair and Decent Way groups. And he heard the cynical jeers of those who thought him the devil incarnate. Of those who believed him a malingerer. A faker. A murderer.

Amid all the noise and clutter, from somewhere in the back of the courtroom, he heard them call her name.

"Ms. Vacanti, are you happy with the verdict?"

"Was justice done?"

"Have you spoken to David Marquette?"

His miracle worker. His Anne Sullivan. She who had made the blind see his illness, who had made the deaf hear the voices only he heard. Assistant State Attorney Julia Vacanti. They continued to shout their questions, but she never answered them. He didn't hear her sweet, defiant voice. Even so, he knew she was there, somewhere behind him, waiting. He could feel her. He could even smell her perfume. Their electric connection was still there, as it had been since the beginning, and he knew she would not leave him until it was all over.

"I find that the defendant most definitely meets the criteria for involuntary commitment and as such am hereby committing him to the custody of the Department of Children and Families. . . ."

He owed her big time. He owed her his life. And it was time to let her know just how thankful he was to have it. It was time to let the world in on the proud little secret that he had been keeping all to himself.

They came for him with their shackles and chains and handcuffs, but he patiently held out his arms because he knew it wouldn't be long before he was free of them. Before God miraculously healed the sick and he would be well again, and they would regrettably have to let him out. He let them lead him away, but he knew she still waited. Until the last second, she waited for him. So he turned around and he made sure he thanked her for all she'd done for him with a big, friendly smile.

Damn, she sure was pretty.

EPILOGUE

"So am I crazy?" Julia asked the stately-looking man with the pleasant but emotionless face in the leather chair across from her. Behind him the towering jungle of New York skyscrapers that surrounded the Weill Cornell Medical College's Payne Whitney Clinic on 68th Street locked the shadows in the small room even on a sunny morning. She could hear the horns honking and the ambulances wailing eleven floors below. She'd come back to New York. Ironically enough, in her search to find answers far away from the claustrophobic microscope of Miami, she'd come back to where it had all begun. Weill Cornell's Department of Psychiatry offered one of the best psychiatric research programs in the country. She clasped her hands together and cleared her throat as she tried to get the next question out. "Do I have it?"

"Are you schizophrenic?" The doctor

shrugged and leaned back in his Chester-field. "I don't know what's going to make you feel better, Julia," he replied with a dry smile, his tone flat. "To know that you don't currently meet the criteria for a diagnosis of schizophrenia or not having a diagnosis for what's been happening to you over the course of the past few months."

She stared at him.

"You don't meet the criteria for a diagnosis of schizophrenia," Dr. Glass repeated. "The fact that you're even here, talking about events that occurred a few weeks back, tells me the possibility is somewhat remote. As you yourself know, a decreased awareness of being ill is a hallmark symptom of schizophrenia. The sleep problems we discussed — the insomnia and restlessness — have they completely resolved them-selves?"

Julia nodded slowly. "I'm with someone now, and he helps me sleep better, I think. No more midnight marathons; he makes sure the doors are locked." She smiled softly.

"Sleep deprivation, with or without a mental illness, could definitely contribute to your feelings of disconnect during the trial. The feeling of being outside your body."

She sighed with relief. "And the phone

calls to my office and apartment? The protesters?"

He shrugged again. "You definitely describe paranoia, but you don't know that someone didn't call you. In fact, it's highly possible that given your situation at the time and the negative publicity your office received, you did receive threatening phone calls. It's hard for me to say they weren't real."

"And when the crucifix, when Jesus . . . I saw him whispering, Doctor . . ."

"Julia, you've been under a tremendous amount of stress. Think about your surroundings at the time. You were at your brother's funeral in the church where your parents had had their funerals. Even absent those stress factors, it could possibly be a profound religious experience." He watched her as she nibbled on her fingernail, still perched on the edge of her seat, ready to run if she had to. "Look, I'm not trying to rationalize your experience over the past few months, Julia; I'm trying to tell you not to panic. You know there is no test for schizophrenia. You definitely experienced a period of psychosis — a disconnect from reality — and that's frightening. But psychosis can happen outside schizophrenia. These factors that we've talked about, taken all together, could be stress-induced situational psychosis — a modern-day nervous breakdown. It's similar to PTSD — post-traumatic stress disorder — and in your case, given that you'd been basically reliving your parents' murders during this situational period, a diagnosis of PTSD wouldn't be far off the mark. Extremely stressful situations can set off a psychotic episode wherein your brain becomes out of touch with reality, with what's really going on around you. Believe it or not, it's your brain's way of dealing with something it otherwise cannot handle. In this case it was the connection between your brother's incarceration and your trial. Your recent reconnection with Andrew heightened your awareness of his illness and the genetic predisposition that you have to it. Think of it like a woman who reads an article about ovarian cancer and recognizes that she has several of the more common symptoms — bloating, backache, fullness after eating — and she successfully convinces herself that she has the disease. So much so that she gives herself the other symptoms she just read about that she didn't have. Now that you have a heightened awareness of the symptoms of schizophrenia, you are more likely to look for any one of those symptoms as an indication of something far more ominous."

She nodded again and tapped her cigarette on the table. God, she wished she could light it. "So you're saying it could all be psychosomatic?"

Dr. Glass was quiet for a long time. Too long. "Listen, I'm not going to lie to you — your family history is of grave concern. And your symptoms do meet some of the diagnostic criteria for the illness. But in situations such as this, where you have the symptoms of schizophrenia but the psychotic episode lasts for a period of less than six months, the diagnosis is schizophreniform disorder."

Her eyes grew wide with fear.

"That means we watch, and we see if it happens again."

"And then?"

"We take it from there. In the meantime, you're out of that stressful environment."

"Yeah, but being unemployed is pretty stressful, I have to say," she said.

"Financially?"

"No, I get unemployment. And believe it or not, I have job offers, too, although so far they've been with the Dark Side. Criminal defense firms," she added when he looked confused. "But . . ." She paused for a long while. ". . . being a prosecutor was my life, Dr. Glass. It's all I know. It's all I think I want to know, and I don't know how to do it again. I don't know if I can."

"Give it time, Julia. Give everything time."

She nodded.

"And your brother?"

She felt her eyes well up. "That's still real hard."

"I'd worry if it wasn't. Grieving takes everyone time. Some more than others."

She nodded again. She still thought of Andy every day. And she still cried every day. It was comforting to know that was normal.

"You've got to let go of the guilt."

She looked away. That was hard, too.

"Your aunt and uncle?"

She shook her head. "She sent me a card, like two weeks ago. It said she wanted to get together. I guess she found out about Andy somehow. Now I can come back in."

"Like I said, grieving takes some people more time than others. She's grieving the loss of you and, to some extent, your mother still; you're grieving the loss of not just Andy but her and your uncle. A card is a first step. Remember, even if she's relieved he's dead, she didn't kill your brother. He did that to himself."

"And with all the recent changes in Andrew's life . . ."

"You're in a good relationship, though?" Dr. Glass asked when she hadn't said anything.

She nodded. "Yes. A very good one. He's a detective. We live together now. He's, you know, he's real worried. He doesn't even want me to work right now. He wants me to . . ." Her voice trailed off again.

"Take it easy?"

"Yes."

"Smart man. Does he know you're here today?"

"He's downstairs in the lobby waiting for me to call him. He's probably got his watch set to the second the hour's up."

"What are you going to tell him?"

She shrugged. "So far, so good. No need to buy me that new straitjacket, I suppose."

"That's one way to put it."

"So we just wait and see?" she asked.

"That's it. And we don't worry and we take it easy, like your boyfriend says. And we check back with me in six weeks. A long, romantic weekend is always a nice excuse to come back and visit New York. Especially in the summer. There's lots to do here."

She smiled and rose to leave. "Thanks again, Dr. Glass," she said, shaking his hand. "I guess I feel better, but there's been something, one thing, that's been . . . well, bothering me. When he — the defendant, Dr. Marquette — you know, when I saw him smile at me in the courtroom, I keep, well, I keep going back to that. What it would mean if it really did happen." She paused as the moment replayed again in her head, as the devil flashed his perfect grin. "Was that, you know . . . ?" Her voice trailed off again.

"Real?" he finished.

She nodded, holding her breath. Part of her actually wanted to hear that she had imagined it. That, like the menacing phone calls, the murderous chants, the whispering Jesus, or the buzzing walls at the SAO, it was all in her head. She wanted to hear that it had never happened. She wanted to hear for once that she was crazy. Because the reality of the truth was far more frightening.

He shrugged again as he opened the door to the waiting room. "I'm afraid that's something only you can answer, Julia. Good luck, now."

Lat was waiting downstairs in the hospital's lobby, pacing like a new father, a cup of Dunkin' Donuts coffee in each hand. When he saw her get off the elevator he stopped dead in his tracks. "How'd we do?"

he asked when she walked up.

"I think I'm here," she said, reaching for a coffee.

"Don't be a wiseass."

"He says wait and see. 'So far so good' were his words. Or maybe they were mine and he agreed. He says I need a vacation."

"I agree with that," Lat said, nodding. He put his arm around her as they started for the door. "Let's go somewhere fun."

"I said I need a job."

"Nah, working's overrated. Let me do that. Let me take care of you for a while." He stopped, gently grabbed her elbow, and turned her to face him.

"I'm fine. I hope," she said while he just looked at her. His blue eyes were probing, worried. "Just stressed, that's all."

He held her close and kissed her head. "Let me take you on that vacation," he whispered in her ear. "Anywhere you want to go. Just name it."

She was quiet for a long moment. Outside the glass doors of the hospital, just a few feet away, the busy Technicolor world went by in fast-forward. "Let's go to a ball game," she said finally. "Are the Mets playing?"

ACKNOWLEDGMENTS

Inspired by the tragic and heartbreaking story of a close friend whose sibling suffers from schizophrenia, *Plea of Insanity* was a labor of love and intense research several years in the making. I'd like to thank the following individuals, without whose help this project could not have been completed, for their wisdom, time, insight, and patience: Dr. Jim Hicks, MD, Director of Psychiatric Services at Kirby Forensic Hospital, and the entire staff at Kirby, including James C. Gilbride, former Chief of Safety and Security, and Anthony E. Rouse, Chief of Secure Hospital Treatment Assistants; Dr. Thomas Macaluso, MD, Medical Director of Psychiatric Services, Memorial Health System; Mr. Dean Mynks, Director of Case Management, Henderson Mental Health Clinic; Dr. Reinhard Motte, Assistant Medical Examiner, Broward County Medical Examiner's Office; Kathleen Hoague, Chief Assistant,

Felony Division, Miami-Dade State Attorney's Office, and Gail Levine, Senior Trial Attorney, Miami-Dade State Attorney's Office, the SAO's resident experts on insanity pleas; Janet Gleeson, Assistant District Attorney, Brooklyn County District Attorney's Office, New York; Special Agents Eddie Royal, Larry Masterson, and Chris Vastine with the Florida Department of Law Enforcement, who still *always* answers the phone for me; Greg Cowsert, Esq., FDLE Regional Legal Advisor; Anita Gay, Assistant United States Attorney, Legal Advisor for the Professional Responsibility Advisory Office; Douglas Donoho, Esq., Professor of Law, Nova Southeastern School of Law; Esther Jacobo, Division Chief, Domestic Crimes Unit, Miami-Dade State Attorney's Office; Priscilla Stroze, Division Chief, Miami-Dade State Attorney's Office; Julie Hogan, Assistant State Attorney, Office of Statewide Prosecution; Marie Perikles, Esq., Florida Office of the Inspector General; Mr. Tyrone Dean and Mr. Richard Gagnon; Marta Marquez, Police Complaint Officer, Miami-Dade Police Department, for a great tour of the Communications Bureau; Wendy Ruth Walker, my editor; and Luke Janklow, my agent. An extra-special thanks goes to great friends

Marie Ryan, Esq., Assistant Commissioner, New York City Police Department, and Joanne Marchionne, MSW, who offered up their time without hesitation when I know they had a zillion other things to do, and to my amazing husband, Rich. He knows all the reasons why. Finally, thanks goes out to my family, especially my parents and my brother, Jack, for their feedback and support.

Schizophrenia is a devastating disease, but there is hope. For more information on schizophrenia or other mental illnesses, please contact the National Alliance for the Mentally Ill (NAMI) at Colonial Place Three, 2107 Wilson Blvd., Suite 300, Arlington, VA 22201-3042, or to find a local NAMI chapter, call 1-800-950-NAMI or visit the website at www.nami.org. Or contact the National Alliance for Research on Schizophrenia and Affective Disorders (NARSAD) at 60 Cutter Mill Road, Suite 404, Great Neck, New York 11021, 1-800-829-8289, or visit the website at www.narsad.org.

ABOUT THE AUTHOR

Jilliane Hoffman was an Assistant State Attorney in Miami between 1992 and 1996. Until 2001 she was the Regional Legal Advisor for the Florida Department of Law Enforcement, advising special agents on complex investigations including narcotics, homicide and organized crime. She lives in Florida. *Plea of Insanity* is her third novel, following the international bestsellers *Retribution* and *Last Witness*.

We hope you have enjoyed this Large Print book. Other Thorndike, Wheeler, Kennebec, and Chivers Press Large Print books are available at your library or directly from the publishers.

For information about current and upcoming titles, please call or write, without obligation, to:

Publisher
Thorndike Press
295 Kennedy Memorial Drive
Waterville, ME 04901
Tel. (800) 223-1244

or visit our Web site at:

http://gale.cengage.com/thorndike

OR

Chivers Large Print
published by BBC Audiobooks Ltd
St James House, The Square
Lower Bristol Road
Bath BA2 3SB
England
Tel. +44(0) 800 136919
email: bbcaudiobooks@bbc.co.uk
www.bbcaudiobooks.co.uk

All our Large Print titles are designed for easy reading, and all our books are made to last.